COLD ZERO

Also by Brad Thor

The Lions of Lucerne
Path of the Assassin
State of the Union
Blowback
Takedown
The First Commandment
The Last Patriot
The Apostle
Foreign Influence
The Athena Project
Full Black
Black List
Hidden Order
Act of War
Code of Conduct
Foreign Agent
Use of Force
Spymaster
Backlash
Near Dark
Black Ice
Rising Tiger
Dead Fall
Shadow of Doubt
Edge of Honor

Also by Ward Larsen

The Perfect Assassin
Stealing Trinity
Fly by Wire
Fly by Night
Passenger 19
Assassin's Game
Assassin's Silence
Assassin's Code
Cutting Edge
Assassin's Run
Assassin's Revenge
Assassin's Strike
Assassin's Dawn
Assassin's Edge
Deep Fake
Assassin's Mark
Dark Vector

BRAD THOR
AND WARD LARSEN

COLD ZERO

A Thriller

EMILY BESTLER BOOKS

ATRIA

New York Amsterdam/Antwerp London
Toronto Sydney/Melbourne New Delhi

ATRIA
An Imprint of Simon & Schuster, LLC
1230 Avenue of the Americas
New York, NY 10020

First Emily Bestler Books/Atria Books hardcover edition February 2026

EMILY BESTLER BOOKS/ATRIA BOOKS and colophon are registered trademarks of Simon & Schuster, LLC

Simon & Schuster strongly believes in freedom of expression and stands against censorship in all its forms. For more information, visit BooksBelong.com.

For information about special discounts for bulk purchases, please contact Simon & Schuster Special Sales at 1-866-506-1949 or business@simonandschuster.com.

The Simon & Schuster Speakers Bureau can bring authors to your live event. For more information or to book an event, contact the Simon & Schuster Speakers Bureau at 1-866-248-3049 or visit our website at www.simonspeakers.com.

Interior Design by Davina Mock-Maniscalco

Manufactured in the United States of America

1 3 5 7 9 10 8 6 4 2

Library of Congress Cataloging-in-Publication Data has been applied for.

ISBN 978-1-6680-6637-9
ISBN 978-1-6682-2896-8 (int exp)
ISBN 978-1-6680-6642-3 (ebook)

To Yvonne Ralsky—
thank you for your invaluable insights,
your exceptional ideas, and, most of all,
your deep and enduring friendship.

—BT

In memory of Scott Miller, agent and friend.

—WL

The best weapon against an enemy is another enemy.

—Nietzsche

CHAPTER 1

Hong Kong

The little car hit a speed bump and hurtled through the air like a shoulder-fired missile. Landing in a spray of glass and broken plastic, it shattered a motor mount and kept going. Two blocks later, as it took flight and slammed back to earth once more, its bent frame groaned like a stabbing victim. Despite all of its damage, the autonomous taxi continued at breakneck speed.

Screaming down the precipitous incline of Hong Kong's Central District, the wind tore at its flimsy shell. As its tires clawed for purchase on the slick asphalt, they unfurled tendrils of hot smoke. Trailing behind, three police cruisers slalomed wildly through the early morning traffic, struggling to keep up.

Horns blared. Klaxons wailed. Wide-eyed pedestrians scattered for cover like startled birds. The madness was only two minutes old, yet the radios crackled with urgency as patrol cars swarmed in from every direction.

With a roar from its engine, an unmarked sedan lurched into the fray, closing the gap quickly with the rogue taxi. Riding shotgun, Captain Ronny Tang of China's Ministry of State Security, or MSS for short, wished he had eaten a milder breakfast. The *mi xian* was twice as spicy coming up as it had been going down.

Using one hand to brace himself against the dashboard, he used his other to work the radio and bark commands. Everything was unraveling.

"Faster!" he yelled at his driver.

The man they had spent weeks tracking was finally making his move. All Tang needed to do was arrest him. But as he moved to apprehend their target, the unexpected had happened—the man had bolted from his hotel. And he hadn't been alone. An unidentified woman accompanied him, adding a layer of mystery to the situation.

At first the woman seemed like a minor hitch, a solvable complication. Then the autonomous taxi had shot straight into the morning rush.

How the hell is that possible? Tang asked himself in disbelief. There was no way the target could have commandeered the driverless taxi. By design, a thick Plexiglas divider cut off access to the front seat.

The alternative possibility was just as crazy—that the car had, of its own volition, gone full-on Formula 1. It had to be ignoring every preprogrammed safety protocol as it traded paint with countless cars and trams as it pinballed downhill.

He looked ahead and watched a police motorcycle accelerate and catch up. The little car braked suddenly and swerved, clipping its front wheel. The bike tumbled to the pavement and its rider went cartwheeling into a curb. The taxi flew into the next intersection, narrowly missing a delivery boy on a scooter. As soon as it was through, the light changed to red.

Tang's driver slammed on the brakes.

"No, no! Keep going!" the captain shouted.

The driver tried to comply, but a bus careened out in front of them. With a last-second jerk on the wheel, they merely sideswiped the bus's front bumper. In a crunch of grating metal, the sedan ricocheted off and kept going.

The captain tried to work the radio, desperate for all the reinforcements he could muster, but he could barely key the microphone as his body was thrown left and right.

"Don't lose sight of him!"

As it turned out, additional radio calls were unnecessary. A massive response had already been initiated by headquarters. Every police car in the district was converging on their quarry, a chorus of sirens that could be heard from miles away. Military units, which had been on alert since last night, were descending from all quarters. Navy patrol boats were locking down the harbor, a ground stop had been ordered at Hong Kong International Airport, and helicopters swirled overhead.

Three blocks ahead a roadblock was hurriedly established. Two rows of eight cars, fronted by spike strips, impeded every inch of road and sidewalk. Backing all of it up were a pair of ZFB-05 armored personnel carriers. It would be absolutely impenetrable. With the streets lined by skyscrapers on either side, and multiple cars in pursuit, the driverless taxi was rocketing toward a box canyon of concrete, glass, and armor.

You won't be running much longer, Tang thought.

The taxi's sensors were on overload. Radar, GPS, cameras, computers: All were working in unison, yet in a way the designers could never have imagined. Safety was no longer paramount. The overriding function had become speed. Two passengers in the back seat held on for their lives, clutching handholds in a death grip as they watched the steering wheel spin ghostlike through oncoming traffic.

As the final intersection before the roadblock neared, a twenty-car-deep traffic jam loomed. The autonomous taxi never slowed for the sea of brake lights. It bounded up over a curb and onto the sidewalk. Pedestrians threw themselves clear and shopping bags went flying. The car plowed over a trash can, clipped two streetlights, and decapitated a fire hydrant. A food cart exploded in a spray of particleboard, candy, and grilled sweet potatoes; the wreckage was soaked immediately by the geyser from the broken fireplug.

By some combination of good luck and technology, not a single person was run down.

As the taxi approached the intersection, the roadblock was not yet in sight. Even so, by some digital prescience, the car sensed the dead end. It swerved left at the corner, its tires smoking through another skid before getting back on track and disappearing.

Tang cursed. "Left. Left!"

"I see him!"

The MSS car rounded the turn trailing by only half a block. At the next intersection the taxi swung hard right and sped downhill. The waterfront loomed ahead.

At each of the next three intersections the pattern repeated. Each time the autonomous taxi flew past, the light changed to red and traffic swept in. Patrol cars joined the chase from all directions, braking and skidding. The end result was nothing short of a demolition derby, auto parts and glass littering the road like a trail of mechanized breadcrumbs.

The taxi neared the waterfront, but instead of turning onto the shoreside road, it crashed straight through a fence and swerved onto the wharf. Dozens of police cruisers and MSS cars followed through the jagged breach. For the pursuers, this simplified their geometry. Patrol cars maneuvered to outflank their quarry, sealing off the only two escape routes. Seconds later, the taxi hit a patch of oil, slewed into a spin, and slammed into a shipping container with a sickening crunch.

Finally, the car had been stopped. One side was crumpled, and the left front wheel was bent severely. Its off-white paint scheme had gone to a virtual rainbow from collision damage.

Squad cars immediately surrounded the taxi, forming a semicircle at a safe distance. Nervous officers bailed out. They drew their weapons and took cover behind doors and quarter panels. Everyone had seen these kinds of car chases on TV, in lawless places like California, but such pursuits in the People's Republic were a rarity.

Captain Tang's sedan, dented and spewing steam from its radiator, wheezed to a stop behind them. Three more unmarked MSS cars arrived and a dozen men spilled out onto the wharf's scarred asphalt. The autonomous taxi was contained. Still, given the chaos of the last ten minutes, no one knew what to expect. *Are the suspects in the car armed?*

Everyone looked to Tang for guidance.

To his credit, he kept calm. At the warehouse behind them, workers were gathering in a doorway. Two forklift operators paused to gawk. A crowd was forming near the breached wire fence. This prompted the captain's first order. He dispatched a dozen police officers to push the onlookers away.

More reinforcements soon arrived, a group of men in full tactical gear who were trained in dispersing crowds. They went to work with shields and batons, clearing the wharf of potential witnesses.

With the scene under control, Tang strode toward the driverless taxi. Five MSS men fell in behind him. The scent of scorched rubber stained the salty breeze. He wrenched open the dented rear door, reached in, and dragged the passengers out one at a time. Both ended up sprawled on the oily tarmac. One was a middle-aged Chinese man in rumpled business attire, the other a black-haired young woman in a sheer blouse, pencil skirt, and stiletto heels.

The man hauled himself up to his feet, indignance in his scowl. He straightened his coat, stared at the captain, and said with all the authority he could muster, “Do you know who I am?”

Amped-up on adrenaline, and frustrated by the turn of events, Tang answered by punching him squarely in the mouth. The blow was more forceful than it needed to be, and the man fell on his ass. He sat stunned and immobilized, blood pouring from his mouth. Two front teeth appeared to be loose. The woman on the ground next to him looked petrified.

Tang leaned into the taxi. He searched the back seat but didn’t see what they were after. He ordered his men to tear it apart. Two raked over the interior. Another used a crowbar to pry open the damaged trunk. Their only find: a silk purse containing a few toiletries.

Tang told them to keep looking.

His men searched the suspects roughly, turning out their pockets and tossing the meager contents on the ground. The car’s seats were ripped out and every compartment was checked.

After ten minutes, two things seemed clear. First was that the object of their search wasn’t here. The second, and more nuanced realization, involved the man on the ground. As he sat moaning and holding a bloody rag to his mouth, the captain suspected he might have made a terrible mistake.

CHAPTER 2

Beijing

A white-hot jolt lanced through Zhang Tao's face, splitting his skull in two from temple to jaw. It was the trigeminal neuralgia again, the vicious antagonist that mocked him with its unpredictability.

Considered one of the most painful ailments on the planet, the so-called "suicide disease" was a souvenir from a long-ago interrogation gone wrong. It was characterized by a searing pain along the trigeminal nerve, which was responsible for sensation in the face. The intensely acute attacks could last for seconds, minutes, or even hours.

His only relief was via an anticonvulsant drug known as Tegretol. It worked by decreasing the nerve impulses that caused seizures and pain. He was already taking 150 percent of the maximum allowable dosage.

The side effects were brutal. In addition to hair loss, the forty-five-year-old was in a constant state of fatigue and plagued by mouth sores. But his problems didn't end there.

He was chief of the Seventh Bureau of the Ministry of State Security, responsible for counterintelligence throughout the People's Republic. It was a position that demanded a certain amount of paranoia. However, Zhang's suspicion of others had morphed into something far more troubling. He was having trouble thinking clearly, had begun isolating himself, and was experiencing early warning signs of psychosis. He shared none of this, of course, with his colleagues.

The mere suggestion of illness would draw unwanted attention—in over twenty years at the ministry, he had made more than his fair share of enemies, and he couldn't afford to show any sign of weakness. Now, as he surveyed the sea of monitors sprawled across the MSS operations center—virtually all of which were tuned to the disaster on the wharf—a mounting sense of dread clawed into his gut.

He had coordinated an overwhelming response. Every available Hong Kong police and MSS unit had converged on the waterfront. Military helicopters continued to swarm overhead like angry wasps. In the background, two Navy corvettes were blockading the pier where the little car lay shattered and spent, its doors flung open and smoke drifting from the wheel wells. No one could accuse Zhang of not using all the assets at his disposal. In his capacity as chief of the Seventh Bureau, he wielded the virtually limitless power of the MSS. Yet the weight of that authority suddenly felt like a noose tightening around his neck.

If Dr. Chen Li, and more important, the item he carried, had somehow vanished into the tangled streets of Hong Kong, it wouldn't just be Zhang's career on the line. His freedom, and even his life, would be on the chopping block.

"Who are they?" Zhang demanded, his voice booming through the cavernous room. He was fixated on the central screen that displayed cell phone photos of the couple who had been dragged out of the taxi. The man was definitely not Chen. The woman was also unknown.

"Facial recognition is running," an analyst piped up from a nearby workstation.

Zhang drummed his index finger against the back of a wheeled chair as his gaze locked on a real-time video feed of the taxi. The stream was sourced from a dash camera on one of the MSS vehicles. His men were tearing the car apart. The seats had been shredded and floor mats lay strewn on the ground. The meager contents of the trunk, a few tire-changing tools and a rubber mat, had been thrown out onto the tarmac.

In the foreground, Captain Tang, the on-scene commander, stood beside the ravaged car. There was defeat in his posture as he raised his phone to place a call. His broad shoulders, usually set with military rigidity, slumped in discomfiture. The phone pressed to his ear looked inordinately heavy.

Zhang's hand shot out, snatching the receiver from the cradle the instant the first ring registered—a silent but forceful message to Tang that his every move was being scrutinized, his failure amplified.

"Well?" he barked. His voice was tight, suppressing his growing panic.

"It's not here, boss," said Tang. "And it's definitely not Chen."

Zhang slammed his fist on the desk. "That's useless information, Tang! Did you find the trackers? The techs put two on Chen—one in his right shoe and another in his overcoat. Both are pinging from the damned taxi."

"Negative, sir. We can't locate them anywhere."

Zhang looked up at the tracking display and saw the twin blue dots glowing brightly, mocking him. "But they're showing right there!"

"We've double-checked the suspects and have practically stripped the car down to the frame. Sir, we've come up empty."

Ignoring Tang for a moment, the counterintelligence chief's eyes darted to a single red dot blinking near the blue ones. "What about Chen's phone? It should be in the car as well."

"Both of the subjects were carrying phones," Tang reported, "but neither is the one we've been tracking."

On another screen, he saw the suspects sitting on the ground in handcuffs, their backs against the fender of a police sedan. The woman, young and expensively dressed, had calmed considerably since getting out of the car. Whoever she was, this wasn't her first tangle with the law. The man, clutching a bloody rag to his mouth, triggered a flicker of recognition in Zhang. He couldn't place him either, but a terrible sense of unease was beginning to raise the hair on the back of his neck.

He bypassed asking Tang about identities. Anything these two offered up, documents or words, could not be trusted. Facial recognition would give them an answer soon enough.

"And the hotel?" Zhang asked. The autonomous taxi had picked up its two occupants at the Landmark Hong Kong, one of the most exclusive establishments in a city that knew luxury.

"We have identified the room. Teams are going over it, but so far there is no sign of either Chen or the device."

Zhang gripped the handset like he might crush it. "Keep searching," he ordered and slammed the phone down on its cradle.

Three weeks. Three grueling weeks they'd spent tailing Dr. Chen Li—ever since he had used a burner phone to make contact with a female CIA officer.

All directors of scientific programs were monitored in the People's Republic, but Chen's recent behavior had brought the watchfulness to a new level.

Chen was the linchpin of China's most classified military project. For nearly a decade, vast national resources had been invested in his game-changing technology, a force multiplier that would allow China's military to leapfrog their Western counterparts.

When alarm bells began sounding at the very top of the regime, Zhang had convinced his superiors to let him run Chen under tight surveillance. The counterintelligence chief's reasoning was twofold. One, if China could arrest a CIA officer along with Chen, it would provide a valuable bargaining chip. Two, by putting Chen on a short leash, they would have time to do a full assessment of the breach and perform any necessary damage control.

Now they had lost track of not only Chen, but also the secrets in his possession.

"We have positive IDs on the suspects!" a nearby analyst announced, cutting through Zhang's churning thoughts. "The man is Luo Sheng. He is—"

"Luo Sheng!" Zhang snapped, the name a punch in the gut. His earlier flicker of recognition, a vague unease, transitioned into full-blown panic. "And the woman?"

"Guan Fei," the analyst replied. "Unemployed. Two arrests last year for prostitution."

Ever so slowly, the landscape of the last twelve hours began to take on a dreadful new light. The way Chen had abruptly booked a room at the Landmark. The wayward blue dots. An errant track on his phone. Fearful of spooking the scientist, or worse, the CIA, Zhang had relied heavily on electronic surveillance. There had always been foot teams on the perimeter, just out of sight, but for long periods, including last night, they hadn't had eyes directly on their target.

Only now did Zhang realize his fatal error. The man they had been tracking, the man entrusted to lead China's most classified project, had been two steps ahead all along. They had been manipulated, played for fools.

On top of it all, his team had just chased down China's minister of culture and tourism and a whore he'd been having a tryst with. Then the leader of the team had punched the minister in the mouth.

Dr. Chen Li had them chasing ghosts.

"So where the fuck are you, Chen?" Zhang hissed, the pain in his face intensifying as his question hung in the air of the operations center like a curse.

CHAPTER 3

Hemisphere Airlines Flight 777

Another glass of champagne, sir?"

Dr. Chen Li looked up from his laptop to see a beautiful flight attendant. A fluted glass was poised perfectly on her tray. Her smile was effervescent, nearly genuine, and her clipped British accent brought back pleasant memories of the old Hong Kong—the vibrant place that had existed before its backslide under the yoke of communism. He wondered if this was intentional. Had the airline selected her for this route with that much nuance?

Having already downed one glass of the wonderful elixir, an exclusive Boërl & Kroff vintage, he decided to take a pause. "No, thank you. Perhaps later."

That eye-catching smile again. "Of course, sir."

Chen was entirely out of his element. Admittedly, as a top-tier research scientist in China, he had enjoyed extensive privileges. A European car, a decent apartment, the promise of a good pension. There had even been a beachside villa on Yalong Bay for two weeks every summer. He would have preferred Bali, but owing to the sensitive nature of his work, he wasn't permitted to travel abroad. Still, it had been nice. But compared to the luxury in which he was now cradled? It was like waking up in a new world.

Hemisphere Airlines was a unique, fresh entrant in global

aviation. An ultra-first-class carrier, its business plan targeted a niche of high-net-worth individuals: those who wished to avoid the headaches of private jet ownership, yet also demanded a discriminating experience. A mere forty seats were spread spaciously across a cabin designed for six times that number. Each "sanctuary" consisted of a plush leather recliner, entertainment suite, separate lie-flat bed, and a mahogany surface that doubled as a workspace and dining table. A mid-cabin lounge offered barstool seating with fine wine and exclusive reserve liquor. In the aft cabin a full-service spa massaged away stress, and private shower compartments allowed passengers to refresh before landing.

All of which, of course, came at a ruinous price.

For the CIA, however, Hemisphere Airlines offered one exceptionally alluring attribute—it operated out of Macau International Airport, a secondary airfield across the Pearl River Estuary from Hong Kong.

Better yet, its security screening and boarding practices were unfailingly discreet. This was not by accident. The airline was a favorite among the Chinese Communist Party elite, who avoided the masses wherever possible, as well as corporate executives and foreign dignitaries. Basic security measures were in place, but the intense surveillance of Hong Kong International or Shenzhen Bao'an International could be sidestepped.

Chen checked the flight display on his private flat-screen monitor. There were no overlays of territorial boundaries, but the map told him all he needed to know. They were closer to Japan than China, which put them in safe airspace. He was, at long last, free.

Glancing across the expansive aisle, he made eye contact with a woman. She was attractive, in an understated way, with ash-blond hair and an engaging smile, probably in her late thirties. It hadn't escaped Chen that she had demurred on the first round of champagne. He imagined the conflict his CIA escort officer must have felt. Declining a drink at the gate would be out of character for a typical Hemisphere Airlines passenger. On the other hand, since they had still been on enemy territory at the time, sobriety was the only responsible course. He guessed that her partner, a young Asian man seated in the mid-cabin who spoke fluent Mandarin, had likely done the same.

Kate—probably not her real name—looked more relaxed now.

She accepted the flight attendant's offer, and as soon as the woman moved on, she raised her glass to Chen in a subtle toast. He grinned, then returned to his work.

His laptop appeared ordinary, a hardened model from a brand-name manufacturer. Yet while the shell had been bought in a store, what lay inside was anything but off-the-shelf.

The laptop interfaced with a revolutionary suite of software contained in its accompanying black case. The system was designed for portability, being intended for use in forward locations. The capabilities it provided were without parallel in modern warfare.

Communication was facilitated by a small satellite antenna, which was presently suction-cupped to the nearby window. The antenna could link to receivers across various bandwidths, which was critical to the system's designed mission. That flexibility was now on display: Chen had locked on to a solid satellite signal, sidestepping the aircraft's Wi-Fi system, which was neither reliable nor secure. And as he knew better than almost anyone on earth, the greatest challenge in any cyber network was maintaining secure communications.

Satisfied that his plush pod prevented anyone from seeing his screen, he called up a real-time feed of the scene at the wharf. Expropriating the feed from MSS channels had been virtual child's play. The battered taxi sat surrounded by police and MSS cars. The bloody minister of culture and tourism was gesturing angrily at a cluster of men in suits. Chen had no grievance with Luo Sheng, nor, for that matter, with the prostitute he had frolicked with last night. They had simply been convenient dupes—in the right place at the right time.

The CIA had expertly orchestrated Chen's extraction—smuggling him out via a delivery truck earlier that morning, changing vehicles three times over in a roundabout route to the airport. Then, finally, a reservation on Hemisphere Airlines, complete with travel documents under a new assumed identity. It had been tense, terrifying, and downright exhausting, but it had worked. *Exquisitely*.

Using the autonomous taxi and manipulating the tracking signals had all been his idea. A smoke screen of distraction to maximize confusion.

The driverless taxi was not only right up Chen's alley, but also a perfect middle finger to the MSS. For years they had experimented with inserting malwares into various Chinese-built cars. Unfortunately, finding practical applications for a self-driving car with a kamikaze mode had proved elusive. After a few hundred cars were shipped out with the hidden software, the project lost funding and had largely been forgotten.

Until the man who had conceived it brought it back to life.

If anything surprised Chen, it was how quickly his hand had been forced. Fully expecting the MSS to be watching him, he had set up tripwires in various internal communication nodes. Three weeks ago, shortly after the CIA had responded to his initial approach, one of those tripwires had gone off. Within days, his name was racing through top-level MSS channels like storm-driven wildfire.

He didn't panic.

Disgusted by the corruption of the regime and its disdain for human rights, he had been plotting his defection for the better part of a year.

The project he now oversaw, *Tianhou*, or Sky Fire in English, was the apex of ten years of work. Chen's transformative application of artificial intelligence could vault China's military to the forefront. For that reason alone, the MSS had ample concern to watch him. What they never took into account, however, was the uniqueness of his position. It never occurred to his MSS minders that they were monitoring him using systems that he himself had created.

With one last look at the scene along the wharf, he input a few final commands. His index finger hesitated slightly, then he tapped the final keystroke. Chen cut the connection, pulled down the antenna, and shut Sky Fire down.

Deep in servers a thousand miles away, in the MSS's most secretive data center, his instructions were executed. In a matter of milliseconds, years of work vaporized in an alphanumeric puff of smoke. Owing to the highly classified nature of his research, the design records and data resided nowhere else. Recovery would be impossible.

The lone prototype of Sky Fire was now his, and his alone.

Dr. Chen Li put his head back and closed his eyes. The sense of relief was profound.

• • •

KASEY SHERIDAN WAS glad to see Chen shut down his laptop. She knew he was using it to facilitate their escape, but in the age of electronic tracking, clipping the only remaining signal was undeniably comforting.

She settled deeper into the oversize leather seat and sipped her champagne. Bubbly wasn't really her thing, but she had to admit it was superb. And it felt good to switch off. The recent weeks had been nerve-racking. Extracting Chen from China had been the most challenging assignment of her sixteen-year CIA career. The mission had been green-lighted from the highest levels, yet its footprint was kept deliberately small. In the final week, she and her partner, Walter Ho, had gone dark. They cut all ties to the embassy, leaving only one secure comm channel to headquarters. They had ducked and weaved through a tradecraft labyrinth, running surveillance detection routes that bordered on marathons in the world's most pervasive surveillance state. It had been exhilarating and exhausting, a once-in-a-career op that could shift the balance of world power. Although she knew only the basics of what Chen was carrying, she knew it was pure dynamite.

And now she and Walter were bringing it home.

Kasey tipped back the last of her champagne, and no sooner had she set down her glass than a good-looking male flight attendant—how many of these people were there, and were any of them unattractive?—materialized to offer a refill.

"Not now, thank you."

Her empty flute was swept away by a white-gloved hand. *Better not get used to this*, she told herself. She figured the karmic odds were high that her next posting would be payback, six months in a pure hellhole in some dark and dusty corner of the globe. The kind of place where no matter how hard you tried, no matter how much the CIA spent, nothing meaningful ever changed.

She got up and walked aft along the main aisle. Walter was seated mid-cabin, and even from a distance she saw him nodding off. She couldn't fault him. Kasey had managed a few hours' sleep at the hotel yesterday evening, but he hadn't gotten any rest in days. The early morning hours had been the worst, transferring Chen to Macau Airport right under the noses of the MSS. The scheme had worked brilliantly, and after arriving at the airport, the three of them had ignored one another in the terminal in the name of operational security. Now, with China in the rearview mirror, contact was acceptable. Better yet, Hemisphere's roomy cabin layout made it simple to stay out of earshot of other passengers.

As she neared Walter's seat, she noticed a young pregnant woman she had seen in the terminal seated across the aisle. The woman appeared too far along in her pregnancy to be traveling, but Kasey couldn't blame her. China was one of the last places she'd ever want to be hospitalized, much less give birth.

One of the flight attendants was in the process of making up the woman's bed, expertly tucking in the thousand thread-count sheets and masterfully plumping the goose down pillows and duvet. It was like watching an artist at work.

Walter, however, was too tired to notice, his head bent lazily to one side.

"We did it," she said, leaning down next to his seat.

His eyes flicked open with a start. "Oh . . . yeah. Although we still have to finish this fourteen-hour flight to New York. I'm not sure if I can stay awake that long."

"I think we've earned a little shut-eye. Might be your last chance for a while." She nodded toward the pregnant woman. Walter's wife was due in nine weeks.

"Maybe so. Did Chen shut down?" He too had been worried about the laptop giving away their position.

"Yep. Sounds like his diversions went exactly as planned. The guy really knows his stuff."

He looked up and down the aisle. "Spot anybody who might be an issue?"

"Chinese assassins on our flight? You're getting paranoid, Walter."

"Isn't that what we're paid to be?"

"Between the two of us, we've put eyes on every person on this jet. Nobody stands out. Chen told me he actually downloaded the passenger manifest for the flight—not sure when he found the time, but I don't doubt him. He ran every name, and not one kicked back as suspicious."

"He was probably using MSS databases."

"True. But those would be better than our own."

Kasey was about to say something else when she noticed that the pregnant woman was trying to reach the overhead compartment to get something down.

Having finished making the bed, the flight attendant had returned to the galley to begin prepping for meal service.

"Can I help you with that?" Kasey asked, crossing the aisle.

"Thank you," the woman replied. "I'm trying to get my bag down. I thought I'd already taken out my AirPods."

"No problem at all. The brown one?"

The woman nodded and Kasey removed the expensive, designer suitcase.

"When are you due?" she asked, as the woman opened her bag and retrieved her AirPods.

"Not for another two months," the woman replied, closing her bag and standing aside so Kasey could place it back into the overhead. "My doctor didn't want me traveling in my third trimester, but I promised this would be my last trip. My husband, not to mention the rest of my family, would kill me if they couldn't be there for the birth of the baby."

"Boy or girl?" Kasey asked, as she hefted the bag back in place.

"We want it to be a surprise. As long as the baby's healthy, that's all we care about," the woman replied.

"Good for you," Kasey said, putting the bag back and closing the bin.

The two chatted a bit, and nothing the woman said raised an alarm for Kasey. She moved back across the aisle and said to Walter, "She works for a private equity company. Can you believe they sent her to Hong Kong? She's due about a week before your wife."

Walter chuckled. "If my wife's boss tried to get her to take a trip at this point, she'd be in his driveway planting pipe bombs."

"Hannah's a tough lady. Probably needs to be in order to put up with you."

He smiled. "What about you? When are you going to have kids?"

"One thing at a time," Kasey responded. "I need to find the right guy first." Shooting a glance up front, she returned to business. "I should probably get back."

"You worry too much."

"I can't help it. It's the first time he's been out of our sight in days."

"I think we're in the clear."

Now it was Kasey who chuckled. "Not until we hand him over in New York."

Walter tapped his display screen, which traced the airplane's flight path over the North Pole to their eventual destination of John F. Kennedy International Airport in New York City. "All we've got to do is get him there. This is the easy part. Relax and have a little more champagne. Everything's going to be fine."

CHAPTER 4

Beijing

How the hell did you let this happen?" said the iron-fisted Minister of State Security, the only man between Zhang and the president himself. The minister was linked in by video as they dissected what had happened that morning. And right now, he was fuming.

Zhang resented his presence. They were in the middle of a massive manhunt, and the last thing he needed was his boss tossing recriminations around the operations center like hand grenades. It not only eroded morale, but also undermined Zhang's authority. With every barb and with every flake of dandruff that dropped off the old man's scalp, Zhang wanted to wrap his hands around his brittle, scrawny neck and squeeze until it snapped. Had the man been in the room, he might have done just that.

Forcing himself to focus, he returned his attention to the security camera footage from Macau International Airport and the lavish boarding lounge of Hemisphere Airlines.

The video they were studying had been taken two hours before the debacle on the pier. There was no mistaking the bespectacled figure of Dr. Chen Li. He was typing furiously on a laptop in the minutes before boarding. The laptop was connected to a familiar black case on the floor by his knee.

"That is the system," said a woman named Wu Mei. She had been the lead AI researcher under Chen and had been summoned to the operations center for the insights Zhang hoped she could provide.

"Are you sure?" Zhang asked.

"Absolutely."

The minister, his face contorting on an adjacent screen, looked like he might pop an aneurysm. "*Where is his airplane now?*"

The researcher called up a map on the main monitor. Hemisphere Airlines Flight 777 was presently transiting Japanese airspace. Its flight path was projected northward on a polar route.

She said, "It will arrive in New York in roughly twelve hours."

"Not if I have anything to say about it!" the minister countered.

Zhang watched as the minister picked up a secure phone without killing the video link. Over the course of the next ten minutes, Zhang and the researcher heard half of two very agitated conversations. The first was with a Chinese Air Force general who confirmed that, if the order was given soon, interceptors could probably catch up with the airliner and shoot it down. In the second call, a Chinese Navy admiral was more confident. He had two destroyers near the airliner's projected flight path, and both carried surface-to-air missiles with enough range to knock the massive jet out of the sky.

The minister then paused before initiating his most perilous call. He set up a three-way videoconference, to include the operations center, before inviting the last participant to join. Zhang knew blame-sharing when he saw it, and he watched nervously as an assistant answered. Sixty seconds later, the well-coiffed visage of the president of China appeared. Two of his closest advisers were visible on the screen, one over each shoulder. The MSS minister confessed what had happened. The fireworks began immediately, a rapid-fire exchange that engulfed all the players.

Potential casualties?

There are forty passengers on the aircraft and sixteen crewmembers. Most are either American or Chinese, with eight other nationalities represented . . .

Yes, the Japanese, the Russians, and perhaps the Americans will see the shoot down . . .

No, we haven't yet come up with justification for use of force . . .

A heated debate ran, and as it did, Zhang found his eyes flicking to a second monitor. The symbol representing Hemisphere Flight 777 ticked farther away with each second.

The discussion digressed into a shouting match between the president's advisers and the MSS minister. Shooting the jet down would resolve their intelligence disaster, but at the cost of generating a political firestorm. The Americans would surely know the real reason for bringing the jet down. Only one point brought consensus. Dr. Chen Li could not be allowed to reach New York with the secrets in his possession.

Zhang suddenly realized that one person was not paying attention to the heated back and forth. Glancing over at the researcher, he saw her typing feverishly on a keyboard. When she finally looked up, she locked eyes with Zhang. Her expression implied that she had discovered something important.

"What is it?" Zhang asked.

The men on the videoconference fell silent, also seeming to notice her pent-up exhilaration.

The AI researcher hesitated. She clearly wasn't used to having the exclusive attention of the most powerful men in China. "Forgive me," she said, "but I think there might be another way."

She explained her idea, an option none of them even knew existed.

Silence followed, everyone deferring to the president.

"Do you have full confidence in this technology?" asked the president.

"Absolutely. I designed it myself."

"How quickly can it be done?"

"I think the better question is, *where* should it be done?" She directed everyone's attention to the map and explained her reasoning. "Doing it that way would give us time to prepare."

The president began a slow nod that gathered momentum. "Very well," he said. "Proceed."

CHAPTER 5

Hemisphere Airlines Flight 777
6 Hours Later

The polar night was a sight to behold. The world *looked* cold. Countless stars jeweled the black sky above. Below was nothing but a darkened void. There were no cities for hundreds of miles, and even if there had been, tonight a dense layer of clouds was obscuring the ground. The isolation was absolute. Like no other place on earth.

First Officer Brett Sharpe checked their position on the flight management system. Roughly halfway through their trip, the latitude showed 88.6 degrees north.

"Not directly over the Pole," he said, "but you can see it from here."

Captain Bill Fowler looked out the side window. Somewhere in the darkness, roughly ninety miles away, lay the geographic point where Robert Peary had planted the American flag over a hundred years earlier. The place where curving lines of longitude met on every map. There was nothing to mark the spot on a permanent basis, no flag or marker, because there was no land upon which to place anything. The North Pole was simply a concept, a geographic curiosity beneath a continuously drifting sheet of ice.

"It's down there somewhere," Fowler agreed. He tinkered with the radar display. "This storm looks wicked."

"Yeah, glad we're above it."

An Arctic low-pressure system was churning up a maelstrom, but they were flying high enough to top out the cloud cover and turbulence. The ride at 34,000 feet was smooth. Better yet, an 80-knot tailwind was giving Hemisphere Flight 777 a solid push to New York.

Long-haul flying over the Arctic and across open ocean was a serious departure from Sharpe's last job—flying F-22 Raptors in the Air Force. Traveling at supersonic speed, turning and burning . . . there was no other flying like that in the world. It was the best job he'd ever had.

At least it had been until he'd been given a "career broadening" staff assignment. It was a misstep the Air Force had been making for years, pulling seasoned pilots at the top of their game out of the cockpit and forcing them into administrative posts. Like so many of his brethren, Sharpe hadn't been interested. He'd made the jump to the civilian world, trading "major" for "first officer."

All told, he'd been with Hemisphere for two years now and was enjoying himself. So far, he had no regrets.

A chime sounded as the jet's satellite datalink downloaded a message. Sharpe called it up but saw a blank text field.

"Huh. Never seen that before."

Fowler glanced at the empty screen. "Me neither, but the sat coverage up here can be spotty. If it's something important, they'll resend it."

Sharpe closed the empty message. "I could use a cup of coffee. You want one?"

The skipper thought it was a terrific idea.

He rang the flight attendant call button.

UNKNOWN TO THE crew, the message wasn't for them. Deep within the jet's labyrinthine network, a digital back door had been cracked open, and a sleeper agent planted years ago, designed by Dr. Chen's capable protégé, stirred from its slumber.

From thousands of miles away, an unseen hand guided the malware's path. The Thirteenth Bureau, the tech-savvy arm of China's MSS, had made its move. In the face of a potential national catastrophe, they had unleashed their ultimate fail-safe.

The silent attack began in the plane's communication system. The message that went unseen by the crew was rerouted, and a spurious signal whispered into the jet's vitals. Four temperature sensors, two placed in the heart of each engine, registered a sudden, impossible spike.

This false data triggered a chain reaction. The digital engine controls, designed for absolute safety, interpreted the phantom heat as a dire threat. Fuel lines clamped shut, and the engines, performing exactly as they had been programmed, began to shut down. Within seconds, warnings were cascading to the flight deck.

Sharpe gaped at the instrument panel, a sea of flashing red and amber lights, and exclaimed, "Engine failure! Both engines!"

CHAPTER 6

The passengers knew instantly that something was wrong. The steady, reassuring hum of the engines changed. The overhead lights stuttered. Most disconcerting of all was the look on the flight attendants' faces. They had frozen mannequin-like while handing out plates of seared Wagyu steak and sole meunière.

Something was *very* wrong.

Kasey looked across the aisle and saw the concern she felt mirrored on Chen's face. They weren't merely worried about *what* was happening. They were wondering *why* it was happening.

For days they had been on high alert, every sense tuned for threats. Now, just as their guard was coming down, a crisis had struck out of nowhere. Like a bolt of lightning on a clear day. And the coincidence of it happening here, happening now, was too ominous to ignore.

Up on the flight deck, both pilots felt the loss of thrust. The sound of the giant turbines spooling down was like a low-pitch death rattle, the last breath of life leaving a dying corpse.

As the engine generators fell offline and battery power took over, the lights flickered. Then the autopilot disconnected, and its frantic alarm added to the cacophony.

Captain Fowler took charge, running the memory procedure for dual engine failure. Hands were racing over controls. Procedures were being run. None of it was helping. They were flying a 200-ton glider.

"Not getting a relight on either engine," Sharpe stated. With the procedures not working, experience became their last resort. "What do you think? Not many things that'd cause both engines to quit. Volcanic ash?"

"Nope, that would have shown high engine temperatures. And the fuel is warm enough, nowhere near the freezing point. All I can figure is contaminated fuel."

"If that's the case, we're not going to get a restart."

The two exchanged a grave look. They were running out of options. The aircraft had been at 35,000 feet when the engines died. Now they were at 28,000. Battling mushy controls, Fowler had reduced the airspeed for a better glide ratio. It would buy a little more time, but not much.

"I'll keep trying for a relight," Fowler said. "Get Burnsy up here—maybe he'll have an idea."

Thirty seconds later, Captain Scott Burns, the relief pilot who had been taking a break in back, entered the flight deck and hopped into the jump seat. They filled him in on the situation. Warnings kept coming, audible alerts and amber lights.

At 20,000 feet the stars disappeared as the aircraft was swallowed by dense clouds. They were no longer above the storm. They were in it.

The jet began rocking in turbulence.

Fowler instructed Sharpe to send a mayday. Position, course, speed, situation. Since they were on a polar route, it couldn't be done by radio; it had to be via satellite.

After three attempts, Sharpe said, "Bill, the mayday's not going through."

"What do you mean?"

He pointed to a series of MESSAGE FAIL responses. "I don't get it. It was working fine earlier."

"Keep trying!"

Sharpe complied while the two senior pilots fought to regain the use of at least one engine.

At 10,000 feet, Fowler made the call they all knew was coming.

"Okay, change of plan. Forget about getting the engines back. We're going down and it's not going to be pretty."

Sharpe expanded his electronic map. "I show the nearest land three hundred and ten miles south." He didn't even bother to look for an airfield, which would have doubled the distance.

"From this altitude, we can glide maybe twenty miles."

"Ditching it is," Burns said, flipping through the handbook to find the correct checklist.

"I guess that's our only choice," Fowler stated. "Problem is, this won't be a straight water landing. We'll be putting down on an ice floe."

It was a situation none of them had ever contemplated. No one had. It wasn't even in the book.

"Will the ice hold if we use the landing gear?" Sharpe asked.

"Four hundred thousand pounds on ten tires? Not a chance."

"Then we're looking at a belly landing," Sharpe ventured.

Fowler looked at the other two pilots. In a silent vote, both nodded. "I guess it's the best bad option. Spreads the weight out. I don't see any way the ice is going to support the jet, but it might help us float a little longer. And once we evacuate it should be strong enough to support our passengers and some survival equipment. Run the ditching checklist, but let's tell the flight attendants that the plan is to evacuate onto the ice."

The captain ordered Sharpe to keep sending maydays, including blind calls on the VHF radio emergency frequency, 121.5 MHz.

Sharpe did so repeatedly but heard no aircraft or ships reply. He wasn't surprised. The top of the world was a lonely place, and there was likely no one within range.

Burns coordinated with the flight attendants to prepare the cabin for ditching. When he finished, he asked, "What about dumping fuel? Seems like we ought to make her as light as possible."

"Do it!" the captain ordered.

Burns worked a few switches and tons of fuel began venting from the wings.

The jet shuddered in a fierce gust of wind. The airframe groaned as if it knew what was coming.

Working the spongy controls, Fowler muttered, "Now I know how Sully Sullenberger felt. Except my Hudson River is going to be a frozen sheet of ice."

CHAPTER 7

The flight attendant gave loud, definite instructions. "*Locate the nearest emergency exit now! Do not evacuate until ordered to do so by a uniformed crewmember!*"

Kasey, who had ignored the routine safety briefing while taxiing out in Macau, clung to every word. Her lap belt was cinched as tight as she could get it. She'd stowed her table. She memorized the layout of the emergency floor lighting and pointed it out to Chen. She counted the number of seats to the nearest exit. If the cabin filled with smoke, she could get them both out by feel if necessary.

Her attention shifted to the passengers around her. She saw a frail older woman who might need help. A muscular young businessman appeared fit and capable. She would enlist his help if needed. She thought about the pregnant woman in the mid-cabin. *Walter will take care of her*, she told herself.

Suddenly, the plane was violently buffeted. A collective gasp erupted and morphed into people screaming, crying, praying. Kasey stole a glance out the window. All she could see was a milky haze in the wash of the landing lights. The monitor in front of her, which had been displaying a map of their journey, had blanked minutes earlier. She tried to recall where they were. Somewhere over the Arctic. Was there even land below? An airport nearby?

"Bend as far forward as you can with your face down! Wrap your arms behind your knees!"

Kasey couldn't stop planning. She grabbed the full-size pillow and thick blanket they'd given her and wedged them at her sides. She caught the eye of the older woman across the aisle. There was panic in her face and her seat belt was dangling free. Kasey mimed buckling it and that seemed to snap her out of her rattled frame of mind. The woman complied.

She glanced back over at Chen. He was wedging his black briefcase between his seat and the bed. It had been beside him the entire flight. The one time he'd gone to use the bathroom, Kasey had kept a constant watch on it.

The flight attendant's instructions kept coming.

"After landing, release your seat belt and go to the nearest exit! Do not take any possessions with you!"

Kasey hoped she lived long enough to break that rule. There was no way in hell she was getting off this plane without Chen. Or without Sky Fire.

CHAPTER 8

Sharpe had stared death in the eye countless times. But this was different. It was a commercial airliner full of passengers and crew—people who had entrusted their lives to him and the other two pilots on the flight deck.

Despite the years of training and experience that had always brought him through before, he knew that this time he was going to need something else. *Luck*. Lots of it.

His attention alternated between the few instruments still functioning and the scene outside. The radar altimeter confirmed they were only 2,000 feet above the Arctic Ocean. The ice-clad sea was rushing at them like a train.

The problem was, with touchdown only minutes away, he still couldn't see the surface. The dense clouds had given way to a blast of oncoming snow. Wind gusts hammered the airframe relentlessly. The flight display showed a wind velocity of 60 knots, almost hurricane force. Fowler was waging a pitched battle with the controls to simply keep the wings level.

"Wind from two o'clock at fifty-eight knots," he stated. "We need to turn straight into it for landing."

"Working on it," Fowler grunted, fighting to turn right. "We'll use full flaps."

The cockpit door was bulletproof, but not so thick that they couldn't hear the flight attendants bellowing commands in the cabin. Burns gave them a two-minute warning on the PA, and they began shouting for everyone to assume the brace position.

"Mark our position," Fowler said.

Sharpe created a new fix in the navigation system and named it Waypoint Zulu. Out of instinct, he committed the lat/long coordinates to memory.

The jet began slowing and, on Fowler's command, Sharpe began lowering the flaps in increments.

By 1,000 feet, the flaps were fully extended, and they were flying at minimum speed. It wouldn't be as much a landing as a controlled crash. Finally, the snow began to thin in the glow of the landing lights.

"We're below the weather but I can't see the surface yet," Fowler remarked. "Still too much snow."

"Five hundred feet," Sharpe noted. "Four hundred."

Obscure reflections finally began registering below. The surface gained contour. It wasn't as smooth as Sharpe had hoped. Ridges in the ice pack creased upward, shiny aqueous pools between them. All of it flashed past in a blur.

"One hundred feet!" Sharpe exclaimed. "Descent rate is too high!"

Fowler tried to pull up, but a burst of Arctic wind countered his inputs. Pushing forward to porpoise the nose down, he overcorrected.

The jet's aft fuselage made impact and the forward belly slammed down hard. Tremors shuddered through the entire aircraft. It was a brutal, ugly landing. And it wasn't over.

With no landing gear, there were no brakes. With no engines, there was no reverse thrust. And with the flaps all the way down, there was no way to create additional drag. There was also no way to steer. They were barreling forward with a tremendous amount of speed, but no control whatsoever.

Directly ahead, Sharpe saw a vague shadow racing toward them. As it got closer, he began to read its contours, and his heart caught in his throat.

It was a hill of ice as tall as an eighteen-wheeler and as wide as a bus station. They had survived the landing only to now crash into a frozen wall. It was a bitter irony.

But seconds before their head-on collision, the jet's starboard engine snagged on a fissure, initiating a spin to the right. It wasn't enough, however, to save them. The airliner struck the ridge in an explosion of ice and snow.

As it did, the cockpit was sent soaring back into the air.

CHAPTER 9

Beijing

The tension in the MSS operations center was crushing. Zhang Tao had just unleashed a withering tirade. Threatening and berating, it left no doubt in anyone's mind that careers were at stake. Every face in the room bore the grim weight of a gamble that they weren't sure would pay off.

Their immediate problem was self-inflicted—they had no way of knowing if their scheme had worked.

One of the most basic tenets of warfare was to control the high ground, making space the ultimate frontier. Leveraging a low-earth-orbit satellite that had never before been activated, China was now jamming all commercial communications in the polar sky. This would cut off distress calls from Hemisphere Flight 777, which meant the world would not know exactly when or where it had gone down.

The MSS, unfortunately, relied on those same feeds.

Zhang's skull felt like it was going to explode. His meds had grown less effective over time and so to compensate, he'd done what he always did in bad moments. He'd popped an extra dose. It was a slippery medical slope, but for now he ignored whatever rocky landing might be waiting for him at the bottom.

"How long can we continue jamming?" he asked.

The operations center chief replied, "There is no technical

limitation, but the longer we keep it up, the more likely our actions will be discovered. Initially, the Americans will view the outage as an atmospheric anomaly. Eventually, however, suspicion will take hold. I think if we continue for more than an hour, they will investigate the interruption and discover our intervention."

Zhang's left eye twitched. The use of the jamming system had been a heated point of debate. It would violate countless aviation and space treaties, but that was of little consequence. Of greater concern was that it would unveil one of their most secretive capabilities. To not use it, however, heightened the risk that Sky Fire would fall into the wrong hands. In the end, the president had made the call, thankfully taking the course Zhang favored.

Flight 777 would slam into the Arctic Ocean, and its wreckage would disappear beneath thousands of feet of water in an ice-clad sea. Any distress calls would be drowned out by the jamming. More important, the signals from the aircraft's two emergency locator transmitters would be temporarily blocked.

The ELTs were tied to the plane's black boxes, and once those sank into deep water, their transmissions would be severely attenuated. The beacons would still function, but it would take a concentrated undersea search to find them.

Yet because they activated on impact, there was a chance one or both might begin pinging before the wreckage sank. By jamming communications for a short time, the airliner's final resting place could effectively be hidden. There would be a narrow window during which only China knew the jet's fate. But even Beijing wouldn't have a precise fix on its position.

Zhang had known from the outset that bringing the jet down was not enough. The device in Chen's possession, the prototype control station at the heart of Sky Fire, had to be recovered. If that wasn't possible, it had to be destroyed, although for Zhang this was tantamount to failure. According to Wu Mei, it would be possible to reverse-engineer the control station, salvaging a decade of work and untold billions of yuan. But that would most likely take years. If the original device was lost, the stain on Zhang's career would be indelible.

Never one to waste an advantage, he did have two things going for him. He knew roughly where Flight 777 had gone down. And he had a head start to reach the crash site.

Two operations to press those advantages were already underway. The first was straightforward. China operated a growing fleet of ice-breakers, which were the best option for a recovery. Better yet, the ship nearest the prospective crash site, the *Xue Long 2*, had precisely the kind of equipment needed for a deepwater salvage mission. She was already steaming northward at full speed.

The second operation was far more nuanced, and one for which Zhang had not sought approval. It was precisely the kind of subterfuge his bureau specialized in.

"What is the status of our insurance policy?" he asked.

The ops center chief referenced a nearby screen that was following a Challenger business jet as it streaked across northern Canada.

There had been no recent tracking updates as it neared the North Pole—that aircraft, too, was subject to the regional communications outage. Still, its progress could easily be extrapolated. "They are getting close. I estimate less than thirty minutes from the assigned target."

"Very well. Give them fifteen minutes beyond that, then terminate the jamming."

Zhang's eyes shifted to another map. An X marked the projected final resting place of Hemisphere Flight 777. It was only an estimate, based on course, speed, and the jet's last known position, but it had to be close. *Triple seven*, he thought. *A sign of good fortune.*

With any luck at all, Sky Fire would be secure within forty-eight hours. At that point the professional peril in which he found himself, a very mortal peril, would be lifted.

Zhang considered how he might celebrate. A good meal, some Kentucky bourbon, maybe arrange for a woman. Or perhaps just down enough pills to get a good night's sleep.

Not once did he give a thought to the fifty-six mortal souls he had just committed to an icy grave.

CHAPTER 10

Above the Arctic Circle

The pilot and copilot of the Challenger 850 were utterly perplexed. Five hours ago they had been in Calgary, Alberta, flight-planning a trip to London when an encrypted transmission with urgent new orders had arrived. They were to fly north at maximum speed to a point above the Arctic Circle, and after that proceed directly to Beijing.

Neither of them had ever seen such a bizarre directive. The pilot plotted the latitude/longitude pairing on a map and saw no significance in the place whatsoever. It was simply a random point in the sky above an ice-blanketed sea. They had also been instructed to verify the operability of one particular piece of equipment. Further orders would be issued en route. And most astonishing of all: the Chinese Minister of Commerce and his entourage, who they had been hauling around the world on an economic junket for the last week, were to be left stranded in Calgary.

Like the exceptional air force officers they were, the pilots carried out their new tasking to the letter. They were part of the Chinese Air Force's most elite unit, a special airlift wing that transported senior ministers and dignitaries, the CCP's equivalent of the U.S. Air Force's 89th Airlift Wing, whose fleet included Air Force One.

"Five minutes to target," said the copilot.

The senior pilot, a colonel, said, "I have us on track. Altitude five hundred feet, speed one hundred sixty knots. I will go prep the package. You have the aircraft."

The major in the right seat took control of the jet, and the colonel unbuckled. He stood cautiously and used his hands to brace himself as he moved aft. The weather was shit and turbulence was pummeling the little jet.

As promised, follow-on instructions had been received on the secure datalink twenty minutes earlier. Both pilots had read that directive twice, and they were struck by two peculiarities. First was the level of detail, including the unusually low speed and altitude to be flown. Second was the task they were to perform when they reached the turn point. They both understood the significance of what they were about to do, but how it could be a vital national priority escaped them. Worse yet, flying low and slow in these conditions bordered on suicidal.

Still, colonels did not become colonels in the Chinese Air Force by exercising good judgment and initiative. They did it by blindly following orders.

The aircraft was already depressurized—this too had been in the directive—and the colonel hauled open the main entry door. A vortex of Arctic air rushed into the cabin. The temperature dropped fifty degrees. He briefly looked outside, and in the dim light he saw nothing but furrowed patches of sea ice all the way to the horizon.

"Thirty seconds!" the copilot called out, shouting to be heard over the wind noise.

The colonel reached down and picked up the device. It was standard equipment on all their aircraft. Roughly the size of a basketball, it had a hardened metal shell and a handle at the top. With his free hand he toggled the lone switch to ON. A green light began blinking.

"Mark!" the copilot shouted.

The colonel hauled back and threw the device out into space. He took one look down but didn't see the device. He shrugged once, secured the door, and returned to the flight deck.

Moments later, the Challenger was clawing back up to altitude in a sweeping left-hand turn.

CHAPTER 11

Arctic Ocean
85°48.6'N, 119°23.0'W
Crash Site

A stinging slap of cold. Then darkness. As Kasey fought her way back to consciousness, her head throbbed.

Only twice in her life had she "seen stars." Once, when she had fallen off her bike as a small child, and then again during high school, when she and a fellow outfielder had run straight into each other chasing the same pop fly. But never had she endured anything like this. It was all she could do to force her eyes open, and only then just to slits.

Memories rushed back in clusters—the terrifying descent, the plane slamming into the ice, the tumbling and lurching. She'd been thrown sideways. Her head had smacked something hard. And after that . . . nothing. How long had she been out? Seconds? An hour?

Everything was dim, shrouded in a hazy, acrid smoke that clawed at her lungs. At first she saw only gray, a few vague silhouettes. From somewhere, she heard crackling noises, along with a rhythmic creak that sounded like an old door swaying in the wind. A woman's screams, raw and desperate, pierced the air.

Kasey felt a wave of panic building in her chest. She forced it down. If she was going to survive, she had to regain control.

Her eyes stung as she blinked them wider and new sensations flooded in. Most involved pain. Her left leg was wedged agonizingly sideways. There was blood on her arm and a frigid wind clawed at every bit of exposed skin. Her joints were stiff, as if rigor mortis was getting a head start.

Not so fast, she thought defiantly.

Slowly her vision sharpened. The bright cabin lights were gone, replaced by a handful of what looked like tiny floods. *The emergency exit lights*. She looked down at the floor and saw the amber strip of lights leading to the emergency exit, precisely as she remembered from her preparation. It was undeniably comforting. She checked the cracked window beside her. The blackness outside was incomplete, a dusky glow painted low on the horizon. Plots of amber flickered in the distance, ground fires where shards of debris lay burning.

The fuselage around her was mostly intact, but when she looked behind, she was stunned. The two seats behind her were empty. The strong young man with the tattoos. A smartly attired Asian gentleman. They were nowhere in sight. Behind that everything had vanished, the tubular fuselage sliced cleanly through as if by a guillotine.

She looked across the aisle for Chen but didn't see him. His seat was gone, nothing left but four fractured steel anchor points. Looking toward the front of the plane she saw a partial human form, the lower half of one of the flight attendants, her uniformed legs and hips motionless on the floor. The upper half of her body was buried beneath an avalanche of serving carts. The carpet around her was drenched in blood.

The screaming she had been hearing fell to a low-pitched moan. Kasey knew she had to move.

With a surge of adrenaline, she twisted her leg. Pain flared, but the bone held. A cracked-open suitcase rolled away, and a half dozen festively wrapped presents spilled out.

Attempting to stand, she was restrained by her tightly cinched seat belt. She unbuckled it as a chemical stench of burning plastic came in waves.

Her leg was sore, but able to bear weight. She performed a quick self-inspection. A gash on her arm was the source of the blood, but the flow had stemmed. She put a hand on top of her head, and felt blood and a large knot. Her midlength hair, which had been in a neat ponytail, was matted and loose.

Looking aft again, she wondered where the back two-thirds of the airplane had ended up. Snow flurries and smoke made it difficult to see, but she could discern a large fire in the distance. It was hundreds of yards away. Nothing hot and bright, but low flames dancing across half a football field. A giant furrow connected the two points, and the ice field between looked like a junkyard.

Walter had been in the mid-cabin. *Where is he now? And what about Chen and Sky Fire? Could the Chinese have somehow caused this?*

She pushed the speculation away. Regardless of what had caused this disaster, there were innocent people around her who desperately needed help. Kasey took a tentative step on the angled floor and wobbled. Three steps later, she was moving freely.

But as soon as she started moving, the cold began sapping her strength, challenging her will. She knew she was in a race against time. And the odds were dramatically stacked against her.

CHAPTER 12

Beijing

Zhang fixed a penetrating glare on Dr. Chen's number two, the AI researcher named Wu. "So?" he demanded. "Have we succeeded?"

"I believe so," the woman replied. "We have ended the jamming by our satellite. The Hemisphere Airlines craft appears to be no longer sending data and is not responding to air-traffic controllers."

"I don't care how it *appears*! We must be certain!"

Wu looked up with barely masked annoyance. "With more warning, I might have built a better plan. I am doing the best I can."

Zhang would have excoriated most underlings for such impertinence. But the researcher was unique, and unfortunately, she knew it. She understood better than anyone what Chen had created; irrespective of whether they recovered the Sky Fire prototype or had to rebuild the system from scratch, Wu would play an instrumental role in repairing the damage Chen had done.

He ratcheted down and addressed the other person he'd summoned to the conference room, the MSS operations center chief. "When the Americans realize contact has been lost with this jet, how will they react?"

The chief said, "Their CIA will coordinate with other intelligence agencies to listen for emergency beacons and monitor radio traffic.

Within an hour, two at the most, it will become clear that the aircraft has gone down. They will monitor the official search and, given the stakes, probably stand up one of their own."

"What about our mission from Canada? Was it successful?"

The chief rotated his laptop screen so everyone could see it. A polar map was presented, and one tiny bright square blinked with the precision of a rapid-fire metronome. The Challenger and its two pilots were on their way back to Beijing. "The crew did well. The decoy was dropped over two hundred miles from our estimate of the true crash site."

"And there are no emergency beacons sounding where the aircraft actually went down?"

The man gestured to the otherwise featureless map. "Complete silence. The beacons would definitely have gone off during the crash, but by now they are on the bottom of the sea. Fortune is with us."

Zhang could not contain his smile, excruciating as it was. "Good. Our head start has gotten larger."

CHAPTER

13

Arctic
Crash Site

Moving through the wreckage, Kasey quickly found two people alive. The first was the seventy-something woman she had persuaded to buckle her lap belt. She also turned out to be the source of the moaning. Still belted in and clearly in shock, the woman didn't have any obvious injuries that Kasey could see. She was helping to make her comfortable when she caught a glimpse of a man outside wandering aimlessly. He looked disoriented and was wearing the remains of a short-sleeve shirt in subzero temperatures.

A vicious wind whipped through the open fuselage, and in her first application of survival skills, Kasey looked around for protection from the elements. She saw multiple blankets strewn about on the floor. She looked up at the ruptured overhead bins and saw what looked like a brightly colored pashmina and the sleeve of a leather jacket. She pulled out the jacket, which turned out to be a men's medium, and gratefully shrugged it on. It was a terrible fit but it cut the cold so she could function. And that was all that mattered.

Having unbelted the elderly woman, Kasey drew a blanket around her shoulders and told her to sit tight. She next hurried to the forward galley and knelt by the flight attendant who was buried beneath the service carts. One of her arms was visible, and a check for her pulse confirmed she was dead.

The floor was a shipwreck of broken wineglasses and shattered china. Kasey spotted two more bodies on the far side of the galley, both flight attendants, a male and a female. The young man was the one who had offered her more champagne hours earlier. Both had been crushed in their jump seats when the bulkhead behind them collapsed. Kasey had seen her share of trauma in war zones, but never anything on this scale.

A thudding noise drew her attention. She looked up and saw the heavy cockpit door rattling as if it was being kicked from the inside. The door was already damaged, two of its hinges broken.

"What can I do to help?" she shouted.

"Stand back," a muted male voice replied.

She complied, and two more kicks did the job. The door fell away, crashing to the floor. An out-of-breath pilot stood in its frame. His white uniform shirt was shot with blood and grime. Judging by his relative youth, Kasey guessed he was the copilot. He took one step into the galley but was then stilled by the scene before him. The bodies of the flight attendants, the gallery of devastation beyond. He absorbed it all silently, a look of agony spreading across his face like shattering glass. These were people he had known and worked with. People he'd likely called friends.

Kasey peered into the flight deck. The left side was crushed, and she discerned at least one body.

He noticed her looking, and said, "The captain and relief pilot are dead."

"I'm sorry."

"Have you seen any other flight attendants?"

She gestured down. "Only the ones here. But I just started looking. There has to be another section of wreckage somewhere."

He looked back at the divide where the fuselage had fractured, and something in his expression faltered.

"Are you okay?" she asked.

"Yeah," he said after a moment. "I'm fine." He looked her up and down. "How about you?"

"A little banged up, but good to go."

"How many . . . ?" He struggled to finish the words.

"There are others who made it. Some of them are injured."

She could almost see his brain switch back on. "Okay, I need a count of how many survivors we've got. You take the main cabin. We'd normally evacuate, but since there's no fire, and given the conditions outside, let's shelter in place for now. Tell anyone who can move to gather at the front of the cabin. I also need to know what kind of injuries we're dealing with. I'm going to go search outside."

"Not like that you won't." She pointed to his short-sleeve uniform shirt. Kasey scoured the overhead bins again. It was early spring, so most of the passengers had come aboard wearing simple outerwear. The only thing she saw within reach was the jacket of a business suit. She retrieved it, noted an Armani label, and handed it over. "I'm sure we can find something better, but this should help for the time being."

"Thanks." He shrugged the jacket over his wide shoulders. It was a tight fit, but close enough. He spotted a knit watch cap on the floor and added that to his ensemble. He set off down the main aisle.

Kasey followed more slowly. She carefully searched each row of seats, clearing away dislodged fixtures and debris. She found three more survivors. Two of them, an Asian man and woman who didn't speak English but appeared to be a couple, had ended up on the floor on the far side of the cabin. They were dazed and bewildered, but seemed to have minimal injuries. Using hand gestures, and the few Mandarin words she knew, Kasey ushered them to the front.

The third person was in far worse shape. A sixty-something Caucasian man in business attire and with a gray crew cut was pinned beneath wreckage. His legs had been crushed. He was barely conscious and obviously in great pain. Not wanting to move him without help, Kasey pulled away some debris and covered him with a blanket. She reassured him she would return soon.

Many of the overhead bins were open, their lids flapping like the wings of big plastic birds. This was the source of the creaking sound she'd heard. What had been inside them—expensive carry-on luggage, laptops, purses—lay flung in every direction. A broken bottle of perfume drenched the air in Chanel Number 5.

Two rows farther on, as she neared the final row before the breach, Kasey saw a sight that sent her spirits soaring—the dark blue shirt Chen had been wearing.

She scrambled across a twisted seat, pulled away a large wall panel, and found him wedged face-down against the sidewall. Her elation ebbed when she realized he wasn't moving.

"Dr. Chen! Are you all right?"

There was no response.

CHAPTER 14

Sharpe stepped outside and was slapped in the face by abysmal conditions. The fierce wind and a temperature in the low 20s conspired for an off-the-scale misery index. Shelter from the elements would be second on his list. But his first priority had to be to locate every survivor.

He encountered three right away. A young couple in their twenties seemed almost unharmed. They were caring for a shell-shocked man in a T-shirt. He appeared to have a head injury and was huddled against the outside of the fuselage.

"You guys okay?" Sharpe asked.

The pair looked up and, in spite of his mismatched clothing, seemed to recognize him as a crewmember.

"Yeah, we're good, all things considered," said the young man.

"We ended up in a snowbank over there," the woman added, jabbing a thumb toward a distant pile of white.

Sharpe knew such things happened in all crashes, random strokes of fortune, both good and bad, that had no rational explanation. "Okay. Get that guy inside and find him something warm to wear. Same goes for you two."

They said they would, and Sharpe continued on.

He walked a wide circle around the fuselage, hoping to find more survivors, but also wanted to survey the damage. Although the left side of the cockpit had been crushed, the fifty feet of fuselage behind it was relatively intact. The belly of the jet had accordioned on impact, and when he reached the far side, he saw the jagged remains of the forward cargo door in the distance. A pile of checked suitcases and cargo had spilled from the opening of the crushed compartment.

One large roller bag had cracked open, and amid the pile of clothing strewn on the ice was a dark trench coat with a wool liner. Sharpe had only been exposed for a matter of minutes, yet he could already feel his hands going numb. Armani might be great for a night at the opera, but it wasn't made for conditions like these. He walked over, switched out to the far heavier coat, which was only slightly small, and committed to returning later to find better gear for everyone.

But first I have to make sure there's no one out here freezing to death.

He kept going, and had nearly completed his circle around the wreckage when he saw a sight that caused his gut to clench. Two contorted bodies lay motionless on the nearby ice. Both passengers were clearly dead, and he paused respectfully.

It wasn't the first time Sharpe had seen such a sight. In addition to being an F-22 pilot in the United States Air Force, he'd been his squadron's flying safety officer. This meant he had been trained to investigate aircraft accidents. He would never forget the horrific sights from his first crash scene. An Air Force executive transport jet had gone down while attempting to land in a storm in Italy. The wreckage of the C-37A, the military equivalent of a Gulfstream V business jet, along with the remains of three crewmen and five passengers, had ended up strewn across the side of a mountain. Those sights and smells, jagged and raw, had been forever seared into his mind.

Equally unforgettable was the accident board's final report, a damning backdrop of poor weather and failed ground equipment. Yet it was the crew's procedural errors, and their lack of situational awareness, that had borne the brunt of the blame. Sharpe wondered if the dreadful scene before him would become his own legacy. His professional tombstone. Had he and Captain Fowler made mistakes? Might they have done something to cause the dual engine failure? What would they be remembered for?

He forced his dark thoughts away. The possibility that others needed help had to be his focus.

The fuselage had separated just in front of the wing, and his circle ended near the breach. A giant groove, obviously made when the forward section had skidded to its resting place, tracked into the distance and disappeared in swirls of snow. If there was more wreckage, it would be at the other end of this rut.

The storm was strengthening, the visibility getting worse. The frigid wind cut at his exposed skin like rusty razor blades. The trench coat was helpful, but his exposed face and hands were going numb. Unfortunately, better clothing would take time—and in these conditions, any delay at all meant others might freeze to death. He put his head down and shoved his hands deep into the coat's pockets, his determination, or maybe his conscience, driving him onward.

He set off, following the icy channel, and told himself that the rest of the jet couldn't be far away. After a few minutes the visibility improved, but only slightly. A glow appeared ahead, and soon after he reached the point where the groove ended. It was the outcome he had both feared and expected.

Bill Fowler's words echoed from the grave. "*Four hundred thousand pounds on ten tires? Not a chance.*"

The captain had been spot-on.

The scene was a hellscape. The colors and the textures were those of death, of devastation. The ice shelf had collapsed under the aft two-thirds of the jet—the heaviest part. Low flames tongued over the frigid sea and the ice groaned from nearby fissures. This was the impact point. The hill of ice they'd struck—he realized now, an iceberg embedded in the pack—had been obliterated, replaced by a temporary lake. The bulk of the jet lay somewhere below. Thousands of gallons of jet fuel, which was lighter than seawater, had risen to the surface and was burning pyre-like. Sharpe scanned across the broad field of debris. Some pieces were floating amid the flames, others scattered across the ice, and tendrils of smoke were being whipped away by the wind. There wasn't a human in sight, living or dead. Even so, he couldn't stop himself from calling out.

No one replied.

He stared for a long moment, reeling from a scene that would surely haunt him for the rest of his life. Bill Fowler had been right about the ice not being strong enough to support a wide-body airliner. But he'd also been wrong. The forward fuselage was light enough, and had struck at a low enough angle, that the ice had held to support it. If they had known that ahead of time, could they have done anything differently?

His thoughts tumbled into a cul-de-sac, a hopeless series of what-ifs, until a glacial blast of wind brought him back to the here and now. There was no time for recriminations. They had done their best in the moment. They had saved a few.

He turned and began walking back, but as he did, nightmare scenarios began to form in his mind. Could the storm outlast their supplies? Would hypothermia set in? What if the ice began to fragment under the weight of the wreckage?

It was a commander's duty to worry—and he would do exactly that until every survivor was safe. Then, perhaps, he would someday be remembered for the passengers he saved.

Not those who were lost.

CHAPTER 15

CIA Headquarters
Langley, Virginia

The champagne cork flew from the bottle with such force it dented a ceiling panel. Bubbly splattered on the floor and a raucous cheer erupted. The party at the CIA's operations directorate was going strong.

Station personnel in Hong Kong had confirmed hours earlier that Dr. Chen Li, Kasey Sheridan, and Walter Ho were safely on board Hemisphere Flight 777. From monitors in the operations center, they had watched the jet take off and seen it depart Chinese airspace. Everyone listened with amusement as the Hong Kong station chief described the madness of an autonomous taxi gone wild. The verdict on that was unanimous, and it reinforced their already glowing opinion of Chen. Not only was the man bringing them national security gold, but he was doing it in style. He had the MSS goons chasing their asses.

As the big jet swept smoothly toward New York, the mood at Langley lightened with every mile. An agency welcoming committee was set to greet Chen at JFK Airport, and a team of technicians were already assembled to exploit the device in his possession.

With the dicey part of the op behind them, and nothing left to do but wait another eight hours, the staff had migrated to the break room for an impromptu celebration. Liquor appeared out of desk drawers. DoorDash beer and wings were retrieved from the lobby.

Shoulders were slapped and bottlenecks clinked. The cheap champagne had appeared out of nowhere. The festivities were just peaking when the first sign of trouble hit.

Deputy Director for Operations David Flynn felt his phone vibrate and saw an urgent message from the overnight skeleton crew in the ops center. New information had arrived from the Federal Aviation Administration. All communications with Hemisphere Flight 777, which was flagged for close surveillance, had been lost.

Flynn immediately dropped his half-full beer in a trash can. In the few minutes it took him to reach the ops center, the situation had changed.

"What's up?" he asked the duty officer.

"We had a temporary disruption of all polar satellite communications. It lasted roughly forty minutes but came back up a short time ago."

"Any idea what caused it?"

"Most outages like that are atmospheric events—solar flares and such. But this feels different. There was nothing in the forecast and it was oddly regional."

"But things are working again now?"

"Yeah . . . and that's the problem. Since the comms came back up, neither Hemisphere Airlines nor Canadian air traffic controllers have been able to establish contact with Flight 777. The jet's automated data-tracking system has also gone dark. Two other airliners, on the fringes of the same airspace, have been contacted without issue."

The DDO didn't need to hear more. Within minutes, everyone in the break room was back on duty. For twenty minutes, rapid-fire queries were sent to sister intelligence agencies, the FAA, and one very concerned Hemisphere Airlines flight dispatcher.

The lack of information from all of them became an answer in itself. The deputy director turned to the comms desk.

"Get me the Pentagon, highest priority. I need to know what assets we've got in the area."

CHAPTER 16

Arctic
Crash Site

Chen was alive, but just barely. Upon finding him unresponsive, Kasey had immediately checked his vitals. He had a thready pulse, his breathing was shallow, and his skin had a chalky, gray pallor. A large welt above one ear suggested head trauma. His right leg was trapped between a seat and the sidewall, and he'd obviously been thrown across the cabin, meaning there was also a chance of internal injuries. Kasey, however, couldn't deal with any of that until she extracted him from the wreckage.

She enlisted the help of the young couple who'd appeared minutes earlier escorting the disoriented man she'd seen wandering outside. That man was now sitting calmly and wrapped in blankets in a seat. The couple, who had introduced themselves as Nick and Sofia, a pair of graduate students, seemed eager to help.

Nick salvaged a long cushion from one of the passenger beds, and together they carefully worked Chen free of the wreckage and lifted him onto it, taking particular care to stabilize his head and neck. They carried the makeshift gurney forward to minimize his exposure to the cold. Once they had him settled, Kasey sent Nick and Sofia to look after the badly injured man across the cabin.

Kneeling down, she took Chen's hand and said to him once again, "Dr. Chen, can you hear me?"

She tried three more times but received no reply. On the last attempt, however, she thought he might have lightly squeezed her hand. Or was it only her mind playing tricks on her? A sudden weight descended upon her. Half an hour ago, she'd thought they were home free. Now Chen was unconscious, seriously injured, and dozens of people were dead.

Her thoughts abruptly pivoted. What about Sky Fire?

She walked toward the back of the cabin, to the spot where she'd found Chen, and began searching for the familiar black case. Given the scale of destruction, she was elated to have simply found the man she and Walter had been charged with protecting. But if she could find Sky Fire as well? That would mean her mission was still fully viable. And it would be the ultimate f-you to China—especially if the Chinese had a hand in the crash.

Her spirits soared when she caught a glimpse of the matte-black case. It had tumbled beneath a broken seat but appeared undamaged. Ever the professional, Kasey tamped down her excitement as she weighed what to do. Since there was nowhere secure to conceal the case, she decided to leave it where it was for the moment. Nevertheless, a bit of camouflage seemed in order. She spotted a bloody sweater on the floor—whose it was and how it had gotten in that state she had no idea, but the matted garment wasn't something that would be scavenged for warmth. She bent down and pulled it over the case.

"How many have you found?" said a voice from behind.

Kasey stood abruptly and saw the first officer approaching. He looked frostbitten. There was snow in his brown hair, and ice had encrusted around his nose and lips. His hands were thrust deep into the pockets of a heavy full-length coat.

She edged away from Sky Fire. She had not yet performed a head count, but with everyone more or less gathered, it wasn't hard. "Nine. Ten including you."

He considered this for a long moment. The pilot looked at the others around them, who were in varied states of consciousness, and beckoned her to the back. Kasey got up and followed him. He paused where the cabin ended, clearly wanting a bit of privacy.

She said in a muted voice, "Did you find any others?"

He drew in a deep breath. “They’re gone.”

“*Gone?* You mean—”

“I mean the rest of the airplane sank.” He pointed to the deep groove that disappeared into the storm. “I followed that to its end, about six hundred yards back. Our landing was almost blind, and at the last second there was a ridge of ice. We hit it hard, and the jet broke into two sections. All the weight—the fuel tanks, the engines, the tail—was in the back. The ice was never going to hold against an impact like that.” He looked up at the surviving section. “This section of the fuselage was lighter and broke off. It was stupid luck, but a handful of us made it.”

She tried to wrap her head around what he was saying. “So that’s it . . . there are only ten survivors?”

“I searched all around where the rest of the aircraft sank. There was no one. So yeah, ten of us made it.”

Walter was dead. As was the pregnant woman across the aisle from him. Fate had reared up in all its random cruelty. Kasey tried not to show any reaction, but failed.

“I’m sorry,” he said, seeing her anguish. “Did you know someone in back?”

She nodded. “A work associate. A close one. His wife is pregnant.”

He allowed her a moment, then said, “Look, this is beyond horrible. I lost colleagues as well. But right now, we have to concentrate on the living. There’s a lot to be done and I could use some backup. Can I count on your help?”

“Of course.”

“Okay. You should understand that our situation is . . . complicated. Normally, when an airplane goes down, first responders are all over it. Minutes away, hours at the most. But this is different. By now the authorities will know we’ve gone down, but this is one of the most remote places on earth. It’ll take at least a day for help to reach us, maybe more in this weather.”

“That’s going to present challenges.”

His voice lowered yet again. “And there’s another problem.”

“Things can be worse?”

“Maybe. I tried a number of times to send a mayday, but I don’t think it went through.”

"Any idea why?"

"No clue. It was chaos on the flight deck, all kinds of systems losing power. But the distress calls should have uplinked. On top of that, the tail of the airplane sank. That means our black boxes, which contain our emergency beacons, are gone with it. There was one handheld ELT on board, but it was stored mid-cabin so that's been deep-sixed as well."

"Are you saying what I think you're saying?"

"Yeah . . . I doubt anyone knows exactly where we are."

"Do you know?"

He looked at her curiously, as if put off by the question. "Of course. I checked the lat/long right before we hit, even marked it in the nav computer. That's the one thing I wish I could have transmitted in a distress call."

Kasey recalled her suspicions when things had first gone south. "Tell me what happened," she said. "Why did we go down?"

"Dual engine failure—virtually unheard-of. We tried to restart them, but nothing worked."

"Of course it didn't," she whispered under her breath.

"What?"

"Nothing. So we can't expect help anytime soon?"

He looked out at the storm-driven world around them. "Like I said, at least a day. Probably more like two or three."

"That's going to be a challenge in these conditions."

"Agreed. Cold like this is life-threatening."

"Okay. Then we start with the basics. We need to get everyone warm, make the injured as comfortable as possible."

"Are there any serious injuries?"

"Two that I know of. One man has multiple leg fractures. He also suffered from heavy bleeding, but I don't think it's arterial, so we can probably control it. Another suffered head trauma and may have intra-abdominal damage."

He looked at her quizzically, almost as if seeing her for the first time. "Are you a nurse or something?"

"No, no. But I've had some first aid training." She didn't want to explain her extensive knowledge of combat medicine.

"We should ask the survivors if any of them have medical training.

If not, you and I will do our best with what we've got. There's a medical kit in the galley. Hypothermia is going to be our biggest problem."

"What about building a fire?"

"The nearest tree is about a thousand miles away. So, we're going to need to figure out an alternate source of fuel. In the meantime, I'll try to figure out some way to protect us from this wind."

"Sounds like a start," Kasey said, suddenly distracted. The weight of losing Walter, of so much death around her. The tenuousness of Chen's condition and having to care for so many others. The fact that her off-rail mission might be the source of so much agony. All of it came crashing down in a torrent.

Sharpe turned back toward the front, then paused. "By the way, I didn't catch your name."

"Kasey," she blurted.

A chill went down her spine. One that had nothing to do with the frigid temperature. She had given her real name and not the false one from her CIA legend. Never in her professional life had she made such a basic error, and she chastised herself for it. In spite of all that had happened, she *had* to stay wired. Had to keep her act together.

"Good to meet you, Kasey. Brett Sharpe."

Their handshake was quick. The cold demanded it. Lives were at stake, and there was no time to waste.

CHAPTER 17

Arctic
102 NM South of Crash Site

Crack, crack. Crack, crack.

Bullets zinged out in tight groupings, the vast majority striking center mass on their targets. Chips of ice and snow exploded into the air. The men kept low as they ran, then fell prone to provide supporting fire. Fighting on drift ice was as naked as it got. No trees, no terrain, no chance of digging in. Absolutely nowhere to hide.

The unit was advancing smoothly, a clockwork flow of fire and maneuver. Only when the commander looked over his shoulder and spotted a new threat—a heavy-coated figure approaching from six o'clock—did he break off the assault.

"Cease fire, cease fire!" he said over the tactical frequency on their radios.

The order was complied with immediately and a stark hush ensued. "Make the range cold, repeat cold," he announced. "We've got company."

Lieutenant Peter Drake's team, dressed in full winter camo, secured their weapons and began heading downrange to retrieve their targets. They were probably already arguing about scores. Drake safed his own SCAR-H rifle, stood, and crunched across fifty yards of ice to meet the interloper. Drake moved effortlessly across the slick surface. He was slightly on the tall side, and he pulled back the hood of his winter camo jacket to reveal an emphatically out-of-regulation mane of brown hair and a scruffy beard.

Halfway across the divide he encountered Commander Trent Hansen.

Hansen was the commanding officer of the USS *Cheyenne*. Tall and angular, with intense blue eyes, he looked the part of a sub commander. The *Los Angeles*–class fast-attack submarine sat stoically in the distance, its sail and hull encircled by cinder-block-sized chunks of ice. The *Cheyenne* was the last boat of her type built, a 688i version with a hardened sail and forward-mounted dive planes for penetrating ice.

Drake knew the *Cheyenne* intimately. He was a former platoon commander in SEAL Team 5, and presently served as an instructor at the Naval Special Warfare Cold Weather Detachment. With the strategic importance of the Arctic increasing every year, submarine-based polar operations had become an emphasis item of the U.S. Military's Joint Special Operations Command, or JSOC for short. The cold-weather schoolhouse was based in Kodiak, Alaska, but with a gap between classes, Drake had jumped at a chance to bring one of his fellow instructors to join two of their Finnish special forces counterparts on a fourteen-day joint training exercise aboard the *Cheyenne*.

They were slated to practice methods of submarine infil and exfil, and test new weapons and support gear in extreme cold. By comparing their services' respective protocols and tactics, training on both sides of the Atlantic could be refined and improved. The Finns were among the most knowledgeable cold-weather operators on the planet. They'd confounded the Wehrmacht in World War II, and their reputation as fierce and innovative winter warriors had helped keep the Russians at bay ever since. Drake owed it to his SEAL students to take every chance to expand his skill set for teaching their unique brand of warcraft.

"Change of plans," the captain said as soon as they converged. "We're pulling up stakes and heading north."

"Are you serious?" Drake said, as he shook his head in annoyance. They had been on the *Cheyenne* for a week now, and bad weather and logistical snafus had preempted much of their planned training.

"Why north?" he queried.

The captain only shrugged.

"Objective?"

"No word on that yet."

"This isn't gonna help our training syllabus."

"Look, I don't know where we're headed or what we're gonna do when we get there. But this doesn't smell like training to me."

"An op? All the way up here?"

"I know, it defies logic. The only conflicts I've seen in these parts involve orcas hunting big fat seals." He paused for a smile. "Whatever the reason, the *Cheyenne* is being repositioned."

Drake gave the captain an appraising look. "Or maybe *we're* getting repositioned."

"Not sure how that would work with the two Finns in your little squad, but we'll find out soon enough. Get your gear back on board and button up. We're under way in thirty minutes."

"Aye, aye."

As Hansen headed back toward the sub, Drake looked out to the horizon. The skies were clear, and in the April twilight he saw drift ice as far as the curvature of the earth allowed. The weather was supposed to hold steady for another twelve hours, but a storm was bearing down like a locomotive. That was another reason they were trying to get some training in now.

He turned and walked toward his team. All three stood waiting for him, no doubt wondering what was up.

"New orders," Drake said. "We're loading back up, getting underway, and heading north. Skipper thinks it's an op of some kind."

"*An op?*" remarked Captain Raine. The senior member of the visiting Finnish contingent, blond and fair-skinned, spoke excellent English but had a heavy accent. "That sounds like a challenge."

"Don't get your hopes up," said PO2 Marcus Williams, Drake's fellow instructor from the Kodiak schoolhouse. "On a boat like this, that probably means we'll be skulking around five hundred feet below the ice chasing a Russki boomer for the next week." Williams was a tall, extreme workout fanatic, but in his full winter gear, he looked more Michelin Man than MMA.

Drake intervened. "That's a distinct possibility, Marcus. But there's not much we can do about it. Let's hit it, boys. Everything back on board."

"Brass?" Williams asked.

Drake looked out and saw hundreds of casings. Having come out hot, they had melted halfway into the ice. "Time over tidiness. Leave 'em where they lay."

"Leave evidence that we have been here?" said Juri, the second Finn. He was small and lean, and like most elite snipers, meticulous about leaving behind traces.

Drake laughed. "Like there are some other crazy-ass operators roaming around these parts? Biggest threat for us on this cruise is going to be overdosing on Navy coffee."

CHAPTER 18

Arctic
195 NM Southwest of Crash Site

Far to the west of the USS *Cheyenne*, the reinforced steel hull of the *Xue Long 2* chewed through the frozen sea, leaving a chevron of loose ice in her wake as she carved a path north.

Translated as "Snow Dragon 2," the icebreaker was one of China's newest additions. Though classified as a research vessel, its true purpose was little different from any of that nation's aircraft carriers or guided missile destroyers. *Snow Dragon 2* was a platform for the projection of Beijing's power.

Despite referring to itself as a "near Arctic state," China held no territorial claims whatsoever above the Arctic Circle. Nevertheless, it had a vital need for shorter sea routes to Europe, and an unquenchable thirst for raw minerals to feed its manufacturing monster. Among the elite in Beijing, the new Polar Silk Road was a natural extension of its long-standing Belt and Road Initiative. With the Arctic Ocean becoming ice-free for longer periods each year, those countries that maintained a presence in the region gained an immense economic advantage. So far, there wasn't a ton of competition.

Out of necessity, Russia had long been the leader in Arctic maritime operations. Canada and the Scandinavian countries took it seriously and had solid capabilities. At the back of the great-power pack was the United States. Its Coast Guard operated two rust-weary icebreakers, both nearly fifty years old, that spent long stretches in port for repairs and refurbishing. Attempts to replace them with newer, more powerful vessels stuttered regularly in Congress—one more can senselessly kicked down America's strategic road.

Sipping a cup of hot tea, Captain Yong Shiu stood on *Snow Dragon 2*'s bridge, monitoring his ship's progress. She was making 12 knots through thin pack ice, which put them ahead of schedule. Soon, however, the ice would thicken and progress would slow.

Snow Dragon 2 was capable of carving through ice ten feet thick, although only at a speed of three knots. Yong had been poring over forecasts since receiving his new orders hours earlier, hoping to steer clear of the heaviest ice as they made their way north. If the forecast could be believed—always a roll of the dice—the denser multiyear ice fields would be far to the east.

The balance of their new orders was being carried out below deck. One team of technicians was readying their most sensitive towed sensor array, and another was preparing a robotic sub for a deep dive. The classification level of the tasking, along with the suddenness of its arrival, was enough to paint a very serious picture.

Something incredibly important had ended up at the bottom of the Arctic Ocean. And the powers that be in Beijing wanted to get their hands on it.

Yong was going to make sure that happened.

Snow Dragon 2 was his first command, having spent his junior officer days aboard a handful of maritime surveillance scows. That might have been the zenith of his career had he not married well.

His new wife, Li-Mei, was shapeless, uninteresting, and the only daughter of the vice chairman of China's Central Military Commission. What his bride lacked in allure, her father more than compensated for with prospect. It was a trade-off Yong was happy to make.

At the most recent promotion board, he had been vaulted to a command billet above dozens of more accomplished officers, and like all good careerists, he felt no regret in having done so. His father-in-law had made their pact crystal clear: *Get your one year at sea, give us a grandchild or two, and the sky is your limit.*

That one year, the minimum required for further advancement, would end in less than a month. For Yong, it couldn't come fast enough.

He was tired of the sea. The cramped quarters, the shitty food. And the weather—*God, the weather.* When the new orders had arrived hours ago, he'd considered sending a message to his father-in-law asking if *Snow Dragon 1*, which was a thousand miles south, and on her way back home, might be given the job. He'd decided against it. The time-critical nature of this mission was obvious. And even his father-in-law had superiors to answer to.

Three more weeks, Yong thought, pulling up his collar against the cold. *Then the only ice I'll ever have to see again will be in a glass filled with extremely expensive bourbon.*

CHAPTER 19

Arctic
Crash Site

Survival was all about adaptation. But in the punishing conditions they were facing, Kasey knew that if adaptation didn't come fast, people were going to die.

"More to the left," she said.

She watched Sharpe and the two grad students drag one of the giant life rafts sideways.

The raft had been Sharpe's idea, a makeshift windbreak to cover the giant opening at the back of the fuselage. The temperature outside was roughly 20 degrees Fahrenheit and the wind was ferocious, making protection from the elements paramount.

Sharpe had extracted the uninflated raft from its ceiling stowage compartment and hauled it outside. When he jerked the activation lanyard, a bottle of compressed air had inflated the rubber shell to its full size in less than a minute. It was bigger than Kasey imagined, over twenty feet in diameter. And its circular shape was a near-perfect fit to seal the cylindrical fuselage. The raft was designed to hold fifty passengers in the open ocean, but it was being converted to a new use in a very different survival situation: protection from ruthless cold.

"That's good, right there!" she shouted.

Nick and Sharpe held the raft in place from the outside while Kasey and Sofia secured it. Using a dozen precut segments of rope from the handhold lines encircling the raft, they secured tie-downs to seats, bin hinges, and whatever other hard points they could find. Five minutes later, twelve anchors were attached. The raft sealed the sheared-open fuselage almost completely.

"Okay, I think that's good," she called out.

Sharpe entered the cabin, shouldering through a narrow gap at one side. He eyed the jury-rigged plug. "Not perfect, but it's almost the same diameter as the airplane."

"It definitely cuts down the wind, and hopefully it will hold in some of the warmth our bodies are generating."

"The raft comes with a canopy. If I hang that across the gap on the left, it can serve as a door." He looked up at the ceiling where one gash remained in the fuselage. "That's the last problem but it should be easy enough to deal with. The gap's only a few inches wide, so we can seal it with torn carpet or clothing."

"What we really could use is a fire," Nick said, appearing from the left.

"That would be a plus," Sharpe agreed. "I'm sure we could find a cigarette lighter or two, but like I told Kasey, the nearest firewood is about a thousand miles south of here."

Kasey surveyed the cabin. "There's plenty of foam and upholstery that looks combustible, but all of that is synthetic. It would be like lighting off a burn pit."

"I agree," said Nick. "Not only would you get chemical smoke, but a fire like that could be hard to control. The last thing we need is to set our only shelter on fire."

Sharpe weighed the dilemma. "We were carrying a fair amount of cargo. I'll go up to the flight deck and see if I can find the manifest. The forward hold is partially crushed, but if I can reach the containers, there might be something in one of them that will burn cleanly. I was planning on going through the checked luggage anyway to hopefully find better winter clothing."

They had already scavenged at least one extra layer of clothing for everyone from carry-ons in the overhead bins. The result was a ridiculous collection of wardrobes—mismatched colors and clashing designer labels, most of it ill-fitting. But it was keeping them alive.

Kasey said, "It's about to get darker in here." She nodded up at one of the four emergency-exit floodlights. All were still illuminated, but their output was distinctly less than it had been an hour earlier. "How long will those batteries last?"

"I have no idea," Sharpe admitted. "Obviously they're going to die, but I found four flashlights in the forward galley, so we'll have those. And even though it's dim outside, we'll have the midnight sun—it shouldn't ever get completely dark."

Kasey's eyes shifted to the front of the cabin where the other survivors were clustered. Aside from the man with two broken legs, who was in critical shape, they looked relatively comfortable. They had carefully moved the severely injured man using a seat cushion, much as they'd done with Chen, but he had passed out from the pain and hadn't regained consciousness since.

Sharpe had inquired whether there were health care professionals among the survivors, and the unfortunate answer was no. The closest was Sofia, who'd taken a few Red Cross courses, and whose mother was a doctor. For that reason, he'd designated her to be head nurse, and she had begun tracking the direly injured man's vital signs. His pulse was irregular, and using the cuff from the emergency medical kit, she'd determined that his blood pressure was dangerously low. They were doing all they could for him with the assets at their disposal, but he seemed to be clinging to life by a thread.

Kasey liked how Sharpe was handling the situation. He had a mission-oriented mindset, which suggested he was former military. As the lone surviving crewmember, it was his duty to assume control, but he was taking it on like a natural leader. She saw him gauging everyone's strengths, delegating tasks. The older couple, who turned out to be Chinese, spoke virtually no English, but Sharpe had used a mix of hand signals and tortured Chinese to have them look after the older woman, whose name was Beverly, and the wandering man who'd taken a blow to the head and still seemed disoriented.

Admittedly, Kasey had a more selfish reason to be glad Sharpe was taking charge. Without him, she herself would have been the most likely candidate to take over. As it stood, she could contribute, but also not lose sight of her reason for being here.

Dr. Chen's condition hadn't changed. His vital signs were stable, but the pallor remained, and he still had not regained consciousness.

She desperately hoped he would turn a corner soon, both for his sake and because she wanted to talk to him about the crash and Sky Fire.

Sofia approached from the front. The look on her face was grim. "He's gone," she said.

They all knew who she was referring to.

"His blood pressure kept dropping, and then . . . he just stopped breathing."

Sharpe took a moment to process the news. Kasey could almost feel his pain. Another passenger had died on his watch. One more name added to an ever-growing list.

"Thank you for your help," he replied quietly. "I know you did what you could."

Sofia paused, as if silently paying her respects, and then asked, "Should we move him somewhere?"

"I'll figure something out. For now, let's cover him with a blanket. We should also go through his pockets, see if he's got any ID so we can match his name to the manifest."

The woman nodded and went back up front.

"I'm sorry," Kasey said.

"I wish I could have done more," Sharpe said.

Kasey felt for the man, but she needed to get him back on task.

"Looks like the windbreak is working," she said. "It feels warmer in here already. What do we need to do next?"

The gears of his mind seemed to reengage. "To begin, we should go through every piece of carry-on. Maybe somebody brought a satellite phone aboard."

"I'll recruit some help and get on it," she replied, knowing that even in a circumstance this dire, the CIA would expect her to continue to keep the existence of Sky Fire top secret.

"Thanks. I'm going to go up front and look for the cargo manifest. We all had a copy on our iPads, and hopefully one of those survived the crash. Between the cargo bay and the luggage in the overheads, there's bound to be a few things that'll help our situation. It'll take some time to go over the manifest. When I'm done, I'll head outside and start digging through the forward bay."

"I can help you with that," Kasey said almost reflexively. "It'll go faster with two people."

"That'd be great." He set off toward the damaged flight deck.

With the injured passengers triaged and their improvised shelter giving them protection from the elements, Kasey watched him head up front. Sky Fire was now her top priority.

She was all but certain that the United States and China would be in a race to reach the crash site, both desperate to learn what had become of Chen and his creation. Having been given a rudimentary briefing on how the system worked, she also realized that Sky Fire—if it wasn't damaged, and if it even functioned at this latitude—could be decisive in determining who arrived first.

The greater concept was as ingenious as it was devious. Sky Fire was essentially a communications device designed to seize control of operating systems. It probed the RF spectrum until a digital handshake could be achieved, after which Chen's unique AI software attacked encryption and bypassed security protocols until Sky Fire took command of the hardware.

Only when Kasey had seen it in operation, when Chen created multiple distractions to facilitate their escape from Macau, did the extent of Sky Fire's potential hit her. A hijacked robotaxi, access to camera feeds, manipulated traffic lights, deceptive cell phone tracking. Used on a battlefield, it would be nothing short of military-grade chaos.

This was Kasey's basic understanding of Sky Fire. For her role in the operation—helping Chen defect—she'd had no need to know more. Now she wondered what the system might truly be capable of. Could it help extricate them from this disastrous situation?

She assumed the device was secured by a password, or possibly biometrics. Either way, only Chen could grant her access and explain how it worked. She realized that if used carelessly, Sky Fire could actually harm their prospects—it was, after all, a Chinese device, and it was conceivable that there was no way to bypass those channels. And the last thing she wanted to do was feed the MSS information. On the other hand, if she could get the system up and running, and connect discreetly to the CIA, she could forward a vital SITREP that would both expedite their rescue and secure Sky Fire.

If nothing else, Kasey realized that her priorities were recalibrating. In the chaotic minutes after the crash, she had made an uncharacteristic mistake by giving Sharpe her real name. Now that the situation had stabilized, the deep-seated code of operational security she lived by was firmly back in place. The fact that Walter had paid the ultimate price today only hardened her resolve to deliver Sky Fire into safe hands.

She glanced discreetly at the black case. It remained wedged beneath a nearby seat and was still covered by the bloody sweater. On appearances it was a generic briefcase, but anyone who opened it would see the unique dish antenna. Sharpe, in particular, would recognize it as a communications device. Until Kasey learned how to use it, how to leverage Sky Fire to affect the *right* rescue, she needed to keep it under wraps.

She shot a guarded look toward the front. Sharpe had disappeared into the wrecked cockpit. Everyone else was assembled in the forward cabin. No one was looking in her direction. Kasey casually sidestepped over a few bits of wreckage, leaned down, and pulled the red-stained sweater away.

For the first time, she took Sky Fire in her hands.

CHAPTER 20

Arctic
105 NM Southwest of Crash Site

The USS *Cheyenne* glided along silently three hundred feet below the surface. There was a storm gathering above, but in the still waters beneath the insulating pack ice the temperature was a constant 29 degrees Fahrenheit, barely above the freezing point of seawater, and the current was at a standstill. Such cold tranquility would normally have infused a sense of ease among the crew, a pelagic tranquility. The urgent new message they'd received minutes earlier, however, precluded any chance of that.

Captain Hansen's reaction had been to summon the leaders of their guest spec ops detachment for a meeting. Lieutenant Drake and his Finnish counterpart, Captain Raine, joined Hansen in the wardroom.

"We are eighty-two nautical miles from our objective," Hansen began once the junior officers had taken seats at the table. "At present speed we should arrive in four hours."

"And what's waiting for us when we get there?" Drake inquired, eyeing a printout resting next to the captain's hand.

"We've gotten word that an airliner has gone down, Hemisphere Airlines Flight 777. Certain unnamed intelligence agencies have given the Navy a bead on an emergency locator beacon that's chirping. We've been tasked to make best speed toward the crash site and search for survivors."

Drake's eyes narrowed. "So that's what this is all about? A SAR mission?" He was referencing the military acronym for search-and-rescue.

"Apparently."

"I guess it makes sense," Drake said. "Not too many first responders in these parts. But wouldn't air assets reach the site more quickly than we can?"

"The message doesn't address that, but I would be surprised if we are the only ones being sent to the area. This search box is beyond the range of helicopters from Canada or Greenland. It's very possible there are fixed-wing aircraft en route, but the weather is shit. And even if an aircraft could locate survivors, they'd have no way to pick them up."

"Which makes us the lifeboat," Drake surmised.

"That would make sense, although our orders are low on details. Headquarters included some ice-thickness projections for the area in question. It's thinner than where we broke through yesterday, so breaching shouldn't be a problem. They want us to surface on these coordinates and stand up a search party."

Drake waited. Raine remained silent. Both men were experienced operators, which meant they had a well-developed sixth sense for when commanders were about to drop the hammer of bad news.

"This whole thing feels strange," the captain finally said. "I hope I'm wrong, but I don't expect to find much. Best case, if this doomed airplane was controllable, the crew might have been able to bring it down in one piece. But the ice in this area is so thin it would never support the weight of an airliner. Conceivably the jet might have floated for an hour or two, but by now it'll be on the bottom—roughly two thousand feet down."

"There might have been time for the passengers to evacuate," Raine ventured.

"Possibly. But carrying that forward, they would find themselves on pack ice in the middle of the Arctic Ocean. They would probably be soaking wet, and according to our surface weather analysis, the temperature is eighteen degrees, and the winds are twenty knots and rising. There's a storm bearing down, and by tonight the winds will be gale force. Any survivors would be facing these conditions with little or no protection. And while the message only gives a window for when they think this crash happened, I estimate they'll have been exposed for a minimum of ten hours by the time we arrive."

"Without proper clothing or shelter, that's not survivable," Drake said.

The SEAL's knowledge of hypothermia wasn't casual—he taught the course on it at Kodiak and had extensive real-world experience. He knew the human body functioned in an extremely narrow temperature range. Lowering the body's core temperature a mere four degrees introduced shivering and mental confusion. As internal temperature continued to fall, hallucinations were common and decision-making faltered. Core temperatures below 80 degrees Fahrenheit brought unconsciousness and, soon after, death. Age, fitness, and training could mitigate the symptoms, but aside from a bullet to the head, there was no more surefire way to kill someone than putting them in subzero conditions without protection.

"I concur," Raine seconded. "But the will to survive can be powerful. We must at least try to reach the site."

"And we will," Hansen promised. His expression turned pensive. "But now we come to the second message."

"Second message?" Drake echoed.

The captain picked up the printout and read aloud. "Advise Captain Raine of pending change of operational command. State Department currently coordinating with Finnish Foreign Ministry for two attached operators deployed on board the *Cheyenne* to fall under temporary command of Lieutenant Peter Drake. Special operational orders undergoing draft, to include rules of engagement and limited authorizations for use of force."

Drake sat stunned. Hansen handed over the paper, and he read it through once, then gave it to Raine, who did the same.

"Limited authorizations for use of force?" Raine said when he finished. "What does this mean?"

Hansen addressed Drake. "Honestly, I'm not familiar with the orders you frogmen typically work under. Does this make sense to you?"

"Joint operations are common," Drake replied. "It usually involves training, but we sometimes go into hot zones and fight alongside allies. What I can't figure is how an air crash in the Arctic equates to a combat op requiring a joint forces agreement. It might make sense if this was a military jet and DOD wanted to safeguard classified equipment. But we're talking about a civilian airliner."

Raine said, "Is it possible they are not telling us the entire story?"

Drake pushed the message back across the table. "I'd say it's a damned certainty."

Raine stated, "I have no issues working with your team, and if the orders come, I will carry them out. But it would be good to know what we are getting into."

Hansen was about to respond when a petty officer appeared at the open door. "Captain, something you should see."

MINUTES LATER, ALL three officers were in the control room.

"What have you got?" Hansen asked.

His executive officer, Lieutenant Commander Adam Bennett, nodded to a headphone-clad sonar operator, who said, "Surface contact bearing one-two-four degrees, range four thousand yards."

"Do we have an ID?"

"We got an instant hit from the library. Chinese icebreaker, *Snow Dragon 2*. Not only is she chugging along like a diesel train, but she's bashing through heavy ice. Sounds like a jackhammer on steroids, sir."

Hansen considered it. There were a finite number of Chinese icebreakers, and all were in the sonar database. Identifying them by acoustic signature was child's play—such vessels were built for brute force, not stealth. If they had crossed paths with *Snow Dragon 2* in the mid-Pacific, it would be a notable oddity. Finding her here, however, was perfectly ordinary. He canted his gaze toward his executive officer, or XO for short, who'd been running the conn. "And your thinking as to why this is relevant?"

The XO said, "We're being sent to investigate the presumed crash of a commercial airliner—one that took off from Macau, and almost certainly has Chinese nationals on board. Could be a coincidence, but it sounds like *Snow Dragon 2* is pushing pretty hard. I was thinking this icebreaker might be under orders similar to ours."

Hansen considered it. "Have you been able to plot her course?"

"Zero-three-five degrees, three knots."

"Well, XO, if you're right, they're headed in the wrong direction. The Chinese will spot this ELT eventually, so we've got a head start."

"Probably. I'm just wondering what they're basing their course on." His exec let the thought hang.

Hansen gave him a jaded look. "Okay, point taken. Hold present course, but let's run this contact up to command. Maybe they'll have a better idea as to whether it's relevant."

"Aye, Captain."

The orders were given. Hansen turned to leave, but then paused. "Anything more on our shadow?" he asked.

"Not a thing," Bennett replied. "It vaporized."

New furrows of skepticism etched the captain's square features.

"What shadow?" Drake asked.

Hansen nodded for him and Raine to follow, and halfway down the passageway the captain paused and crossed his arms. "Yesterday, right before we surfaced so that you guys could start shooting ice blocks and building igloos, our sonar registered a brief contact. There were only a few hits before it ghosted away, but my best sonar guy thinks it might have been legitimate."

"Meaning?"

"I think it's very possible that somebody was tracking us."

"As in another submarine?"

"Yes."

"Who could it be?" the Finn asked.

"We didn't get enough data to make an ID, but in these waters . . . there's really only one suspect."

CHAPTER 21

Arctic
102 NM Southwest of Crash Site

Captain First Rank Arkady Khurtin stood behind his ship's sonar station, his eyes locked on a display showing the fading acoustic signature of the USS *Cheyenne*. The Americans were getting away, but that was of little consequence. Today's battle was already won.

He had been playing cat-and-mouse with the *Cheyenne* for two days now, a silent stalk he viewed as a resounding success. Khurtin commanded the *Aurora*, the first of the Russian Navy's new *Laika*-class nuclear attack submarines. His boat was, technically, still in the developmental stage. The war in Ukraine had sapped funding for most big-ruble military projects, and the *Laika*-class program had fallen years behind schedule. Yet *Aurora* was, undeniably, the future of the Russian Navy. Her initial sea trials had proven so promising, so potentially game-changing, that the Kremlin had ordered her to be tested in the real world.

In truth, the voyage was also a bit of gamesmanship. As with its newest fighter jets and hypersonic missiles, Russia had learned that fielding the next generation of weapons, even if they weren't completely battle ready, spawned panic-stricken headlines from foreign news services. Such glowing reviews of fearsome new technologies not only triggered worry overseas, but when echoed in official state media they distracted ordinary Russians from the fact that troops on the front lines were being slaughtered by the tens of thousands.

Yet in the *Aurora*'s case, unlike many other new weapon systems, the panic was warranted.

During her initial exercises with the Northern Fleet, she had not only matched the capabilities of Western boats—she had surpassed them. Her hull was coated with new composites, giving an acoustic signature so low that, under most conditions, it was absorbed by the ocean's background noise. Her jet propulsion system was proving remarkably silent at low and midrange speeds. She was fitted with the latest weapons, including Tsirkon hypersonic cruise missiles. Taken together, *Aurora* offered capabilities never before available to the captains of Russia's attack fleet.

And no one appreciated that more than the man standing in her control room.

The neatly cropped gray at Khurtin's temples attested to his experience, but the smile on his face was more telling. For the first time, he truly felt like he had the upper hand on an American boat.

"We will lose her soon," said Captain Second Rank Grekov, his executive officer and second-in-command. "Do you wish to increase speed?"

"No, let her go," Khurtin replied. "Make speed ten knots and continue present course and depth. She is sailing a straight line. We can pursue her at our leisure and make contact later if she slows."

Grekov echoed the order, then asked, "Why do you think the *Cheyenne* darted away?"

Khurtin was wondering the same thing. When they had first acquired the *Cheyenne*, two days earlier, she had been in no particular hurry. Nor had her crew been under orders to maintain silence. Pots could be heard clanging in her galley, toilets were flushing, and tools got dropped by mechanics. She had surfaced yesterday, punching through the ice to undertake some kind of exercise on the ice pack. This wasn't unusual, and it suggested a low-priority training mission. Then, with little notice, the *Cheyenne* had submerged and set off at high speed, once again making no attempt to minimize her noise signature.

"Do you think she noticed us?" the exec asked.

"Certainly not," the captain said assuredly.

There were a dozen crewmen around them in the control room, manning various stations. Khurtin had long ago learned the importance of showing confidence in front of his crew, yet his last response was not completely truthful. His initial take on the *Cheyenne*'s maneuver was that they had indeed detected the *Aurora*. If that was the case, then bolting might have been an attempt to entice the *Aurora* to follow. And while his boat might be the quietest in the Russian Navy, no submarine could be stealthy at 20-plus knots.

"Captain, there is an alert in the new message," said a seaman at the communications station.

Ten minutes earlier they had found a small break in the ice and raised a tethered buoy for a burst communication. Khurtin edged over and looked at the screen.

"What is it?" inquired Grekov from across the room.

"Headquarters has forwarded a news release issued by the Americans."

"A news release? What possible news from America would we care about?"

"It seems that air-traffic control authorities have lost contact with an airliner in this area. Hemisphere Airlines Flight 777. It was traveling from Hong Kong to New York. There were no distress calls, but the Americans are working with Canadian authorities to coordinate a response. We are to monitor the area and report any possible responses."

"So there is our answer," the exec conjectured. "This is why the *Cheyenne* is running north at high speed."

Grekov was a thinly built man with a sharp intellect. He could quote Navy manuals with the adeptness of any officer, yet there was a shrewdness to his intellect, a flair for extracting nuances from complex tactical situations, that the captain respected.

As was often the case, Khurtin agreed with his second-in-command. "Yes, I think you are right."

"For once, Fokino has given us useful information," Grekov said, referring to Russia's Pacific Fleet Headquarters.

"Let's see." The captain meandered toward the sonar station, and after a thoughtful pause, said, "Remove the filtering on surface contact Three. I want a position and course plot."

The operator repeated the command and began working.

Half an hour earlier, the *Cheyenne*'s fading acoustics had been drowned out by an icebreaker thundering overhead. At the time, Khurtin had thought little of it, viewing the ship, which they easily identified as a Chinese icebreaker, as a mere acoustic obstacle to tracking the nearly silent Americans. This new message, however, potentially altered that calculus.

A map flashed to the primary screen and the geometry of both vessels, relative to the *Aurora*, was presented.

The captain swapped a glance with his second.

"One Chinese and one American, heading in different directions," the exec commented.

And there it was again. Grekov was in line to get his own boat soon. When he did, Khurtin would miss his company, and even more so his keen mind.

The captain nodded distractedly. "Another excellent point. The question is, why?"

CHAPTER 22

Arctic
Crash Site

For all the cruel turns of fate that day, Kasey finally caught a break. Dr. Chen Li regained consciousness.

"How are you feeling?" she asked him.

"Like I was run over by a bus," Chen replied weakly.

She held a water bottle to his lips, and he took a tentative sip.

He had begun stirring minutes earlier, and she'd taken a seat next to his makeshift bed. What began as a series of spasms and moans stabilized when he opened his eyes and saw her. Kasey tried to project an aura of calm to counter the chaotic scene around them. It seemed to work. Chen was obviously in pain, but with each passing moment he became more lucid and clear-eyed.

"What ran over you was a lot bigger than a bus. Tell me what hurts."

"There is pain in my ribs when I move or cough. And there." He looked down at the bloody bandage on his leg.

"I suspect it'll be sore for a while, but I don't think there's any permanent damage done. If you need pain meds, there are some in the emergency medical kit."

"That would be appreciated." He studied the faces around them. "Where is your partner?"

Kasey shook her head. "Only nine of us made it."

He took a moment to process this. "My condolences. I know the two of you worked together, but I sensed you were friends as well."

"We were. I'm going to miss him."

Chen took in the greater scene: the shattered hull of the jet, the rubble of fixtures, the strewn personal belongings. "It is a miracle anyone survived."

"It is." She looked over her shoulder. Chen was somewhat isolated from the others, but all the same she lowered her voice. "But my mission hasn't changed. I'm going to get you safely to the United States."

His gaze went to the nearest oval window. "Where are we?"

"On an ice floe somewhere in the Arctic. The first officer survived and he's in charge now."

"That is good. He will know what to do."

"He does. But there's a bad storm outside and he thinks it could be a day or two before help arrives."

Something in Chen's expression deepened. Notwithstanding his physical injuries, his brilliant mind was recovering quickly. "But who will come?"

She gave a subtle nod, happy with how quickly their thoughts had merged. "That's the million-dollar question." She looked around cautiously, wishing they had more privacy. In the tight confines of their makeshift refuge, having a private conversation was going to be a challenge.

She lowered her voice further. "Could the Chinese have brought this airplane down?"

"Tell me what happened."

"According to the copilot, both engines shut down without warning and wouldn't restart."

He thought about this for a long moment. "One of my research associates was working on exactly such a capability. She was removed from my team and assigned to the MSS. They wanted to exploit a related technology—hidden malwares in chips exported from China in recent years."

"So it wasn't Sky Fire?"

He shook his head. "The prototype I carried out is unique, and before I shut it down on the flight, I executed a final command that destroyed all the existing databases and design records."

She looked at him incredulously. "You had that much control over the program?"

"It's not unusual. For a scientist living in the PRC, the best way to advance is to make oneself indispensable. All my colleagues keep their greatest innovations hidden as long as possible to provide leverage for advancement. But perhaps, in the back of my mind, I also knew it gave me the power to destroy everything."

"What was your reasoning?"

"The program had been metastasizing in ways I never envisioned. Sky Fire was originally designed as a defensive system."

"Defense against what?"

"China is an autocracy, and all such governments have one thing in common—those at the very top are forever nervous. Threats from within are usually a greater concern than those from abroad. The ability to 'take away the keys' from an internal military rebellion allows leaders to sleep better at night."

"And that was Sky Fire's goal?"

"Originally, yes. But when the first tests showed remarkable success, its offensive potential became apparent. The regime is desperate to leapfrog America militarily. They ordered that Sky Fire be expanded globally to target the digital architecture of as many Western civilian and military systems as possible. Seeing the project being increasingly weaponized, I became nervous. I had envisioned Sky Fire as a stabilizing force. When I made the decision to defect, I inserted a kill switch into the primary server. Ten years of work, tens of billions of dollars spent on research. I was able to wipe all of it out in seconds."

Chen coughed and his face furrowed in pain.

When his eyes opened again, Kasey said, "We need to think this through. If we allow that they *did* take the airplane down, then they did it here, in the Arctic, for a reason. Chances are, they assumed that neither you nor Sky Fire would survive. They failed on both counts."

Chen's eyes scanned the cabin. "You found the case?"

She nodded.

"Where is it?"

"In a safe place."

"Then the question becomes, does Beijing realize there are survivors."

"At some point they will, but probably not yet. That gives us a window of opportunity."

Chen looked at her quizzically, clearly not following. He was a genius when it came to controlling the binary world, but clandestine operations were far more capricious than ones and zeros.

"We need to tilt the playing field in our favor. The first officer told me the crew weren't able to send a distress call as we were going down—something about a satellite communications outage."

He reacted with a slow, contemplative nod. "Yes, that makes sense. If the Chinese were willing to risk bringing down an airliner, it would be a small additional step to jam communications. That would help hide their crime and also make a search more difficult." She could see his thoughts accelerating. "The capabilities of the device in our possession are virtually limitless and would take years to replicate. The MSS knows this and will make it their highest national priority to get it back."

"Won't they assume it's at the bottom of the Arctic Ocean?"

"Probably, but that might not matter. The control unit is designed for the field, hardened for combat conditions. It could conceivably be damaged beyond repair in a severe air crash, but right now the MSS can't know how it fared. Even if the critical drives are exposed to seawater, they're recoverable if they can be salvaged quickly. If found and returned to Beijing, there's a good chance the entire system could be reconstructed—which would save years over starting from scratch. I assure you, the MSS will stop at nothing to find Sky Fire.

"Conversely, if we can deliver it to your compatriots and they're able to exploit the prototype . . . we would be handing them a blueprint for a new weapon that could devastate the Chinese military."

"Which is why nobody but the Americans can be allowed to get their hands on this thing."

"Exactly."

"Then here's my question. Can we use Sky Fire to send a message to the CIA right now? One that the MSS won't see?"

A deep look of concern washed over Chen's face. "I think I could get a message through to your headquarters. But to do it without giving away our position to the Chinese . . . that might be difficult."

"Difficult or not, we need to find a way. Otherwise, we're as good as dead."

CHAPTER 23

Kasey was wired to be a forward-thinker. She always preferred to have a plan. The extreme situation in which she found herself, however, was unlike anything she'd ever faced.

To this point, she had mostly been reacting, making decisions in the moment to keep people alive. But now the situation had stabilized. And more critically, Chen was slowly getting back in the game. It was time for Kasey to seize control—but without drawing attention to the fact.

She found Sharpe in back, going over the cargo manifest. The life raft was holding, although it trembled with every gust of wind, and puffs of cold air crept in around the edges. The storm continued unabated, the scene through the cabin windows a steady blur of wind-driven snow in the constant twilight.

"You found it," she said, pointing to the iPad in his hand.

"I did," he replied as he scrolled through electronic pages.

"Anything of use?"

"It shows three containers in the forward bay. The belly of the airplane took some damage, but I think I can reach them and hack my way in."

"Hack?"

"The way the containers are loaded, I can't access the doors. The only way to get inside is to breach a sidewall." He pointed to the floor, and she saw a sturdy hand axe with an awl on the backside.

"Where did you get that?"

"Crash axe. Every airliner has one in the cockpit. In theory it's a firefighting tool, along with asbestos gloves and a couple of fire extinguishers. I shouldn't have any problem chopping through the side of a cargo container."

"Okay. What exactly are we after?"

"There's a load of auto parts encased in wooden packing crates. The crates should burn pretty well. There's also a huge shipment of books from something called the Confucius Institute."

"In any other situation," said Kasey, "I'd be against book burning. But the Confucius Institute is a Chinese propaganda outfit aimed at American college students. It also beats freezing to death."

"I'm sure we'll come across paper and cardboard as well," Sharpe replied. He then gave her a curious look, probably wondering how she knew about the publisher and its propaganda aims. He seemed to move on. "The passenger berths are trimmed in some kind of hardwood," he added, pulling a small piece from his pocket. "I pried this off no problem. Also found a cigarette lighter in a purse. It'll take some work, but I think we can scavenge enough to get a small fire going."

"If nothing else, it'll boost morale."

"I figure a day and a half, and we'll be out of here. It's conceivable we could get a supply drop before then. The big variable is the weather—the sooner it breaks, the sooner help will arrive."

"Then let's hope for clear skies."

Kasey made no mention of what Chen had just told her: If Sky Fire could acquire a good satellite signal, they might be able to send a call for help that included their precise location. The challenge was to keep it from careening through the system's normal channels back in China. If that happened, there was no telling who would be first to their Arctic doorstep.

Sky Fire needed to be outside for its antenna to acquire the strongest signal. Unfortunately, since Chen hadn't tried moving yet on his injured leg, the job of sending the message fell to Kasey. He told her how to configure the system to contact the CIA directly. Not wanting to do that with Sharpe looking over her shoulder, she had to come up with a reason to go outside alone. She didn't like keeping him in the dark, but if she could expedite a safe rescue, everyone would come out ahead. Everyone, that is, except the murderous MSS.

Her chain of thought broke when one of the raft's tie-downs came loose in a heavy gust of wind. Kasey hurried over and resecured the line.

"This is going to take some maintenance," she said.

"No doubt." He turned up the collar of his trench coat. "Okay, no time like the present. You up for a treasure hunt?"

"Let's do it."

She pulled on a pair of wool gloves she'd found. They loosened the canopy at the entrance and stepped outside.

The cold hit like a frigid wave, biting into every inch of exposed skin. They put their heads down and shuffled alongside the hull. The jacket Kasey had scavenged from a carry-on bag had worked well inside the cabin, but against the raw wind it was far too thin. She would have to come back outside later to send the message, and there was no telling how long that might take. Finding better protection moved up on her list of priorities.

The damaged opening of the cargo bay loomed like a dragon's lair. It was dark inside, but Sharpe had come prepared. He pulled two flashlights from his pocket and handed her one.

"There used to be a door," he said, raising his voice over the wind and pointing into the distance, "but it ended up fifty feet over there." He dragged away a few suitcases that were blocking the entrance, and soon they were inside.

The interior was equally cold, but the lack of wind was a relief. The cargo bay was roughly five feet high—Kasey had to crouch a little, but she could stand. They swept their flashlight beams to survey the place. Forward and aft, the big composite cargo containers were mostly intact, only a few dents where the hull had compressed inward. In the spaces between, suitcases of all shapes and colors were piled against the far wall, a tideline of canvas and plastic.

"You go through those," he said, pointing to the luggage. "I'll try to break into these containers."

"Got it."

The first suitcase Kasey opened was useless—it contained shopping bags full of makeup, a half dozen pair of high-heel shoes, and perfume. Someone with an unhealthy fetish for Christian Louboutin and Chanel had spent an outrageous amount of money. The next case was locked, and to deal with that she borrowed the crash axe from Sharpe. After three careful blows, the latch gave way with a *crack*.

The suitcase fell open like a giant clamshell and she handed back the axe. Kasey was buoyed by the first thing she saw: a pair of lady's fur-lined leather gloves. She tugged them on, and it was like putting her hands in an oven. Beneath these she found a heavy winter jacket. It was two sizes too small for Kasey but would probably fit the older Asian woman perfectly. She started a pile of "keepers." In the background she heard Sharpe hacking away at one of the containers.

They battered and sorted for thirty minutes. Kasey requisitioned two underlayers and a nice weatherproof jacket for herself, as well as a duffel bag full of gear for the others. Sharpe came out of a dim corner dragging a plastic box full of books, clothing, paper, and folded cardboard.

"I'd say this is a good start," he said.

She handed over a men's parka with a liner and hood, and a pair of leather gloves.

"Outstanding." He took off the trench coat he was wearing and switched to the new jacket. "Not a bad fit."

"Things are looking up," she said. "I figure next on our list should be food and hydration."

"That's easy. We've got enough steak and lobster, not to mention nuts, cookies, and assorted snacks, to feed everyone for several days. And last I checked, the bottled water hasn't frozen yet."

"If it does freeze, we can thaw it using the fire."

"There are also about three hundred liquor minis, although as I recall from my training, getting shit-faced isn't a priority in a survival situation."

Kasey grinned, less at the joke than for his willingness to attempt it. "Are you former military?"

"Yeah, Air Force."

"Bet you thought you were done with survival stuff when you took this job."

"Definitely. But it's not like we'll be out here for weeks. Help is probably already on the way. I only wish we had some kind of comm. I take it you didn't find any sat phones in the luggage?"

"No such luck," she said evenly.

"I came across one surprise." He diverted to a shadow near one of the containers and pulled out an elongated case. Sharpe opened it and extracted a rifle. He expertly checked the chamber to ensure it wasn't loaded.

"What kind is it?" she asked, knowing perfectly well it was a Winchester Model 70.

"Bolt-action Winchester—millions of them out there. There's ammo and a scope as well. It's tagged for a connecting flight to Montana, so I figure somebody was headed there for some hunting."

"Might come in handy if anyone starts a mutiny," she said lightheartedly, hoping to hide her dead-serious approval of the find.

Sharpe laughed for the first time, his blue eyes crinkling at the edges. It was easy and natural, and Kasey imagined that on most days he did it a lot.

He slid the rifle back into the case and returned it to the shadows. They stepped outside hauling their bounty. The icy wind struck again, but its effect was muted by their new and improved outerwear.

They were halfway back to the cabin entrance when Sharpe paused. He set down his box and stared into the distance.

"What is it?" she asked.

"There's something else we need to deal with." He pointed to two mounds of snow fifty feet away. "There are two bodies over there. We also have the flight attendants in the forward galley and the man who just passed away. I think we should move them into the cargo hold."

Kasey nodded. "Seems like the decent thing to do . . . for everyone's sake. What about the other pilots?"

His light demeanor, which had flickered moments earlier, vaporized completely, crushed by the burden of reality. "I closed the door to the flight deck. It's probably better to leave them where they are."

"Okay."

"I should do it," he said, more to himself than to her.

"No," she countered. "We agreed that food and drink are next on the list. You're the only one who knows where everything is. I'll deal with the remains. Nick can help me."

He gave her a long look that was something between relief and gratitude. "Thank you, Kasey. It really helps to have somebody I can count on."

"Glad to help," she said. "Come on. Let's go get our passengers warm."

As they returned to the protection of the cabin, Kasey lagged slightly behind. She scoped out the immediate area. She would be coming back soon, although not only to relocate bodies. In her years in the CIA, she had performed more than a few strange tasks in order to complete a mission. Never before had she volunteered for mortuary duty.

"First time for everything," she whispered.

Her words went to vapor in the howling wind.

CHAPTER 24

Arctic
14 NM South of Crash Site

Snow Dragon 2 had slowed to a crawl, her bright red hull driving ahead at a mere three knots. It was the best she could manage for now. The ice was one factor—it had thickened to five feet, and her massive diesel engines were straining to batter ahead, thick clouds of black belching from her twin stacks. The raging storm only made matters worse. Yet even if they had been in open seas, blessed with better weather, her speed would not have been higher. The reason was simple. For the last hour, her crew had begun executing their mission.

"Depth?" Captain Yong inquired.

"Pinger locator is at five hundred meters," said a technician at the operator's console. He was working a joystick, his eyes fixed on the green-shaded control screen. While the operator "flew" the towed pinger locator to keep it at the desired depth, a man next to him listened on a headset.

Yong looked on sullenly. An hour earlier, more details on their tasking had come through. In his opinion, headquarters was asking them to do the impossible.

Their immediate objective was to locate the emergency beacons from Hemisphere Flight 777. When an airliner crashed on land, its black boxes emitted satellite and VHF radio pings that could easily be pinpointed. A deep ocean search, however, was far more problematic.

Because satellite and radio signals were attenuated by water, an alternative system was activated. An underwater locator device, or ULD, was triggered upon immersion, sending an ultrasonic pulse, once every second, on 37.5 kHz.

This was where *Snow Dragon 2*'s façade paid dividends. She was officially owned and operated by the Chinese Academy of Science, a paper-thin veil to suggest that she was a maritime research vessel. She was equipped accordingly, with a large complement of towed underwater scanning devices and UUVs, or unmanned underwater vehicles. Indeed, few other ships in China's military and civilian armada carried the specialized equipment needed for finding underwater emergency signals—a pinger locator that could be towed low and deep behind the ship on a cable. And by assigning *Snow Dragon 2* the task, China could plausibly deny direct military involvement.

Yong's proficiency in searching for ULDs was limited to a single training exercise, and he had but one recollection from the experience: He knew it was a laborious process. Even ULD pings attenuated in deep water, meaning that *Snow Dragon 2* would have to sail within a mile of the device to have any hope of hearing it. Making matters worse, bathymetry maps confirmed that the depth of the seabed varied greatly in this area. The contours resembled those of a minor terrestrial mountain range, with ridges rising to within 650 feet of the surface and trenches plunging half a mile. Finding the crash site could take a day, or it might take a year—it all depended on the accuracy of the starting point they had been given by headquarters.

If they did get lucky and find the beacon, the second step of their tasking order was relatively straightforward. They would use a towed side-scan sonar array to map the debris zone. Only then could they begin the third, and seemingly impossible, endgame. Using their best underwater drone, they were to locate and retrieve what appeared to be—based on pictures sent by headquarters—a standard black briefcase.

The more Yong thought about it, the deeper his mood descended. The odds against success seemed insurmountable. He had grilled two of his junior officers, both of whom had more experience in such operations, and they had agreed there was little hope of quick success. It was akin to finding a specific stone in the Great Wall. An air crash would have sent debris exploding in every direction. As the pieces sank in thousands of feet of water, they would spin through currents and tumble down subterranean hills, leaving a wreckage field strewn over miles of ocean floor. As if that weren't damning enough, the deep waters of the Arctic were as black as outer space, and a visual search using the drone's cameras and lights would progress at a snail's pace.

Yong realized he was already plotting his excuses for failure, and as he did a ray of hope emerged. If he could fulfill his two simpler objectives—finding the ELT and mapping the crash site—his competence might not be questioned. How a simple briefcase could be worthy of such trouble, he couldn't fathom, but the fact that it was might also be in his favor. In the time it would take them to find and survey the crash zone, other vessels might be sent to share the burden of retrieving the case. And, from Yong's point of view, share the blame if they could not.

"Distance to turn point?" he asked.

The helmsman responded, "Nine miles, Captain."

Yong had delegated the details of the search to his executive officer. They had begun at the center of the search box and were stair-stepping outward using twenty-mile legs. The first two passes had come up empty.

"These parallels seem too tightly spaced," Yong complained to his exec.

The junior officer pointed to a map of the submarine terrain. "The depth here varies greatly. If these ULDs sank into a trench, they might be difficult to hear. Thankfully, we have good charts for this area. Perhaps if we—"

"Captain!" the sonar operator said excitedly. "I have a signal on 37.5 MHz!"

"Transfer it to speaker!"

Moments later, everyone on the bridge heard a warbling tone on the overhead speaker. It was faint but steady—the unmistakable pulse of a ULD.

"Can you get a bearing?"

After a lengthy pause, the operator said, "Ten degrees right of our present course."

Yong looked at the map. They were nearly centered in the search box. It had to be their missing airliner.

"Steer new course zero five zero," he ordered.

No sooner had the order been carried out than the technician said, "The signal is getting stronger. And I have a second tone on the same frequency." This was further confirmation. One ping would be the cockpit voice recorder, the other the flight-data recorder.

The exec said, "We are lucky to have found them so quickly."

Yong felt immense relief. "How long will it take to map the area with the towed array?"

"We must still triangulate a precise position. And it is important to remember that the wreckage could be spread over a wide—"

"*How long?*" the captain snapped.

"In eight hours, we should have the first side-scan images of the area around the beacon."

"Eight hours," Yong repeated, his frustration clear.

When no one offered a more promising assessment, he said, "Very well. Prepare to send a message to headquarters. We will advise them of our success."

As Yong mentally composed a message reflecting maximum credit on himself for locating the wreckage, it occurred to him that an additional request might be in order: a plea for any additional information on where the sunken briefcase might have been on the jet. The aviation authorities in Macau would presumably know the seat assignment of whoever was carrying it, so if the fuselage remained at least partially intact, their search could be considerably narrowed. Otherwise, they would be groping blindly in very dark waters.

In truth, Yong, along with the other officers on the bridge, never realized how tantalizingly close they were to success. Their great mistake was in assuming that all of the wreckage lay where the flight recorders had ended up. It never occurred to anyone that parts of the aircraft might be stranded on the ice, or that deepwater currents had carried the primary wreckage field, as it sank into the abyss, far from its original impact point. Adding to that separation was the movement of the ice pack on a storm-driven sea.

It didn't help that the ship's radar showed nothing but electronic clutter, overlapping fields of ice on the horizon all around. And white-out conditions had made posting lookouts pointless.

The agonizing reality: In that moment, the forward section of Hemisphere Flight 777, containing the briefcase China so desperately wanted, was a mere fourteen miles off *Snow Dragon 2*'s port beam.

And it was slowly drifting away.

CHAPTER 25

Arctic
165 NM West of Crash Site

Within minutes of arriving at its targeted coordinates, the *Cheyenne*'s sensors began registering erratic hits. It took only minimal fine-tuning to lock down a hard emergency locator signal.

"We've got it, Captain," said the comms supervisor. "Strong ELT directly above us on VHF emergency frequency."

"Right where they said it would be," Hansen remarked. "Bring her up to one hundred feet and ready the camera."

While those orders were carried out, Hansen cross-checked other variables. Temperature and pressure measurements, estimates of currents that might suggest upwelling columns of water.

Soon a video feed was up and running from the mast-mounted upward-looking camera. Vague grayscale images of the ice above filled a primary monitor. The camera was designed for low-light conditions, and software helped highlight variances in the thickness of the ice. They were looking for an answer to one question. Was the ice, as satellite reconnaissance had suggested, thin enough for the *Cheyenne* to penetrate?

The camera swept left and right, and a definitive answer emerged.

"Video and surface ice projections concur," said LCDR Bennett. "We're looking at less than a meter overhead, no significant fissures noted."

Hansen locked eyes with his XO, got a nod, and said, "All right, let's do it. Prepare to surface and configure for breaching."

"Am I the only one who sees the problem here?" Drake interrupted. The SEAL had been watching from the perimeter.

Hansen looked at him and cocked his head. "Let me guess. If this is where our airplane crashed, then why isn't there a giant hole in the ice?"

"Seems like there ought to be."

"I admit, it crossed my mind. But ice up here can be tricky. This jet went down ten hours ago, and the pack is moving constantly. Pressure builds up, and one ice sheet can roll over the edge of another. We make a pretty big hole with the *Cheyenne* when we surface. Sometimes it stays there for a month, other times it's gone within hours. As far as this downed airplane goes, I figure most of the wreckage sank. But apparently a few pieces, including this ELT, must have ended up on the surrounding ice. The big breach probably filled right back in."

Drake appeared placated, but not completely convinced.

Hansen didn't blame him because he was feeling it as well. The rushed tasking, the brief shadow they had noted on sonar, a Chinese icebreaker steaming full bore in a different direction. Instincts he always trusted, but could never quite quantify, were shouting for caution.

Cheyenne's periscope and masts were retracted, and her dive planes rotated to the vertical position. As the slow rise began, all eyes went to the depth gauge.

First contact was gentle, a slight thumping noise and a tremor in the deck. Then the grating became louder. Within thirty seconds, it sounded like the *Cheyenne* was churning through a giant rock-crusher.

BY THE TIME the access hatch opened, Drake and his team were suited up and ready to go. They stepped out on deck in full winter gear, their SCAR-Hs on chest slings.

They normally wouldn't have weaponed-up for a simple search on an Arctic ice field, but soon after the *Cheyenne* had burst through the ice, they'd received updated orders. Drake's team was to search for a hardened black case that had been on the airliner, and a photo was included. There were no specifics as to what it contained, other than a vague description of a "device that is vital to U.S. national security." They were also warned that an adverse foreign power might also be seeking the device.

Williams then reminded his fellow operators that their joint operations agreement with the Finns had been revised with laserlike speed, including a "use of force" authorization. It was enough to put everyone on edge. There was consensus on only one point, and it mirrored Hansen's concerns: They still weren't being told the entire story of what was going on.

Drake and his men moved forward and gathered at the base of the sail. On the bridge above, Captain Hansen and two junior officers were scanning in all directions with binoculars. The weather was marginal, with low scudding clouds and a strong wind. According to weather reports, a storm was approaching from the northeast, but conditions here would remain stable for a few more hours.

"Any luck?" Drake called up.

Hansen lowered his optic. "I don't see anything, but the visibility is lousy. We're still getting a solid ELT on a due-east bearing." He made a chopping motion with his hand toward the starboard beam.

Drake performed a comm check on his secure handheld radio, and a seaman in the *Cheyenne*'s control room responded clearly. After descending to the ice field, he addressed his team. "Okay, we start in that direction. Line formation on me, left and right, fifty-yard stagger."

The commandos formed up and set out cautiously. The thin ice that had been favorable for breaching in a submarine might be less so for hiking with gear. After a hundred yards, Drake decided the surface was solid, and he picked up speed.

For ten minutes they saw nothing but snow-dusted ice and the occasional fissure. Then, on the far right, Juri shouted, "Over here!"

The group joined up around him, and soon everyone saw it. A hundred yards in the distance, a yellow object of some kind sat alone on the ice. Minutes later the team was standing around it in a semicircle. The device resembled a large medicine ball, and its steel shell showed two substantial dings. There was a handle on top, and beneath that was a toggle switch and a blinking green light.

"Is that what I think it is?" Williams asked.

"Has to be," Drake answered. He bent down, picked the device up, and turned it by its handle. The back side was stamped with instructions and manufacturing information—scripted in Mandarin, French, and English. "Gentlemen, I give you one portable emergency locator transmitter."

"I did not know they made such things," said Juri.

"Standard equipment on airliners and business jets. Helps rescue crews find you if you go down."

"Or gullible navy intelligence units," Williams said dryly.

Four sets of eyes scanned across the ice, both near and far.

Raine said what they were all thinking. "There is no other wreckage here."

"And no black case," Williams added. "Only one ELT in the middle of nowhere."

Drake nodded and said, "Quite clearly, somebody is screwing with us."

"Maybe somebody Chinese," Williams speculated.

"Could be, but that's not a slam dunk. If we send in some pictures of this thing, include the manufacturer and serial number, we might get an answer."

They were back at the *Cheyenne* ten minutes later, Drake hauling the ELT. Having seen them coming, Hansen had descended from the towerlike structure atop the vessel, known as its sail, to deck level.

Drake dropped the device with a thud on the sub's steel deck. He said nothing, only watched Hansen as he ran the same thoughts they already had.

"I'll be damned," the captain said. "And that's all you found?"

"Nothing else man-made in sight. And definitely no black case."

"Okay, I'll send a report up the chain." He gestured to a petty officer, who began taking pictures of the ELT with a tablet computer.

When the man finished, Drake asked the captain, "Where do you want me to stow this?"

"Are you kidding? Bring an electronic beacon on board my boat? Might as well tie some tin cans onto the rudder while you're at it."

"So what do we do? Just leave it here? This thing might have intelligence value."

"What if we turn it off?" Raine conjectured. The Finn reached down and flicked the switch. The green light kept blinking.

"Probably can't turn it off," Hansen surmised. "It's a survival tool, and once it's activated, it'll probably chirp until the battery dies."

Everyone pondered the problem, until Williams said, "I'll take care of it, Lieutenant."

He picked up the device, heaved it out onto the ice, then leveled his SCAR-H and took careful aim. After six 7.62x51mm rounds, Drake walked out and performed an inspection. "Looks dead to me," he said. "Green light is definitely not blinking. Permission to come aboard, Captain?"

Hansen smiled cheerlessly and waved the SEAL aboard.

CHAPTER 26

Arctic
Crash Site

Kasey wasn't sure precisely why the critically injured man had died. Some combination of blood loss, internal injuries, and trauma, she guessed. He had never regained consciousness, and his vital signs deteriorated until his heart simply stopped.

Sharpe had found no identity documents in his pockets, and while that would be sorted out in the coming days, to Kasey the man's anonymity was oddly comforting. As she and Nick hauled his body outside, using blankets as a makeshift body bag, the fact that they knew nothing about him gave a measure of detachment. The same was true of the two snow-covered bodies outside that they respectfully relocated.

The lifeless flight attendants were different. Their name tags and uniforms verified who they were and what they did. For hours Kasey had interacted with them, receiving their smiles and appreciating their service. The last minutes of their lives had been dedicated to keeping everyone safe. They had perished in the course of their duties, but their professionalism had saved others.

Sharpe helped extract their bodies from the debris, and the anguish on his face was clear. These were people he had known and worked with, and extricating one woman in particular, a stunning blonde, had brought tears to his eyes. Had he dated her? Kasey wondered. Been her lover? These were questions that couldn't be asked. Not now.

Probably not ever. But she was glad for one thing: By volunteering to take the bodies outside with Nick, she was easing his burden.

Admittedly, however, her true motivation wasn't quite so pure.

The storm was abating, but only slightly. The polar wind whipped at the sleeves of her jacket as she and Nick dragged the last body into the cargo hold—a natural, if soulless, temporary resting place. When they were done, the two of them stood back for a quiet moment.

A gravedigger's pause.

"Thanks for your help," she finally said. "You've been a rock."

He nodded appreciatively. "Same to you. This whole thing sucks, but there's no way I can feel sorry for myself. Sofia and I came through with barely a scratch, while so many others . . ."

His words trailed off, and Kasey said, "I know what you mean. I lost a good friend today."

A tiny tornado of snow whipped past.

"Guess we should head back inside," he said.

She followed him to the canopied opening, and the moment she entered the cabin, Kasey felt relief. It wasn't exactly warmth, but there was no wind, and the cold was ten degrees less excruciating. Sharpe had built a makeshift fire pit using metal baking sheets from the oven and layers of aluminum foil that had been covering hot meals. His first attempt at a fire had taken nicely. He kept it small, slowly adding books and tightly wrapped cardboard. The fire was situated centrally in the cabin, and its smoke channeled up and out through a small breach high in the sidewall.

Kasey saw all the other passengers huddled in the forward section. Some were eating. Others had used the fire to warm mugs of what was probably tea or coffee scrounged from the galley. She tugged at one of her gloves, then said to Nick, "You know, these are pretty tight. I might go back to the hold—I think I saw a pair that would be a better fit. If Sharpe asks, tell him I'll be right back."

"Will do."

Nick padded ahead, removing his gloves and rubbing his hands together.

Kasey loitered near the back long enough to make sure no one was watching, then retrieved Sky Fire. She had repositioned it deep in a crevice of twisted metal near the makeshift door.

Seconds later she was outside. Shouldering close to the hull, she moved halfway toward the cargo hold and then sat down on the ice. She flipped open the case and powered up the system. The interface was essentially that of a laptop—a standard keyboard and monitor. As promised, the machine booted up quickly. She pulled out the password, which was scrawled on a piece of paper in her pocket, and began typing. It was twenty-six characters in length, an alphanumeric stew of upper- and lowercase letters, numbers, and special characters. How Chen remembered it she had no idea, but the screen unlocked immediately.

She quickly found a communications application Chen had described and began inputting commands—these, too, she had written down. Snow swept over the keyboard, but the system seemed impervious to the elements. Prompted by a message on the screen, Kasey removed the thick disc antenna from the carrying case, plugged it in, and walked it away until the cable went taut—Chen had emphasized getting as far away as possible from the hull of the jet.

Back at the keyboard, she performed a signal-integrity check. A circular icon spun as the test ran. Chen told her that the last time he'd used Sky Fire, he'd configured the protocols to ensure that uplinks weren't routed through MSS servers. She'd sensed equivocation on this point, and when she challenged him, he admitted that he couldn't be absolutely sure—it depended on which satellite the system locked on to for its connection.

They had debated the issue for a time, but in the end, Chen had won her over with math—he told her that the odds against the signal being compromised were better than 90 percent.

When a green check mark confirmed a solid signal, Kasey typed in a destination address and then slewed the cursor into the message field. Sometime in the next minute, the precise coordinates of their position would land in either Langley or Beijing.

Possibly both.

Ever so tentatively, she removed her gloves, put her fingers to Sky Fire's keyboard, and began to type. Having already composed the message in her head, it flowed quickly. In less than a minute she hit the send button. Sky Fire seemed to hesitate, as Chen had told her it would. He'd tried to explain the secure routings and connections required to reach Langley, but even for an experienced intelligence officer it was too arcane to follow.

Kasey was so fixated on the screen, and the howling wind so loud, that she never heard the footsteps approaching on her right.

"*What are you doing?*" bellowed an authoritative voice. "*And what the hell is that?*"

CHAPTER 27

In Kasey's many years with the CIA, she had acquired a sixth sense for how far she could stretch lies and deception. Each situation, of course, was unique. Facts, personalities, and risks combined for a broad range of outcomes that had to be measured against the ever-constant goal of mission success. In essence, Kasey knew that bullshit, no matter how well backstopped or how convincingly conveyed, always had its limits.

And at that moment, she knew she'd hit a wall with Brett Sharpe.

She looked up and met his gaze. Had she been caught out by anyone else on this ice floe, she might have tried to talk her way out of it. But Sharpe would know, even if only vaguely, what he was looking at. He'd already brought up the subject of communication and had told her point-blank that rescuers might not be aware of their precise location.

"It's a satcom device," she said.

"I can see that." He came closer, hovering over her, a clear attempt at intimidation. He looked down at Sky Fire and said, "My first instinct is to ask where you found it . . . but something tells me this isn't something you just stumbled across."

"I can explain—"

"*Explain?*" he cut in. "No, let *me* explain that one of my passengers just died for lack of medical care. Let me remind you that I entrusted you with the knowledge that I wasn't able to send a distress message before we landed. If we don't get rescued soon, under these conditions, more people are going to die! You and I talked about this, and all along you had the means to send for help?"

"It's not that simple. Please, just listen for a minute."

Sharpe was livid, the muscles in his neck straining. But he remained quiet, giving her a chance.

"Look, I understand your anger. But there's a complication you're not aware of."

"Something more important than the lives of nine people?"

"Actually, yes. The lives of thousands, even millions could be at stake!"

He recoiled ever so slightly. Indignance surely, but also a trace of indecision. He stilled and his eyes narrowed. "What are you talking about?"

She glanced behind him, as if checking whether anyone else was outside. It was a subtle bit of manipulation, but one Kasey felt justified in employing. By implying secrecy, she would emphasize the importance of what she was about to say. "I work for the CIA." She looked down at the case by her feet. "My partner and I were in Hong Kong on a mission to retrieve this, along with the man who designed it."

She half-expected him to challenge her claim of working for the agency. It was the kind of thing delusional people said. People who had cracked under the stress of extreme situations. Like airplane crashes. He gauged her for a few beats, measuring and assessing. Then his gaze went down to the black case and the backlit screen.

After a thoughtful moment, he said, "Your name." Not a question, but an accusation. "When I was going over the cargo manifest, I had an impulse to check the passenger list as well. There was no one named Kasey on this flight. No female with the initials K.C."

She nodded. "You got me . . . I slipped up. But that only proves my point. I'm traveling under an alias. In those first moments after the crash, I was out of it. I shouldn't have divulged my real name. Trust me, I rarely make mistakes like that."

She saw him mentally challenging her every word. In truth, she would have been disappointed in him had he not.

Kasey continued, "My partner, Walter Ho, was in the aft section. He didn't make it. We've been working together for years. He was my best friend at the agency."

She hadn't embellished any of these words, nor the tone in which she'd delivered them. Her confession was raw and real, and came straight from her heart. It seemed to have an effect. Ever so slightly, she saw a softening in Sharpe's bearing.

"I'm sorry," he offered.

She nodded her appreciation.

When he spoke again, his suspicion wasn't completely gone. "You say the two of you were bringing back this . . . whatever it is, along with someone else?"

"Dr. Chen Li. He's China's leading researcher in the military applications of artificial intelligence."

He glanced at the fuselage. "Did he survive the crash?"

She nodded. "You won't see his name on the passenger list either. He's the Asian man who was unconscious for a time. That's why I didn't try to use this sooner. I had no idea how to operate the system. I needed Chen to explain how to gain access so I could send a message to Langley."

"This guy is defecting?"

"That's right. And the technology he's bringing with him is priceless. It would have given China a big war-fighting edge against the U.S. and its allies."

He looked skeptically at Sky Fire. "What does it do?"

"I was only given a pencil-sketch brief. But honestly, if I did have a deeper understanding, there's a lot I wouldn't be able to tell you for national security reasons." She paused, expecting him to argue exigent circumstances or something along those lines, but he didn't. Sharpe was ex-military. He understood which side of the need-to-know threshold he stood on. "Basically," she confided in him, "it uses sophisticated artificial intelligence to allow ground commanders to seize control of military hardware."

"AI battle management?"

"Something like that. Except it can attack and take control of both friendly and enemy assets."

He seemed to measure his words, before saying, "You and I are here because our airplane simultaneously lost both engines. I've been in aviation a long time, and that's a one-in-a-billion failure. Now you're telling me we had a scientist on board with a device that can take control of things. I'm not into conspiracy theories, but does that not seem highly coincidental?"

Kasey nodded. "It's one of the first things I asked Dr. Chen when he regained consciousness. I pressed him on whether the Chinese could have brought down our airplane."

"And?"

"Not with this system—it wasn't active at the time, and this is the only prototype."

"Then what happened?" Sharpe pressed. "Commercial aircraft just don't drop out of the sky."

Kasey nodded. "Chen told me one of his protégés had been working with the Ministry of State Security on a new program. They're trying to leverage China's manufacturing dominance by burying viruses in the control software of electronic components. Most simply gather information, but there are also destructive variants that remained latent, serving as hidden weapons that can be activated in a crisis. Direct strike, irregular warfare, cyberattack, sabotage . . . the potential for devastation is massive."

"And one of these malwares, embedded in our engine controls, was the last chance to stop Chen's defection?"

Kasey nodded.

Sharpe stood tall. She could see his rage building.

"To bring down a civilian airliner with passengers on board?" he said, as if trying to wrap his head around the idea. "That's the kind of thing that could start a war."

"I agree. Which tells you how important Dr. Chen and this system are to the Chinese."

He looked at the screen. The connection was still processing, the usual spinning wheel. "The message you're sending to the CIA right now—what does it include?"

"I told them there are nine survivors, and that they needed to reach us quickly."

He looked at her fatalistically and said, "Because we're all going to freeze to death? Or to rescue this defector and his prize creation?"

"I told them Dr. Chen and Sky Fire both survived the crash. Honestly, I don't care which is a bigger motivator for them to get us the hell out of here. But there's something else to consider. Chen wasn't one hundred percent sure this message wouldn't be intercepted by the Chinese. Even if that doesn't happen, they already have a rough idea of where we are."

He looked up at the hard gray sky. "They brought us down here intentionally."

"It's one of the most inhospitable places on earth."

"The edge of the old mariners' maps where they used to draw dragons."

"Exactly. In all honesty, I'm glad you walked out here when you did. I could use your help. Right now, there's a race on to reach us. We have to do everything in our power to make sure the good guys win."

Sharpe pointed his gloved hand at Sky Fire. "And this device might make that happen?"

Kasey looked at the screen. The wheel of death had stopped spinning, and in its place two words appeared: MESSAGE SENT.

"I think it just did."

His gaze shifted to the horizon, the icy void where the main wreckage had sunk into the abyss. "I hope you're right. Because if Chinese did cause this, and they got here first . . . so help me, I'd get that rifle and shoot every damned one of them."

"Hopefully it won't come to that. But if it does, I'll be right there helping you reload."

Kasey no longer had any doubts. Sharpe was on her side. That could prove critical in any number of ways. Yet it also came with risks. The anger inside him was continuing to grow, like a massive thundercloud waiting to sling a bolt of lightning onto the world. And anger, blind and uncontrolled, could do more harm than good.

She was about to tell him exactly that when a great roar in the distance intervened.

It reverberated in the cold but was definitely not related to the storm. It wasn't the howl of the wind or the keening of sleet against the hull, but a resonant animalistic roar.

The two exchanged a stunned look, yet neither bothered to ask the obvious question. Because only one thing here was capable of such a primal noise.

Kasey raced toward the cargo hold and retrieved the case containing the rifle.

CHAPTER 28

Langley

The mood at CIA headquarters was bouncing like an overinflated basketball. At first the mission to extract Dr. Chen from Hong Kong had seemed like a rousing success. Then the aircraft bringing him home had vanished in the Arctic.

In the hours since, only one new bit of information had arrived: Polar communications satellites, which had suspiciously gone offline for a time, suddenly came back to life and registered a solid emergency locator beacon. This was strong evidence that the airliner had indeed crashed.

Now the operations center was digesting a report from their only asset in the region, the USS *Cheyenne*, which had rushed to the presumptive crash zone. Unfortunately, that only muddied the picture further.

"ARCHEX-AP3," said an analyst from the technology section.

He and the deputy director were hunched over a monitor studying the photos sent by the *Cheyenne* of the device they'd recovered. "It's built by a Chinese manufacturer, one of their bestselling models. Portable emergency locator transmitters, or ELTs, are standard equipment on airliners and business jets."

"You say this is a *portable* device?" DDO Flynn asked.

"That's right. The ELTs in the tail section of a jet activate automatically if it goes down. But in a ditching scenario, those beacons sink with the wreckage. With one of these on board, you can load the passengers into life rafts and take an ELT with you."

"Okay, I guess that makes sense. Could this be from Hemisphere Flight 777?"

"No, I already looked that up in the jet's maintenance records. The portable ELTs that Hemisphere Airlines uses are from a French manufacturer."

"So how did this one end up in the middle of an Arctic ice field?"

"That's the million-dollar question. But when you add in the fact that there's no trace of any other wreckage . . . it seems pretty clear. Somebody put it there."

"To get us chasing ghosts."

"I think that about sums it up."

"China," concluded Flynn.

"That's the most logical answer, but it's not a slam dunk. These beacons are manufactured in Tianjin, but they're sold all over the world. Anybody could get a hold of one."

"I don't understand how it got where we found it."

"I suppose it could have been brought in by boat—a sub or an icebreaker. But given the time constraints as we know them, there's a more likely answer." The analyst magnified the best available image and pointed to a large dent on the device's housing. "These transmitters are built to survive air crashes, and you can see where this one took a pretty good hit. If I were to guess, I'd say somebody dropped it out of an airplane or a helicopter from low altitude."

"Seriously?"

"Technically, it's perfectly feasible. But it does imply a certain amount of desperation."

The DDO thought about that. If China had realized that Chen and Sky Fire were on their way to New York, desperate is precisely what they would be. But to down a commercial airliner with passengers on board? That seemed incomprehensible, yet it was where all the evidence was pointing. Before he could pepper the analyst with more questions, the operator at the comm station said, "Sir, I've got an incoming message."

"From who?"

"I'm not exactly sure. It came via an irregular routing. None of the usual agency protocols. The team downstairs decided to forward it due to the implied geolocation."

"Geolocation?"

"The source of the transmission was triangulated through two polar satellites, and the coordinates correlate with a lat/long that's embedded in the message itself. We're working to verify all this, but it appears to have come from very high up in the Arctic Ocean."

"Put the fix on the map!"

A blue circle flashed to the main screen at the head of the room. It was well over a hundred miles from the spot where they'd sent the *Cheyenne* after a decoy. The dot was also nearly on top of a second symbol—the Chinese icebreaker they had been tracking.

And just like that, the basketball bounced again.

After chasing their asses for hours trying to locate the crash site, they now knew where it was to within an accuracy of two meters. More intriguingly, someone had just sent them a message from that very spot, but it hadn't followed the appropriate secure communications protocol. Either they didn't know what they were doing, or they were taking one hell of a risk of their transmission being discovered.

"That ship we've been tracking is just south of this new fix?" Flynn queried, wanting to be sure about the picture before him. "The icebreaker the *Cheyenne* sent us a heads-up about?"

"Yes, sir. The *Snow Dragon 2*. The two are separated by fifteen miles."

The DDO turned to the NRO liaison, and said, "Do we have an ice survey for this area?"

The woman began typing furiously. "We do," she replied.

"How old is the data?"

"Six and a half hours."

"Give me an overlay."

The map changed again, and in a cool magenta hue the current topography of ice fields in the area was added to the display. With the complete scene presented in high-def clarity, Flynn stood awestruck. Roughly 200 meters from their new blue dot was a hole in the ice pack the size of a football field. There were no similar breaches anywhere else on the screen. It was exactly the kind of aberration they had been searching for 160 miles west. And most jarring of all: Just over the horizon from their new reference point, a Chinese icebreaker was loitering in the pack ice.

"Well, I'll be damned," Flynn said.

The comm officer announced, "The rest of the new message is arriving on your console, sir. Alphanumeric security protocol verifies it as being from Orion."

Flynn saw a text field blink onto the screen.

> **3WLE6BT. Hemisphere Flight 777 down this position. 9 survivors including Orion and Falcon. Package intact and operable. One surviving crewmember, FO Sharpe. Need extraction ASAP for all. Chinese involvement in downing likely. Will check for response this address at 2000Z and include secure challenge.**

Silence froze the room as everyone processed the implications of the message. Orion was Kasey Sheridan. Falcon was Dr. Chen Li. The package could only be Sky Fire, and it was up and running. The fact that Walter Ho, code name Nike, had not been mentioned could only mean that he wasn't among the survivors.

Flynn was stilled by this realization, but not for long. His voice erupted in a ragged tenor of urgency. "The Chinese may have beat us to the scene. But we are not out of the fight yet, ladies and gentlemen. We have ninety minutes to come up with a plan." He sprayed orders across the room like an overcaffeinated machine gunner.

Only after the workstations around him were humming in overdrive did Flynn reach for the blue phone. Taking a deep breath, he placed a call to the White House.

CHAPTER 29

Beijing

Zhang Tao felt something warm on his chin and realized all too late that a rivulet of drool had escaped the corner of his mouth. In his periphery, he noticed an attractive young woman at a nearby workstation staring at him. He wiped away the saliva with the sleeve of his shirt before turning his head and locking her in a glare. Her head snapped back to her screen.

His senses were faltering, as was his mind. Zhang desperately needed sleep, but it was out of the question at the moment. The meds would probably have prevented it anyway, but the ongoing crisis killed any chance of respite. Nothing kept one awake at night more than the prospect of a bullet to the head. And if he could not successfully retrieve Sky Fire, that was the most humane outcome he could expect.

"How deep is the water there?" he asked, his attention riveted on *Snow Dragon 2*'s salvage effort.

"Three hundred and ten meters," replied the weary ops-center chief. "Shallow for this area. The bathymetry maps also show the immediate area to be mostly flat. This will speed our recovery operation substantially."

"What of the Americans?"

"*Snow Dragon 2* reports no vessels or aircraft in the area."

Zhang was encouraged, but not convinced. Icebreakers weren't equipped to detect enemy aircraft and submarines. If the Americans were closing in on the crash site, they might not be detected. Indeed, the lack of any clear response by the Americans felt ominous in itself. He turned to Wu, who was, as usual, engrossed in something on her laptop.

"Do you have any other tricks up your sleeve?" he asked.

"I brought down your airplane," she said distractedly, not taking her eyes off the screen. "Is that not enough?"

Once again, Zhang bristled at her insolence. He tamped it down but made a mental note. He needed this woman's expertise more than ever, but her usefulness was perishable. If he survived this crisis, he was going to make her pay. It might take months, or even years. But he would not forget.

Perhaps sensing his vindictive mood, she looked up and said, "If I had Sky Fire in my hands, I could make good use of it. But things are going as well as can be expected. Captain Yong has located the wreckage, and the mapping has begun. Sky Fire may be at the bottom of the sea, but if it can be recovered, I can rebuild the controller quickly. And I promise you, when I do, it will be better than Chen's original."

Zhang wasn't swayed. As a long-serving intelligence officer, he was profoundly familiar with hollow promises. They were the stock in trade of all upward-aspiring bureaucrats, even the technology experts.

That thought cascaded to another growing concern. Before today he had never heard of Captain Yong Shiu, but with his career riding on the man's competency, he had researched the *Snow Dragon 2*'s skipper. What he found was not encouraging. By all accounts, the man was a poster child for *guanxi*—the career advancement via nepotism that ran rampant in the PRC. This was hardly a surprise, but it instilled further anxiety.

The unknowns of what was happening began to weigh on Zhang. How long would it take to locate and retrieve Sky Fire? How were the Americans responding? What assets had they deployed? He knew the decoy ELT was in place, but had they taken the bait?

He pinched the bridge of his nose, careful to limit the pressure.

"Sir, a new image has just come in!" the chief said excitedly.

Zhang hurried to the man's workstation and saw a single photo. They had diverted a satellite for a fleeting pass over the decoy. The image was dim and grainy, taken near the edge of the storm half an hour earlier. Despite the poor quality, there was no question what they were looking at. Like a great lumbering dragon, a submarine had surfaced next to their lure at the end of the earth.

An American submarine.

Just like that, many of Zhang's questions were answered. And the game entered a brand-new phase.

CHAPTER 30

Arctic
20 NM South of Crash Site

More than the commanders of any other weapons system, submarine captains made their living off of instinct.

In large part, it was a consequence of operating in the blackest environment on earth. Enemies were often "seen" in momentary acoustic pings, which meant their movement could only be predicted. Attempting to highlight an adversary with active sonar meant giving away one's own position. There were decoys and false echoes in a sea of acoustic mirrors, and in far-flung regions like the Arctic Ocean, bathymetric data to identify undersea obstacles was of dubious accuracy. What's more, unlike most naval assets, support from friendly surface ships and command centers was limited by difficult communications. The end result was that submarine warfare was little different from what it had always been: a quasi-blind contest of wills between commanders.

And Captain Arkady Khurtin wouldn't have had it any other way.

"Range to target," he said to the sonar operator, his voice calm and assured.

"Twelve thousand meters," came the reply.

"Make speed four knots."

The command was repeated and carried out. The *Aurora* slowed to a crawl, giving Khurtin time to assess the situation.

Hours earlier he'd made a decision that many of his crew, judging by the looks on their faces, had found highly questionable. They'd broken off their pursuit of the USS *Cheyenne* and were instead chasing down a thundering Chinese icebreaker. Their success in shadowing the Americans had been an extraordinary triumph and was a testament to the abilities of Russia's new *Laika*-class design. The *Aurora* had easily caught up with the *Snow Dragon 2* and was now ghosting at a safe distance—hardly a challenge, since icebreakers weren't equipped to detect submarines.

Aside from a brief discussion with his exec, Grekov, Khurtin had not explained his reasoning to the crew. Initially there had seemed little benefit in chasing after the Chinese vessel, yet the report of the downed airliner had stirred his imagination. Everything he saw from both the vessels he had been tracking—their speed, their straight-line courses, and a complete lack of defensive measures—supported the idea that they were responding to the crash. Yet their divergent geometry had transfixed him, and on little more than a hunch he'd broken off to tail the icebreaker.

Now Khurtin was increasingly convinced he'd made the right call, although the benefits of having done so remained elusive. If his instincts about the vessels responding to the air crash turned out to be correct, he didn't see how following either boat would further the interests of the Russian Navy. Still, he felt there was something going on, and like a shark sensing a whiff of blood in the water, he'd taken up pursuit.

Khurtin racked his brain, wondering how he might get more information. Communication, as ever, was a constraint. The original message regarding the air crash had been received from a buoy antenna they'd deployed in a patch of open water. To transmit a message to headquarters from here, perhaps requesting guidance on how to proceed, would mean breaching the ice. That would give away their position. More to the point, he doubted Pacific Fleet Headquarters would have anything useful to add to the equation.

No, Khurtin was certain he was better off making his own decisions.

To that end, he decided to make use of the *Aurora*'s onboard sensors, some of which were unlike any he'd previously had at his disposal. Most relevant at the moment was a new upward-looking camera system. A network of three low-light lenses, designed expressly for Arctic operations, passively tracked minute variances in ambient light and correlated them to grid coordinates. The end result was a near-real-time map displaying the thickness of the ice overhead.

Khurtin thought it might be telling. *Snow Dragon 2* had paused her search pattern, and ever since had been mapping the bottom with a side-scan sonar device—easily noted by the *Aurora*'s own passive listening system. This suggested the Chinese ship was zeroing in on what she was looking for.

Which made Khurtin more curious than ever.

He addressed the communications officer. "Was there a new ice map in the download we received from the buoy?"

Russia's multispectral satellite capabilities were not up to the standards of the Americans, but they were getting better. And thankfully, Arctic coverage was a high priority. The most recent ice map in their area of operations was supposed to be included in every burst communication, although reliability was always an issue.

The comm officer confirmed that there were indeed new images. He handed over printouts and Khurtin spread them out on the chart table. What he saw confused him at first, and he beckoned his exec to join him.

"This is the latest surveillance of our area," the captain said.

Grekov eyed the satellite images. Khurtin eyed his exec.

He watched the younger man's face, and saw his eyes drift to the same spot, fifteen miles north, that had seized his own attention. A light blue area that denoted very thin ice.

Grekov tapped an index finger on the disparity. "This doesn't look like a polynya," he said, the Russian term for naturally occurring gaps in ice coverage. "The shape is wrong—not linear and tapered, but almost perfectly round. It appears to be slowly freezing over."

They both stared at the great hole in the ice.

Khurtin carried the idea brewing in his mind a step further. He carefully checked the deep water current estimates, and also considered the drift of the ice pack in the current high winds.

Grekov nodded knowingly. "Do you think it is possible? Could the wreckage have drifted that far before it hit bottom?"

"It's the only thing that makes sense. The Chinese have clearly found something."

"I suppose it makes sense. But at this point I would say it's academic."

"Probably. But what if—"

Their conversational thread was clipped by the sonar operator.

"Sir, I have a new contact from above. Bearing three five zero. Three echoes, very distinct."

Khurtin exchanged a surprised glance with his exec. There was nothing to the north but their round patch of thin ice. "Can you tell what made them?" the captain asked.

"Yes. Analysis clearly identifies the sounds as gunfire."

CHAPTER 31

Arctic
Crash Site

Kasey lowered the Winchester.

"I think you missed," Sharpe said sarcastically.

She frowned at his assessment.

The polar bear had appeared out of the gloom, a hulking figure meandering closer with the species' distinctive swaying gait. Kasey had seen her share of bears before, in the Eastern mountains and the Rockies. This one was in a different league. It had to weigh half a ton, and its size was accentuated by the dim twilight and desolate backdrop of ice.

The bear wasn't moving aggressively, but it was definitely headed their way. When it was half a football field away, Kasey fired three rounds into the air, hoping to scare it off.

It seemed to work. The creature startled and scurried away, but it stopped before disappearing. After a hundred-yard retreat, the bear half-turned and lifted its nose into the air. Then it lumbered away and disappeared in the swirling snow.

"He'll be back," she said.

"I agree," Sharpe seconded. "It's the bodies. Bears are as much scavengers as they are predators. He also might not be alone."

"Actually, polar bears tend to be solitary. Conditions out here are tough and there's not enough food to support competition."

"Does the CIA teach all its agents about polar bears?"

"First of all, I'm not an agent, I'm an operations officer. And what I know about polar bears came from a report I wrote in middle school biology." She dropped the Winchester to a low ready position. "Anyway, it's a good thing you found this."

"It might come in handy."

"Are you a good shot with a rifle?" she asked.

"When you grow up in Texas *and* your last name is Sharpe, you really don't have a choice."

She couldn't suppress her grin. "Okay. Bottom line, this shit's getting real. On top of everything else, we've now got an apex predator lurking out there. With only one gun, it needs to be immediately available to either you or me at all times."

"Agreed. Why don't you keep it for now. I'll double-check the cargo bay to see if there's more ammo."

"That would be helpful."

He pointed to Sky Fire. "Are you going to leave that powered up?"

Kasey considered it. Chen had told her battery power wasn't an issue—he had charged the system during the flight. On the other hand, batteries didn't like extreme cold, and further charging was out of the question. "It'll take some time for Langley to come up with a plan. I told them I'd check back in a little over an hour, so I think it's best to shut down until then."

She began typing, and Sharpe headed toward the cargo bay. As Sky Fire's screen blanked, Kasey recalled his anger. He seemed to have recovered, but she wanted to be sure.

"Brett . . ."

He paused and turned.

"I told you that the Chinese were probably behind this crash. But if I've learned one thing in my years of intelligence work, it's that you can't let emotions cloud your judgment."

He thought about that and said, "I'll do my best."

"Good. Because people who can't . . . a lot of them end up dead."

CHAPTER 32

Arctic
140 NM West of Crash Site

Full house!" Raine said, slapping his cards down on the table of the *Cheyenne*'s wardroom.

Drake frowned. With a flick of his wrist, a lousy two pair went spinning to the center of the table. Williams and Juri were right behind him. The Finn commander had been kicking their asses.

Raine raked in the meaningless pot: a pile of 7.62x51mm NATO-standard cartridges. In an era when no one carried cash, it was the best they could come up with. The value, of course, was little more than symbolic—the team had brought eight thousand rounds, all of it technically property of the United States taxpayers. And if they could get any training in at all, it would be expended before they returned to Kodiak.

Raine, the dealer for the next hand, smiled and began shuffling.

Working in elite special operations units had more than its share of excitement—firefights, HALO jumps, submarine infiltrations. That said, no soldier could completely escape the interminable curse of military service: long periods of boredom between the rushes of adrenaline.

Drake's eyes shifted to the digital clock on the wall.

An hour earlier, when the *Cheyenne* had still been on the surface, he had typed up a hasty mission report, attached photos of the dented

ELT, and launched it into the ether via encrypted satcom. The moment MESSAGE SENT was confirmed, Captain Hansen had ordered the boat rigged to dive. Drake and his team had stowed their gear, and soon after the poker game had broken out.

There was never any question as to which direction they would sail. The Chinese were almost certainly the ones yanking their operation chain, and the sonar techs had very clearly tracked the Chinese icebreaker *Snow Dragon 2* crashing eastward. It didn't take a genius to make the connection.

Raine was dealing the next hand when the *Cheyenne*'s captain appeared from the companionway.

"I've got an update," Hansen said. "Came in right before we submerged." He paused a beat, taking in the table full of bullets. "It's as we suspected. The CIA has confirmed the crash site. Roughly one hundred sixty-five nautical miles east of our little detour."

"Which means the Chinese beat us there," Williams surmised.

"That's the funny thing," Hansen said. "There's still a chance we can win the race."

"How?"

"This device the CIA wants so badly—somebody used it to transmit the exact coordinates of the crash site to Langley."

"No shit?" Drake said. "You mean there are survivors?"

"Nine, apparently. Along with this mystery black case that's got everyone spun up. The Chinese are in the area, but they got distracted."

"Distracted by what?"

"Most of the wreckage sank, and the *Snow Dragon 2* has apparently locked on to the signals from the airplane's black boxes—the real ones. They ended up in deep water. But the section of wreckage with the survivors is sitting on an ice floe fifteen miles away."

"Somebody's smiling down on us," Williams replied.

"Time will tell. At any rate, we have new orders. We're to make best speed to the scene and recover both the survivors and this precious black case."

"Will the ice be thin enough for us to surface?" Raine asked.

"When the plane crashed it made a hole in the ice pack that's more than big enough. The breach is starting to freeze back over, but for our purposes—it'll be like punching through a wet paper bag."

"How long until we arrive?" Drake asked.

"At present speed, six hours."

Glances were swapped all around the wardroom table. "A lot can happen in six hours," Drake said. "The Chinese might spot the survivors."

"That's a possibility," Hansen replied. "Unfortunately, we won't be able to receive any comms until we arrive. If the situation changes, it'll be up to us to figure out how to respond."

Raine swapped glances with his team and asked, "What's our part going to be in all of this?"

"That remains to be seen," continued Hansen. "For the time being, we haul ass east. When we arrive, we'll stop and listen. I doubt we'll have any trouble finding the icebreaker again. If we find her in the same place, idling to hold her position, then we surface in the big hole, give aid to the survivors, and lock down the black case."

Juri looked at him. "And if she's on scene and has already collected everything?"

"Then things get more complicated," the skipper admitted. "But headquarters made one thing very clear—our absolute priority is to find that case."

"Do you think the Chinese might be after it as well?" Williams asked.

"There's been no mention of that, but out of caution we should assume they are."

Drake saw concern cloud over the captain's expression. "Is there something else?" the former SEAL inquired.

Hansen cocked his head. "I'm still concerned about that sonar hit we got earlier, the one that ghosted away. We're making good speed at the moment, but we're also making a lot of noise."

"Wouldn't anybody tailing us be just as loud?"

"Yes, and we haven't picked anything up on passive monitoring. It's just one of those things that keep captains awake at night."

"So don't sleep," Williams said. "It's only six hours."

Hansen grinned wearily. Saying, "I'll let you know if anything changes," he disappeared down the companionway.

The wardroom fell silent.

Raine set down the deck of cards and said, "Am I the only one thinking about our new orders?"

"The use-of-force provision our governments pushed through with uncharacteristic efficiency," Drake stated, the exact same thought on his mind. "Somebody in D.C. thinks this could go hot, and they want legal cover to put every available gunslinger into the fight."

Williams said, "The order talked about 'limited authorizations for use of force.' But the more I hear, the more I see the limitations disappearing."

Drake pushed back from the table, stood, and gestured to the cartridges on the table. "We've got six hours, gentlemen. Better tidy these up—we might need them for something more than target practice."

CHAPTER 33

Arctic
Crash Site

For fifty minutes after picking up the sound of gunshots, the acoustic realm around the *Aurora* reverted to what it had been.

The two ELTs from the downed airliner were loud and clear, manic electronic metronomes shrieking for attention. The *Snow Dragon 2* remained busy, her twin screws and thrusters churning to maintain a constant position. An underwater drone could also be heard, the electric hum of its battery-operated propellers distinct in the frigid water, its accessory motors whirring intermittently to position instruments. All of that made perfect sense.

The gunshots, however, had been an outlier. They simply didn't compute. And now, having closed in on the area from which they'd come, the *Aurora*'s sensors were picking up more.

"I have unidentified returns on the same 340 bearing," the sonar operator said. "Very irregular, random frequencies. If I were to guess, people moving equipment around."

"Can you tell if this is coming from above or below the ice?"

A pause, then, "No way to tell, Captain."

Arkady Khurtin's blue eyes drilled into his chart.

He had *Aurora* on the move, crawling in a pattern as her upward-looking cameras charted the light above. Her helmsman corrected for drift, keeping a precise grid, and her ballast tank pumps worked to maintain a constant depth of 50 meters. Aside from that, she listened.

Everything had made perfect sense . . . until the damned gunshots. And that *was* what the sonar had picked up, as verified by acoustic analysis. Now someone was clattering around in the same general area, and he strongly suspected this was coming from the surface as well.

"What do you make of it?" he asked Grekov. "The shots came from a northerly bearing, nowhere near the icebreaker."

The younger man tilted his head in conjecture. "I can only think of one explanation. The Chinese initially locked on to the main wreckage field where the ELTs are chirping. But then they saw the big hole in the ice, perhaps like we did by downloaded satellite images. They might have sent a party to investigate."

Khurtin hesitated. "Walk across the ice? Fifteen miles in such weather? The ice pack must be a maze of fractures and ridges."

"It would be dangerous, yes. But not impossible."

"What about the gunfire?"

"Perhaps they encountered a polar bear."

It sounded preposterous to Khurtin. Less so, however, because it was the only explanation he himself had been able to come up with. Polar bears were the dominant predators in this region.

Save for one.

"Sir," said the navigator, "we have completed the scanning operation." He directed their attention to a screen where the thickness of the ice above was displayed. It meshed perfectly with the satellite map they'd downloaded. A circular breach, roughly 100 meters in diameter, lay just to the north of their present position. If the measurements were accurate, the thickness was a mere 10 centimeters.

"It correlates with the SATRAD data," Grekov said, referring to the satellite report.

This breach was, by their present knowledge, the only place within thirty miles where the ice was thin enough to punch through. The captain saw but two options. They could surface here and find out what the hell was going on topside . . . or they could remain hidden.

If they surfaced, he gave even odds on *Snow Dragon 2*'s radar discerning their presence. And if the Chinese had indeed sent a search party to the area? Then the *Aurora* would be seen without question. Yet even then, Khurtin suspected the icebreaker's captain would simply go about his business. His mission was not to chase submarines.

Conversely, there was only one other vessel known to be in the area, the USS *Cheyenne*. And her captain was tasked to do precisely that. If Khurtin ran quiet and deep, he could surely remain hidden, and perhaps track the Americans again if they reappeared.

The tactical intricacies were unlike any he'd ever faced. The *Aurora* was not technically an operational boat, and surfacing would expose the new *Laika*-class design in unknowable ways. Khurtin had the rebel tendencies of all good sub commanders, but he also knew how to cover his ass. If he surfaced now and his boat was seen, he had a simple excuse. He could say he had done so in order to establish communications with headquarters. A request for guidance in a complex situation.

He looked at Grekov and saw similar thoughts running through his head.

"If we surface," the exec said, "the icebreaker might see us on radar."

"Possibly. It depends how her system is configured. Our reflection could be filtered out as just another hill of ice. More worrying to me is that they might have sent a team to scout the area."

Khurtin's thoughts churned, but in the end he succumbed to the most basic of human instincts: curiosity. Surfacing was the only way to find out what was going on topside.

"I say we do it," Grekov said without being asked.

It was all the captain needed to hear.

He gave the order to prepare for breaching, which was echoed around the control room. He then addressed his exec. "If the Chinese have sent out a search party, then we should do the same. Assemble a detail to go ashore. Six men from the security roster." Owing to cramped quarters, submarines were not manned with a dedicated security force of naval infantry like larger ships. Instead, fire control technicians, cooks, and mechanics underwent additional training and took over that role.

"Yes, Captain," Grekov said.

"And make sure they are armed."

The exec looked at him questioningly.

"It's probably nothing. But until we understand the reason for the gunfire, it seems a wise precaution."

"Of course."

Khurtin turned his attention to the control room to monitor the preparations for their ascent. As he did, he felt an extraordinary sensation.

The captain was already doubting the decision he'd just made.

CHAPTER 34

Kasey cranked up Sky Fire right on schedule. A message from Langley was waiting. This time Sharpe sat in the snow beside her, both of them huddled against the shell of the shattered fuselage. The silence was freighted as the message downloaded—both of them had been enduring off-the-charts stress, and a shot at salvation finally seemed at hand.

"Is there any way to tell whether the Chinese got copied in on these messages?" he asked.

"Chen told me it was doubtful, but he couldn't guarantee it. I included a challenge-response protocol in my original message that only Langley could verify. They'll send one back. If everything checks, the content of the message is solid. We just can't be sure who's seeing it."

A full page of text filled the screen, and they read it side by side.

"Protocol checks," she said.

The news was encouraging. A submarine, the USS *Cheyenne*, was en route and expected to arrive in five and a half hours. The plan was to surface in the thin ice where Hemisphere Flight 777 had gone down. All survivors would be taken aboard, the ship's medical staff would care for the injured, and Sky Fire was to be locked down.

"More than five hours," Sharpe said, venturing a look into the distance. The visibility had improved, and he could see the distant crash site. The flames on the water had subsided but he could still make out shards of wreckage and discolorations in the snow and ice.

"Yeah, it's gonna seem like a long time."

"At least a sub won't be affected by this weather."

A second message pinged to the screen. Langley had saved the bad news for last.

> **Be advised, Chinese icebreaker Snow Dragon 2 is currently 15 NM south your position. Vessel is stationary and appears to be conducting deepwater survey of main wreckage. At this time they do not seem aware of your presence. DO NOTHING TO HIGHLIGHT YOUR POSITION. This includes visual, thermal, and acoustic disruptions.**

"Shit!" she said. "The Chinese are already here."

"Almost. But fifteen miles is a good distance away."

"We should douse the fire."

"I don't think it's making much difference in the thermal signature of the fuselage."

"But the smoke from our improvised chimney might be seen."

He nodded. "Fair point—we should err on the side of caution."

"How do we explain it to the others?" Other than Chen, no one inside was aware of the full situation. Kasey reckoned that Sharpe would leave it that way, and his response proved her right.

"I'm in charge, so it's on me. I'll say it's a safety issue. Embers drifting into the wrong place."

A clatter rang out from inside the fuselage. They both knew what it was. Sharpe had asked Nick and Sofia to make more room in the forward cabin, and they'd been tossing empty carry-on bags and debris toward the cluttered aft section.

"I'll go put a stop to that," Sharpe said. He got up, walked toward the cabin, and disappeared inside.

Alone in the cold, Kasey stared at the screen and wondered what to do next. Her first thought related to electronic security. She had no idea whether a Chinese icebreaker could register emissions from a satellite device, but there was an easy solution. Satisfied that no more files were inbound from Langley, she shut down Sky Fire. She would check back periodically.

"Five and a half hours," she said to no one as the screen went blank.

She scanned the horizon carefully but saw no sign of the bear. She stood and grabbed the rifle, which had come with a sling, and shrugged it over her right shoulder. After stowing Sky Fire, she headed for the canopied entrance.

She was almost there when a strange crackling noise caught her attention. It came and went quickly. Not an animal this time. More . . . tectonic. She paused and listened.

The storm was moderating, its constant shrill lessening.

She heard it again, a distant popping noise. Not gunfire. More like low-frequency fireworks. This time the sound lasted long enough to suggest a direction. She looked toward the wide crater of ice where the jet had struck and immediately saw the source.

A half dozen black poles were rising out of the sea. That was followed by a massive black fin. The ice on either side of the fin began to fracture like sheets of glass, jagged shards heaving upward and outward, until a great matte-black tube appeared. It was a sight Kasey had never seen, but there was no doubt as to what she was looking at.

Her first instinct was elation.

Then she considered the timing, and her euphoria flipped to dread.

She shouldered into the cabin and heard Sharpe saying, "Yeah, a couple of people are trying to sleep, Nick. Let's not move any more of that stuff for now to keep the racket down."

Sharpe glanced back and saw Kasey standing at the entrance. Then he registered the look on her face.

He hurried aft. "What's wrong?" he said in a harsh whisper.

She nodded sharply for him to follow. When they were outside, she pointed into the distance.

All he could say was "It hasn't been five and a half hours."

"It hasn't been ten minutes. Even if Langley composed that message an hour ago, it doesn't add up. That can't be the USS *Cheyenne*."

"How can we be sure?"

"You were in the military. Wasn't there training on submarine recognition?"

A humorless laugh. "I flew fast jets in the Air Force. Give me a

MiG or a Sukhoi, and I can ID it from five miles away. Boats aren't my thing."

"We need to figure this out, because if that *is* a Chinese sub, it's game over. Shouldn't there be a flag or an emblem or something?"

"I think subs fly flags, but only when they're underway on the surface."

"I don't see a flag anywhere."

"Hang on . . ." Sharpe quick-timed back to the cargo hold and disappeared inside. Thirty seconds later he emerged with a pair of camouflaged binoculars.

He rushed back and said, "I came across these earlier, but I didn't see much use for them at the time. Probably owned by the guy who was going hunting."

He trained the optics on the sub and studied it at length.

"Well?" she asked, her gaze fixed on the distant sharklike form.

"I still don't see anything. It's just black, no insignia of any kind. There's a . . . wait." He adjusted the focus and said, "I see a stenciled warning near a hatch. I have no idea what it says, but the characters themselves are an answer. Cyrillic."

"*Russians?* What would they be doing here?"

"I don't know . . . but I suspect we're about to find out."

CHAPTER 35

Langley

The CIA operations center went silent. There was no typing. Hushed conversations between workstations stopped. Every phone call paused. It was as if the world had frozen when the new image appeared on the main screen.

It was sourced from the NRO, which was finding its stride. Satellite passes were increasing in frequency, and a growing stream of overheads had been flooding in. Yet one crystal-sharp image of a surfaced submarine, captured moments earlier from a hundred miles above the North Pole, had caught everyone off guard.

"What the hell is that?" the deputy director of operations inquired, ending the stunned silence.

When no answer came, he surveyed the room. His eyes settled on an analyst at the ISR desk. Intelligence, surveillance, and reconnaissance. The man was junior, but he wasn't young. Deep into his forties, he was a double dipper who'd served twenty years in the Navy before transferring to the CIA. It was a common track that put experienced people to good use. Unfortunately, at that moment, even the ex–Navy man looked baffled.

Realizing all attention was on him, he began by stating the obvious. "It's definitely not the *Cheyenne*. In fact, I'm pretty sure it's not one of ours. The aft sweep, the configuration of the planes, masts, and sail. All very subtle, but it wasn't built by General Dynamics or Huntington Ingalls." He was referring to the only two manufacturers of U.S. submarines.

"Chinese?" Flynn ventured.

"Possibly, but . . . hang on. Let me run it through the analytics."

The wait seemed interminable but was actually only thirty seconds.

"The image IDs with a very high confidence," the ISR man announced. "We're looking at the *Aurora*, a prototype of Russia's new *Laika*-class hunter-killer."

"A Russian prototype?" Flynn echoed, trying to wrap his head around it.

"It's a boat they've been working on for years. The *Aurora* is the first of this new class and has been undergoing sea trials." The man referenced another screen. "Last time we had a bead on her was five weeks ago. She was leaving Rybachiy for the WESTPAC," or Western Pacific Region. Rybachiy, on the Kamchatka Peninsula, was Russia's main submarine base in the east.

"She damned sure isn't in the Pacific anymore. Why would a boat that's not even operational be skulking around in the Arctic?"

"It's not uncommon for them to field new weapons before they're fully tested. It might have tracked the Chinese icebreaker there."

The DDO felt a need to press ahead. Now wasn't the time for analysis paralysis. "Well, the damned thing is at the crash site and it's a threat to our mission. How long until the *Cheyenne* arrives on station?"

The duty officer said, "We show her ETA five hours and six minutes."

"Can she pick up the pace?"

"I'd have to ask the Navy about that."

"Do it, and if they give you any pushback, tell them the White House is watching this situation closely."

The comm officer initiated a call to Pacific Fleet Headquarters.

"Let's draft a message to Orion. We need to warn her about this Russian sub . . . if she hasn't already seen it for herself." He turned to the ISR man who had quickly become his source for all things Navy. "Give me your best guess. Why are the Russians sticking their nose in here?"

The analyst considered it. "I don't see any way they could know about Sky Fire. Most likely, they sent this new boat up to the Arctic as an extension of her sea trials. You know, to see how she performs in harsh, real-world conditions. But how she came across our crash site? I'd only be speculating."

"So speculate."

The ISR man thought about it. "From an acoustic point of view, the Arctic is pretty quiet. There's a lot of background clutter from grinding ice, but very few man-made noises. Maybe they heard *Snow Dragon 2* battering along and decided to follow her."

"That still doesn't explain why they surfaced."

The duty officer chimed in. "Could they be working jointly with the Chinese?"

"That doesn't compute," Flynn said. "The Chinese have a vessel of their own fifteen miles away. If they'd known about the wreckage on top, they would have been there hours ago."

The subsequent silence forced Flynn's hand.

"Okay. For now, let's put aside *why* the Russians showed up. We have to assume they'll spot the wreckage. When they do, they're obliged by international law to give aid to the survivors. Since there are no critical injuries to deal with, time is on our side. We need to slow-roll their response, and Orion might be able to help. If she can buy a few hours, the *Cheyenne* can take over when she arrives on scene."

The ISR man said, "Actually, from a legal standpoint the Russians would have on-scene command of the rescue since they were the first vessel to arrive."

Flynn bristled, a nerve having been hit. He arced an index finger across the perimeter wall and said, "Do you see any law books in this room?"

The chastised analyst said nothing.

"The moment the *Cheyenne* arrives, we are taking charge, and no lawyer in the country is going to tell me otherwise." He walked to the comm station and said to a young woman, "Compose a message to Orion. Tell her to buy time. And make sure she secures Sky Fire. The last thing we need is for the Russians to get their hands on it."

The comm tech began typing, the DDO hovering at her shoulder. After a few minor edits, she hit the send button. Within seconds, a reply flashed to the screen. MESSAGE FAIL/RECEIVER FAIL.

"What does that mean?" Flynn asked.

"Our connection with Sky Fire has been lost," the comm tech said.

"*Lost?* Is it a satellite problem again?"

"No, we have signal integrity, but the device isn't responding. Orion must have shut it down."

Flynn felt anger rising, but he knew it was more his fault than Orion's. He hadn't included comm protocols in their initial message. He should have told her to keep the system up and running. Chances were, she was trying to keep electronic silence to avoid giving away her position. Or possibly conserving battery power. Either way, there was little he could do about it until she turned Sky Fire back on.

In their favor, there was no one Flynn would have trusted more in this situation. He'd seen Kasey Sheridan fight her way out of countless tight corners. She was a rising star at the agency, and he had handpicked her for this mission. That said, the pressure she was under had to be extreme. The importance of Sky Fire, having survived an airplane crash, the extreme cold. Not to mention the loss of her partner, Walter Ho.

One more star in the Memorial Wall, he thought despondently.

Flynn looked at the big map, where a handful of varied symbols were converging in an icy wilderness. A desolate point on the globe that had, until today, never meant anything to anyone. And one that now held the key to the next generation of warfare.

CHAPTER 36

Arctic
Crash Site

As soon as the all-clear was given, Khurtin climbed to the platform atop the sail. The cold hit like a tsunami, but as was often the case with submariners, he didn't find it particularly hostile. They had been submerged for weeks, and even though the *Aurora* was a new boat with good ventilation, she was still a sub. Compared to the stale, recirculated air below, the glacial wind was rejuvenating.

Grekov was right behind him, and both men turned up the collars of their winter jackets.

"It reminds me of Siberia," Grekov said, looking out across the ice-clad seascape.

"We are a thousand miles north of it."

The *Aurora* had surfaced at the edge of the breach, and Khurtin instinctively checked the condition of his ship. His gaze swept down to the thin pool of ice to starboard. It looked fragile, a wafer-thin crust slowly congealing on the sea. What he saw to port was different, the endless sheet ice of the drifting Arctic pack. Thankfully, he saw no sign of damage to the *Aurora*. The newest ship in the Russian Navy, her finish was faultless, and no rust had yet accumulated. She was as pristine as a warship could be.

Khurtin's gaze strayed outward, and the scene changed. He easily picked out shards of debris. A torn sheet of aluminum the size of a canoe testified to the cataclysmic forces of the crash. Farther out he saw an uninflated life jacket, cracked composite panels, and a shredded seat cushion. Scorch marks on the ice had been blurred by snow. This was indeed ground zero.

He surveyed the southern horizon and easily found what he was looking for—the swirling black smudge that gave away *Snow Dragon 2*. "There she is."

Grekov trained a pair of binoculars on the spot. "I don't think she's moved."

"Hopefully it will stay that way."

"As soon as we surfaced, her radar sweeps registered." *Aurora*'s passive receivers were tuned to sense shipboard radar.

"It makes sense. But I still don't think she will pick us up through the clutter. All the same, post a lookout topside. If she moves even an inch, I am to be told immediately."

"Yes, Captain."

The exec began scanning with his binoculars, and halfway through a wide arc he snagged to a sudden stop. "Captain!" he said excitedly. "Over there!"

Grekov pointed to a dull shadow in the distance and handed over the optics.

Khurtin raised them and studied an irregular shape on the broad field of ice. The cylindrical object was mottled by snow, but there was no question as to what it was. "A section of the jet is intact."

"Could there be survivors?"

Khurtin kept scanning, and soon he saw them. Two figures standing at the edge of the wreckage. "It would appear so."

"I wonder how many?" the exec said, seeing them unaided with his sharp eyes.

After a lengthy pause, Khurtin lowered the binoculars and said, "It makes no difference. We have a lawful duty."

"Are you suggesting we give aid?"

"Are you suggesting we do not?"

"Captain, *Aurora* is the most closely guarded secret of the Russian Navy. She is the future of our submarine force. We cannot risk bringing foreign civilians on board."

"What alternative do you propose?"

"Notify the Chinese, tell them to open their eyes. They could secure their equipment and be here in less than an hour."

Khurtin considered it. "Give them an unearned win?"

"It's not a game."

"That is where you are wrong, Grekov," the captain said, his voice rising but steady. "I give you great latitude, my friend, and we generally reach the same conclusions. But you forget why we have come to this godforsaken place. The *Aurora* is, as you say, at the vanguard of the Russian Navy. But that is not something to hide. The world should know it. This is the perfect opportunity to demonstrate what she is capable of. If we are reading the situation correctly, and I think we are, the Chinese and the Americans have been stumbling across the region trying to find this crash site. But the *Aurora*, with virtually no knowledge of the situation, is the first to arrive on scene."

The exec argued no further, knowing Khurtin's decision was made. He said, "If we use the forward hatch, and if there are not too many of them, we could convert the crew's mess to a holding area. That would keep them from getting a look at the control room and fire control area."

"It would also force our crew to eat cold meals in their bunks." Khurtin grinned and put a hand on his exec's shoulder. "I never said we would take them aboard."

Grekov looked at him curiously.

"I will lead the shore party. Have the medic join us with supplies, and also Senior Seaman Andreyev—my English is decent, but his is better and he also speaks Mandarin. There is no telling who we will encounter. We will provide aid—medical care, blankets, food, clothing. Most important of all, we will bring a camera to document our good and benevolent work."

A slow smile. "And I will contact headquarters to advise them of our heroic actions."

"Now you are seeing it. Headquarters will contact the Chinese, and the *Snow Dragon 2* will arrive in due course. By that time, we will have the poor wretches warm, fed, and bandaged, and news outlets around the world will be praising the star of the Russian Navy."

"But an icebreaker is far better suited to transporting crash survivors than a submarine. They have a helicopter deck in case any critically ill survivors must be transported immediately."

"You see? It is only common sense."

"We get the credit," said Grekov appreciatively.

"And they bear the burden. When the Chinese arrive, we will give them a quick briefing and submerge before anyone begins nosing around the *Aurora*."

A flash of motion caught the captain's eye, and he raised the binoculars again. The two people outside the shattered airplane were waving at him.

Arkady Khurtin grinned and waved back.

CHAPTER 37

Kasey saw one of the two figures atop the submarine return her wave. Both men on the platform were in uniform. Both were watching them intently. A hatch on the main deck popped open, and two crewmen scurried out hauling gear.

"We need to buy time," she said to Sharpe.

"Five hours for our sub to arrive?"

"That's not realistic, so I'm working on Plan B." She backed toward the cabin. "I'll explain in a minute. Right now, I need to go back inside and talk to Chen. Stay here and keep an eye on the Russians."

"No. I have to tell the other passengers about this."

It was a fair point. The others had been going outside occasionally to relieve themselves. On top of that, the sub could probably be seen on a sharp angle through the starboard windows. There was no logical reason to keep the sub's arrival a secret, and it only made sense that Sharpe would be the one to announce it. "Okay, hold off for a minute, then follow me inside. When you tell them, stick to the basics. Say that a submarine surfaced nearby and should be providing assistance soon."

"In other words, don't mention that it's Russian."

"That'll become clear soon enough. Tell them that you and I are going to determine how to make contact. While we do, everyone should stay inside."

"Okay."

Sharpe sounded suspicious. He was trying to decipher what she was up to. Without explaining, Kasey ducked inside.

She was surprised to almost bump into Chen at the entrance. He was standing gingerly and using a seat back for support, but he had clearly walked all the way aft. When she'd last talked to him, Kasey had inquired about his mobility. Chen had been flat on his back since the crash, and he said he wasn't sure if his injured leg would allow walking. Apparently, it did. When he let go of the seat, there was only a slight wobble.

"Easy," she said.

"No, I'm fine. It actually isn't painful. My leg is just stiff."

"Good, because I need you to do something for me." In a low voice, she told him what had happened, and what she had in mind.

When she was done, he whispered, "A Russian submarine?"

"I know. None of us saw that coming. Are you sure you can do what I'm asking? If not, we'll find another way."

"No, your plan is a good one."

Kasey's "plan," to the extent that she had one, was for her and Sharpe to walk to the submarine and intercept whoever came ashore. She wanted to buy as much time as possible, allowing Chen to work his magic with Sky Fire on the far side of the fuselage. They desperately needed to send a message to Langley to explain the situation. It would be an unmitigated disaster for China to get Sky Fire back. But allowing the Russians to take possession was the next-worst thing.

Sharpe came inside, and in a hushed voice Kasey explained her scheme. She hadn't wanted to lay it out until she was sure Chen was up to it. Sharpe didn't argue, either because her plan made sense or, more likely, because he couldn't think of a better one.

He took a few steps forward and gave his passengers the good news. While they were distracted, Kasey retrieved Sky Fire and slipped outside with Chen. She saw a half dozen men on the sub's deck now, and a gangway was being lowered on a steep angle to the ice.

"Over here," she said, leading Chen to the port side where there would be no line of sight to the submarine. While he booted up the system, Kasey walked the antenna away from the hull.

She said, "You should use our code names in the message. Yours is Falcon, mine's Orion. After you establish contact, keep the connection open for as long as you can. But keep an eye on me and Sharpe. When the Russians start heading this way, shut down Sky Fire and hide the case where I had it. Any questions?"

"No."

Sharpe emerged and circled to the port side.

"I didn't hear any cheering," she said.

"Oh, they're happy. Just too exhausted to shout about it. I told everyone to sit tight until you and I got back. I also told them not to worry about Chen—I said I'd given him a small chore outside."

She looked at the rifle, which was resting next to the canopy. "We should leave that behind."

"Your reasoning?" he asked, his eyes going to the last point where they'd seen the bear, as if expecting it to reappear.

"Tradecraft 101. We're air-crash victims, and the first impression of lugging around a rifle doesn't reinforce the desired image. Once we've met these guys, then we tell them about the Winchester and why we're keeping it handy."

"Okay. But if our friend comes back, you know what they say . . . you don't have to outrun the bear, only the person you're with."

"And here's what you should know—I ran track at the D-one level, hundred-and-ten-meter hurdles. Fourth place at the NCAA Finals."

Sharpe grinned, and they set out across the ice field, heads down into the wind.

The sub had surfaced less than half a mile away. Sharpe edged in front, keeping a good pace.

"Slow down," she said. "And try to look a little more unstable." Kasey feigned a stumble. "We need to look like we're suffering."

As they walked, Kasey tracked the Russians' every move. The gangway was now in place. No more than fifteen feet long, it was some kind of lightweight aluminum ramp that gave a steep angle down to the ice. It seemed hardly ideal, but Kasey supposed it made sense—a submarine wouldn't have space for something larger, and they probably only carried it for those rare contingencies when they weren't at a proper dock. She counted ten men in the shore party, and a few of them were carrying rifles. The group waited on the ice until one last man descended to join them. If Kasey wasn't mistaken, it was one of the men who'd waved to her. The Russians began walking toward them.

"Let me do the talking," she said.

"Won't that seem odd? I mean, with me being the uniformed crewmember?"

"Maybe. But I need to steer this conversation carefully and we can't be passing notes."

"Okay, I'll chime in with some meaningless drivel, but you can run the show."

"Thanks for understanding."

They were halfway to the submarine when Sharpe said, "I think we just got a good break."

"What's that?"

"Check the ice ahead, about eighty yards out."

Kasey lowered her gaze and saw it right away. A fissure had developed, maybe ten feet wide. Two massive plates of ice had been driven apart by the storm and currents. The break ran as far as she could see both left and right, a frigid river separating them from the Russians.

"That *is* good," she said.

"They'll probably figure some way around it, but that'll take time."

She paused and looked back at the shattered fuselage. Kasey couldn't see Chen, but she imagined him typing furiously. Sharpe was right. The icy gap was in their favor, but the Russians would find a work-around. The direness of their circumstance settled like an anchor.

In spite of Chen's efforts, Langley wasn't going to have a magical solution. She doubted the U.S. Navy had any asset closer than the *Cheyenne*. The weather was improving but probably still precluded an air rescue. Conceivably the CIA could approach Russia through diplomatic channels, but what would they say? *You have a CIA officer, a Chinese defector, and a secret technological marvel in your grasp. Would you please set them aside for us?*

The more she thought about it, the more isolated Kasey felt.

Sharpe, Chen, Langley—they were on her side. The Chinese and Russians most certainly were not. Kasey was trapped between them all, her control of the situation hanging by a thread. And she could think of only one way to strengthen her hand.

Soon, probably very soon, she would make a move that surprised them all.

CHAPTER 38

Langley

The ping hit like a hammer blow.

"Sky Fire is back online!" said the comm officer. A green circle flashed to the main screen, confirming the contact. "Message downloading now."

All intake of breath paused around the room.

Russian submarine has surfaced nearby. Orion and First Officer crossing to meet. Request friendly submarine expedite to scene. Must log off soon and conceal package to keep from falling into Russian hands. Will attempt to delay Russian intervention until arrival of Cheyenne. Standing by for immediate reply. Falcon.

"They figured out the sub is Russian," said the duty officer.

Flynn's first reaction was relief. Kasey was thinking along the exact same lines they were. Delay as much as possible to give the *Cheyenne* a chance. And above all else, keep Sky Fire secure.

"Shrewd," he said under his breath.

He looked at the edge of the map and saw the symbol representing the *Cheyenne*. Since she was not capable of direct communication, her position was only an estimate reflecting a straight-line course and the predicted currents.

"What did the Pacific Fleet Headquarters say about the *Cheyenne* picking up the pace?" the DDO asked.

The duty officer said, "I just heard back. They say she's capable of a wartime dash, but it wouldn't make a significant difference in her arrival time. It could also overstress her nuclear propulsion system. And the problem remains that unless she surfaces, which would only slow her down, headquarters has no way to issue the order."

"I'll take that as a no. What about air assets? Is this storm ever going to let up?"

"The latest weather forecast does predict moderation, but I'm not sure if it would be enough to permit a rescue flight."

"All the same, get with DOD. I want to see every option; whatever aircraft can retrieve two people and one package from an ice floe. I have no problem with letting the Russians handle the other survivors. The quickest alternative they come up with needs to be put on alert. Maybe we can position assets forward to expedite. That way, if the weather lets up, we'll be ready to go."

Flynn's orders were carried out at desks across the room.

He went to the comm station and dictated an immediate reply to Falcon.

> **Monitoring your situation closely. All efforts being made to expedite but unless weather changes expect USS Cheyenne arrival at 0100Z. Concur with your plan. Delay as able. Recovery of Sky Fire and Falcon are priority. Will monitor this channel continuously.**

Sadly, Flynn could think of nothing else to add. He gave a final nod, and the comm technician hit the send key.

The DDO returned to his chair feeling woefully inadequate. The greatest intelligence coup in years was almost within his grasp, one that could kneecap China's military for a decade. The resources of the entire nation had been put at his disposal, courtesy of the White House. But in that moment, he could do nothing more than tell one exhausted operator to keep up the good work.

He racked his brain, desperate for alternatives, but kept coming back to the same fundamental answer. One set of boots on icy Arctic ground.

Until help arrived, Kasey was on her own.

CHAPTER 39

Arctic
Crash Site

We're so glad to see you!" Kasey shouted when the Russians were within earshot. It would have been far more satisfying to give them the middle finger, but probably not conducive to mission accomplishment.

She typically had keen instincts for how to control situations. How to playact and blend into circumstances. The current scenario, however, had her completely confounded. She was one of the few survivors of an airplane crash, and for the last day she'd endured one of the harshest climates on earth. Now rescuers had finally come to give warmth and comfort—and she wanted with all her heart for them to go away.

Still thirty yards distant, the man leading the pack waved but didn't reply to her greeting. She and Sharpe were standing at the edge of the break in the ice. The gap seemed stable, and on closer inspection was roughly eight feet wide at its narrowest point. Kasey wished it was bigger. Wished it was an ocean.

The Russians drew to a stop on the opposite side.

"Thank God you've come!" Kasey called across the divide. She said it in English for two reasons. First was to play the part of the dumb American, one of her go-to moves. Most Yankees assumed the rest of the world spoke English, a predictable if self-diminishing trait. Her second reason was more calculating—Kasey, in fact, spoke fluent Russian. And that could be turned to her advantage.

"Hello," said the man in the lead. He wore the insignia of captain first rank. "Our headquarters notified us that there was an air crash in the area, so we joined the search. We were lucky to find you quickly."

The captain's English was good but heavily accented. Kasey concentrated on what he'd said. Hemisphere Airlines Flight 777 was overdue, so it made sense that news of the crash had gotten out.

"I am Captain Arkady Khurtin. You are one of the pilots?" the Russian inquired, addressing Sharpe.

"First Officer Brett Sharpe. I'm the only remaining crewmember."

The captain gestured to the distant wreckage. "I trust there are others?"

"Unfortunately, many were not so fortunate. There are nine of us altogether."

The captain exchanged a look with his men. "I am sorry for your loss. But know that you are now safely in the hands of Russia's finest submariners."

Kasey said, "A few of the others are injured, but none critically."

"Rest assured, my team will assist you. We have a capable medic on board, and doctors are standing by to offer advice until we reach a hospital." The captain gestured then to the icy fissure that was separating them. "It appears we have a difficulty. But this can be dealt with."

He half-turned to give an order in Russian that Kasey correctly interpreted. Two of his men set off back toward the submarine, their job to retrieve the gangway. They would drag it here and attempt to use it to cross the breach.

And it's probably long enough to work, she thought, struggling to come up with another way to buy them more time.

As the men rushed off, Kasey said, "Why are you carrying weapons?"

"I was hoping you might tell us. A short time ago our sonar registered the sound of gunfire."

Kasey held steady. This had not occurred to her, and it was a solid explanation for why they were armed. Though not necessarily the only one. "A polar bear was approaching. We used a rifle we discovered in our cargo hold to frighten it away."

She watched the captain closely and saw neither affirmation nor doubt. The man was calm and collected, and she guessed he was a good submarine commander. But right now, he was out of his element.

"Have you reported that you've found us?" she asked.

"Not yet. I wanted to evaluate the situation myself before advising headquarters."

She turned to Sharpe and said, "Might be a good time to tell Captain Khurtin what happened—just the basics."

Sharpe went over the crash in a general way, describing the failure of both engines. He left out their suspicions of Chinese involvement in the disaster. He then described the condition of all nine survivors.

As he talked, Kasey watched and listened.

Four of the Russians were armed, but they didn't look alert. In fact, based on their stances and eye movement, they weren't particularly well trained. If she were to guess, she was looking at four ordinary seamen who'd been told to grab rifles.

She noticed two of the other men fiddling with their phones. This confused her at first. There wasn't a cell signal within a thousand miles, and she doubted a military sub would provide an alternate connection. More to the point, no self-respecting captain would permit such a distraction by a working detail. Then one of the men raised his phone and began taking pictures . . . of her and Sharpe, with the wreckage in the background. And just like that, Kasey understood.

In the distance, the two sailors who'd been sent back to the boat were gesticulating toward a third man on deck. On appearances, a minor argument had erupted about how to disassemble the gangway.

Arguments were good, Kasey thought.

Arguments took time.

Sharpe was now droning on about the weather. A minute here, a minute there. The two of them were doing well.

She only hoped that Chen was making the best of it.

CHAPTER 40

Beijing

A distant rattling noise startled Zhang awake. He bolted upright, his arms shooting out as if he were falling. One by one, his senses came back online. The light at the doorway to the main room seemed stunningly bright. He was drenched in sweat and gasping for air. His heart felt like it might burst out of his chest.

He took a moment to gather his bearings. He'd been in an unusually deep sleep. It could have been because he hadn't gotten any real sleep in two days. More likely it was the drugs and bourbon. His breathing slowed and his eyes adjusted.

Another rattle. Hard and insistent.

Someone knocking on the front door.

The executive suites in the Yidongyuan complex were located directly across the street from MSS headquarters. They had been built as a convenient and exclusive getaway for the agency's top brass, and no expense had been spared. The furnishings were opulent, the staff indulging, and delicious food could be ordered from a private kitchen where the finest chefs in the city were on call 24/7.

As was always the case in the supposedly classless People's Republic, these extravagances had to be concealed. In Yidongyuan it was simple. The entire MSS complex was sealed off from greater Beijing, meaning that what happened behind its bastion walls remained a mystery to the masses. The executive tower went even further, being off-limits to the 10,000 intelligence officers, analysts, and support staff who worked at the ministry. For senior leaders it was the ultimate safe haven and reflected a zeal for personal security that bordered on paranoia. Yet there was a flip side to having such a privileged sanctuary.

An unexpected knock on the door, particularly in the middle of the night, was nothing less than a harbinger of doom.

Zhang checked the clock on the bedside table: 4:20 a.m. Next to the clock he saw a pharmaceutical train wreck, toppled pill bottles and capsules spilled across the polished mahogany.

He rose unsteadily and trundled to the door. Looking through the peephole, he saw long black hair, a slender body beneath. It was a young woman, her head canted down toward a phone or a purse. He was confused at first, trying to recall if he'd arranged to have a girl sent up. Then the woman looked up and he recognized Wu Mei.

Zhang opened the door. Wu immediately did a double take. In his sleep-addled state, it hadn't occurred to him that he was wearing only boxers and a wrinkled undershirt.

"I'm sorry, sir," said a flustered Wu. "I had hoped I wouldn't wake you."

Zhang looked at her curiously. As far as he could remember, it was the first time she had called him "sir." His state of undress clearly had the woman rattled. *Good*, he thought. *Rattled people are always easier to control.*

He turned and walked inside, leaving the door open as an invitation.

Wu entered and, after a brief hesitation, shut the door.

Zhang saw his bathrobe discarded on the plush sofa—how it had gotten there, he couldn't remember. It was tempting to remain in a partial state of undress to keep Wu off-balance. He could offer her a drink or tell her how pretty she looked. Zhang reveled in making others uncomfortable, but this was not the time. The researcher would not put herself in such an awkward position without good reason. He retrieved the robe, shrugged it on, and sank heavily onto the couch.

"Tell me what's happened," he said.

"There are two developments."

"I hope one of them is that *Snow Dragon 2* has succeeded in locating Sky Fire?"

"No, sir. And she will not . . . at least, not where she is looking."

Zhang's stomach knotted. "What are you talking about?"

"Something very unexpected. I knew that the search our icebreaker is undertaking would proceed slowly, so I considered ways to help them. I remembered that the crew had requested additional information regarding where Dr. Chen was sitting on the airplane. The staff at headquarters have been working with airport officials in Macau to determine this, but I approached it from a different angle. I went back and looked at Sky Fire's position logs."

"Position logs?"

"Each time the system is turned on, it connects to at least one satellite and transmits its position."

"But you said Chen had destroyed our access to Sky Fire."

"He corrupted the design records and databases, yes. But I installed a backup locator packet a few months ago. It was a small project Chen assigned to me, and he might have forgotten about it. Sky Fire's position data is highly accurate, so I thought if we had gotten pings from the airport in Macau, it would be a quicker way to determine where he was sitting than sorting through passenger manifests."

"Not the worst idea you've had. And did you have any success?"

"With his seat assignment, no . . . I never got that far."

Zhang sensed something in Wu's demeanor he had not seen before. Something approaching fear. He had thought her anxiety was a reaction to his state of undress, but now he knew otherwise. She had come bearing bad news. *No, catastrophic news.*

"Spit it out, woman!"

"Thirty minutes ago, I ran a backlog of Star Fire's third-level cache—"

"Spare me the technical rubbish!" he shouted. "Why did you wake me in the middle of the night?"

"Sky Fire was active twenty minutes ago. And also on two other occasions in the last few hours."

Zhang took a moment to process these words. "You are telling me that Sky Fire is *up and running*? From the bottom of the ocean?"

"The system is up and running, yes. But not from underwater. Its position is twenty-four kilometers north of where *Snow Dragon 2* is now searching. And precisely two point three meters above sea level."

Zhang sat stupefied.

Wu, having had more time to consider the bombshell, gave the only rational explanation. "There is only one person who could do this. Dr. Chen is alive, and he is in possession of Sky Fire—operating it."

Zhang's lips pulsed soundlessly, like a fish hauled into a boat. A dozen questions flooded his mind all at once.

"But . . . how could that be?" he finally managed.

"*Snow Dragon 2* has located wreckage from our crashed airliner. But possibly not all of the wreckage. Maybe the airplane broke apart, or perhaps Chen was thrown clear. Whatever the details, my traitorous colleague appears to have survived."

"Why would Chen be using Sky Fire?"

"I can only see his position, so we are left to speculate. But one thing comes to mind."

Zhang was wide awake now, his deep-seated instinct for self-preservation having injected a surge of adrenaline. He completed the shocking thought. "He is trying to contact the Americans to coordinate a rescue."

Wu nodded.

Zhang nearly vaulted off the couch. He headed for the bedroom, tore off his robe, and began searching for his pants. "What has been done so far to address this situation?" he shouted through the open door.

"I have told no one else, so no action has been taken. I thought you should be the first to know."

"You did the right thing," Zhang said. Now wasn't the time to dwell on it, but he realized how closely tied his fate and Wu's had become.

Two minutes later, he was dressed and on the move. As he rushed to the door, it occurred to him that one phone call could not wait.

He pulled out his secure handset and placed a call to the People's Liberation Army, Northern Theater Command. Before falling asleep, he'd put one particular unit on alert. Now it was time to activate that contingency plan. The order he gave was within the bounds of his authority, but only just. Zhang was sticking his thick neck out further than he ever had, yet there seemed to be no alternative. If what Wu was telling him was true, this might be his last chance at survival.

Thirty seconds later, he was out the door, Wu trailing in his wake as they hurried in a cold drizzle toward the operations center.

ZHANG'S PHONE CALL initiated a torrent of follow-ons. They ended four hundred miles northeast of Beijing, at Shenyang Beiling Air Base, China. There, twenty-four commandos from the PLA's 78th Special Forces Brigade, the Ice Wolves, began double-timing toward a waiting Y-20 aircraft. The four-engine transport was fully fueled, and its crew were running through the last of their preflight checks. The unit's tactical gear had been loaded an hour earlier, including parachutes for a free-fall jump.

The Ice Wolves had been on alert for three hours, and while they still didn't have specific orders, there *were* hints as to where they were going. The unit specialized in cold-weather operations, and they had been briefed to prepare for the "harshest conditions." In Ice Wolves lexicon, that translated to somewhere above the Arctic Circle.

The officer in charge, a captain, had served twelve years in the Army. That being the case, he'd seen his share of short-notice call-ups. In his experience, most such deployments were mere training exercises. This one, however, felt different.

He'd sensed it in his colonel's voice when he had issued the assignment. In the speed with which their weaponry had appeared from the armory. The pilots told him they'd taken on a maximum fuel load, giving a range of over 5,000 miles. This was unheard-of for a training mission. And if that weren't enough, he'd been told that elements of the 134th Airborne Brigade had also been called up and would be deploying behind them on three more Y-20s.

Soon the last man was on board, and everyone belted into the webbed troop seats along the sidewall. The jet's big aft ramp motored upward, locking into the hull with the finality of a sealing tomb. At the last moment, a man the captain had never seen boarded using the forward stairs near the flight deck. He wore thick glasses and was dressed in civilian clothes, a dark overcoat, and a fur hat. In the crook of one arm, he cradled a thick manila envelope, as if it held the secrets of the universe.

The stranger glanced back once, as if to make sure the Ice Wolves were on board, then turned away and disappeared into the cockpit. The captain didn't know precisely who this man was. But, like most Chinese military officers, he knew a cocksure goon from MSS when he saw one.

The thought came again. *Yes, this one feels very different.*

The big, slate-gray Y-20 began to taxi.

Moments later, it was thundering down the runway and lifting up into the night.

CHAPTER 41

Arctic
Crash Site

To Kasey's disappointment, the gangway worked like a charm.

She had been hoping for snags. Hoping for broken hardware or incompetent deckhands. But aside from a brief dispute over detaching the ramp from the sub's deck, everything went smoothly. The crewmen dragged it across the ice effortlessly. As they closed in, Kasey recognized it as a passerelle, a telescoping, lightweight boarding ramp commonly used on luxury yachts to get well-heeled owners ashore. By all appearances, it worked equally well on ice-clad nuclear submarines.

After arriving at the breach, the crewmen stretched the ramp to its full length in seconds. Roughly fifteen feet long, it easily bridged the gap between the ice sheets. The captain was the first across, and he walked tentatively, his arms stretched out like a man on a high wire. The passerelle seemed stable enough, but the wind was still gusting.

Khurtin stepped off on the near side and said, "There, you see? Our problem is solved." He shook Kasey's hand, followed by Sharpe's.

"Good thing you had that on hand," she said, gesturing to the ramp.

The captain regarded the fissure. "In English, I think, these gaps are called 'leads.' We Russians are experienced in Arctic operations. Normally, they are but a minor problem. Sometimes, however . . ."

His voice trailed off as Khurtin turned and signaled for his crew to join him. One by one, they began to mount the passerelle and traverse the divide.

The men with phones documented the operation, paying particular attention to two men hauling supplies. Five minutes later, everyone was across.

Khurtin gestured to two of his men and gave instructions in Russian that Kasey had no problem understanding. The pair hauled the ramp onto solid ice, presumably so it wouldn't be lost if the shelves started drifting apart. He then told one man to remain behind to monitor the lead. If it began to widen, the captain was to be notified immediately. Khurtin, Kasey realized, had not been exaggerating—for him, the ice was familiar ground.

"Now," the Russian said, clapping his hands together. "We should see to the others."

Kasey led the way to their shelter. When they reached it, Khurtin paused to study the makeshift canopy covering the entrance.

"Very clever," he commented.

"Credit to our first officer," she said, nodding to Sharpe.

They went through, and the instant the passengers saw the Russian captain they broke into applause.

Khurtin beamed, and one of his men was quick enough to capture a video.

"Thank you for the warm reception," he said. "I am Captain Arkady Khurtin of the Russian Navy." He launched into a speech that seemed almost rehearsed. He began by expressing sympathy for the terrible ordeal they had endured, then followed with confident assurances that their troubles were near an end.

Kasey's eyes drifted to the starboard side. She saw a corner of Sky Fire's case beneath the pile of wreckage where she'd been concealing it. Chen had done well.

Khurtin came in for a landing. "We are coordinating with headquarters to determine the best way to transfer you to a safe port. This may take time, as the weather is difficult. Until then, you will be safe and secure here. We have brought portable heaters to make you more comfortable. My men and I now wish to talk to each of you individually. We would like to know your full name, country of citizenship, and also please detail any injuries you have suffered. This information will be transmitted to the authorities immediately. I am sure your families are eager to hear of your good fortune."

One of the crewmen broke away and began talking to the elderly Asian couple in fluent Mandarin. A medic began tending to the man they'd found wandering outside, who Kasey suspected had suffered a serious concussion.

Khurtin took out a pad of paper, poised a pen, and said, "I will begin with the two of you."

Sharpe provided his name and nationality, and said he had no significant injuries. Kasey did the same, sticking to the legend she had been booked under for the flight.

When the Russian was done writing, Kasey asked, "Do you plan to take us aboard your submarine?"

The captain cocked his head. An overt display of indecision from a man whose job title precluded it. "We shall see. Certain measures would have to be taken to bring guests aboard the *Aurora*. I also doubt she is the most expeditious route to safety."

"Are there any other vessels in the area?"

"None that I am aware of."

For the first time, Kasey saw a red flag. A Chinese icebreaker lay just over the horizon, and any competent captain of a warship would know it. Which meant Khurtin was either inept or lying. She doubted it was the former.

"But do not worry," he added. "If the weather worsens, or if other serious troubles arise, then of course we would welcome you onto *Aurora*."

"Good to hear."

Khurtin held her in an appraising stare. "I am wondering, Miss . . ." He referred to his pad. "Johnson. You seem very involved in this situation."

"First Officer Sharpe is in charge. But I saw that he needed help, so I volunteered to assist."

Appearing placated, Khurtin said, "Good of you to do so." He moved on to Nick and Sofia.

The Russians not involved in taking names began handing out supplies. Blankets and chemical heat packs were distributed. Hot coffee was poured from a thermos into Styrofoam cups. Two portable butane heaters were fired up. A folding stretcher was expanded to its full length and mounted between broken seats to create a bench.

The crewman who spoke Mandarin interviewed Chen. As soon as that exchange ended, Kasey gave Sharpe a subtle elbow. Together they edged over to Chen, and when all of the Russians were out of earshot, she quietly asked, "Did you get through to Langley?"

"Yes. The news is not good." He checked his watch. "The *Cheyenne* is still more than four hours away. We are to delay as best we can until then."

"Four hours is a long time," Kasey replied, "but it might be doable. We were just talking to our U-boat commander, and I got the impression he doesn't want to take us on board. I'm guessing there's a lot of tech on that sub they don't want us to see, but nevertheless, it suits our purposes."

"I read it the same way," Sharpe agreed. "But I might ask him if I can go aboard anyway."

"Why?" Kasey asked.

"In a situation like this, my duty would be to establish comm with a dispatcher at Hemisphere Airlines to initiate their accident response plan. At least, that's what I'd do if you and Sky Fire weren't in the mix."

"That actually makes sense," Kasey said. "See? You're starting to think like a spy."

"Of course, if you two *hadn't* come aboard . . ."

"Point taken. Go ahead and bring it up with Khurtin. Chances are, he'll say no. If he does, we lose nothing, and you'll have done what would be expected of you."

"And if he says yes?"

"Then go for it. But remember, they'll be watching. You can't mention our ability to communicate with Langley."

"Understood. And while I'm at it, maybe I can get a look inside the boat. I'm no expert on Russian submarines, but this one looks pretty new. Maybe I could get a picture or two."

"Absolutely not! I don't want you going all secret agent on me."

"I wouldn't be an agent. I'd be an intelligence officer."

She shot him a hard look.

He grinned back. "Got it, no pics." He turned away to find Khurtin.

"One other thing," she said.

Sharpe paused.

"You should mention the bodies in the cargo hold."

He nodded. "Yeah, that'd give the captain something to think about."

"Every hurdle we give them is in our favor."

"Right. And you're an expert on hurdles."

Sharpe set off, still smiling.

Kasey noticed Chen staring at her inquisitively. "I'll explain later," she said. "Did Langley say anything else?"

"They promised to monitor the comm channel continuously. But they understand that Sky Fire must remain shut down."

"Okay, then that's it. We wait."

Kasey put on her gloves and stepped outside, wanting a moment to herself. The cold slap of the wind was bracing, but she was getting used to it. The *Aurora* lay in the distance, a menacing, sharklike presence save for her stillness. Somewhere beyond lurked the *Snow Dragon 2*, and the *Cheyenne* was closing in.

Kasey was struck by the symbolism of it all. She was no expert in geopolitics, but she knew that the Arctic had become a battleground. Not in a war fought with bullets, but a theater of sharp-elbowed diplomacy, territorial overreach, and military intimidation. Unfortunately, if her present dilemma was any indication, America was a distant third. At that moment, Russia and China had the positional advantage; their vessels were nearby, and Sky Fire was almost in their grasp.

But not quite.

Kasey was determined to keep it that way. As had been the case for hundreds of years, America enjoyed one great combat advantage. Authoritarian nations, by definition, kept strict top-to-bottom chains of command. A field commander rarely made a move that wasn't authorized by headquarters.

Kasey, however, was not so constrained. American combat doctrine held that those on the front line were in the best position to recognize tactical advantages, and as such, they were given broad latitude to react as necessary. Whatever choices Kasey made, she would have to account for them later, defend their legality and soundness. But in the heat of battle, the decisions were hers to make.

And down to her marrow, that's what she believed was coming.

A battle was near.

And she would be ready.

CHAPTER 42

Patience was an essential trait for intelligence officers. Kasey had always sucked at it. She couldn't stop planning. Couldn't stop overthinking, visualizing the pitfalls. What if the *Cheyenne* was running late? What if she never made it here at all? If that happened, there were only two vessels anywhere near that could spirit the survivors to safety. For Kasey, getting on either one with Chen and Sky Fire was a complete nonstarter.

Dozens of scenarios coursed through her head, and for each one she drew up a contingency plan. More and more, one common denominator emerged. Unfortunately, it was a move that she wasn't even sure was possible.

The mood among the passengers had brightened. Rescue was imminent. After spending an hour inside the wrecked hull, Khurtin and most of his crew had gone back to the *Aurora*—according to the captain, to obtain a second load of supplies, as well as to coordinate a plan to get everyone back to civilization.

Sharpe had made his pitch to the captain to go aboard the *Aurora*. Not surprisingly, Khurtin shot the idea down. He explained that his crew would happily relay all the pertinent information to Hemisphere Airlines. Sharpe had pushed back, but only slightly. He and Kasey had both expected the captain to kill the idea.

Two Russian crewmen had stayed behind, one of them carrying a handheld VHF radio for communication with the *Aurora*. Kasey kept a casual eye on them, but she saw nothing beyond a pair of enlisted men who were glad to be ashore for a few hours. Yet when the one with the radio answered what sounded like a routine call, something stirred in the back of her mind. The thought soon coalesced into a new complication—one she hadn't considered before.

The photos and videos the crew had taken.

Their only use was as propaganda for Moscow, so the images would be transmitted to headquarters. Soon after that, however, they would be headlining newscasts. She imagined the crawl at the bottom of the screen: Russian submarine *Aurora* rescues passengers from Arctic air disaster.

It was as predictable as it was disastrous. If such a headline aired, the Chinese would see it almost immediately. Minutes after that, *Snow Dragon 2* would receive new and urgent orders. Kasey tried to think of a way to forestall that sequence of events, but nothing came to mind. Even booting up Sky Fire to query the agency would do little to alter the equation.

Kasey realized there was no sense dwelling on it. Exposure was imminent. She could only be ready.

She spotted Chen near the improvised door of their shelter. She had encouraged him to walk up and down the aisle to work on his mobility. She'd phrased it in a way that a physical therapist might have, but her true motive was more self-serving. Chen seemed to be improving, although he was still limping on his injured leg.

She strolled up the aisle, timing her approach to intercept him midway—the most private place in the cabin at that moment.

"Looks like you're moving better," she said.

"The pain is less, but I doubt I will be running a marathon anytime soon."

"Hopefully we did all our running back in Hong Kong."

Chen looked forward and aft. With no one near, he said in a hushed tone, "It might be helpful to check for updates. Is it possible you could distract the guards while I take Sky Fire outside and make a connection?"

Kasey was struck by his word choice. *Guards*. It felt strangely apt.

"No," she said, "we can't risk it. The Russians say they've come to rescue us, but we can't forget they're a military unit. If they caught us using an advanced communications device, they would confiscate it in a heartbeat. They'd also start investigating our backgrounds, and that's a hole you and I don't want them to dig."

Chen nodded, his disappointment evident.

"Maybe we'll get a chance later," she added. Kasey then gave him an appraising look. "That jacket looks a little thin."

"I wasn't cold when I was outside earlier."

"Yeah . . . but all the same." On a nearby seat, she saw a pile of winter jackets the Russians had brought. They had Velcro on the chest for attaching nametags and epaulets for rank insignia. They had obviously been requisitioned from enlisted men on the *Aurora* whose duties precluded them from going ashore.

She sorted through to find what looked like the best fit and handed it to Chen. He removed the jacket he was wearing and tried it on.

"That looks better," she said.

"The other one was more comfortable."

"You can still wear it. But keep this one handy in case we get a chance to go outside and use Sky Fire."

Chen said that he would and then set off toward the front.

Kasey moved in the opposite direction. She paused near the pile of debris that Nick had built near the exit. The edges of the covering canopy vibrated in the wind, tiny swirls of snow pulsing inside.

Kasey retrieved a discarded backpack from the pile. She unzipped it and removed a neck pillow, a phone charger, and a spy novel she'd heard about but never read, *The Elias Enigma* by Simon Gervais. She kept the empty backpack and tossed the rest back on the pile. Kasey began building a mental inventory of what she would need for her last-ditch plan. She hoped to never execute it, but laying the groundwork was a good distraction. It kept her busy, made her feel like she was doing *something*.

She returned to the front of the cabin and offered words of encouragement to the passengers. She smiled at the two Russians, neither of whom spoke more than a few words of Hollywood English.

Then, ever so discreetly, Kasey began gathering what she would need.

CHAPTER 43

Beijing

Critical intelligence sometimes came from the most unexpected sources. This was one of Zhang's mantras, and it pounded in his brain as he stood in the headquarters operations center.

By mere chance, Wu had stumbled upon evidence that Chen and Sky Fire had survived the crash. That was a possibility Zhang had never considered. Even the researcher herself seemed stunned to have uncovered it. Earlier, as the two of them had walked through the cold rain from the executive suites, he'd pressed her mercilessly on whether she might be mistaken. Wu insisted there could be no doubt. Sky Fire had gone active near the crash site, and only one person could be responsible.

Zhang was convinced. But he was not going to share this new information with those above him. Not yet. The survival of Chen and Sky Fire raised the stakes immeasurably. The complex salvage operation being undertaken by the *Snow Dragon 2*, which he'd expected to take weeks, had been rendered moot. The only viable response now was direct intervention.

He had already issued orders on two fronts. He'd launched the rapid reaction force from Shenyang Beiling Air Base, and the Y-20 carrying the Ice Wolves was now speeding north. The second order he'd issued with more trepidation—he had instructed the captain of the *Snow Dragon 2* to suspend her salvage operation and prepare to reposition. These procedures, Zhang had been told, would take the best part of an hour, as the ship's underwater drone had to be retrieved, and various sensors hauled on board.

While all that ran its course, Zhang was left to ponder a looming decision.

His preference was for the Ice Wolves to take possession of Sky Fire and its creator, yet they would not reach the crash site for hours. The alternative was to muster a shore party from the *Snow Dragon 2* to do the job sooner. The icebreaker carried a few light weapons, and Zhang expected no resistance. On the other hand, the crew were little more than merchant sailors, technicians, and scientists, none of whom would have a tactical bone in their soft bodies.

"Where is that reconnaissance?" he growled. Thirty minutes earlier, Zhang had requested a satellite pass on the coordinates where Wu had detected Sky Fire, a radar imaging platform that wouldn't be affected by the cloud cover. He needed the best possible information for what he knew was coming: a very difficult call to the president.

"New images arriving now," said a technician.

The picture that flickered to the screen caused confusion around the room. It was very similar to a scene they'd all seen hours earlier. The USS *Cheyenne* surfaced in an ice pack.

"No," Zhang bellowed. "Show me the one from the crash site!"

"That *is* the crash site," replied Wu in a low voice. "Look at the coordinates."

Zhang checked the bottom corner of the image. She was right. The latitude and longitude were correct. Then he noticed subtle differences from the earlier image. The submarine had surfaced next to a rounded lake of thin ice. A large cylinder nearby could possibly be the partial fuselage of an airliner.

Zhang stared slack-jawed at it all.

"How could the *Cheyenne* have moved so quickly?" the chief wondered aloud.

"Could it be a different boat?" Wu speculated. "The Americans must have other submarines in the region."

Zhang studied the submarine more closely. Its lateral lines were obscured by a skirt of ice . . . yet something about the silhouette did seem different. This wasn't the *Cheyenne*. He was about to order analysts to identify the boat when the operations center chief interrupted.

"Sir, there is something you must see on television."

"*Television?*" Zhang barked. "Nothing takes precedence over what is happening in the Arctic!"

"But sir," the man persisted, "this is about the crash. A newscast on Russia-1."

Zhang twisted around to view the television on the back wall. He could decipher none of the words at the bottom of the screen because he didn't speak Russian. The video, however, held him like a vise. A camera panned across a group of bedraggled individuals. Halfway through its arc, he saw a face he recognized. The unmistakable profile of Dr. Chen Li.

And just like that, Zhang's world whipsawed again.

Surely this is all a dream, he thought. *A dream meant to drive me mad.*

His personal phone vibrated in his pocket. He pulled it out and saw a call from his boss, the Minister of State Security. Zhang tapped on the green button.

"The president just called me!" shouted the minister. "He is furious. Something about a Russian newscast."

Zhang stood speechless. His left cheek twitched.

Critical intelligence sometimes came from the most unexpected sources.

CHAPTER 44

Langley

DDO Flynn sat transfixed in the CIA Operations Center. He, too, was watching Russia.

The video was amateurish. The camera lens jittered and the audio was muffled, all of which only heightened its authenticity. It was exactly what one would expect from a maelstrom at the top of the world.

He watched the crew of the *Aurora*, Russia's newest and most deadly attack submarine, hand out blankets like Red Cross volunteers. A medic wrapped a bandage around a survivor's head. Flynn caught a glimpse of Kasey as the camera settled on a group of passengers. Her hair was askew and there was a contusion on her forehead. But the alertness of her gaze, the control in her posture, told the real story. Kasey was switched on.

"When did this first air?" the DDO asked the room.

A comm technician answered, "2123 Zulu. Sixteen minutes ago."

"The Chinese are seeing it as well," said the duty officer.

"Stands to reason," agreed Flynn. "Has the *Snow Dragon 2* moved?"

This question was directed to the junior CIA analyst in the room. He had been given one vital task—using all available reconnaissance, he wasn't to take his eyes off the icebreaker.

"Her position hasn't changed," the young man said. "But there has been some activity."

"Activity?"

"I'm getting images at ten-minute intervals. In the most recent three I see changes on deck. They've pulled in some kind of sonar sensor, and in the newest photo the UUV has surfaced. It looks like they're hooking it up to a deck crane."

"And when were you going to mention this?" the duty officer admonished.

Flynn also felt a spike of annoyance. The ship hadn't moved, but the kid should have said something about the change of status. He held his irritation in check.

"Sorry," the young man stated.

"Learn from it," said the DDO. "We're looking at a fishing boat that's reeling in all the lines. *Snow Dragon 2* about to move to a better spot, and we all know why."

"How will the Chinese deal with this Russian submarine?" the duty officer wondered aloud.

"There's no telling," replied Flynn, "but we have to assume the worst. They'll find a way to get Chen and Sky Fire on board, at gunpoint if necessary."

"And probably Orion as well," said the duty officer. "We need to warn her the Chinese are inbound."

"No way to do that unless they boot up Sky Fire, which we specifically told them to not do."

The young analyst offered, "If they see *Snow Dragon 2* approaching, they might initiate comm anyway."

Flynn looked at the kid and nodded. "Good point." He ordered comms to watch continuously for a signal from Sky Fire. Then he shot a look at the workstation labeled DOD. "Any word yet on some kind of air asset to get our people out of there?"

"Arriving now, sir," the tech replied. She read off the specifics of the proposed rescue mission.

"Seriously?" asked a stunned Flynn. "Does the Air Force realize where they'd be landing that monster?"

"We were very specific about the operating area. They say it's doable. Tasking is being sent to the unit as we speak."

Flynn spat a humorless laugh. "I hope to hell they know what they're doing."

• • •

THE TASKING FROM DOD dropped like a brick through a maze of command channels. It landed with a thud in the hands of an aircraft commander of the New York Air National Guard.

Lieutenant Colonel James Driscoll, seated next to a space heater in a chilly prefab building, stared at the one-page printout. He didn't know what to make of it.

From a theoretical standpoint, the mission proposed in the message was feasible. That said, it was the kind of flying stunt he and his buddies typically debated in the squadron bar, and even then, after considerable lubrication. No one had ever actually *done* it. The consensus was, it was an op that would never happen because higher headquarters would never approve it, the risk level being off the charts.

Now, out of the blue, higher headquarters was actually *assigning* it.

He folded the printout and stuffed it in a pocket of his winter flight jacket. He needed to show it to his copilot, who would likely have the same first thought he'd had. *If this had come at the beginning of the month, I would have written it off as an April Fool's prank.*

Driscoll bundled up until every inch of skin was covered, put on his goggles, and stepped outside into a clear evening. The scene, as always, was awe-inspiring. The cold was extreme—on last check minus-30 degrees—and in the dim twilight the heavens seemed boundless.

He was standing squarely in the middle of the Greenland ice sheet, the second largest body of frozen water on the planet. Save for a few distant mountains to the east, the ice stretched as far as he could see in every direction. He'd been told it had an average depth of one mile, and that if it ever melted, it would raise the world's oceans by 24 feet.

Which, obliquely, was why Driscoll was here.

Summit Station was a year-round research facility situated centrally on the ice shelf, and his unit, the New York Air National Guard's 109th Airlift Wing, was the primary provider of logistics. Indeed, it was the only squadron in the entire Air Force equipped to do so, flying the LC-130—the largest aircraft on earth that operated on skis.

A hundred yards away, his airplane squatted on the ice like a snowbound colossus. Ground units were presently pumping warm air into the four turboprop engines, a typical preparation for starting in extremely cold temperatures. His copilot, Captain Doug Harrison, was in the cockpit running preflight checks. They had originally been scheduled to depart in an hour, a three-flight hopscotch back to their home base in Schenectady, New York. Since the aircraft's skis were retractable, landing in the spring thaw there didn't pose a problem.

Now those plans were shredded.

Driscoll set out across the snow-swept ice. As he made his way to the airplane, he studied the surface. The runway, if it could be called that, was like few others on earth. It wasn't composed of concrete or asphalt, or for that matter even hardpan dirt. It was simply a block of ice 6,000 feet thick.

The good news was, there was little snow at the moment. If they could get the airplane started without any critical systems crapping out, they should be able to get airborne. And then? Driscoll recalled recently watching one of the *Mission: Impossible* movies, and the series' ever-present opening line came to mind: *Your mission, should you choose to accept it . . .*

"Why do *I* never get a choice?" he muttered, his breath going to vapor.

He climbed up the boarding stairs and found Harrison programming the navigation computer.

"Hold off on that," Driscoll said. "We've got a change in destination."

The copilot looked up. He was a compact man with dark hair and a permanent five o'clock shadow. "Will we still get home tomorrow? I've got a trip starting the next day." A part-time Guardsman, Harrison's "day job" was as a first officer with Southwest Airlines.

"Doubtful."

"Where are we going?"

"North," Driscoll said, unable to think of a better way to put it.

"North? Thule?" Thule, Greenland, was the only airfield in that direction certified for Air Force operation.

"No, farther."

Harrison blinked. "There aren't any airfields north of there."

Driscoll removed the message from his pocket and handed it to his copilot. "Yeah . . . that's the problem."

CHAPTER 45

Arctic

Captain Yong Shiu was overwhelmed.

Messages were crashing in at a rate he had never before seen. And from sources he barely knew. The *Snow Dragon 2* was, on paper, operated by the Polar Research Institute of China. This was thin cover for her nationalized missions, yet in Yong's experience, operational command and control had never wavered. Orders in the past had *always* come from the institute's headquarters in Shanghai.

The messages lighting up their primary comm channel now were altogether different. They were coming from a host of important agencies across the People's Republic. They could only be legitimate, because the link was secure. Some were from the PRI, but there were also three from the PLA Navy, specifically Northern Sea Fleet headquarters in Qingdao. The Ministry of State Security had also entered the fray, its instructions threatening that Yong would be stripped of his command if he did not comply. Another came from an agency he'd never even heard of.

The instructions hadn't been coordinated in any way. Indeed, they were confusing and contradictory. The MSS told him to muster a large shore party for armed intervention—the mysterious black case, it seemed, was not underwater after all. The Navy wanted him to cut every cable on his research gear and steam north immediately, while the PRI instructed that he secure all hardware before moving. Two of the dispatches also mentioned, almost casually, the presence of a Russian attack submarine in the area.

Yong was left to settle on two commonalities in the messages. First was that he was to move *Snow Dragon 2* fifteen miles north. The second was the sheer desperation in their collective tone. Whatever was happening just over the horizon, it had the most important people in China in a state of panic.

Altogether, it was enough to make a captain's head spin.

"UUV is secure and ready to raise, Captain," said a junior officer.

"Yes, bring it aboard," Yong replied.

"Sonar lines have been recovered," said an enlisted man.

"Three new messages arriving," said the man at the comm station.

Already overloaded, Yong ignored the incoming messages and requested a course plot.

"Course to new objective is three five two degrees, twenty-four kilometers," said the navigator. "I am also showing a new radar return in that area, possible surfaced submarine."

Yong held steady. The radar contact was at the edge of his equipment's range in these conditions, but they probably should have discerned it earlier. Would he be held accountable for the mistake? *No, I can blame the navigator.*

He guessed the new messages were from the MSS and the Navy. They were probably wondering why *Snow Dragon 2* hadn't moved yet. Yong had elected to recover the submerged equipment. In part it was because he had received the PRI's message first. Yet he also thought it the most rational course of action. All the hardware they had deployed was connected by cables and umbilicals. To cut wires haphazardly and begin moving risked fouling the propellers. If that happened here, it could cause a delay of hours. Worse yet, there would be no way for Yong to dodge responsibility.

Trying to keep a clear head, he said, "As soon as the UUV is in its cradle, we will get underway."

Five minutes later, the deck was secure.

"Make course three five zero, speed three knots," Yong ordered.

Snow Dragon 2 rumbled as her engines engaged. Ever so slowly, she battered ahead. The rudder began to respond. Great slabs of ice cleaved around her bow, creating claps that resonated like cannon fire. With a massive cloud of black smoke spewing from her stacks, the ship carved a broad turn and began pounding north.

CHAPTER 46

Arctic
Crash Site

Anywhere else on the high seas, a distant black stain on the horizon might have seemed innocuous. Here, for Kasey, it was nothing less than the coming of the Apocalypse.

Her first clue that the situation was degrading had been the young Russian sailor with the handheld radio. He'd received a call that seemed urgent, and while Kasey couldn't hear the conversation, the man had immediately slapped his partner on the shoulder, and they'd rushed outside.

Kasey waited a few beats, then cautiously followed. Outside, she saw one of the men pointing into the distance. And just like that, her fears were confirmed. A trail of black smoke billowed on the horizon, a brutish silhouette below. The Chinese were coming. Coming for Chen and Sky Fire.

Probably for her as well.

She hurried back inside and found Chen sitting on the floor near the forward galley.

"What's going on?" he asked, having noticed the commotion.

She bent down and said in a forceful whisper, "We have to go . . . now!"

He stared at her blankly, not understanding. "Go? Go where?"

In a move that would have impressed any drill sergeant, she

reached down, hauled him to his feet, and ushered him toward the back. They ended up near the crevice where Sky Fire was hidden. Kasey retrieved the backpack she'd prepared from the big pile of debris. She shrugged it over one shoulder and said, "The Chinese icebreaker Langley told us about—it's on the way. We can't be here when it arrives."

"What do you propose?"

"You can walk, right?"

"A little, yes. You're saying that we should . . . walk out into this storm?"

"The storm is letting up, and we have warm clothes."

"Where would we go? There is nothing but ice for hundreds of miles."

Kasey tried to think of a good reply, something convincing and logical. Nothing came to mind. She'd been gaming this scenario for hours but always hit the same dead end. There *was* nowhere to go. There was only ice and wind and frigid water. But staying here was tantamount to surrender, or worse.

"We'll figure something out," she said.

Sharpe came up the aisle and joined in. "What's up?"

Kasey told him about the approaching icebreaker. "We've got ten, maybe fifteen minutes. Dr. Chen and I are going to make a run for it."

She saw his thoughts stutter. He was hitting the same practical roadblocks Chen had, seeing the Arctic as an insurmountable obstacle. But then a steely calm overtook him. The way it probably did when, back in the day, Sharpe had spotted an enemy fighter on his wingman's tail. Instead of asking questions, instead of telling her it was hopeless, he said, "How can I help?"

Kasey was stunned by the relief those four words brought. And also by her reflexive response. "You could come with us."

Sharpe hesitated. "I can't just leave these people."

"They'll be okay. The Chinese are only after us, and the Russians are here to take credit for a rescue. The survivors will be taken care of either way."

She could see his struggle. A responsibility to his passengers versus duty to country.

"Actually," he said, "it might be better if I stay behind. I could help you get clear. The Russians will eventually figure out you're missing, and the Chinese are going to come looking for you no matter what. If we're lucky, I can run cover for you with both of them."

Kasey thought about it and nodded. It was a valid point. "All right. Any time you can buy us would be appreciated."

Chen said, "We should update Langley first."

It was another good thought. Proactive and helpful. Both men were stepping up their games. She said, "You're right, the agency has to get moving on an alternate plan to get us out of here."

"What about the guards?"

"They're both outside, on the right side of the fuselage. Go to the opposite side and set up Sky Fire. I'll keep an eye on them."

Chen unsteadily bent down to retrieve the black case.

As he did, Sharpe pulled Kasey aside and asked, "Are you sure he's up to walking out of here?"

"Not really. But I don't see any choice. If we can make a mile, maybe two, we'll have some separation. The ice has a fair amount of snow on it, but with this wind our tracks should get covered quickly."

"Okay, but humor me. You make a mile or maybe two . . . then what? If his leg gives out and he can't walk anymore, that's a death sentence out there."

Not having an answer, Kasey simply shot him a hard look. "One crisis at a time."

"What's in the backpack?"

"Some supplies. Food, water, heating packs."

"The food and water will freeze."

She looked at him plaintively.

"Sorry, I'm not trying to be a downer. I just want to get everyone out of here alive." He glanced toward the entrance. "You should take the rifle."

Kasey didn't know if he was thinking about the polar bear or the Chinese. "I'm going to be hauling a lot and Chen might need help walking. But yeah, it's probably a good idea."

"How will you handle those leads Captain Khurtin mentioned? Chances are, you're going to come across more than a few."

"I was thinking about that as well. Chen and I are just going to have to keep moving, even if it's not in a straight line."

"All right. Let me know when you're good to go. I'll figure out a way to distract our two minders."

"You know what, Sharpe? You're not half bad at this. If you're ever in the market for a career change, I'll put in a good word for you with the agency."

"From a pilot who just crashed his airplane to spook. Seems like a totally natural transition."

Kasey couldn't contain her smile.

He smiled back.

"Thanks," she said.

"For what?"

"For giving me a moment to think about something besides life in a Chinese prison or being mauled by a polar bear."

"You're welcome."

A crackle from the radio outside interrupted. Kasey heard one of the sailors acknowledging instructions.

"I've got some prep work I need to take care of," she said.

Sharpe pulled a box of ammo for the rifle from his pocket and zipped it into her backpack. "I think we both do."

CHAPTER

47

Five minutes later, Kasey was outside. She saw the icebreaker no more than two miles away, its bright red paint scheme unmistakable. It was moving slowly, layers of ice driving up its hardened bow as it hammered through the pack. On top of the *Aurora*'s sail three men stood watching, and Captain Khurtin was surely among them. All had binoculars fixed on the approaching icebreaker, but they didn't seem concerned.

And why would they be? she thought. *Their boat already has the glory. They'll be happy to let someone else do the yeoman's work of getting the survivors back to civilization.*

The pair of crewmen who'd stayed behind to act as guards were watching it all play out. Neither had noticed Chen when he slipped to the far side of the fuselage. Kasey positioned herself a few steps behind them—she wanted to be close enough to overhear any radio calls that came, and also be in a blocking position to keep Chen isolated.

At this point, she knew it was all down to timing. When to grab Chen and make a run for it. She wanted to give him as long as possible to connect with Langley. Ideally, the operations center would quickly come up with a rapid alternate plan.

It felt like time was compressing.

She wondered where the Chinese ship would stop. The most

logical place, in her admittedly nonnautical mind, would be somewhere near the *Aurora*, in the tiny harbor of thin ice. But given that it was an icebreaker, the ship could theoretically drive straight up to the wreckage.

Wherever it stopped, Kasey reckoned there would be an interval—ten minutes at least—before a shore party could make its way onto the ice. But probably not much more. She and Chen had to be out of sight before anyone realized they were missing. In their favor, the visibility had begun to drop—the wind had lessened, and wisps of ice fog were beginning to form.

Their two Russian minders seemed transfixed by the approaching ship, and Kasey decided to risk getting an update from Chen. She quietly moved to the far side of the fuselage.

She found him typing furiously near the crumpled nose section.

"Any luck?" she inquired.

He glanced up briefly. "Yes, I have made contact and explained what's happening. It appears they are aware of the situation."

Kasey wasn't surprised. Langley likely had every available space-based asset focused on this little slab of ice. The same for Russia and China. It could practically melt from the electronic barrage. "Did you tell them that you and I are about to make a run for it?"

"Yes. They said to remain connected for as long as possible while they come up with . . ." he paused and read from the message, "'an alternate means of extraction.'"

"We can't wait much longer," she said. "We need to be gone by the time the Chinese arrive."

Chen stopped what he was doing and looked at her with unusual directness. She saw something in his expression, something brewing in his head. If she were to guess, given his apparent level of discomfort, it was something outside his engineering wheelhouse.

"What is it?" she asked.

"There might be a way to buy more time."

"What's that?"

Chen looked down at Sky Fire. Then he explained what he had in mind.

"Is that possible?"

"I can't be sure. It depends on a great many things. Software packages, signal strength, how various systems interact. But it is exactly the kind of thing Sky Fire is designed to do."

"Then why do you look like you're about to jump off a cliff?"

"I . . . I never anticipated that I would be in the field. The one giving such commands."

"You're facing a crisis of conscience?"

He nodded.

"Well, I can help you with that. Do it, Dr. Chen—that is a direct order."

CHAPTER 48

Captain Yong no longer needed binoculars. He could see the Russian attack sub less than a mile away. Slightly beyond it, intermittently visible through a scudding mist, was the tubular shape that was their objective, the partial remains of the downed airliner.

The MSS had sent photographs of three people they were to search for and detain. Two were Americans, both suspected CIA operatives—an Asian man and an Occidental woman. The third was a Chinese national named Dr. Chen Li. Most important of all, they were not to depart without having the prized black case on board. Yong didn't know what to make of it all, so he concentrated on those things he could control. The most important of which, at that moment, was guiding *Snow Dragon 2* to the crash site.

The ice thickness had been constant, roughly two meters. Just ahead, however, he saw the far thinner floe he had been told to expect—the place where the airliner had crashed the previous night.

"Prepare to reduce revolutions when we encounter the thinner ice. Keep the speed a constant three knots until we identify a place to stop."

The helmsman acknowledged the order.

A low-frequency tremor caressed the ship as it cleaved ahead, a combination of the rumbling engines and a fracturing ice pack. The wind was down to 20 knots, far less than it had been hours earlier.

At least the sea is on my side, thought Yong.

"Sir," said the watch officer, "we have a warning light on the port engine. Digital control has gone offline."

Yong tried to recall the procedure to correct the malfunction.

"Would you like me to activate the standby system?" the watch officer prompted.

"Yes, immediately." Yong waited one held breath, then asked, "Did that correct the malfunction?"

After an extended silence, the watch officer replied, "No, sir. And now I show the same warning on the starboard engine."

"How could that—"

Yong's words were cut off as the engine noise began to rise.

"Both engines are accelerating," said the helmsman. The roar was getting louder and the deck shuddered violently.

"All stop!" Yong shouted.

The helmsman transmitted the commands. Nothing changed.

"Engines not responding to commands. Approaching red-line revolutions!"

It felt like the ship was tearing herself apart as the propellers exceeded their maximum rotational speed.

The watch officer said something else, but Yong couldn't hear it over the thundering of the engines and the rattling of fixtures. The floor shook as if from an earthquake, and cups of tea spilled over and shattered on the deck. Yong grabbed the chart table to keep from falling. Everyone on the bridge was shouting—the watch officer, the helmsman, the navigator. All seemed to have a different idea about what to do. Cut electrical power. Steer in a circle. Take an axe to the fuel lines. It was like a team of surgeons arguing over a flatlining patient.

To Yong it was nothing more than noise, accelerants to the madness.

Snow Dragon 2 was gaining speed. The gauge showed only 6 knots, but in heavy ice such forces on the bow could prove catastrophic. Yong looked ahead and saw the thinner ice approaching. *That will save us*, he thought.

When the ship reached the thin patch, her bow, which had been riding high on the thicker ice, dropped noticeably. The vibrations lessened somewhat, but then the props dug in and speed began to build.

Ten knots.

Twelve.

"Shut the engines down!" Yong shouted.

The watch officer replied, "Captain, chief engineer reports the engine controls are not responding!"

Yong had never felt so powerless. He was riding a ship that wasn't responding to his commands. The crew kept working to shut down the runaway engines, but *Snow Dragon 2* seemed to have a mind of her own, countering every input. Yong ventured a look ahead. What he saw was catastrophic. They were headed straight for the Russian submarine.

"Come hard to port, twenty degrees!" he said.

The helmsman responded, "Sir, rudder is jammed."

With the submarine less than 100 meters away, the impending disaster was clear.

"Speed sixteen knots," said the watch officer. "Sir, we must sound the collision alarm!"

Yong stood rooted, immobilized. He couldn't believe this was happening. The black hull of the sub filled the forward windshields. He saw men scrambling down from its sail, others running across its deck and jumping onto the ice.

"Activate the collision alarm!" said the watch officer.

The alarm siren blared. Red warning lights flashed. Lost to the bedlam, Captain Yong Shiu stood statue-like, his hands white as they knuckled the chart table in a death grip.

Fifty meters.

Twenty.

Steel met steel in a titanic collision of forces. *Snow Dragon 2*'s reinforced bow slammed into the nuclear attack submarine 30 meters from its own bow. The inches-thick steel plating of the icebreaker tore through the sub's pressure hull like a razor blade through a sheet of paper. Everything inside the *Aurora*—its wiring, its ductwork, its stringers—was instantly crushed and severed. Pipes spat steam and lights flickered to emergency power. What didn't remain attached sank in a long journey to the bottom of the ocean.

When the submarine was carved completely through, *Snow Dragon 2* slammed into the heavy ice beyond. A deckhand tumbled over the safety rail and plummeted overboard. Her bow vaulted out of the water and everyone on the bridge was thrown to the deck. Captain Yong flew head over heels into the base of the helm. His head struck something hard.

And then the world went black.

CHAPTER 49

Kasey had seen automobile accidents before. They happened in a heartbeat, and came with a metallic smack that sounded like a clap of thunder. In comparison, the disaster playing out before her seemed to unfold in slow motion.

The sounds of crunching steel and fracturing ice shattered the quiet. The size and momentum of the vessels sustained the collision for an interminable length of time. The forces translated through the ice, feeling like an earthquake beneath Kasey's feet. It took half a minute for the ships to grind to a stop.

The din of the collision was replaced by Klaxons and frantic shouting. A rising cloud of steam and smoke shrouded the scene for a time, but soon two surreal silhouettes emerged. *Snow Dragon 2* was the first to appear. Her bow had come to rest vaulted onto the ice sheet, like a breaching whale that had departed its element and become stranded. She was listing to port and there were massive gouges in her hull.

The *Aurora* was in worse shape. She had been sliced clean through, the forward thirty feet of her bow simply gone. The rest of the submarine lay smoldering, canted down at the bow with flames licking up at the edges. Her matte-black hull glimmered in the reflection of the fires.

Kasey thought the sub might sink immediately, but it didn't seem to be dropping lower. Not yet. She knew submarines were fitted with ballast tanks and watertight doors, so maybe there was a chance the boat wouldn't sink. The next thought that came to mind, a bit too late, was that the *Aurora*, like all newer Russian submarines, was almost certainly nuclear-powered. Had she and Chen just instigated the next Chernobyl?

Chen was standing next to her. He looked ashen. "That isn't what I intended," he said in a hollow voice. It was probably the understatement of his life.

Kasey gave him a perplexed look. When he had told her Sky Fire might be able to seize control of the *Snow Dragon 2*, she'd guessed it might shut down the engines or steer the ship toward the North Pole. Wholesale destruction had never entered her mind.

She wondered if the disaster Chen had just instigated—no, she corrected, the disaster *I ordered* him to instigate—might constitute an act of war. That thought subsided as quickly as it had arisen. This was precisely what Sky Fire was capable of, proof of its lethality. Kasey had merely turned the system against the country that created it, a Frankenstein moment for the digital age. There would be attempts to cast blame in the days ahead, but those were arguments better left to diplomats and politicians.

Two immediate impacts, however, were inescapable. The ante had been upped incredibly. And she and Chen needed to leave right now.

"I think our work here is done," she said. "Shut Sky Fire down. Time to move."

While Chen complied, Kasey edged toward the back of the fuselage. Upon reaching it, she peered around the corner and searched for the two Russian guards. They were nowhere in sight. Then, suddenly, faraway flashes of movement caught her eye. Their two minders had just crossed the makeshift bridge and were sprinting toward the wrecked ships. The sailor that had been assigned to watch the passerelle was also gone. He, too, must have rushed to aid his shipmates.

On the decks of both vessels crewmen were scrambling and shouting. A sailor was inflating a life raft on the *Aurora*'s crumpled foredeck and Russian crewmen were tumbling down onto the ice. She saw the sheen of an oil slick on the trail of open water behind the icebreaker, and fire flickered ominously from a hatch on the *Aurora*. The scene was apocalyptic.

And Kasey wasn't going to waste it.

She hurried back to Chen and, as soon as he had Sky Fire in its case, she snatched it up, ready to move. Studying the barren ice-scape ahead, she searched for references in the distance, a landmark of any kind. There was nothing but ice and mottled sky for as far as she could see. Bands of low gray clouds whipped past above, and the ice seemed to sway on unseen swells. It had been there all along, but now, as she was about to face it head-on, the surrounding world of white took on a far darker aura.

Together they began walking away from the wreckage that had become their refuge. Kasey watched Chen carefully and set the quickest pace he could manage. For the first few minutes, she kept turning around to check their six, hoping no one had noticed their departure. At one point she saw Nick emerge from the shelter, but he disappeared to the far side. Two others came out and followed suit. It made perfect sense. Everyone inside would have heard the catastrophe, and it was only natural that their interest would be piqued. Kasey was thankful to have their attention locked in the wrong direction.

After roughly a quarter mile, she took one last look over her shoulder. The fuselage had all but faded into swirls of snow. Moments before it disappeared completely, however, a man suddenly appeared. Her heart skipped a beat when he looked straight at them, but with great relief she realized it was Sharpe.

He held out his arm and gave a wave.

Kasey waved back, but not quickly enough. Sharpe had vanished in a sweeping curtain of mist.

CHAPTER 50

Arkady Khurtin was so incensed he barely felt the pain in his arm. He was quite sure it was broken. He was standing in the control room, ankle-deep in glacial seawater. The lights blinked on and off like a disco gone haywire as *Aurora*'s emergency electrical buses, where many of its critical circuits converged, ping-ponged between power sources. The blackness, he knew, would win. The only question was how long it would take.

He had witnessed the collision sequence from atop the sail, ordering the *Aurora* to general quarters as the icebreaker bore down on his boat. There had not been enough time to rig for a dive. Khurtin could do nothing more than stand his ground and prepare for the worst, seized by a sense of helplessness he had never before felt. The crash had sent him flying to the deck, and his left arm took the brunt of it, striking the base of a solidly welded stanchion. The pain was immediate, although not incapacitating. Realizing that his arm was broken, he had quickly fashioned a sling from a torn life jacket. That kept the discomfort to a minimum. Truth be told, after fifteen minutes of appalling casualty and damage reports, he found the pain . . . invigorating.

Khurtin was convinced the ramming of his ship was intentional. The only questions were, Who had ordered it and why? Was the icebreaker's skipper carrying out instructions from his headquarters? Had some member of the crew, perhaps the captain himself, gone insane and caused the collision? There had to be irrationality at some level for an icebreaker to attack a Russian warship without provocation. A warship that had been, until that moment, engaged in giving aid to the survivors of an air disaster.

Yet some of what Khurtin had seen in the final moments seemed incongruous. He'd noticed a crewman near the bow, no doubt a man on watch duty, screaming and flailing, waving his arms toward the bridge in warning. Khurtin had heard the icebreaker's collision alarm clearly, meaning those in command were aware that impact was imminent. Yet the ship had taken no evasive maneuvers, and she was traveling at what had to be flank speed.

None of it made sense.

Could they really be that incompetent? he wondered.

"Captain!" Grekov said as he descended into view from the sail.

Khurtin had put his exec in charge of the topside emergency response. His face was a bloody mess from a head wound, but he seemed perfectly lucid. "We have recovered three bodies from the water. Eighteen men are now shoreside, sixteen missing. The rest are manning their battle stations. Damage control reports that compartments eighteen, nine, and six are fully flooded."

"The pumps?" Khurtin asked as he shifted his bad arm.

"Only half are working, and power to those is intermittent. We are losing the battle."

In line with his nature, Khurtin fell inordinately still. This had always been his temperament, as if something in his brain was miswired. The more fury he felt, the more dire the situation, the greater the calm that enveloped him. It was the ideal disposition for a sub commander, and never more so than now.

"Should we abandon ship?" Grekov prompted.

The captain checked the roll and pitch indicators. *Aurora* was listing 10 degrees to starboard. Far more worryingly, what was left of her bow was down 18 degrees. He knew the situation was hopeless. They had been rammed full speed by a ship four times their size that had a hardened bow. *Aurora* would not survive. Yet she wouldn't go down without a fight. The doors would hold for a time and the pumps would buy a bit longer. He gave it an hour, perhaps two. Enough time to tend to his casualties and salvage some equipment.

"Comm," he said, "any luck sending that mayday?"

"No, Captain. The communications buses are down, most likely flooded. The backup satcom has no connection, probably damage to the antenna. And the communications buoys were all in the forward section, which . . ." He didn't need to finish that thought.

"I'm going topside to have a look," Khurtin said.

One-handed, he climbed the crooked ladder to the platform on the *Aurora*'s damaged sail.

The scene was absolute bedlam. Fire, smoke, bodies being hauled from the ice-clad sea. The bow section of the *Aurora*, what had been the forward torpedo room, was simply gone, completely sheared away. It was probably just now settling on the bottom, a half dozen training torpedoes rattling around inside. At the front of the boat now were the gaping remains of the crew's quarters, a forest of jagged metal and torn wiring. These two sections, he knew, were where the fatalities had been suffered.

He stared venomously at the ship that had wrought this destruction. The big icebreaker had settled, her bow lower than it had been immediately after the strike. A gash along her side was taking on water, but her pumps were working furiously, gushers of water spewing from every exhaust port. Unlike *Aurora*, the *Snow Dragon 2* would probably sail another day.

Khurtin stood statue-like, his blue eyes lasering in on a group of a dozen Chinese. They were gathering on the ice near a gangway, midway along the icebreaker's waist. Central among them was a man in uniform wearing captain's stripes. Three of the men around him held weapons, what looked like old Type 56 battle rifles—China's knockoff of the venerable AK-47. All of them wore the working clothes of merchant seamen. On the ship's main deck, ten other men stood along the safety rail gawking at the scene.

Khurtin estimated that such a ship would run with a crew of between fifty and seventy, a mix of merchant seamen, technicians, and scientists. He contrasted this to his own ship's complement, seventy-two of the best sailors in the Russian Navy. That number had been halved by casualties, but he still had under his command a solid contingent of highly trained men. All of whom, in light of what had just happened, were highly pissed-off.

He regarded *Aurora* solemnly. The pride of the Russian Navy, she had been placed under his stewardship. On another day, in another place, he might have used the last of her faltering battery power to drive her onto a sandbar. But here? *Aurora*'s final resting place was written in stone. Or actually, ice. Khurtin could make a case that he had done all he could, and his men would back him up. Even so, it would be a stain on his record that could never be erased. This would be his last command.

My last command. Those words looped gravely in his mind. His expression remained blank, and his heart rate was metronomic. But his eyes drilled into the Chinese captain.

"Grekov!" he bellowed down the ladder.

His exec appeared quickly.

"Do your best with the boat. I am going ashore."

"Ashore, Captain?"

"Yes, and I want ten men to accompany me. They are to bring a stretcher and a blanket. Have the remaining crew who are not directly involved in rescue operations standing by." When he explained his plan, his exec smiled, which Khurtin took as tacit approval.

Grekov added, "You should take our Mandarin speaker with you, Andreyev."

Khurtin nodded with otherworldly composure. "Yes, an excellent idea."

CHAPTER 51

Langley

The CIA operations center sat in stunned silence as they watched the disaster play out via a multispectral NRO satellite hovering overhead. They witnessed the two vessels collide and saw people scrambling across the ice. They noted the bodies floating in the frigid sea in the aftermath. More critically, and almost unnoticed on the periphery, they saw two lone forms trekking off into the Arctic wilderness.

For a full minute no one spoke—a virtual eternity in the fast-paced hub of the world's preeminent intelligence agency. Finally, DDO Flynn pierced the quiet by announcing, "Ladies and gentlemen, our battle has shifted."

The next twenty minutes were a barrage of amended requests, new information, and realigned priorities. There was no need to emphasize the urgency of the situation.

"What's the status of our LC-130?" Flynn inquired.

"The Hercules is fueled and ready to go at Summit Station," replied the duty officer. "Flight time to the crash site is roughly four hours. But gas will be tight for the round-trip, and we can't launch without choosing a landing zone. Once we provide coordinates to the crew, they'll need an hour to survey the ice conditions to determine if a landing is even feasible."

A minimum of five hours, Flynn thought. He cast a hard look at the operating area on the map. "What about the *Cheyenne*? Where is she now?"

The duty officer replied, "She's almost to the crash site, but I don't see how her surfacing in the middle of this goat rodeo does anything to advance our cause. Chen and Sky Fire are already a healthy distance away. We could tell them to turn back. There are no guarantees that the *Cheyenne*'s crew, even with the four Spec Ops personnel on board, could take control of the situation there."

The duty officer had a good point, Flynn thought, and he privately expanded on it. The Chinese were hell-bent on regaining possession of Sky Fire. Chen, however, fell into a slightly different category. The MSS would very much want to take him back to Beijing, where they could mainline drugs, remove body parts, and administer electrical shocks until he gave up every scrap of information, both on his work and his planned defection. More important, however, was that Sky Fire's chief designer couldn't be allowed to spill the contents of his brilliant mind to the Americans. The simplest means of ensuring that was a bullet to his brain in the Arctic.

This cemented the start of Flynn's new plan. The last place Chen and Kasey could go was back toward *Snow Dragon 2*.

He said speculatively, "On Orion and Falcon's present course, is there anywhere the ice is thin enough for *Cheyenne* to break through and surface?"

All eyes shifted to the ISR specialist, who gestured to the map and said, "It's hard to say without knowing exactly where they are. But I do show one thinner area roughly thirty-five miles northeast of her present position."

"Thirty-five miles?" Flynn exclaimed.

The duty officer said, "It's not as bad as it sounds. The *Cheyenne* could get there pretty quickly, assuming we can get in touch with them to give the order. If we can put her within a reasonable distance of the weather station, the SEALs can go out and pick them up."

"Do they have transportation?"

"What, like snowmobiles?"

The DDO nodded.

"No, attack boats aren't designed for loading and unloading heavy equipment. They don't have deck cranes, and the hatches are too small.

The SEALs would likely be on skis. But in our favor, that's exactly what the team on board *Cheyenne* specializes in. They're cold-weather experts and can move over ice like nobody else on the planet. It would take some time, however."

There was nothing but ice for hundreds of miles around Orion and Falcon's estimated position. "I'm not sure how much time they have," Flynn replied. "They're completely exposed and probably already freezing their asses off."

The ex–Navy man at the ISR desk interjected, "Sir, I might have a stopgap option. I've been looking over some NOAA charts and—"

"NOAA?" The National Oceanic and Atmospheric Administration had never been a go-to agency in the CIA operations center.

"Yes. They operate a small chain of Arctic weather stations. Each summer they deploy two or three on the drift ice. While teams of scientists come and go, the equipment is mostly automated and streams data all year long. These outposts generally don't survive more than a season or two, but at the moment a handful of them are active.

"How many, specifically?"

"Six," the man at the ISR desk responded. "One of which is fairly close to our area of operations."

"How close?"

"Nine nautical miles. East–southeast."

On the lone image they'd captured of Kasey and Chen leaving the crash site, they had appeared to be heading east. Flynn took this as half a win, which was better than no win at all.

"What do these stations consist of?" Flynn asked.

A new map appeared. NOAA's logo was at the bottom, and it depicted the Arctic Ocean flecked by six blue X's, including one that was reasonably close to the crash site.

"Not much," the ISR man stated. "No personnel or provisions. But there is a small prefab building—more of a shed, really, assuming this storm hasn't blown it away. It could provide protection from the elements until help arrives."

The duty officer chimed in, "It would also give us a point of reference. When Orion and Falcon are within four hours of this place, we could launch the LC-130."

Flynn was skeptical. "Can they walk nine miles in this storm? With Chen injured?"

"That's going to be the least of our problems," said the duty officer. "If this storm doesn't let up, the Herc won't be able to get in. The pilots have to be able to see the surface in order to attempt any landing."

The DDO kept staring at the big map. Even if Orion and Falcon could reach this weather station, it would take half a day for them to get there. If they fell short, they'd be stranded out in the open. Nevertheless, a plan, albeit risky, was beginning to form in his mind.

As the circumstances changed, the team at the operations center was changing—adapting to what was available and narrowing the possible outcomes.

Which, in a more desperate sense, three thousand miles to the north, was exactly what Kasey and Chen were doing.

Only they were a lot colder.

CHAPTER 52

Arctic
East of Crash Site

Kasey brushed away the icicles from her lashes, which were threatening to freeze her eyelids shut. It was the only part of their bodies they'd left exposed and the steam rising from their face coverings froze instantly upon contact.

She and Chen had been traveling over the windswept ice for a good half hour. The crash site was no longer visible, although for a time wisps of smoke marked the area, the fire on the *Aurora* still burning.

When the smoke finally disappeared, Kasey wondered why. Had the fire burned out? Or had the *Aurora* sunk? She figured any answer at the moment was academic—the Russians, at least, were no longer a threat.

The Chinese, however, remained very much in the game. Eventually they were going to figure out that Chen and Sky Fire had instigated the disaster, which would put more pressure than ever on Beijing to track them down. The guardrails of politics and diplomacy, if any had been there to begin with, now lay smoldering at the top of the world.

Kasey kept moving, willing herself forward, but with each step she sensed their progress slowing. Chen was weakening, and she noticed he was favoring his bad leg. She recalled seeing a walking cane in a wrecked overhead bin and now wished she'd brought it.

Compounding their problems was a lack of navigation aids. Without so much as a compass, maintaining a proper heading and walking in a straight line was virtually impossible. Nevertheless, Kasey did her best to keep them headed in the same general direction.

Initially the smoke had been her reference point, but with that now gone she could only rely on the murky glow of the southern horizon. Catching glimpses of the sun through the swirling snow and fog, she kept it on her right, which allowed them to maintain a roughly easterly direction.

This was fieldwork like she had never experienced before. In this environment, standard tradecraft was all but useless. There were no surveillance detection routes to run, no dead drops to make. No ducking into doorways or doubling back. It was, in a sense, the most artless of missions. Yet like all good operators, Kasey forced herself to adapt. With nowhere to run and nowhere to hide, she only had one job—to keep her charge alive in the world's most unforgiving climate long enough to be rescued. A single rifle, two days of food and water, and a communications device like no other. That was what she had to work with.

But would it be enough?

She could feel the cold wearing her down, reaching deep into her bones. Her hands were going numb, and her limbs were slow to react, as if the signals from her brain were firing through slush. She and Chen had layered up as best they could, but inevitably there were gaps in their outerwear. The wind clawed at bits of exposed skin, and heat escaped through loose seals. Kasey's concerns were amplified when Chen stumbled and dropped to a knee.

"Are you all right?" she asked, quickly going to his side.

"Yes," he mumbled unconvincingly.

Kasey helped him stand, and they paused for a moment. She removed a water bottle from inside her jacket. She had transferred it there from her backpack, reckoning the water wouldn't freeze if she kept it close to her body. They shared it, and she pulled out an energy bar and unwrapped it. She broke it in two and gave half to Chen.

Kasey knew she'd need to ration what little food she'd brought. The energy bar was a brand she'd had before, but it had never tasted so good.

Looking at Chen, she noticed his hand trembling slightly as he ate. He, too, was beginning to succumb to the elements. She would have to keep a very close eye on him.

"How is the charge holding up on Sky Fire's battery?" she asked. She tried to pose the question casually, but there was no masking its importance. If they lost comms out here, in the middle of the Arctic, they would be doomed.

"When I last checked, it was strong, still over sixty percent."

"Good to hear. All the same, let's plan on keeping our activations brief."

She pulled out a chemical hand warmer, courtesy of the Russians, and offered it to Chen. Once activated, it would provide temporary relief to his chilled extremities.

"No," he said. "We may need them later."

Kasey nodded and returned the package to her pocket.

"We should keep moving," Chen prompted, mustering a modicum of stoicism.

She nodded in agreement, and as they set out again, she tried to support him by the elbow. Ever the trooper, Chen waved her off, insisting that it wasn't necessary. Kasey admired his resolve, but she knew it had its limits.

"How far do you think we've gone?" he asked.

She had been wondering the same thing. Other than when Sky Fire was active, they had no GPS information. There was no terrain elevation for reference, only a flat and featureless horizon, and the choppy ice had made for uneven progress. Ridges and draws, carved into the surface by the wind, made footing in the lower areas quite slick, which had required them to proceed slowly and with extra caution. Thankfully, they hadn't encountered any major leads to further stymie their progress. The two they'd run across had been small and easily bypassed.

"Two miles," she speculated. "Maybe a little more."

"And how far should we go?"

It was an excellent question, and one for which Kasey had no answer. They were moving without an objective. Not going *to* any particular point but simply separating from where they'd been. Getting off the X, the point of greatest danger, as it was referred to in the military. Her intent was to run far enough that they wouldn't be followed, but not so far that they were beyond rescue.

"Let's move for another twenty minutes. Then we'll stop to rest and set up Sky Fire. Hopefully Langley will have a plan by then."

Chen nodded, but he couldn't conceal his worry. He was thinking the same thing she was.

We can't go on like this for long. If something doesn't change, soon, we'll be facing a lonely and very cold death.

CHAPTER 53

Sharpe decided to keep his distance from the spectacle playing out between the Russians and the Chinese. He doubted he could be of any practical help, and inserting himself into the fray wouldn't do his passengers any good. Holding in place was also probably the best way to help Kasey and Chen get as far away as they could. *Sometimes, the best move is no move at all.*

Watching the aftermath of the horrific collision unfold, he noticed that the Russians were more organized—an unpredicted development since they had taken most of the casualties. He saw three bodies laid out on the ice, all of which had been pulled from the water. Two crewmen in a tiny inflatable boat were on the far side of the *Aurora*, banging on something with a hammer. Whatever they were doing, it had a distinct air of hopelessness. The sub was resting at a strange nose-down angle. The base of her sail was submerged, and part of the rudder was visible. Twenty crewmen milled about on the ice, caring for the wounded and glaring at the Chinese ship.

He wondered how many had been on board the *Aurora*. Fifty? A hundred? How many had survived? Sharpe hadn't formed any particular bond with the Russian captain, but having faced his own recent disaster, including loss of life, he felt a pang of sympathy for the man.

The *Snow Dragon 2* was in better shape. She was listing slightly and, although there was no longer smoke coming from her stacks, a brightly lit deck proved that she still had electrical power. There were a handful of crewmen on deck, and Sharpe saw shadows moving in the windows of the bridge. There was also a group of about a dozen gathered on the ice at the foot of a gangway.

The timing of the disaster wasn't lost on Sharpe. He had seen Chen working on Sky Fire minutes before the crash, and he wondered if the two were related. Probably, he surmised. After being told by Kasey that similar technology might have brought down his airliner, the concept of making an icebreaker go rogue was well within the bounds of this new reality. It also meshed perfectly with what happened next: Kasey and Chen had disappeared in the ensuing disarray.

Sharpe's eye was drawn to movement at a midway point on the ice. A wave had sloshed onto the ice sheet not far from the passerelle. He soon realized what had happened. A second lead had formed, perpendicular to the existing one. It seemed to be widening, as was the original gap. For whatever reason—perhaps the force of the pileup?—the ice was moving. The passerelle had been left behind in all the chaos, forcing crewmen to slide down the sub's hull or simply jump to reach the safety of the ice. Now it was in danger of falling in.

On pure instinct, Sharpe began running toward the lead. Several times he lost his footing on the slippery surface, but mercifully, he didn't go down. He was nearly there when the far side of the passerelle dropped into the sea. The edge on the near side began sliding, and he launched himself toward it. He glided on his stomach like a seal, skidding over the ice, and his outstretched hand gripped the last corner of the ramp as it dipped into the water.

Sharpe dug in with his toes to keep from gliding any farther, and his face ended up inches from the edge. He squirmed backward, thankful that the ice shelf was thick enough to support his weight. He had a good grip on the edge of the passerelle and so started to haul it in. Then he froze.

Conflicting thoughts began lurching through his mind, a fusion of the vastly altered situation around him. The Russians, the Chinese, the destruction. The state of his own passengers. Kasey and Chen. No matter how he worked the variables, he kept arriving at the same solution.

Sharpe let go of the passerelle and watched it sink into the ink-black sea.

Empty-handed, he rose to his feet and stood still for a moment. He was completely out of breath, his lungs burning from the cold. He surveyed the scene of the collision. No one seemed to have noticed his scramble to save the ramp. Everyone was too busy recovering bodies, tending to their ships. The loss of the passerelle would be noticed, but not for some time. With the lead widening, it would simply be one more complication for the Chinese and the Russians to deal with.

He walked back to the shelter, and as he arrived, a brutal gust swept past, throwing a gyre of snow. The wind and cold were incessant, but his upgraded clothing helped—for short exposures it dialed down the misery. He kept going until he reached the cargo hold, where his gaze was drawn to a canvas tarp he had discarded twenty minutes earlier. He had originally discovered it when he and Kasey were conducting their treasure hunt. The size of a bedsheet, the tarp had been covering a consignment of machine parts. Because it was greasy, he'd tossed it aside at the time, reckoning it was of little use. Now his mind had changed. He could use it to help cover Kasey and Chen's escape.

Following their tracks for about a quarter mile, he then laid down the tarp and began sweeping it back and forth, obliterating their footprints, along with his own. In some areas the footprints were deep, the snow having compressed, and it took considerable effort to erase them. He worked all the way back to the fuselage, paying particular attention to the first fifty feet of the trail.

Now, looking over his work, Sharpe saw that their tracks were barely visible, a hazy runner of white. They would soon be further obscured by windswept snow. It wouldn't hold against a concerted search, but at the moment the Chinese were fully distracted by damage control.

Sharpe once more studied the two wounded ships. One was on the verge of sinking, the other severely disabled. Their crews were scrambling to respond, but it seemed pointless. All of them, whether they realized it or not, were subject to the same fate of his own little group inside the fuselage—survivors in need of rescue.

He reckoned both of the vessels had already sent distress calls. Help would be on the way very soon. Would the Chinese be the first to arrive? The Russians? Canada had to be in the mix, owing to mere proximity. Sharpe didn't care who it was. At some point in the next twelve hours, rescue would arrive and all the poor wretches who'd been stranded on this sullied patch of polar ice would be saved. Finally, his passengers would be safe.

All, that is, except for two, one of whom is injured. Kasey and Chen might have escaped, but would they be safe, out there alone, against the elements and without shelter? The thought gnawed at him. Regardless of who they were and why they had been on his plane, they remained his passengers; his responsibility. Too many had already died.

With his sense of duty tugging at his mind, Sharpe's thoughts veered in an entirely new direction, one that quickly ventured onto dangerous ground. But no sooner had it ventured onto that ground than he committed to a course of action.

There were countless variables to weigh. Critical risks to evaluate. His gloved thumb tapped his thigh in agitation.

What he had come up with really was a bad idea. A monumentally bad idea. Even so, he knew he had to try it.

CHAPTER 54

It took twenty minutes to assemble the special shore detail Khurtin had requested. During that time, he kept a close eye on his boat. And an even closer eye on the Chinese.

In particular, he watched the group that had rushed ashore. A junior officer was shouting commands, while the man with captain's stripes anxiously looked on. Khurtin couldn't understand what was being said, but the group had split into two distinct details, each composed of five men. One of the details headed toward the *Aurora*, where the Chinese sailors began helping his own men. The language barrier was evident, but they immediately tended to the wounded and assisted in the search for survivors. It was a symbolic effort at best, but at least they were showing some compassion. An adherence to maritime rescue law.

To Khurtin's surprise, the second detail, led by the nervous captain, didn't approach the *Aurora*. Instead they struck out toward the wrecked airplane, which only fueled Khurtin's simmering wrath.

There had been a handful of messages between the two vessels, exchanged via short-range VHF radio in the immediate aftermath of the collision. The Chinese had cited a catastrophic malfunction of their engine controls as the cause of the disaster, and assured Khurtin that they would provide any and all assistance to the *Aurora* that could be spared. What they hadn't offered was any sort of apology.

The fact that the Chinese captain was now prioritizing a far less critical situation enraged Khurtin. The consequences of the man's incompetence were all around them: dead bodies, wounded, a foundering submarine. Seeing the Chinese captain simply shun the stricken *Aurora*, and shun any sense of accountability, was beyond baffling.

When the second Chinese detail reached the lead, they hit the same roadblock Khurtin and his crew had when they'd first tried to reach the crashed airliner. Curiously, his own solution, the passerelle, had vanished. He didn't see it anywhere, and wondered if the ice might have shifted from the force of the collision, causing it to fall into the sea. The man he had stationed to mind it was gone, having rightly returned to aid his shipmates. The ramp, at some point in the confusion, appeared to have been lost.

For ten minutes, he watched the Chinese contingent stand in disarray. They gestured and argued, and their captain seemed unwilling to make a decision. One of them shouted in the direction of the wrecked fuselage but received no reply from the crash survivors. This Khurtin thought curious, but he wrote it off to the wind. In the end, the stymied Chinese turned around and began walking back to their ship.

Khurtin assessed his own vessel. *Aurora* remained afloat, but her electrical buses had failed completely. This rendered the pumps inoperative and would hasten her demise. Procedurally, one of his primary concerns was the boat's nuclear reactor. The reactor was centrally located and had not been exposed to the brunt of the collision. Its critical cooling system was operating normally on backup power, and there were so far no warnings from the radiation monitors. All that would change, but probably not before *Aurora* ended up on the bottom of the sea.

Khurtin actually felt a measure of solace in this, which was a testament to how far he had fallen. Only minutes ago, he had commanded the most cutting-edge vessel in the Russian Navy. Now he was grateful that the nuclear disaster unfolding on his watch had at least occurred in one of the most inaccessible places on earth.

He strove to keep his composure. This was not the time for stray thoughts. His crew had salvaged everything possible from the *Aurora*: food, medical supplies, survival gear. In his mind, all that could be done had been done. It was time for the next step, which had been brewing in his mind since he'd realized his ship was doomed. He descended a ladder to the ice, ignoring the groans that emanated from deep inside *Aurora*'s hull. His special shore detail was waiting, along with the items he'd requested. Khurtin gave his men a meticulous briefing on his plan.

He led his contingent toward the Chinese who were returning from the lead. His own crew complied perfectly with his detailed instructions. To a man, they appeared more consumed by shock than anger; more in need of help than posing any sort of threat. Khurtin was in front, and at the rear were two men carrying a stretcher. One of his sailors was on the stretcher. His eyes were closed, suggesting that he was either dead or seriously injured, and his lower body covered by a thick blanket.

Khurtin brought his men to a stop, letting the Chinese traverse the last 20 meters to reach them. The second Chinese shore party paused their aid work and rejoined their captain. The air was redolent with the scents of the disaster—burning oil, charred wiring, singed flesh.

The Russians arranged themselves precisely as Khurtin had instructed—a wide arc, with Andreyev directly behind Khurtin and the stretcher at the very back. The two groups ended up ten paces apart. The Chinese eyed them warily. Unlike his own men, they were clumped in a tight group. Their captain stood at the front, and the three men carrying weapons mingled with the rest, their rifles hanging loosely on their shoulders.

Khurtin locked eyes with his Chinese counterpart but said nothing. Previously anxious, the man now feigned confidence—even borderline bravado. It was an inappropriate posture in such a volatile situation, which called for contrition. A long and awkward silence ensued.

Finally, the Chinese captain exchanged a few words with the man directly behind him in their native tongue. Khurtin heard a distinct cough—Andreyev by his own shoulder. This was the prearranged signal. Confirmation, based on what Andreyev had heard, that there were no Russian speakers among the icebreaker's crew. More critically, they apparently assumed that there were no Mandarin speakers on the Russian side.

Conceding to the usual default language, the Chinese skipper said in heavily accented English, "I am Captain Yong of the People's Republic of China. We are officially taking command of this rescue."

Khurtin remained silent.

"It is regrettable that you and your crew have suffered injuries." He looked directly at the stretcher, then at Khurtin's limp arm. "As we previously informed you, our ship suffered a technical malfunction affecting our engines and steering."

"We have suffered more than just injuries," Khurtin growled, struggling to keep his temper in check. "Three of my crew are dead, and sixteen are missing."

The Chinese skipper turned his head and said something to the nearest man with a rifle.

Andreyev whispered a translation in Khurtin's ear. *If you have to shoot, take the captain first.*

Khurtin had had enough. "Now!" he shouted.

It happened in a flash. The man on the stretcher threw off the blanket, revealing six fully automatic AK-12 battle rifles. Rounds had been chambered, and the fire selector levers were set to semiautomatic. It took mere seconds for the six men Khurtin had designated to retrieve weapons and train them on the Chinese crewmen that mattered—the three who were armed.

The Russians had deconflicted their fire in advance: left, center, and right. Two barrels were leveled at each of the three armed Chinese. Only one made the fatal mistake. The rightmost guard lowered the rifle from his shoulder. Before he could get anywhere near the trigger, he was cut down in a hailstorm of 5.45x39mm rounds. Eight of them connected at minimum range, and he was dead before he hit the ground. The man standing next to him staggered, a stray bullet having caught him in the arm.

The Chinese captain looked horrified, but he said nothing. Did nothing.

Khurtin gave a hand signal, and eight more of his men appeared in the distance. They were also carrying weapons, the last from the *Aurora*'s armory. They sprinted toward the *Snow Dragon 2*'s gangway.

Khurtin stepped forward until he was looking Yong straight in the eye. With his good right hand, he pulled a Makarov from his pocket and directed the barrel straight at Yong's forehead.

Andreyev bellowed in Mandarin, "Everyone on your knees! Hands behind your heads!"

Captain Yong was the first to kneel. His men followed his example.

Khurtin saw a walkie-talkie on the junior Chinese officer's belt. He ordered one of his men to confiscate it. He then said to Andreyev, "Tell him I want his entire crew assembled on the ice in fifteen minutes. If even one man remains on board, the captain will be shot. Anyone carrying a weapon will be shot."

Andreyev translated, and Yong ordered the seaman nearest the ship to carry out Khurtin's instructions. The poor man set out with his hands in the air, Andreyev accompanying him.

The act of piracy was concluded quickly. With three minutes to spare, sixty-one officers, crew, and scientists from *Show Dragon 2* were sitting on the ice floe under guard. That was where they would stay, cold be damned, until transportation could be arranged for everyone, including the air crash survivors, on a Russian Navy vessel.

Khurtin was soon on the bridge of *Snow Dragon 2*. One of his technicians reconfigured the communications suite, first to cut all connections with Beijing, and then to initiate contact with the Russian Navy. Khurtin knew that the icebreaker was not seaworthy. Her hull had been damaged, which meant that battering her way to open water was out of the question.

Through no fault of his own, the *Aurora* was lost. But he had at least taken control of the situation. From the bridge of the *Snow Dragon 2*, he glared at his Chinese counterpart, who sat shivering on the ice. Yong looked back with abject fear. Khurtin suspected his terror wasn't driven by his present predicament, but rather the one he would face when he returned to China.

Both men were so engaged in their stare-down, one reveling in a dark victory, the other dazed in ignoble defeat, that neither noticed the periscope that had emerged half a mile away.

CHAPTER 55

Langley

Holy crap . . ." Adam Bennett muttered as digital images from the *Cheyenne*'s photonics mast hit the display monitor.

Captain Hansen stared at a scene that was nothing short of cataclysmic. In the low-light images, *Snow Dragon 2* lay dead in the water. She was nosed into the heavy pack ice and her hull was seriously damaged. The remains of a submarine—the class surprisingly escaped him, but he suspected it was Russian—lay bow-down at a hard angle and was on the verge of sinking. If he were to wager, he would guess this boat was the shadow presence they'd registered the previous day.

Hansen had been on edge for the better part of an hour. They had been fifteen miles away, running at high speed, when a spike sonar contact seized everyone's attention. The noise was so loud it had overwhelmed their own signature. Even more disconcertingly, it was distinctly steel-on-steel. According to the sonar operator, who'd been forced to pull his headset off, it had sounded like a train wreck.

That description, as it turned out, was disquietingly accurate.

"The analytics were dead-on," Bennett remarked as he studied the scene. "There really was a collision."

The control room fell silent, everyone transfixed by the stunning images. There was no mistaking the scale of what had occurred. Dead and injured men were splayed out on the ice, and the submarine was on fire, a one-way trip to Davy Jones's locker all but assured. They were looking at the aftermath of a massive maritime disaster. Notwithstanding the fact that the nations involved were undeclared enemies, everyone in the control room felt a sailor's regret for the loss of life.

"How the hell did that happen?" Hansen asked, probably rhetorically.

Drake, standing on the perimeter, said, "More to the point, how are we going to insert ourselves in that mess to pick up the people and hardware we've been ordered to retrieve?"

"I'm not sure we are," Hansen replied. "The situation has changed drastically."

The captain considered his next move.

He had brought the *Cheyenne* to periscope depth as a precaution. After registering the distant collision, and knowing there were very few ships in the area, his personal DEFCON level had redlined. Something unexpected had happened, and he wasn't going to expose his boat until he knew what it was.

With that in mind, on reaching the target area Hansen had ordered the upward-looking cameras put to use. These had immediately registered an open channel above. Roughly sixty feet wide and arrow-straight, it could only be a path the *Snow Dragon 2* had plowed. The new ice was barely crusted over, and although Hansen had no intention of bringing the *Cheyenne* fully to the surface, he'd realized that the channel would be the perfect place to rise to periscope depth.

Now they had their answer. Not only were the photonics giving a perfect picture of the situation, but he had been able to deploy an antenna to communicate with PACFLT.

"Sir, new message," said the PO2 at the comms station, validating Hansen's plan.

He moved to look over the man's shoulder, read the message once, then summarized it for the crew. "Our command authorities are aware of this collision and have ordered us to remain clear. Our objective, this black case, remains the priority, but it's now on the move. Apparently, two individuals are transporting it across the ice. We've been given a new coordinate set where the ice should permit us to surface. Our orders are to proceed there at best speed, punch through, and deploy our Special Forces friends to facilitate the exfiltration of two individuals and the device they're carrying."

Hansen glanced at Drake, but the former SEAL's expression gave nothing away.

"Oh," Hansen added as an apparent afterthought, "headquarters claims to have identified this submarine as a Russian attack boat—a *Laika*-class prototype, the *Aurora*."

"*Laika*-class?" Bennett remarked. "Since when did those go operational? And what would a *Laika* be doing up here?"

"Two good questions, and I don't have any answers. But I would say that she hardly appears operational anymore." He studied the low-light images on the monitor. "Looks to me like the *Snow Dragon 2* plowed straight into her, and I can't imagine it was an accident." He turned to address his crew. "Ladies and gentlemen, we need to all be on our A-game. This is the kind of thing wars break out over. I don't know what this device is that everyone is after, but it obviously has national security implications. From this point forward, we will operate accordingly."

Hansen began issuing orders.

"Pull down the photonics mast before somebody spots us. Comms, before we pull the antenna, let's send a SITREP to PACFLT. Include a few of the images we just captured. We need to be sure everyone back home is aware of the urgency of the situation here. As soon as we get an acknowledgment, we'll dive and sprint for this new point. It's only forty miles, so we should be there in less than two hours." As Hansen spoke these last words, he was looking directly at Lieutenant Drake.

"Aye," the former SEAL said, before turning and heading toward the wardroom.

"I'm getting something new, captain," said the sonar man.

"Another mystery contact?"

"No, this one is very identifiable. Permission to go to speaker?"

Hansen nodded.

The control room went quiet as the audio went live. The sounds were metallic, like metal being bent in a vise. Which, in essence, was exactly what it was. The *Aurora* remained on the surface, but she was lower now. And she was going through her death throes. Compartment walls were warping, watertight doors bursting under the pressure of tons of seawater. The creaking and grinding worsened, the wails of a dying warrior.

Hansen sensed the mood in the room turning grim.

"Cut it," he ordered.

The tech tapped his keyboard and the speaker went silent.

Every set of eyes was on the captain. Hansen met each of them, one by one, before saying, "There is no room for error, people. No room at all."

CHAPTER 56

Beijing

"How can we lose contact with our own ship?" asked a disbelieving Zhang.

The veins in his neck were visibly pulsing as his attention bounced between Wu and the red phone on the table. They were in a conference room adjacent to the operations center. Wu had come in moments earlier to deliver the bad news: All contact with *Snow Dragon 2* had been lost.

It only added to his sulfurous mood. The red phone loomed—the president of China was set to call in five minutes for an update. On their previous call, Zhang had hinted that success was imminent. *Snow Dragon 2* was underway and her captain expected to retrieve Sky Fire and Dr. Chen within the hour. Now their ship had fallen off the face of the earth. No radios, no satcom, not even a ping from her Automatic Identification System transceiver.

"The communications people don't know what's happened," Wu admitted. "Captain Yong sent one message after they arrived on scene. He said there had been an incident. But he also gave assurances that he was personally leading a shore party to recover Chen and Sky Fire."

"How long ago was that?"

"Nearly an hour. We've tried three different satellite channels, but none are able to connect."

"An incident," Zhang mused aloud. "Perhaps the Russians are interfering, or even the CIA." Then he was struck by a more disturbing thought. "Could this be Chen? Might he be using Sky Fire to interrupt our communication links?"

Wu gave a speculative nod. "It *is* the kind of thing Sky Fire is capable of . . . so in theory, yes."

"Then Yong will take possession of the device, and the interruption will end."

"Not necessarily. We have provided Yong no instructions on how to operate the system. We simply told him to find the case and secure it on board. If Chen initiated an attack on our communications, it could be ongoing." Wu hesitated, then added, "But I don't think that is the case."

"Why not?"

"Because we see a ping every time Chen activates Sky Fire. He can't stop that, and we haven't seen one in over an hour, which is roughly the time *Snow Dragon 2* arrived on scene."

Zhang slammed his fist on the table. The red handset rattled in its cradle. He would not have any satellite imagery for another six hours, until the next Chinese satellite was overhead. He was running blind, with no way to know if his nightmare was near an end. Satellites, electronic pings, imagery. This new way of fighting, this digital warfare, was changing so fast he could barely keep up. He longed for the days when state security had been simpler. Neighbors ratting out neighbors. A few thugs at your side. A midnight knock on the right door. *How simple it had been then.*

"Where are the Ice Wolves?" he demanded, forcing himself back on track.

Wu referenced a computer. "Their jet is still five hours away."

Five hours, Zhang thought miserably. Until then, he had but one source to keep him abreast of what was happening in the high Arctic: *Snow Dragon 2* and her worthless captain.

So where are they?

CHAPTER 57

Arctic

Kasey had confronted countless adversaries in recent days. The MSS in Hong Kong, a plane crash in the Arctic, the Russian Navy, and a rogue Chinese icebreaker. What she faced now was more formidable than any of those: bitter, bitter cold.

Every human had their limit, and she and Chen were approaching theirs. The temperature had plummeted, and in spite of her layered clothing and heavy jacket, cold was assaulting every part of her body. Only the warmth of her core was preventing her body from turning to ice. Even beneath her hat, her ears were numb, and in her gloves her hands had grown weak.

She'd been forced to reconfigure her load, the Sky Fire case being too heavy to carry by hand. She'd removed the sling from the rifle and attached it to the case, and it was now slung over her shoulder. The rifle she had been able to sheath into the straps of the backpack. It was awkward and unbalanced, but the only way she could haul all their essential gear.

Despite keeping a measured pace over the uneven surface, Chen was struggling. He could barely walk unassisted. If his staggering worsened, he could be at risk for even greater injury. To sprain an ankle out here, or to suffer even the tiniest of fractures, could quickly become a life-threatening situation.

"Should we stop and make contact with Langley?" he asked, his words plaintive and vaguely slurred.

Kasey wasn't wearing a watch, but she guessed it had been nearly an hour since they'd last discussed it. That was longer than she'd originally intended, but she desperately wanted to get away from the crash site. Or at least, that's what she told herself. In truth, she had begun to question whether Langley could even come up with a plan that would save them before they froze to death. The remoteness of this place, the lack of assets in the region, would have the agency scrambling for solutions. Delaying contact with them, she'd reasoned, might provide more time for analysts to come up with something viable. But she also had to consider Chen. The very fact that he was asking to stop was a message in itself.

"Okay, let's do it," she said.

She stopped and unloaded everything: the backpack, the rifle, the Sky Fire. She felt instant relief from having the weight off her shoulders.

While Chen powered up the system, Kasey looked back west. She saw no sign of smoke, no trace of anyone following them. The world looked the same in every direction, a swirling curtain of white. The only aberration was the twin tracks they were leaving in the thin snow. With any luck, those they had left at the outset were already obliterated. Sharpe had said he would try to erase them.

She turned to the east and regarded the horizon in that direction with far more trepidation. A sector of dark sky in the distance portended possibly worsening weather. Leads were another concern. The few they had encountered so far had been small, requiring only minor deviations. She hoped that would continue to be the case, since their only recourse was to route around them.

The sound of Chen's typing drew her attention. The tapping of the keys seemed frail in the brittle air, a reminder that Sky Fire was their lifeline, their sole connection to the outside world. It also dredged up another thought: Chen's sabotage of *Snow Dragon 2*.

"I've been meaning to ask," she said. "What exactly happened back there with the icebreaker?"

He paused his work. "I have been trying to understand that myself. I designed Sky Fire to receive tactical inputs from its human operator. The internal AI software then attempts to establish contact with the targeted hardware, and searches for weaknesses in its control systems. Once pinpointed, Sky Fire determines the best path to meet the objective."

"What input did you give it?"

"I told it to search for weaknesses in *Snow Dragon 2*'s engine and navigation controls. If any were identified, Sky Fire was supposed to disable her. I never imagined it would go to such an extreme. It must have calculated that striking the *Aurora* would do more damage than simply crashing the icebreaker into the ice sheet."

"Either that, or it realized it had two birds it could disable with one stone," she mused. "That's potentially some scary third-order thinking."

Chen readdressed his keyboard and changed the subject. "I have a good signal," he announced. "There's one new message."

They read it simultaneously.

Proceed to coordinates below for rendezvous. NOAA remote weather station there can provide shelter. No staff or provisions on site. Rescue team from USS Cheyenne enroute. Estimate team arrival at shelter 0630Z. Will escort you to exfil point. Suggest you make contact hourly for updates.

A latitude/longitude pairing was included at the bottom.

"Can you plot that fix on a map?" Kasey asked.

"Yes."

Chen began typing and a map appeared. It seemed to be a military-grade chart, although without the terrain contour lines Kasey was familiar with. *Because when you're standing on a frozen ocean, there is no terrain*, she thought. Their own position and the rendezvous point were displayed.

"Seven miles southeast of where we stand," she said.

"Seven point two," countered the engineer.

"Can you add the crash site to the map?"

"Of course." Moments later a third reference point was shown.

"We've only covered three and a half miles so far," she lamented.

Chen smiled wearily. "We're making progress."

"I like that attitude—glass half full. Can you handle it?" she asked.

"Do I have another choice?"

"Nope."

His expression went to grim determination. "I can do it."

Kasey looked out across the ice in the direction she guessed was southeast. As she did, a new problem came to mind. "Navigating to a precise point is going to be a challenge—Sky Fire is our only reference."

Chen checked the corner of the screen. "The cold is starting to have an effect on the battery. We're down to forty percent. We can't leave it running continuously."

It was yet another obstacle Kasey had never been trained to deal with. Navigation with intermittent references. Sky Fire could be used for occasional snapshots of their position, but nothing more. If there was a mountain on the skyline, distant city lights—those could be used as a guide. But here she had only one primitive reference for orientation.

"So we'll take an initial bearing, then shut down Sky Fire and move. If I keep the glow of the sun at my two o'clock position, we'll be headed more or less in the right direction. In an hour we'll boot up, get any news from Langley, and update our progress. As we get closer to the rendezvous point, we'll check our position more often. If we can get within a mile of this weather station, we should be able to see it. At least, as long as the visibility doesn't worsen. Does that make sense?"

"Yes." Chen tinkered with the map, then gave her a precise course to the NOAA station. Kasey imagined herself standing on a compass rose and carefully noted the bright glow on her right, relative to her shoulder. It was a ballpark estimate, but hopefully it would be close enough.

Chen shut down the system and they shared another water bottle. Kasey felt a cramp in her calf, and hoped the hydration would help. The idea that a rescue team was inbound was reassuring. But it was only part of the solution. Langley was going to take them out using a submarine. But would they rendezvous later with an icebreaker or a helicopter? She had no doubt every national asset was on the table, but in such extreme isolation even America's considerable arsenal of military and intelligence strength could be stretched to the breaking point. Possibly beyond.

They set out again at a steady pace, temporarily invigorated by the brief rest and hydration. But even more revitalizing for Kasey was that they had a destination. And with it, hope of salvation. If they could reach the weather station, they could connect with the rescue team. Exactly how it would play out after that was mere speculation. Right now, she and Chen were in the homestretch.

But it would be the most demanding final dash of their lives.

CHAPTER 58

Langley

It was often said that timing was everything. For DDO Flynn, it had never seemed more critical than right now.

"I need an *exact* flight time," he said to the working group assembled in the conference room.

As soon as Orion had acknowledged their latest message, he'd convened a planning session with the key players. Everyone was bone-tired, running on strong coffee and carts of subpar food hauled up from the CIA cafeteria. By choice, however, not a single person had gone home. The watch team, the desk analysts, every agency liaison—all remained on duty, because they knew lives were at stake. Not to mention the biggest intelligence coup in generations.

The DOD coordinator answered, "According to the crew of the LC-130, the flight from Summit Station in Greenland to PAWS 24916 will take three hours and fifty-two minutes."

PAWS stood for Polar Area Weather Station. Unit 24916 had been in place for five months, an automated system that transmitted wind, temperature, and other atmospheric data on a three-hour cycle. Now that desolate outpost had become the center of America's national security universe.

The DOD specialist went on: "According to the aircraft commander, the best site for landing the LC-130 is one mile south of the weather station. This is based on his evaluation of ice-thickness plots and satellite analysis of the surface conditions."

"I take it the SEALs will escort our people from the weather station to the LZ?"

"That's the plan, sir. They will also, of course, provide security if any elements of the Chinese or Russian contingents take up pursuit."

"Is there any evidence of that?" Flynn inquired.

"No," replied the ISR man. "We're still watching the crash site from overhead, although there are occasional gaps in our coverage. The anarchy we saw earlier has given way to a tense quiet. The *Aurora* has sunk, and it appears that the Russians have commandeered the *Snow Dragon 2*."

"Commandeered?"

"That's a bit of speculation on our part, based on what we're seeing and some communications intercepts from inside Russia. The salient point is that we've seen no indication that anyone from the crash site is trying to chase down Orion."

"What about the weather?"

An Air Force meteorologist who had been called in for her Arctic expertise answered, "Visibility is the most critical factor for LC-130 to land on the ice sheet. Before they even try to put down, the pilots will have to make a few passes over the LZ to assess the surface. Right now, the conditions look marginal. The most recent webcam image from this PAWS station shows one mile visibility. That wouldn't be enough to land, but it's an improvement over what we've had for the last day. The wind and temperatures are still extreme, but those are less of a factor for landing."

"All right, people," Flynn said uneasily. He wasn't happy with the preliminaries, but he knew they had to move on. "We've got three variables to sequence. The arrival of Orion and Falcon at the weather station, the arrival of our SEAL Team soon after, and the projected landing time of Logair 51." This was the call sign of the LC-130 mission. The 109th Airlift Wing typically used Skibird, but that had been a nonstarter. Using their unit call sign, on an open-air traffic control network, could compromise the mission by telegraphing that a highly specialized aircraft was headed toward the area. The Chinese, they suspected, had already brought down one aircraft, and the MSS had a nasty penchant for doubling down on their mistakes. Logair was a call sign normally assigned to logistics flights flown by DOD contractors, and one that likely wouldn't pique anyone's interest.

The DOD specialist picked up: "The LC-130 is our limiting factor. It can't arrive early because fuel will be extremely tight, and the plan is to leave her engines running. Once we have a reliable estimate of when everyone will be in place at the weather station, we can time her takeoff to arrive soon after."

"All right," Flynn said. "Three hours and fifty two minutes, maybe add twenty minutes for slop. We'll call it four hours and fifteen minutes total. All we have to do now is figure out arrival times for Orion and the SEAL team."

"Orion and Falcon should be the first to arrive. The nearest ice the *Cheyenne* can punch through, unfortunately, is almost thirty miles away. That means the SEALs will arrive roughly an hour behind them. I'll send messages to both requesting their best estimates."

"Speaking of the *Cheyenne*," the DOD specialist stated. "Does she stay on station after the SEALs disembark or does she go back under the pack?"

The ISR man said, "I think she should stay in the area as a backup. Just in case anything goes wrong with Plan A. That said, I wouldn't leave her on the surface. Too much chance of a satellite spotting her, especially if the weather improves."

"I agree," Flynn replied. "Let's order her to submerge as soon as she drops off the SEALs. But I want her to stay in the loop. Have her use a buoy or her communications mast, whatever it takes to maintain a signal. Our evacuees already have limited comm, and we don't need any more holes in the network. What about logistics for the LC-130's landing?"

The DOD specialist answered, "As I mentioned, the crew plan to keep the engines running after touchdown. That should help minimize the chance of mechanical issues. For the same reason, they're not going to lower the aft ramp. It'll be a hot load for our exfils, engines running, but that's not a problem. The loadmaster can guide them to the side boarding door. Six people and one small case come on, and then they take off immediately. With any luck, the aircraft won't be on the ground more than five minutes."

Flynn thought that sounded like a dream. *And it probably is.*

"The aircrew also sent some special instructions to be forwarded to the SEALs for marking the landing zone."

"Aren't they trained to do that?" Flynn asked.

"They're well trained in establishing LZs for a variety of aircraft and conditions. But landing a four-engine transport on the Arctic ice pack isn't in anybody's syllabus. Truth is, a landing like this has never been attempted at such a high latitude. The LC-130's skipper wants the SEALs to bring as many flares and lights as possible to illuminate the LZ. We're talking about low-light conditions on the best of days, and getting a visual on the landing surface is going to be critical. Suffice to say, this is not the time nor place for a hard landing."

He released his team to make it all happen. There were a lot of moving parts to the mission, a lot that could go wrong with equipment, weather, and communications. But what worried him more than anything was the Chinese. They appeared to be cut off for the moment. *Snow Dragon 2* was damaged, stuck on the Arctic version of a sandbar, and if the intel could be believed, it was currently under Russian control. But if the Chinese were anything, it was tenacious. They wouldn't surrender Sky Fire without a fight.

He was certain that if they could come up with the means to do it, they would strike. But how and when?

Flynn needed to get Kasey and the others out of harm's way—and do it before the Chinese got their act together. If he could do that, he would have Sky Fire once and for all.

And there it is again, Flynn thought. The key to everything. *Timing.*

CHAPTER 59

Beijing

At this point, Zhang was profoundly attuned to the moods of the operations center. He could sense the trill of excitement when good news arrived, recognize the nose-to-the-grindstone drive when everyone was on task. But more than anything, his private radar could detect trouble with unfailing accuracy.

And that was why he was walking down the hall to the men's room.

He had seen the communications officer stiffen in his seat. Seen the sharp intake of breath from the woman at the adjoining workstation when the man had directed her attention to his screen. When the comm officer immediately turned and looked at Zhang, the look of dread on his face was irrefutable.

More bad news had arrived.

Not sure if he could handle it, Zhang retreated.

He burst into the washroom, the door smacking into the interior wall. He saw only one other person inside, a vaguely familiar bespectacled man who, after taking one look at Zhang, cut short his visit to a urinal and bolted like a horse out of a burning barn.

Zhang went straight to the nearest washbasin. His face flaring with pain, he reached a trembling hand into his pocket and retrieved the pill bottle. He fumbled to extract two capsules and slurped them down, cupping water into his hands from the washbasin. Then he took four more. He had completely lost count of how many he'd downed in recent days. This bottle was nearly empty, but supply was never a problem. Bureau chiefs of the Ministry of State Security never stood in line for pharmaceuticals.

Tentatively, Zhang dipped his head down and gently dabbed cold water on his cheeks. On some days, this seemed to help. Today it felt like a Taser on his face. He bolted upright, his entire body going rigid. He heard a ringing in one ear, a new symptom, and one that, if it persisted, would surely drive him mad.

All too slowly, the pain subsided. The high-pitch cymbal in his ear abated.

Zhang breathed deeply, deliberately, and when he finally regained his composure, he looked into the mirror. The face that stared back at him was unrecognizable. The tan from his recent vacation to Thailand was gone, replaced by a pallor the color of clay. Bloodshot eyes rested above hollowed-out cheeks, and the stately grooves in his forehead had turned to weary chasms. His hair was snarled and skewed, and had gone shades grayer seemingly overnight.

He stood in front of the mirror for the best part of five minutes, not thinking or moving. Simply waiting for the agony to fully pass. At one point someone opened the door halfway, but after seeing the disheveled bureau chief, the interloper put his bodily functions on hold and disappeared.

Finally, Zhang dried his hands with a paper towel and straightened the collar of his shirt. He considered finger-combing his matted hair but decided it wasn't worth the discomfort.

He went back to the operations center with all the dignity he could muster. Pretending not to notice the guarded side-glances from his underlings, he sank into the wide seat at the head of the room.

"Tell me what has happened," he said, ready to get the news of their latest misfortune over with.

The short straw of delivering it was held by the operations center chief.

"The minister has just sent a message," the man said. "Our president received a difficult call from the president of Russia. He was very upset about an incident in the Arctic."

Zhang was struck by the word *incident*. This was the exact term

Captain Yong had used in the pathetic message, sent an hour earlier, that otherwise lacked any useful information; it was the last communication sent from *Snow Dragon 2* before she had gone silent. Spymasters made their living off of information, and Zhang suddenly found himself on the outside looking in. Something very bad had happened in the Arctic, and now, thanks to Yong's incompetence, he was going to find out what it was via the president of China himself.

The chief continued, "*Snow Dragon 2* has collided with the Russian submarine *Aurora*. The *Aurora* has sunk, and there are many casualties on the Russian boat. Four fatalities, sixteen missing, many others injured. The *Snow Dragon 2* was severely damaged and is presently disabled. The Russian president is in communication with the surviving crewmen from the *Aurora*. They have taken control of *Snow Dragon 2* and detained her crew. The Russian president insists the collision was a deliberate act and is insisting that China take full responsibility."

Zhang sat still, his innards seeming to swell. He felt like an overfueled boiler waiting to blow. That explosion was contained by the only thing he had left: an unwavering instinct for self-preservation. His future, in every sense, was hanging by a thread, and his only chance of survival was to make good on his primary mission. He *had* to retrieve Chen and Sky Fire. Without that, all the disasters of the recent days would be laid at his feet.

The chief was still talking, covering details of the Arctic calamity as relayed by the Russians. Zhang heard none of it.

He had risen to command the Seventh Bureau of the MSS with good reason. He was technically proficient, but far more important, he was skilled in the internal politics of China's authoritarian world. He knew how to steal credit from others, how to shunt blame when necessary. And most important in that moment: He knew when to cut his losses.

Inserting *Snow Dragon 2* into the situation had been a failure on every level. Her captain had not only botched acquiring Sky Fire and its creator, even when both were easily within his grasp, but he had now embarrassed his nation with an international incident. Zhang couldn't help but wonder if Chen and Sky Fire might have played some part in the disaster—it was, after all, just the kind of chaos the system was designed to create—but in the end, it didn't matter. The specifics of what had happened. The race to assign blame. All of that Zhang had to put in his rearview mirror. Because there was only one remaining path to success, slim as it might be.

The Ice Wolves.

"Wu!" he bellowed. "Where is she?"

Heads around the room swiveled and eyes searched. No one answered. Wu was an enigma here, not part of the regular operations center team. Then, as if hearing his summons, she burst through a side door and made a beeline for the front of the room.

Zhang didn't wait for her to arrive. "The situation has changed," he said. "We must send a message to the aircraft that is transporting . . ." His words trailed off. Something in the researcher's expression. In her hurried pace.

As she neared, Zhang thought she looked naked without her laptop. She approached his chair, leaned down, and whispered into his ear.

His eyes went wide. "When?"

"Nine minutes ago."

"Where?"

"Three miles east."

Zhang leapt to his feet. "Show me!"

CHAPTER 60

Arctic

Dammit!" Kasey fumed as her foot sank into a pool of slush. She quickly extracted her already half-frozen shoe, but it was hopeless. Frigid seawater was sloshing inside.

She looked back at Chen. He was ten yards behind and limping heavily, his head bent down against the cold.

"I need to stop for a minute," she said.

Kasey dropped her load and sat on Sky Fire's case, turning the world's most advanced AI weapon into a seat. She dug into the backpack, thankful she'd had the foresight to pack extra pairs of heavy wool socks for them both.

Chen finally caught up as she was unlacing her shoe.

"Do you need a fresh pair?" she asked, holding up the socks.

"I think mine are dry," he said, "but perhaps I could wear them on my hands. These gloves aren't very thick."

She handed over the socks and watched him fumble to pull them onto his hands and over the forearms of his jacket.

"How are you doing?" she asked.

"Okay," he said weakly.

"We can take a break if you want. I'm guessing we've got about four miles to go. We'll stop in another twenty minutes or so to check for messages from Langley and update our position." She retrieved a small towel from the backpack and used it to mop out her right shoe.

Once she began lacing back up, Chen set out again to get a head start. He'd only gone a few steps when he stopped and said, "We may have a problem."

Kasey stood and went to join him. He pointed ahead and she saw what he was referring to: a wide lead was blocking their path. They walked closer to get a better look, stopping just short of the breach.

"Any luck we may have had appears to have ended," Chen said.

Only a few minutes earlier, Kasey had remarked that they'd been fortunate. They'd encountered only a few leads so far and had gotten around them with minor deviations. This gap was six feet wide at its narrowest point and stretched endlessly to both the north and south. As far as the eye could see, their path to the weather station was blocked.

Chen said, "There's no way we can cross that, and I don't see an end in either direction."

Kasey studied the icy terrain but saw nothing encouraging. The break had to stretch half a mile in each direction before curving out of sight. "It would be a half-hour detour, probably more."

"Or we might never find a way across."

"Is there any way Sky Fire could help us?" she asked.

"We could contact Langley. They would see our precise position and be able to cross-reference their most recent ice maps. I don't know if they have enough resolution to see these small channels, though."

Kasey didn't know either, but it was worth a shot. A logical course of action that entailed minimum risk beyond pulling power from the device's battery. Nevertheless, she had a terrible feeling the news would be grim. An alternate route, if there even was one, could conceivably add five or ten miles to their trek. And Chen, she was certain, wasn't capable of that. In truth, Kasey wasn't sure if she was up to it herself.

Her methodical nature, her relentless need to process and plan, kicked into overdrive. Could the SEALs come to their aid? Not anytime soon. Was there another weather station not blockaded by the sea? Probably none that were closer. At every turn, with every fresh idea, Kasey hit a wall. A wall of ice and wind and glacial water. She was deep in thought when a single hushed word broke her concentration.

"Kasey . . ."

She looked at Chen.

His face was mostly covered, but all she needed to see was his eyes. They were shot with concern as he stared at something behind them. Kasey turned, scanned into the distance, and had no trouble spotting what had seized his attention. A man was approaching, probably a hundred and fifty yards back. A lone figure hauling something on his back. He was perfectly aligned with the tracks they were leaving.

"He's following us," Chen said.

"No doubt about it."

In heavy clothing and with full facial coverings, there was no way to tell who it was. The figure's weary stride, and the absolute lack of any local population, guaranteed it was someone from the crash site. The possibilities of who this was ranged from helpful to disastrous.

"Do you think it's the Chinese?" Chen asked.

"It's a possibility."

"What do we do?"

Kasey didn't reply.

"If that lead was half as wide, we could jump across."

"But it's not. So we wait."

"Wait for what?"

Her eyes narrowed, straining to see through the mist. Soon, fifty yards behind the man, she saw another hulking silhouette materialize out of the gloom.

Kasey quickly dropped her gear and extracted the Winchester. She lifted the rifle to her shoulder, settled the scope, and took careful aim. "Whoever it is," she said in a low voice as she looked through the optic, "he's definitely not alone."

Her half-numb finger put pressure on the trigger.

CHAPTER 61

Summit Station Airfield, Greenland

"Start number one," Lieutenant Colonel Driscoll ordered.

Across the cockpit, Captain Harrison began to start the outboard port engine. They were keeping to the standard start sequence: 3,4,2,1. Once the last turboprop was up and running, the enormous LC-130 Hercules would be ready to roll.

The plane was already pointed down the frozen runway, which Driscoll had walked in its entirety twenty minutes earlier. He had seen few imperfections, the surface having been groomed by machines and checked for loose ice to ensure a smooth takeoff roll. The next runway he would encounter, if all went as planned, would have none of those guarantees.

He looked out the window and saw clear sky above the Greenland ice shelf. "Hope we get some of this at our destination," he said.

Harrison chuckled. "That's not the forecast. If we can get a look at what we're landing on before touchdown, I'll be happy."

"Is our takeoff data still valid?"

"Numbers are good," Harrison replied. "Temperature holding steady at negative twenty-two Fahrenheit."

Driscoll didn't even flinch. All of Greenland was cold due to its latitude, most of its landmass being above the Arctic Circle. Summit Station, however, had the unfortunate additive of high altitude. Its

10,000-foot elevation subtracted 35 degrees from the temperatures on the coastal lowlands.

"It's going to feel downright balmy up at the North Pole."

The loadmaster, Staff Sergeant Robert Carruthers, poked his head into the flight deck. "Doors and cargo bay are secure, Colonel. All equipment outside is clear."

"Sounds good. Grab your seat for takeoff."

The sergeant disappeared into the cargo bay. Carruthers was an old hand in the squadron, a part-timer who was an Albany cop in his day job. Driscoll couldn't think of anyone he'd rather have riding in back today. Carruthers was the only other crewmember on board. A second loadmaster and a crew chief had been on the original manifest for the flight home, but headquarters insisted on using a bare-minimum complement for this mission. Driscoll didn't know if that was for the sake of simplicity or something more ominous, but he'd decided not to dwell on it.

"Any last-minute revisions?" he asked. They had received the green light for the mission half an hour earlier, but also been told to check for updates before takeoff.

Harrison referenced the communications log. "Nothing new. We're good to go."

Driscoll gave a mock frown. "I was kind of hoping they'd scrub us at the last minute."

Harrison grinned. Dark humor was going to rule the day.

The aircraft commander added power, and the big transport began sliding forward on the ice. He lined up carefully on the runway. The surface had been swept one last time after he'd walked it, and the edges were marked by a long line of banners mounted on fiberglass poles. They stood out as well as the painted lines on any conventional airstrip.

Driscoll shoved the throttles forward and the four big turboprops bit into the cold air. He felt the familiar push, heard the deepening thrum. Clouds of snow washed back in their wake, a maelstrom that enveloped a cluster of the station's outbuildings in a fleeting blizzard. The ride was bumpy but the acceleration smooth as they raced down the runway. They were airborne quickly, and Harrison retracted the skis, which clamped tight to the hull for better aerodynamics. He then extended and retracted the skis a second time to knock off residual snow and ice.

The climb-out was smooth, and all systems were operating normally—not always a given after the brutal conditions of Summit Station.

"Time to IP?" Driscoll asked, the "initial point" being their intended landing zone.

"Three hours and forty-six minutes."

"Okay. Let's send a report that we're airborne."

As Harrison busied himself with that task, Driscoll wondered what he'd forgotten. He was headed out on a mission that, until today, had never been attempted: landing a heavy transport on a high Arctic ice floe. He had pored over every available map for the landing zone's ice condition, and the predictive weather maps were all but stamped in his mind. They had removed all nonessential equipment from the aircraft to minimize weight, and Harrison had run the numbers for takeoff and landing with a dozen different variables. On paper, there was no reason a landing and subsequent takeoff shouldn't be feasible.

But he didn't see paper now. He saw cold sky out the forward windshield and a steady fuel flow on the gauges in front of him. The risks were high, so he wasn't undertaking them lightly. He had done all the necessary planning, taken every precaution, and with good reason. Lives were on the line.

Driscoll adjusted course slightly, turned on the autopilot, and settled back in his seat. Established on its northerly course, the LC-130 blended swiftly into the dim polar night.

CHAPTER 62

Arctic

Sharpe's head was down, his shoulders forward. He was putting maximum effort into every step. For hours now, he had been lugging the folding stretcher on his back like some sort of Arctic sherpa. He'd easily been able to strap it on his back, but it was heavy and seemed to have a penchant for picking up snow and ice, increasing its weight. He'd already stopped twice to knock off the worst of it, but it was becoming a regular chore. And Sharpe didn't like stopping, because that slowed him down. The twin tracks he was following were getting less clear, and he was all too aware of what would happen if he lost his bead on Kasey and Chen's trail.

Put simply, he would be screwed.

A muted sound registered above the sound of his crunching footsteps. He couldn't source the direction, but when he looked up, he immediately saw twin dark shapes in the distance. Human shapes. Sharpe stopped and his spirits soared. It was Kasey and Chen. They had stopped and were looking back at him.

His elation was cut instantly when he saw a muzzle flash.

Before he could even react, the report of the gunshot echoed across the ice. He dropped to the ground sensing that a round had just whizzed past his head. His face smacked into the snow and he wondered, for an instant, why the hell Kasey was shooting at him.

Probably because she can't recognize me at this distance and thinks I'm one of the Chinese or Russians coming to steal Sky Fire. Then he heard the muted sound again. Finally, he realized that muted sound hadn't come from in front of him, it had come from behind—a low, massive growl.

Sharpe whipped around and saw the enormous polar bear fifty feet behind him. It had gone sprawling onto the ice, but its momentum was in his direction. The beast had been charging him. The huge paws scrambled, and the monster got back on its feet. A bloodstain was clear on its giant white shoulder.

The beast stood staring at him, panting. Tendrils of steam rose from his flared nostrils.

Sharpe pushed away an instinct to run. Instead, he stood up tall. He shrugged the folding stretcher off his back, snapped it open to full length, and hoisted it over his head. He wanted to appear as large as possible. He began shouting, and with no particular message to give, he let loose a torrent of expletives.

The bear took a tentative step backward.

Sharpe yelled like a madman and waved the stretcher.

He looked over his shoulder and could barely distinguish Kasey. She had the rifle poised for another shot, but didn't take it. Sharpe thought it was the right call. A second bullet, if it didn't strike something vital, might only enrage the brute and cause him to charge again.

Whether it was the bullet, the shouting, or waving the stretcher, something seemed to work. The bear began backing away.

It moved slowly, sidestepping to keep Sharpe in sight—more caution in its posture than aggression.

Sharpe waited until the bear was at least a hundred yards away. At that point he stopped shouting and very slowly lowered the stretcher. He didn't move until he had another hundred yards of separation. He folded the stretcher, turned, and began walking toward Kasey and Chen. He glanced over his shoulder repeatedly to make sure the bear didn't change its mind.

KASEY KEPT THE Winchester ready all through Sharpe's approach. Even though she couldn't see his face, she knew it was him.

She recognized his somatic signature, his build and gait. And who else would have come all this way lugging what appeared to be a folding stretcher? If she wasn't mistaken, one of the Russians had brought it to the crash site. *Which is exactly what we need.*

Sharpe had a knack for things like that.

Soon the polar bear was barely visible to the naked eye. Even so, Kasey kept tracking him with the scope.

As Sharpe neared, he said, "Thanks . . . I think." He brushed snow off his jacket.

"Do you think you hit him?" Chen asked Kasey. The scientist had been silent through the entire event.

"She did," Sharpe answered. "Right shoulder."

"Will he come back?"

"Depends on how hungry he is."

In any other situation, Kasey might have said something self-deprecating about her marksmanship. But she was too tired, battling too many problems. "We know he's in the area, so we need to keep an eye on him. But the bear isn't our biggest threat. The cold is what's going to kill us." She looked at the stretcher. "I don't know what impresses me more: the fact that you hauled that thing all the way here, or that you tracked us down from the crash site."

"I actually lost your trail twice. Had to go back and do a sawtooth pattern to pick it up again."

"Clever."

"I discovered that it helps to err to the north side out here when you're trying to pick a trail back up. The footprints in snow stand out better in the reflection of the southern sun. I'm learning a lot about tracking over ice."

"Amazing what you can do when your life depends on it."

"Yeah. I probably didn't think this through as well as I should have. It occurred to me after a couple of hours that if I didn't catch up with you, I'd probably end up dead. I've got no comm, no way to navigate, and I doubt I could find my way back to the crash site."

Kasey thought about that. The risks he'd taken to reach them were indeed immense. If the weather had turned, if new snow had obliterated their tracks, Sharpe would have died an agonizing death. But still he had kept coming.

"I think you knew exactly what you were getting into," she said. "So thank you."

He pulled down his gaiter and smiled, his ice-encrusted features conveying a genuine warmth.

He then said, "Can I ask where the heck you're going?"

Kasey explained the new plan.

"A weather station?" He couldn't help but laugh. "I don't know why anybody would bother. From what I've seen, there's only one kind of weather here."

"Don't expect much when we arrive. From what we've been told, there's nobody in residence and not much in the way of supplies. It's just a shack of some kind."

"How far away?"

"Four miles, assuming we can do it in a straight line."

He regarded the lead, then took the stretcher off his back and unfolded it to full length. "Do you think it's long enough to get us across?" he asked.

"Let's hope," Kasey said. "Because Chen and I were discussing the alternatives right before you showed up."

"And what did you come up with?"

She reached for the stretcher. "You don't want to know."

CHAPTER 63

They picked a spot where the gap was narrow, and where the ice shelf on both sides looked stable. Sharpe and Kasey each took one side of the stretcher and gently lowered it into place. It barely reached to the far side, only a few inches of the handle having purchase on each frozen edge.

Sharpe was the first across, and he took his time. Kasey and Chen held the handles to keep their makeshift ramp from moving. Thankfully the stretcher was built for combat and not comfort. The thick canvas was mounted tautly on its frame, providing a solid platform. He got down on his hands and knees, and moved deliberately.

He reached the far side and said, "It's more stable with your hands in the center."

Chen was next, but before he mounted the ramp, Kasey carefully tossed her backpack across the divide. Sharpe caught it without incident. She wouldn't, however, take that risk with Sky Fire. With only the black case and the rifle, she felt far lighter.

Kasey and Sharpe stabilized the stretcher's handles, one of them on each side of the divide. Chen lowered himself and began crawling across. He started out smoothly, but when he was a yard short of the end, the icy edge on the opposite side fractured beneath one of the handles. Sharpe couldn't hold it in place and Chen lost his balance, tumbling into the icy water. He didn't fall in completely, his belly landing squarely on the stretcher, but from the waist down he splattered into the glacial sea.

Sharpe dropped immediately to his belly, and reaching out one of his long arms, he snagged a handful of Chen's jacket. As he dragged him closer, Kasey kept a death grip on the stretcher, knowing she couldn't let it sink. She watched Sharpe wrestle him back onto the ice. Thankfully, he also had the presence of mind to grab one of the stretcher's sinking handles. He pulled it up and set both handles on what looked like firmer ice.

Chen lay writhing. He was shocked by the cold and gasping for breath.

"Come on," Sharpe said. "I've got it on a thicker edge. We need to get you across so we can tend to Chen."

"Okay," Kasey said, trying to force what she'd just seen from her mind.

She checked that the handles on her side were on stable ice, then lowered herself onto hands and knees. She adjusted the rifle and Sky Fire to keep them from shifting. Sharpe was concentrating intently on steadying his end. Kasey kept her weight as central as she could, moving inch by inch. It was like walking a high wire without a net, except that a fall wouldn't kill you directly. The cold would do it far more agonizingly.

On reaching the far side she felt a wave of relief.

Sharpe hauled in the sodden stretcher.

Kasey immediately went to Chen's side. His entire body was shivering. "Are you all right?" she asked. "Any injuries?"

"I . . . I don't think so," he said through chattering teeth. "At least, nothing new."

"Okay, we have to get you dry."

For ten minutes they did their best to warm Chen, although they had little to work with. Sharpe removed the sweatshirt he was wearing as an outer layer, and they used it as a towel. Once they had Chen's legs and feet somewhat dry, Kasey put the last pair of dry socks on his feet, then doubled up with the ones on his hands.

It helped, but only marginally. Prompted by Kasey, Chen tried to stand. His legs buckled instantly, and he fell into a sitting position.

To this point, the scientist had surprised her with his strength and resilience. But now, for the first time, Kasey saw defeat in his eyes. She bent down and put a hand on his shoulder. "Don't worry, we'll figure this out."

Chen's breathing was shallow and choppy, the cold and adrenaline fusing ominously. "I can't go on," he said through quivering lips. "You should leave me here. Sky Fire is more important."

"Not gonna happen," she said with certainty. Yet when she looked at Sharpe, and saw his dire expression, her own confidence wavered. Kasey stood up, ostensibly to retrieve the rifle, which was well back from the water. She gave Sharpe a subtle nod, and he followed her.

"Now what?" he asked in a hushed voice. "There's no way he can walk four more miles."

"I know."

"What if you booted up your system and explained to Langley what's happened? Could they come get us?"

"I could try, but it's doubtful. Whoever is coming to fetch us, they're still hours away. The idea was for us to head to this weather station so we'd have protection from the cold while we wait."

"Yeah, well . . . the cold for Chen just got a whole lot worse." He looked all around, and finally his eyes settled on the stretcher. "I think that's our only option."

She followed his gaze. "What, put him on it and carry him?"

"I don't think you and I could manage that. But maybe we could use it more like a sled. I've already hauled it this far. The stretcher itself isn't too heavy, and I saw that you brought some extra line from the life raft. There's enough that I could attach a pull loop to each of the handles."

"Both of us drag him?"

He nodded.

Kasey thought about it for a moment. "I don't have any better ideas. Let's give it a try."

They explained their plan to Chen, who reluctantly agreed.

"But if it doesn't work," he insisted, "you must continue without me."

"It'll work," Kasey said, not yielding to his ultimatum. *And if it doesn't work*, she thought, *we'll find another way*.

She turned to Sharpe and said, "Before we try this, we need to send a report to Langley. It's going to take longer for us to reach the weather station now. And they need to know you've joined up with us."

"Both good points," he agreed.

She began setting up Sky Fire, the shivering Chen unable to do little more than offer advice. As the system spun up, Kasey was struck by a subtle change in their power dynamic. Out of necessity, it had been Sharpe's duty to take command at the crash site. But now, somewhere in the intervening hours and miles, she had assumed the position of leadership. It was a shift steeped in practicality, since she was better versed in the procedures and operations, in her world better known as tradecraft, that would get them safe. All the same, she was very happy to have Sharpe as a sounding board.

Once the connection had been established, Kasey fired off a SITREP. Langley acknowledged their transmission and said the extraction plan would be updated to include Sharpe. Before shutting down, she carefully noted their position.

"Looks like we're more or less on track. Four miles to go, maybe a little correction to the right. If we don't hit any more leads, and if the sledding's not too tough, we should get there in a couple of hours."

"Let's hope," replied Sharpe.

Together they helped Chen lay on the stretcher and made sure he was secure. Then they set out for a trial run. The resistance with Chen's extra weight was significant, but they quickly discovered that faster was better. They paused to work through the logistics.

Sharpe said, "When we get up to a fast walk, the drag really lessens."

"Yeah. Problem is, I don't think either of us can maintain that."

They experimented as they went, and found that five minutes of hard pulling, followed by two minutes of rest, was optimum. Kasey felt like she was running wind sprints on her old track team. Only here, the cold seared her lungs and her feet continuously slipped on the ice.

Pausing again after five cycles, with both of them panting for air, Sharpe said, “Well? You still up for this?”

Not wanting to waste a single breath, Kasey simply nodded.

They went through the sequence again, and they would keep doing it with every remaining reserve of their strength and willpower. Because if they couldn’t find shelter soon, Dr. Chen was going to die.

CHAPTER 64

Arctic
28 NM Northeast of Weather Station

The parting of the ice was biblical as the *Cheyenne* shattered once more through the pack. Great blocks of white heaved upward and outward, and the black deck became covered with chunks of frozen rubble.

Once the maneuver was complete, it took less than a minute for the main hatch to open. Sailors began hauling gear out on deck, and then down to the ice. The four men central to the show, however, remained below a few precious minutes longer.

Drake led his team down the passageway to the control room. He had been giving a final briefing until a few minutes earlier. The four operators had downed a big meal and hydrated heavily. The traditional "last supper" for a unit that might be very busy in the coming hours.

Drake turned the corner into the control room and saw that it was fully staffed for the breaching maneuver. "Any parting words from home?" he asked.

Captain Hansen referenced the latest message traffic. "Your green light remains. The best estimate is that your exfils should arrive at the rendezvous point in a little more than two hours. And they somehow came up with a plus-one."

"A what?"

"Two individuals has turned into three."

"How does the CIA come up with stragglers on an Arctic ice pack?"

"No telling. Oh, and your ride home just called airborne."

Drake turned and looked at his team.

Having witnessed the situation back at the crash site, they were all aware that the Chinese sailors were fucked. Better yet, there was nothing in their update about new threats. As things stood, it looked like a cut-and-dried mission. Hump across twenty-eight miles of flat pack ice to secure two—now three—CIA assets, along with one very valuable device, and escort them a mere mile south where everyone would be picked up by an LC-130.

It sounded simple. Sounded safe. They'd break a sweat on the cross country leg, but there would be no jihadis crawling out of wadis, no rebel militias careening in with .50-caliber-mounted Toyota Hiluxes. Even so, Drake felt a nagging concern. It was the ops that looked simple that bit you in the ass.

He didn't know exactly why the Russians and Chinese were here, but he doubted it had to do purely with the crash of the airliner. And after locating the fake ELT signal, he knew that the Chinese, at least, were screwing with them. The assets being deployed by everyone, the United States included, were significant. The sense of urgency was palpable, bordering on desperation. This from the most powerful nations on the planet.

Regardless of the isolation, and notwithstanding the lack of firepower endemic to the region, this mission was big-league. Whatever they were chasing, it was very, *very* valuable.

Which, in Drake's eyes, meant the coming hours could prove exceedingly risky.

TEN MINUTES LATER, Drake and his team were outside and gearing up.

They had spent the hours en route from the crash site fine-tuning their load. Each of them carried a fully automatic SCAR-H rifle. There was ammo, survival gear, radios, and three satphones. They had left behind their NODs, since darkness wasn't an issue, and gone with limited provisions to reduce weight.

Their entire outer layers, right down to goggles, ski masks, and plate carriers, were either Arctic white or winter camo. All four of their rucks were stuffed to the breaking point, and they'd chosen the best skis for the difficult ice conditions. To assist in traversing any leads, they carried both a sectioned folding ladder and an inflatable two-man raft.

"That's a lot of stuff for a half day's work," Williams commented, hefting his ruck onto his back.

Drake replied, "They wanted us to bring a lot of lights and panels to mark the LZ."

"Since when is that a big deal?"

"This won't be a tennis-court-sized patch of dirt for putting down a Black Hawk—you can draw that circle with a can of spray paint. We've got a sixty-ton Herc riding in on skis, and that requires a lot of runway."

"How much?"

"They say it depends on conditions, but something in the neighborhood of half a mile."

"We got to mark all that?"

Drake laughed. "We'd need an airdrop for that many runway markers. We're supposed to identify the best area and lay out the first five hundred feet. The pilots get to figure out the rest."

"Let's hope they know what they're doing, since they're *our* ride out."

"Let's hope."

Raine and Juri approached. "Can we get a comm check?"

They went through the motions, everyone receiving and transmitting on the tactical frequency.

"All good," Drake said. He shuffled his skis to point southwest.

"I'll take the lead, medium stagger. Let's keep heads up and eyes open. Everyone ready?"

Three nods in return.

Drake looked back and saw the captain watching from atop the sail. He gave a lazy salute and called out, "Good luck, skipper, and thanks for the lift."

Hansen gave a crisper salute back. "See you back Stateside, Lieutenant."

Drake set his skis in a wide V, pushed off, and worked into a powerful skating rhythm. The others fell in behind, Williams muscling ahead, and the two Finns looking infuriatingly at ease. This was their element.

From his vantage point high on the *Cheyenne*'s sail, Hansen watched the team go. Within minutes they were mere dots. Sub commanders rarely had to deal with weather, but he did a double take on the western horizon. It looked foreboding, low black clouds hanging like a heavy curtain. The four men who'd just skied away were among the most capable anywhere, but even they weren't invincible. And for Hansen, leaving them here just didn't feel right. He descended the ladder to the *Cheyenne*'s control room.

Bennett was waiting. "Send a SITREP and rig for dive, sir?"

"You read my mind, XO. You never know when a rogue Chinese icebreaker might come barreling along." His exec grinned at his black humor.

As his crew took care of business like the professionals they were, Hansen still couldn't shake the stark image of the four operators skiing away. He wished he could do more to help them. Wished he could provide some kind of backup. As it stood, he was trapped in this hole, and very soon beneath it. It was the only place where *Cheyenne* could remain in contact and stay in the game.

All they could do now was listen and wait. But if a chance arose to do more, Hansen would be all in.

CHAPTER 65

Keep going, one more minute!" Kasey shouted.

"Two," Sharpe countered.

It was turning into a competition: Who could endure the most misery? Kasey tried to think of it as a positive thing. They were pushing one another, each demanding more of themselves, while at the same time making headway.

Her thighs burned and her hands ached. The strain on her back was unrelenting. There was enough rope that she could wrap it once around her waist, but she still had to hold the end firmly with both hands. Sharpe was now carrying Sky Fire, but Kasey had kept the rifle and backpack on her own shoulders. Combined with the dead weight of Chen on the sled behind them, it was a backbreaking load. But none of it could be left behind.

She and Sharpe pulled for all they were worth, storm be damned. Kasey looked back guardedly at Chen. His eyes were open but seemed unfocused. It was as if the cold had him in a coma, stunned and immobilized. He had at least taken some water the last time they'd stopped, but she'd had to hold the container to his chapped lips. She suspected his hands were suffering from frostbite, and probably his feet as well. But now wasn't the time for field medicine. It was the time to find shelter or die.

Aside from the cold, their biggest problem was visibility. The dark squall she'd been watching for hours had crept closer and closer. Then, twenty minutes ago, the world around them had disappeared in a wall of gray. She couldn't see more than ten feet in any direction.

This introduced a number of problems. She and Sharpe had encountered three leads since Chen had fallen in the water, but all had been either narrow enough to step across or simple to circumnavigate. If they came across a larger one now, it would be dangerous to negotiate since they couldn't see left and right. The dense precipitation, a mix of snow and sleet, had also made the footing more difficult. Kasey kept losing traction. She had scavenged a quality pair of athletic shoes from a suitcase, and while they seemed almost impervious to moisture, they were a size too large and caused her to skid under the weight of her load. Sharpe was also having trouble with his footing.

If all those genuine troubles weren't enough, the prospect that the polar bear might be lurking behind them kept drumming in Kasey's mind. It was a danger, she knew, that was mostly in her head, but it was hard to shake a vision of snarling teeth, bloody white fur, and massive claws charging out of the gloom.

The biggest problem, however, was one Kasey hadn't anticipated. The last time they'd referenced Sky Fire, twenty minutes ago, it had shown them to be nearing the weather station, no more than a quarter of a mile away. She'd originally figured they would only need to get within a mile of the outpost to spot it, but now they were stumbling around in near white-out conditions.

She and Sharpe had kept a steady pace for the first hour they'd been hauling Chen, but their progress was slower now as they slipped and staggered through this frozen world. Every step was a challenge, every pause a risk. They had pushed to their limits time and again, and although Kasey hated to admit it, their bodies were shutting down.

The storm also cut the dim natural light to near darkness. Distance was hard to estimate, direction nearly impossible. For all she knew, they could be walking in wide circles and going nowhere. They could be within a stone's throw of the station and never see it. The only alternative, she knew, was to fine-tune their position using Sky Fire. But every power-up would drain its waning battery.

"Shouldn't we be there by now?" Sharpe asked.

They drew to a stop.

"Seems like it," she said. Kasey was heaving for air, her voice brittle in the cold, her throat raw.

"We could just about be within spitting distance and not see it."

"It's possible we overshot, but it couldn't be by much. Let's give it five more minutes. If we don't see it by then, we'll spin up Sky Fire."

"You can try, but that might be a challenge. This storm is getting worse, and precipitation, particularly the frozen kind, degrades satellite reception."

Kasey knew he was right. If they couldn't find the station *and* lost their only means of navigation . . . they were doomed. Yet she also knew that some satellite connections were more susceptible than others, and Sky Fire was a state-of-the-art device. The only way to find out was to try to connect.

"Five more minutes," she reiterated.

Sharpe concurred with the plan, and they started out again, willing their bodies into motion. The cold was like a great slab, weighing down arms and legs, every part of their bodies. Inches felt like yards. Sharpe was close beside her, and Kasey could feel his exhaustion almost as much as she could feel her own. All synchronization in her stride was gone, only jerky twitches as muscles contracted and tendons strained.

Kasey tried to come up with positive thoughts. When that failed, she just got pissed. She simmered at what the Chinese had done to them. The mortal agony inflicted on Walter, so many innocent passengers, and the Russian sailors on the *Aurora*.

Her thoughts began to drift, and Kasey tried to recall when she'd last slept. Other than a couple of short naps, she'd been going full throttle for days. Her mind blanked, confusion setting in. One of Walter's ridiculous maxims floated into her head: *If I feel like I'm getting tired on a long drive, I just drive faster.*

Kasey picked up her pace.

It actually seemed to work. Perhaps it was the increased blood flow, the jolt of adrenaline, but she felt stronger and more focused. Then she tripped over something and face-planted hard in the snow.

She cursed and scrambled up to her knees.

"You okay?" Sharpe asked, stopping beside her and lowering his side of the stretcher.

"I'm fine." Kasey looked back, searching for the offending chunk of ice. But that wasn't what she saw. Just behind the stretcher was something unexpected. Something that didn't exist in nature.

A small ridge of snow that formed a perfectly straight line.

CHAPTER 66

Kasey scrambled back on her knees and dusted snow off the aberration that had snagged her attention. She had actually tripped over some kind of metal anchor, and beneath it was a cable of some kind.

"Look at this," she said to Sharpe. Kasey wiped snow from a wider segment of the insulated line.

"Any idea what it is?" he asked.

"Mid-gauge UF cable."

"A what?"

"Underground feeder. Hot and neutral wires, plus a copper ground, all wrapped in a heavy plastic sheath. It's what you use underground and outdoors to connect to a power supply."

He looked at her curiously. "You're also an expert on wires?"

"It's a practical skill for somebody like me. Wires, antennae, plumbing, cameras. You can gain a lot of intel with a working knowledge of things like that."

He leaned down and began uncovering another section with his gloved hand. "Well, all I can tell you is that it's the first man-made thing I've seen in hours."

"And that's no accident." She looked left and right, following the conduit's path. It disappeared into the icy fog in both directions.

She looked at Sharpe. "The station has got to be nearby. I'll go right and you go left, but not too far. Turn around if you lose sight of the cable—we can't afford to get split up."

They set out, and within a minute Kasey encountered a tiny forest of vertical poles and antennae. Atop one of the poles was a device she had seen before, although she couldn't remember what it was called. It measured wind, and at the moment it was weathervaning with the gusts, the spinner on top whirling like a helicopter rotor.

She called out to Sharpe, "This way!"

He shouted back that he was reversing.

Kasey saw two other poles supporting instruments, one of which she recognized as a small parabolic satellite antenna. She kept going, still following the cable, and a bulky shadow emerged out of the mist. It looked like a standard garden shed, and the cable ran beneath one wall and disappeared inside.

She bypassed the structure, but there was nothing else on the far side.

Kasey turned back as Sharpe appeared out of the murk.

"That's it?" he asked, looking at the shed.

"Langley warned us not to expect much."

"The cable runs to a wind-powered generator in the other direction."

"That makes sense. Solar wouldn't be much use up here."

She regarded the shed more closely. It was roughly eight feet by twelve, and it looked flimsy, its corrugated walls rattling with every gust. Anchors at the base corkscrewed into the ice.

"Well, it's not much," Sharpe said. "But it's probably been here since before winter, so it ought to last one more day."

Kasey shuffled toward the only access point, a flimsy door with a single handle. She sank the handle, which took some effort as the frozen mechanism unseated bolts both above and below. She pushed the door inward, stepped inside, and felt immediate relief from the wind. The interior was dark. Kasey pulled a flashlight from her backpack and flicked it on.

Sharpe followed her inside, and together they stared at the muddled scene. There was barely room to move amid what looked like a tiny junkyard. Crates and boxes, many empty, were stacked against the back wall to the ceiling. Two empty plastic buckets appeared frozen, their edges rimmed in ice. There were discarded oil cans, unused hardware, and an ice axe with a broken handle. Metal stakes and poles leaned on the wall, and remnants of wire lay strewn on the plywood floor. The cable from outside ran to a row of three batteries that were linked in a series. The air was laced in a chemical tang, as if one of the batteries had leaked acid.

"Hallelujah!" Sharpe said. He pointed to a small camping heater that was screwed onto a quart-sized propane bottle. He picked it up, shook the bottle, and his smile collapsed. "It's almost empty. See any more bottles?"

She scanned across the scattering of junk. "No. But we can dig around later. Right now, we need to throw anything we can't use outside to make room for Chen."

They both began chucking boxes and debris through the open door. There was little that seemed to have any practical value in their survival situation. Kasey kicked a pile of food wrappers and construction debris from one corner, sending it out the door. A half-gallon plastic Buc-ee's cup caught the wind and disappeared.

Sharpe threw out every empty box and stacked the full boxes against one wall. Soon they had half the floor clear.

"Okay, close enough," she said. "We need to get Chen in here now."

AFTER SO MANY grueling miles, so much pain and cold, moving Chen the last few feet was like a victory lap. They carried him inside on the stretcher, which barely fit through the door. As soon as they set him down, Kasey returned to the door and shut it securely. Chen was fading in and out of consciousness, but he seemed to realize that their surroundings had taken a turn for the better.

Sharpe found a wand-type butane lighter and immediately went to work on the camping heater. When he got it running, the small blue flame looked laughably feeble, but Kasey could feel a tinge of warmth. It also provided enough light that she could turn off her flashlight to conserve battery power. She moved the heater closer to Chen while Sharpe ransacked the boxes for more fuel bottles.

She realized the shed's small size was actually a blessing. What little heat they were generating with their bodies, plus the few BTUs generated by the sputtering heater, would be contained in the tight confines of its four thin walls. Kasey was utterly exhausted. She needed to fire up Sky Fire soon to tell Langley they had arrived at the rendezvous point, but the idea of going outside, even for a few moments, to deploy the antenna was daunting. She decided it wouldn't hurt to thaw out for a minute.

She lay down next to Chen, hoping her body would give him just a bit more warmth. His eyes were closed and his breathing remained irregular.

"I can't find any more propane," Sharpe said.

"I'm not surprised. Let's hope that one lasts a while."

He sat down on the opposite side of Chen. "I can't remember ever being this tired."

"Hopefully this rescue team will arrive soon."

"What's your guess on how they'll get us out of here?"

"The message said they were coming from the *Cheyenne*, so I'd guess that's our ticket home."

He closed his eyes. "I hope it's not too far away—for Chen's sake."

She looked at the scientist with concern. "I agree. He can't take another hike like the one we just had."

Minutes later the blue flame flickered. Then it disappeared completely. The interior of the shed went pitch black. The walls rattled like they were possessed.

"Now what?" Sharpe asked.

Kasey searched blindly until she found the black case. She extracted the laptop and turned it on; its dim backlighting instantly filled the void. "Now we contact Langley." She picked up the antenna and cable, willing herself to go outside.

He looked up at her from the wooden floor. "Do you ever rest?" he asked, his voice sleepy.

"Whenever I can. But right now, keeping us all alive is more important."

CHAPTER 67

By the time Kasey's message arrived, DDO Flynn was convinced he had leveraged every possible source of information to monitor the ongoing rescue in the Arctic. As it turned out, he was wrong.

"NORAD?" Flynn repeated. He directed his comment at the ISR man, who was proving to be invaluable.

"Yes, sir. I've been working with them on a new bit of intelligence." He launched into a detailed explanation.

On nothing more than a hunch, he had reached out to North American Aerospace Defense Command. NORAD was a joint command responsible for monitoring the air and space borders of the United States and Canada. The network of advanced radar stations of its North Warning System was one of the most advanced on earth and kept a close watch on polar airspace. And while its primary mission was strategic, to detect inbound intercontinental ballistic missiles and bombers, other aircraft were also tracked.

With every space-based asset focused on what was happening on the ground, it occurred to the ISR man that what was happening in the skies above might also be relevant. He'd put in the request half an hour ago, and four targets of interest, which were already being watched closely by the Point Barrow long-range site in northern Alaska, had been forwarded.

Hours earlier, the system had begun tracking a lone Chinese aircraft in the vicinity of Wrangel Island, and a second group of three appeared roughly an hour behind it. The targets didn't seem particularly threatening except for one notable fact.

"They're all headed straight toward our area of operations," the ISR man said.

"The crash site?" Flynn asked, wanting to be clear.

"Actually, their present course will take them slightly to the east. It looks like they're making a straight line for our weather station."

"You can tell that from so far out?"

"This radar is *very* accurate."

"Have you got anything to suggest this is more than a coincidence?"

"Yes."

He explained that NORAD could cross-hatch with other intel sources to determine where an aircraft had taken off from. And in this case, the NRO had even acquired communication intercepts suggesting who was on board. "These aircraft are Y-20 military transports. The first departed roughly seven hours ago—about the time when the *Aurora* first showed up at the crash site—from Shenyang Beiling Air Base in China."

Flynn felt his stomach roll. But the analyst wasn't done.

"And according to the NRO, the PLA's Seventy-Eighth Special Forces Brigade, the Ice Wolves, were activated for a deployment at this same airfield, as were elements of the 134th Airborne Brigade. The Ice Wolves are a spec ops unit, and since they're a rapid reaction force, I'd guess they're on the first aircraft. The trailing jets are probably carrying airborne infantry from the 134th, which would have taken longer to organize and load."

Flynn stared at the four new blips that had been added to the big screen. "You said airborne infantry. Does that mean we're not talking about these jets landing on the ice sheet?"

"Not a chance. The Y-20 is a heavy airlifter, nothing you could put on skis. But an airdrop is very much within its capabilities."

Flynn turned to his DOD specialist. "How many men could these jets be carrying?"

"It depends on how they're equipped. With just troops, close to a hundred on each one. But jumping into an environment like this would require a fair amount of equipment. If this lead jet is hauling the Ice Wolves, it's probably one or two platoons, which would roughly equate to either twenty or forty men. The jets in back are probably carrying twice that, an overall force of at least a hundred."

Flynn stood and stared at the big screen. "This is a *lot* of speculation."

"Yes, sir, it is," said the ISR man. "But is it something we can afford to ignore?"

The DDO's eyes narrowed in concentration. "Just to play along, is there a projected time of arrival for this first jet if it goes directly to our weather station?"

"At present speed, it will arrive ten minutes before our LC-130 does."

After a brief silence, Flynn said, "Is there some way we can prove or disprove this theory?"

A long silence took hold, until a woman at the comm station said, "I think I might see some proof." She pointed to a hovering blip on the screen, the single aircraft in the lead. The altitude tagged next to its track number was changing. "It's descending now. And there aren't any airports within a thousand miles."

Flynn shook his head in disbelief. They were *so close* to making the extraction work, and now the entire plan was at risk. Kasey, Chen, the first officer of the airliner. Not to mention the SEAL rescue team, the crew of the LC-130. And, of course, the ultimate prize itself: Sky Fire.

The DDO wasn't 100 percent convinced they had it figured out. But if there was a Chinese force inbound, he had to come up with a counterpunch.

"We have to assume this threat is real. And if that's the case, our SEALs will be outnumbered, in the very best case, five-to-one. What can we do to change that equation?"

The silence was prolonged. In the end, it was the DOD specialist who came up with the idea.

"Is that even possible?" Flynn asked after hearing it.

With only a slight hesitation, the man said, "Yes."

"How long will it take to put in motion?"

"Thirty minutes."

"Okay. Make the call."

IT TOOK ONLY twenty-six minutes.

Four F-35 Lightnings from the 354th Fighter Wing at Eielson Air Force Base, in central Alaska, were prepped to fly. Bombs and missiles were loaded, fuel topped off, and the runway was cleared of snow.

A senior flight commander, a major, had been assigned to lead the flight, and he'd selected three of his most experienced aviators. They convened for what turned out to be an astonishingly short flight briefing. This was in part due to the urgency of their tasking, which had been littered with phrases like "maximum speed" and "without delay." In truth, even if he'd had more time, the flight lead wouldn't have known what to discuss.

They had been given few details on what was clearly a fluid tactical situation: Potential threats and specific targets would be briefed en route, and the lone reference to friendly forces was oddly vague; they were being launched in aid of a "Special Operations unit supporting vital national security objectives." This was as equivocal as it was unnerving. On arriving at the target area, they were to establish contact with a ground unit via secure comm links.

It smacked of being a JSOC mission, and to the pilots there was a sense of being thrown into the sky like so many lawn darts. Or as one wingman commented, "Get your ass in the air, fly fast, and we'll tell you what you're doing when you get there."

But the dead-serious tone of the tasking wasn't lost on anyone. This was no training exercise, proven by the fact that they were hauling live ordnance. Multiple tankers were being launched to support their mission, a necessity since the target area was 1,200 nautical miles north, which exceeded their round-trip range with the load they were carrying.

Beyond that, the pilots were left to read between the lines. They were flying toward a point near the North Pole to, potentially, drop 12 tons of high explosives. Who those bombs might land on, and for what reason, hadn't been mentioned.

Indeed, this was the most peculiar part of it all. One wingman's cursory search had uncovered no maps of the target area, for the simple reason that there was no terrain. Even if they'd been ordered to fly to a point in the North Pacific, they might have made sense of it. This could have suggested that a ship needed to be sunk, and there were no available U.S. Navy assets to do the job. Yet even that didn't compute for this target area. They would be headed for a barren sheet of white on the top of the earth. No people, no maritime routes, and virtually no military activity.

But somewhere in the middle of this cold nowhere, something *very* important was happening.

In less than half an hour, the first of the four jets began its takeoff roll, a massive cone of fire shooting from its afterburner as it shrieked down the runway. At ten-second intervals, the other jets followed.

All four pilots kept the afterburners cooking a little longer than necessary, a subconscious mix of showboating and adrenaline. They climbed to 40,000 feet and kept the throttles up. They would slow their speed to rendezvous with the first tanker in thirty minutes, but otherwise would hold maximum Mach.

The flight lead pushed his throttles to the stops, then cranked them back ever so slightly, giving his wingmen a bit of thrust to play with so they could maintain formation. He had no idea whom they were supporting, or what kind of threats they might face.

Only two things seemed clear: Lives were on the line, and time was of the essence.

CHAPTER 68

Beijing

Zhang looked up and saw Wu staring at him.

"Are you all right, sir?" she asked.

"I'm fine!" he barked.

He knew this wasn't true. He wasn't well at all, and he knew it was obvious. His face contorted constantly from the shooting electrical pains, and he had difficulty concentrating—that had to be the drugs. His stomach reminded him that he hadn't eaten in days, but the very thought of eating, of putting something in his mouth and chewing, was abhorrent. It would be like getting waterboarded.

He and Wu had again entrenched themselves in a private room. Compared to the loud, pulsing operations center, Zhang found the relative silence soothing. And it insulated him from the constant looks of pity.

Save for one.

"How long until the Ice Wolves reach their target?" he snapped at Wu.

"They are closing in," she said evenly. She canted her laptop to show him a map that displayed the position of their forces. "The latest update shows that our first transport will be overhead in ninety minutes. The reinforcements are one hour behind them."

Zhang pummeled his mind for what else he could do to retrieve Chen and Sky Fire. Nothing came to him.

Wu excused herself to use the restroom, but she left her laptop behind. The screen glowed brightly in the dimly lit conference room—Zhang had insisted on turning on only half the lights. In recent days, full illumination felt like knives stabbing from behind his eyes.

He concentrated on the screen and tried to force away his distraction.

The hits from Sky Fire's periodic activations were noted on the map. The markers tracked east of the crash site at a relatively steady rate and were now roughly ten miles away. It wasn't a perfectly straight line, yet there was inherent purpose to its geometry.

What are you up to, Chen?

Zhang knew virtually everything about the traitorous scientist. The man was smart and disciplined, but trekking off into Arctic wilderness simply wasn't in his skill set. Somebody was helping him, most likely either one or both of the CIA agents who had spirited him out of the Landmark Hong Kong to a luxury airliner in Macau. According to the Russian news feeds, there were only nine survivors from the original crash. Among them, surely, had to be one of his American escorts.

The pain in his face throbbed. Zhang ignored it.

It made sense that Chen and his minder would have run when they'd seen the *Snow Dragon 2* approaching. Had Captain Yong been less incompetent, he could have tracked them down quickly and taken them into custody. *Captain Yong . . . perhaps the only man in China with worse prospects than my own.*

His gaze settled decisively on the most recent hit from Sky Fire. These were the coordinates sent to the pilots of the Ice Wolves' transport. This was their updated target. But was Chen still moving? He decided it didn't matter. The Ice Wolves would move faster.

Soon, however, his thoughts took a new and dismal turn. This movement by Chen. What could be the objective? Was he not simply running away from the crash site but running *toward* something else? If so, was it a potential rescue?

The very fact that Sky Fire was intermittently active suggested

Chen was using it to communicate. And that pointed to the Americans. They would devise a plan for getting Chen and whoever was with him out. But how would they do it?

Zhang considered all the information he and Wu had been poring over. Satellite imagery in the area was spotty, in part due to the storm, but more owing to a lack of coverage at that latitude. China's space-based reconnaissance was improving, but not yet comprehensive. Still, nothing they'd seen in the images held any hint of a rescue mission. Information was also flooding in from other agencies, some he had never even heard of. The recovery of Sky Fire, not surprisingly, had become China's highest national priority. In all that data—troop movements, communications intercepts, human sources—he had seen nothing to indicate what the Americans were up to.

All he could do, Zhang realized, was fortify his own plan to every possible extent.

Snow Dragon 1, the sister ship of the icebreaker now in ruins on an ice floe, had been turned around hours earlier from her homeward journey. She was now steaming at best speed to the area. She would be the ticket home for Chen, Sky Fire, and the deployed Chinese airborne forces. The fate of the *Snow Dragon 2*'s crew, who were presently in the hands of the Russians, had become nothing more than a footnote to the entire affair.

Any way Zhang figured it, the Ice Wolves were his last hope. They would soon be on the ground, and they would hunt down Chen ruthlessly. Once he and his device were in their custody, reinforcements would arrive to establish an unassailable defensive perimeter until the *Snow Dragon 1* reached them.

Still, Zhang worried. The CIA had to be up to something. *But what?*

He heard a muted conversation in the hall outside and recognized one of the voices. Wu's tone carried an unusual tenor of excitement, although her words were indecipherable. Soon she bounded through the doorway waving a piece of cardstock. It turned out to be a photograph, and she sent it spinning across the oval table.

"Our satellites have finally captured something useful," she said.

With two fingers, Zhang righted the photo and saw a satellite image.

Wu said, "It was taken an hour ago, roughly thirty miles from Sky Fire's current position."

He studied the photo and saw the black cigar shape of a submarine surrounded by ice. It was, he would wager, the same submarine they'd seen on the surface many hours earlier over a hundred miles to the west. Next to her on the ice now were four men. The resolution was high enough that he could see they were wearing skis and heavy packs. And if he wasn't mistaken, all were carrying battle rifles.

Zhang felt an undeniable wave of relief.

Here was his answer. This submarine was the Americans' nearest asset, and they were sending out four crewmen to retrieve Chen and Sky Fire. This was obviously the closest the boat could get to its objective, leaving the men a great distance to travel. And leaving them exceptionally isolated. Soon that team would find themselves up against twenty-four of China's most elite warriors. Not to mention over a hundred paratroopers dropping down right behind them.

Zhang was ecstatic. He could almost taste the victory.

But now was not the time for celebration or complacency.

He dictated a message to Wu, to be transmitted immediately to the Ice Wolves. It explained this new development and left no question as to how it should be handled. "If you encounter any resistance whatsoever, you must respond with overwhelming force. Show no mercy until your objectives are firmly in your hands."

CHAPTER 69

Arctic
7 NM Northwest of Weather Station

Lieutenant Drake kept a solid rhythm, his skis gliding over the bumpy surface. He veered only slightly left and right, and his men followed in his tracks. His heart rate was elevated, and in spite of the brutal cold he was sweating beneath his layered outerwear.

They'd had to stop for one lead so far, but it had been easily negotiated with the ladder. The two-man raft probably wouldn't be necessary, but it was a comforting backup in case they encountered any wide stretches of open water. Comforting for everyone, that is, except Williams, who'd drawn the short straw and had the extra ten pounds strapped to his back.

They were making good time, and Drake had been in regular contact with Langley. The three satphones his team were carrying were the latest technology, and they had no trouble acquiring and holding a signal, even at such an extreme latitude and in lousy weather. As they closed in on the weather station, he decided to get one last update on the situation.

He drew to a stop, took a quick swallow from his hydration pack, and pulled out his phone. The others were soon standing next to him. Williams was panting from the exertion. The Finns still looked maddeningly fresh. It was as if they'd been born on skis.

"I'm checking for a last update," Drake said. He turned to Williams and added, "What's our ETA?"

Willams pulled out his own device and went to nav mode. "I show six point one miles, estimated arrival 0632 Zulu."

Drake began typing and hit send, and in less than a minute a lengthy response arrived. It was full of bad news, things that hadn't been mentioned before. And it was exactly the kind of complication Drake had been worried about. As he read the message, his face went to stone.

"What is it?" Raine asked, seeing his concern.

"Pretty much the worst-case scenario. We've got a suspected enemy force inbound to our location."

"*Enemy?* What enemy?" asked Williams incredulously. "And inbound how?"

"Headquarters has detected four Chinese transport aircraft making a beeline for our weather station. The first should arrive not long after we do."

"Can these transports land on the ice like our Herc?"

"No. We're talking about heavy jets, way too big for that."

Williams said, "Well if it's not going to land, then . . ." His words drifted off as the answer became apparent.

"Yeah. Consensus at JSOC is that we've got airborne units inbound. There's one aircraft in the lead, and the others are roughly an hour behind. Based on where these aircraft departed, along with some SIGINT, the three trailing aircraft are thought to be carrying a force drawn from the 134th Airborne Brigade."

"And the aircraft in the lead?"

"There is a high likelihood it's bringing in elements from the PLA's Seventy-Eighth Special Forces Brigade."

The four operators exchanged glances. Like specialists across all the services, they were intimately familiar with their counterparts in other militaries. Particularly Russian and Chinese units.

"The Ice Wolves," Juri said. "How large a force are we talking about?"

"It's only speculation at this point. Given that they're a spec ops unit, like us, and the size of this transport . . . probably one or two platoons."

"So at least twenty," Williams said. "Versus the four of us."

"Almost evens the odds, doesn't it?"

Nobody laughed.

"Is there anything about the ETA of our own ride?" Raine asked.

"That's the good news. Sounds like our Herc is right on time. The question is, can they land in this weather."

Raine said, "If they can't, then we'll be on our own to face this Chinese force . . . and seriously outnumbered."

"I suspect headquarters is acutely aware of that. And I would also guess they'll move heaven and earth to keep us out of a firefight with the Chinese."

"No," Williams said. "I think somebody saw this coming all along. We got that use-of-force authorization right off the bat."

"True. But maybe the powers that be were just proactive for once. Either way, if we find ourselves facing an imminent threat, we are cleared to respond. And there is one other ray of hope," Drake added. "We may get some close air support."

"CAS," Williams said. "Where would that come from?"

"An Air Force base in Alaska, apparently. Four F-35s are on the way, but it's unclear if they can get here in time."

"You're telling me our lives now depend on the United States Air Force? The least they could've done was send some damned A-10s."

This got a smile from Drake. The A-10 was every ground-pounder's CAS aircraft of choice. But the Warthog couldn't hold a candle to the F-35 when it came to speed. And right now, that was essential. He pocketed his phone and gripped his ski poles. "If you ask me, I hope everybody is late to this party . . . except, of course, our LC-130. If I don't have to shoot anybody today, I'll be a very happy man."

CHAPTER 70

After making contact with Langley, Kasey had retrieved the antenna and lay down on the floor of the shed next to Chen. She had wanted just a moment to close her eyes, to catch her breath. At least that's what she had told herself an hour earlier.

She was sleeping so soundly, she never heard the door of the shed creak open. Never felt the burst of frigid air sweep inside. At first she didn't even feel the hand on her shoulder.

Then the hand shook her and she bolted upright.

A stranger in winter camo looked back at her. He was down on a knee, and there was ice on his bearded face. His goggles were pulled up over military headgear. He was wearing a large ruck and had a battle rifle slung across his chest. A similarly geared-up African American man stood behind him at the open door of the shed. Both had American flag patches on their uniforms.

"Kasey Sheridan, I presume?" the man said.

She nodded guardedly.

"I'm Lieutenant Peter Drake, United States Navy."

Regaining her equilibrium, Kasey studied the two men more closely. She had spent enough time downrange to recognize a special operator when she saw one. The top-end gear, the focused gaze, the slack grooming standard. "You guys part of our exfil team?"

"We're exactly half of it. Petty Officer Williams and I are instructors at the SEAL Cold Weather Detachment in Kodiak. Outside are two good friends, Raine and Juri. They're counterparts of ours from Finland."

"Finland?"

"Long story. We were sort of the only cops in the neighborhood."

"Well . . . I'm very glad you're here."

Sharpe, who had been sleeping deeply, began to stir. Chen was laid out on the stretcher between them and remained motionless.

"Sounds like you've had a tough couple of days," Drake said.

"We have."

The SEAL regarded Chen. "And this would be Dr. Chen Li?"

"Yes." She then introduced Sharpe, adding, "He was the first officer on our airliner."

"Okay, all good to know," Drake said, rising off his knee. "We can exchange our life stories over tea and biscuits later. Right now we are in a shit-serious hurry."

Kasey stood, but a bit too quickly as aches in her legs reminded her of what she'd endured to get this far. "Why are we in a hurry? I checked in with Langley about an hour ago, right before I dozed off. They said there was a C-130 on skis coming to fly us out."

"Yeah, an LC-130. And that's still the basic plan. But a lot has changed during your nap." He told her about the inbound Chinese special ops unit, and the airborne force right behind it.

Kasey wasn't even surprised. That was how this mission had been going. One minute she was relaxing in a luxury airliner, the next she was stranded in the Arctic. Each time she topped some seemingly insurmountable obstacle, another would take its place. "How soon until they get here?"

"That's the big question. As of twenty minutes ago, the Chinese transport was just barely behind our own ride. And this storm is a problem. If the Herc can't land due to the weather, things are going to get dicey."

"What can we do to make the landing happen?"

Ever so slightly, Drake straightened. "I like that attitude, Kasey." He looked around and his eyes settled on Sky Fire. "Is that the black case everyone is so fired up about?"

"That's the one."

The lieutenant regarded it for a silent moment, obviously wondering what secrets it must hold. Then he refocused and nodded toward the Winchester, which was leaning against the wall in a corner. "Where did that come from?"

"We found it in the cargo hold of our aircraft," Sharpe said.

Kasey added, "It's actually come in handy." She explained about the polar bear.

"Yeah, there's a lot of them up here, and they can be a nuisance. How much ammo?"

"One box, minus a few rounds."

"Good. Bring it." He diverted to the door and started issuing orders to the men outside.

Kasey and Sharpe exchanged a long look.

"Looks like we're not quite out of harm's way," he said.

"He's just being cautious," she replied.

But Kasey knew otherwise. She heard it in Drake's clipped tone. Saw it in the team's professional but rushed movement. These guys were concerned.

And in her experience, when professionals like this were worried, it meant all hell was about to break loose.

ONCE AGAIN, THERE was a shift in authority, and Kasey had no problem with it. She watched Drake and his team organize the exfiltration with skilled proficiency.

Williams and Raine were sent ahead to mark the landing zone. The location, which was based on a satellite survey of the ice conditions performed by the Hercules pilots, was half a mile from the shed. Williams and Raine would fine-tune the location, looking for the smoothest section of ice available.

Drake and Juri remained behind to prepare Chen for transport. They elected to leave him on the stretcher and wrapped him in Mylar survival blankets they'd brought. This would both keep him warm and hold him in place. The jostling seemed to stir Chen, and his alertness ratcheted up, which Kasey took as a good sign. It didn't last long, and soon his eyes closed again. Kasey realized his state of relative incoherence took a weapon off the table—it was possible that Sky Fire could be leveraged to help them avoid the oncoming Chinese platoons, but with Chen in his current state that wasn't going to happen.

Drake put Kasey in charge of Sky Fire, and Sharpe would carry the Winchester. Anything nonessential was to be left in the shed. The SEAL commander was wearing earbuds and kept in continuous contact with JSOC. For all that could still go wrong, they now at least had the backing of America's defense and intelligence networks. The LC-130 was near, but the first Chinese aircraft was close behind. Drake and Juri grabbed the stretcher's handles and they set out to the south, their skis strapped to their backs. Over the short distance, they hauled it in the normal manner, making far better time than Kasey and Sharpe had when they'd been forced to drag Chen for miles.

The wind persisted, giving Kasey the usual slaps in the face, but it somehow didn't bother her. She felt invigorated as they crossed to the LZ. Perhaps it was the hourlong rest, or having an interval of relative warmth. More likely, she suspected, was that she was buoyed by the prospect of rescue. Of getting out of this frigid prison and delivering Chen and Sky Fire to safety. Whatever the source, she felt fresh and alert as they hurried across the ice.

She saw the landing zone long before they arrived. Williams and Raine had it lit up like a carnival. Two rows of highly candescent white lights bordered the best landing surface, and a third smaller segment at one end, these red, signified the landing threshold. There was also an electronic beacon of some kind at the end—she presumed something the pilots could home in on.

As they neared the LZ, Kasey found herself scanning the sky. The conditions were vacillating wildly. At the moment, the clouds looked devastatingly thick, and she wondered if the LC-130 could get beneath them to land. Sections of the surrounding horizon were particularly dark, and snow continued to whip past in flurries. But not all of that was bad. She had never gone through jump qualification, but she knew a little about airborne assault. Conditions like this were every bit as dangerous for paratroopers as they were for aircraft. If the Hercules could make it in, the turbid sky would also provide cover in those minutes when they were most vulnerable.

Four sets of footsteps crunched over the ice, quick and determined.

They reached the LZ to find Raine and Williams fine-tuning their work.

"All set?" Drake asked as they put down the stretcher.

"All good. Beacon is activated and the lights are on. I skied out for a full half mile and saw no serious issues with the surface."

"Did you send a report on that?"

"Yeah, JSOC forwarded it to the pilots. They'll be arriving any minute."

On Drake's orders, everyone continued another quarter mile ahead, remaining roughly a hundred yards to one side of the LZ. "All right," he said, "this should work for a staging area. As soon as the Herc stops, we wait for an all-clear from the crew on the comm net. The loadmaster will open the forward boarding door. Engines are going to be running, so stay clear of the props. Sharpe and Williams, you're on the stretcher. Raine and I will bring up the rear to watch for threats. Everyone else board up fast. We should be able to do this and be out of here in less than five minutes.

There were nods all around. No questions. The world was once again encompassed by the sound of the storm.

Less than a minute later, Kasey heard a faint new sound on the wind. It was the one she wanted to hear. She saw the SEALs exchanging glances.

"That's not a jet," Kasey said. "Those are turboprops."

"You are correct," agreed Drake.

All of them looked skyward with a shared realization. The next ten minutes would determine the course of their lives.

It was now or never.

CHAPTER 71

Three minutes!" the Chinese captain bellowed.

The Y-20 buffeted wildly, rocking from side to side. The airframe creaked and groaned as metal joints were strained to their limits. Small articles of loose equipment—a tie-down strap, a can of lubricant, and a clipboard—slid over the deck in rhythm with the turbulence. The Y-20s designers had been given many specifications, but comfort was not among them. The cargo bay was cold and industrial, and the acrid scent of oil and hydraulic fluid was intense. The heating system barely worked. This last point, at least, was not an issue today.

Ice Wolves never complained about the cold.

To a man, they stood in line waiting for their commander's signal. Every soldier was bulked up by gear and heavy winter clothing. The captain wore a headset that connected him to the flight deck. The pilots had expressed reservations about even attempting the jump. They voiced concerns about descending to low altitude in such terrible weather. Aviators, the captain knew, were trained to avoid risk.

He, however, was wired very differently. He was perfectly aware of the risks of jumping in such conditions. The strong winds on the surface would have been far out of limits for any training jump. But this was not an exercise. This was a mission of vital national importance to the People's Republic.

Still, he thought it wise to take every precaution. Even though his men were highly trained, he shouted a last-minute briefing. He reiterated the techniques for landing in high winds and added that they would likely not get a good look at their landing surface. He reminded everyone that bent legs, along with a tight roll, were a must for dissipating energy on solid ice. Most important of all, he told them to release their chutes quickly to avoid being dragged away by the fierce winds.

He left unmentioned that the landing area did have certain advantages. They didn't have to worry about hanging up on trees or power lines, and snowdrifts in certain areas might cushion their landings. Best of all, if the most recent intelligence assessment was correct, the opposition force would be minimal: one or two CIA operatives, along with four U.S. Navy sailors from a nearby submarine. And barely worth mention: one traitorous Chinese scientist. If the ragged group put up any resistance at all, it would be quickly put down. As something of a footnote, he reminded his men that the scientist should, if at all possible, be taken alive.

The men checked each other's gear, patting harnesses and tightening ruck straps. Being a combat force, they were mostly loaded down with weapons and ammo. In addition to battle rifles, there were grenade launchers and mortars. The more mundane supplies, things like food, snowmobiles, and tents, would be dropped in the second wave after the Ice Wolves had secured the area and seized their objectives.

The captain received the signal from the flight deck. "One minute!" he shouted.

The side door opened and subzero air filled the cabin. In that moment, the poor cabin heat actually worked in their favor. Had it been warmer inside the aircraft, some of the men might have sweated, and perspiration would freeze almost instantly as they dropped through the frigid sky.

The jump signal light went from red to green.

With a final shout and a slap on the back, the first man launched himself through the door and disappeared. The rest followed right behind him. The interval was kept to a minimum, allowing the platoon to land in a tight group and organize more quickly.

In less than a minute, all twenty-four men were falling through the stormy Arctic sky.

CHAPTER 72

The LC-130 was rocking and rolling. It was 2,000 feet above the Arctic Ocean, this measured precisely by the aircraft's radar altimeter. The barometric altimeter, the usual reference for flight, correlated perfectly. The reason that they matched so well was an oddity: Even though they were in one of the remotest places on earth, hundreds of miles from any outpost of civilization, they were receiving current and accurate barometric pressure and wind information for their landing zone. Courtesy of the weather station known as PAWS 2164.

"I hope the surface winds this station is reporting are accurate," Harrison said from the right seat.

"They've been consistent," Driscoll reasoned, checking the wind vector on his navigation display. "We're showing fifty-two knots up here, but they're almost always less at ground level. What's the distance to our projected LZ?"

"Four miles. But I'm still not seeing the ice."

Both men looked down and saw nothing but gray clouds. They had been stairstepping lower, a thousand feet at a time, trying to get beneath the base cloud layer.

"I'm going to take her down to fifteen hundred," Driscoll said. He kicked off the autopilot to hand-fly the Herc. It turned out to be serious work. The controls gyrated his hands like a wobbly jackhammer as wind gusts battered the hulking aircraft. He fought to keep their flight path steady, and slowly the altimeter edged lower.

At 1,800 feet the clouds went ragged. At 1,500 they broke into the clear, such as it was.

"I can see the surface," Driscoll said, "but it's pretty dark. There's not much natural light up here on a good day and this storm is making it worse."

"You want me to turn on the landing lights?"

This was a double-edged sword. They would need the lights in the endgame to see the landing surface. But turning them on now, in the mist, would be like flicking on the bright lights of a car in the fog—it might only wash out what they could see in the distance.

"Hold off on that. What's the latest visibility at the station?"

"It was terrible an hour ago, but now it's two miles."

"That's generous. I'd say one and a half at best."

"I've got a solid beacon at the landing zone. Two point five miles to go."

Driscoll eased the aircraft down to a thousand feet, thankful there was no terrain to worry about. The fog lessened. "Okay, give me the landing lights. I want to get the best possible look at what we're going to touch down on."

Harrison flicked on the landing lights. This aircraft had been upgraded to new LED bulbs and turning them on under normal conditions was like switching on the floodlights of a stadium. They illuminated in all their brilliance, reflecting off wisps of cloud above and the ice sheet below.

"A mile and a half," Harrison announced.

"There!" Driscoll pointed slightly to the right. Two rows of steady white lights were fronted by a single row of red lights. Driscoll banked right and descended, flying directly over the LZ at 500 feet and two hundred knots. Harrison marked the precise position of the front edge of the improvised runway in the navigation computer. Both pilots tried to gauge the surface. The first 500 feet, which was illuminated by the edge lights on the ground, looked relatively smooth. Beyond that, there wasn't enough light to make a determination.

"Did you see anybody?" Driscoll asked.

"No, but that's hardly surprising in this weather. Headquarters has been in contact with them, and they say everyone is positioned for the exfil. Do you want to make more low passes before we land?"

The aircraft commander considered it. "Normally I'd want two or three more, but we don't have the gas."

"One?"

It was a tough call. Before landing on any unprepared surface, it was a virtual requirement to perform multiple overflights at low altitude to gauge the conditions.

"Yeah," Driscoll said. "We've gotta take one more look." He banked the airplane and raised the nose higher, beginning a box pattern to the left.

"Even with one more, we're putting a lot of trust in the guys who set up this LZ."

"This ground team supposedly knows what they're doing."

A new message chimed via secure comm.

"What now?" Driscoll asked, unable to divert his attention from flying the airplane.

"Message relayed from JSOC. They say we need to land ASAP. There's an enemy force inbound."

"*Enemy force?* What enemy force?"

As if in answer, another chime sounded. Harrison read the follow-on. "It says enemy infantry approaching LZ. Take all necessary precautions and expedite exfiltration."

"Precautions? What the hell does that mean? This isn't a damned Spooky gunship. We don't even have chaff or flares loaded in the dispensers."

The pilots exchanged a brief glance.

The 109th Airlift Wing's aircraft were rarely rigged with combat in mind. The unit's mission was, almost exclusively, to support research cold-weather stations in the Arctic and Antarctic. There had been no mention of ground threats in previous communications. Apart from all that, this seemed like the unlikeliest place on the planet to encounter an enemy force. That said, the rushed nature of this mission, the risks they were being ordered to undertake—everything about this op was unique in both their experiences.

"I was afraid we might be looking at something like this," said Harrison.

"Yeah, it was in the back of my mind too. But now we've got friendlies on the ground who are going to be in deep trouble if we can't get them out. You up for giving it a try?"

"Let's do it!"

"Then here we go."

Harrison programmed navigation references to line them up with the improvised runway. Driscoll gave Carruthers an update on their situation, telling the loadmaster to strap in tightly, and emphasizing that their time on the ground had to be kept to an absolute minimum. The loadie acknowledged the order and then asked, "Want me to put up the flag in the cargo bay?"

"Great idea," Driscoll replied. They kept an American flag on board to fly the colors on high-profile missions. *And what better time than now?*

Driscoll flew onto the programmed final approach referencing his instruments. Soon they were below the clouds again, and the lights of the LZ emerged from the mist. From four miles away it looked impossibly small. Both pilots alternated between their duties and scanning outside, paying particular attention for the telltale flickering of small-arms fire.

So far there was nothing. Only a tiny island of lights in the middle of a frozen wilderness.

CHAPTER 73

Minutes earlier, Kasey and the others had watched the LC-130 fly past with a mix of hope and apprehension. Its brilliant lights seemed to fill the dark sky, and the drone of the big turboprops reverberating through the polar air was like an invitation back to the civilized world.

But the aircraft hadn't landed.

"What are they doing?" Kasey asked as the big aircraft climbed out again and disappeared into the clouds.

"He'll be back," Drake said, his eyes locked on a point behind them.

Kasey turned and noticed the other operators were also facing away from the landing area. Their eyes were fixed on the muddled horizon. Then Drake pressed a finger to one ear, in the way one did to adjust an earbud. Kasey heard him talking in a low tone on the secure comm net.

When he seemed done, Kasey asked, "Is there a problem?"

Drake didn't answer right away, but she sensed a tension in him that hadn't been there before. He gave a hand signal, and the two Finns moved away from the group. Spreading thirty yards to either side, they both dropped to a low crouch.

Sharpe, too, recognized the warning signs. He put both hands on the Winchester.

"Lieutenant!" Kasey said more forcefully.

Drake turned toward her. "The lead Chinese transport we were worried about is in the area. It passed directly over the weather station a few minutes ago."

"Sky Fire," Kasey said reflexively.

"What about it?" Sharpe asked.

"Chen mentioned something when he first turned it on. He said he couldn't be sure the Chinese weren't tracking it."

"And you used it at the station," Drake said.

"I had to tell Langley we'd arrived. Now, the fact that these transports came here, to the precise place where we last activated it—they must have found a way to do it. They know where we are."

"The question of *how* they found us is history," said Drake. "They're here and we have to deal with it. If they've already dropped, we could be taking fire in a matter of minutes. It all depends on how long it takes the Ice Wolves to get their act together."

Williams added, "We have to assume they saw what we just did. That Herc was lighting up the sky like a lighthouse. It'll draw them in like moths."

"The LC-130 crew have been advised that there's a possible enemy force in the area," Drake stated. "They know it's now or never."

The planner in Kasey wanted to ask what they would do if the Hercules couldn't land. She decided it best to focus on making the existing plan work.

"What about our CAS?" Raine asked from the right flank.

"Close air support?" Sharpe queried.

Drake nodded. "JSOC launched four F-35s from Alaska a little over an hour ago. They're en route and flying fast, but I don't think they can get here in time. Which means if we don't board this LC-130 soon, we're going to come under heavy fire with no backup."

"Do you really think the Chinese would instigate a shooting war?" Sharpe asked.

"You tell me," Drake replied, looking at Kasey. "Is this gadget of yours that important?"

She considered Sky Fire, and also Chen. In an unexpected thought, it occurred to her that the scientist might be the bigger prize. Sky Fire was his creation, a product that not only reflected his technical expertise, but also his determination—something that had been on prominent display in recent days. "Yes," she said, seeing no need to verbalize her opinion. "It is absolutely that important."

"Then there's your answer."

He ordered everyone to lie down, offering the lowest visual and infrared profiles to anyone who might be searching. And also, Kasey realized, to present the smallest possible targets.

Drake, who was nearest to her, reached across the ice and offered Kasey a handgun. She recognized it as a SIG Sauer P226.

"You any good with one of these?" he asked.

She took the weapon in hand and checked to make sure a round was chambered. "Never go into a gunfight empty-handed."

Apparently happy with her answer, he slid two full magazines toward her across the ice. Kasey snatched them up and put them in a pocket for easy access.

In the dim light everyone looked toward the weather station in the distance. It wasn't visible at the moment in a passing maelstrom of snow, yet that quadrant became their focus. The four operators lay motionless in prone positions, weapons poised and scanning constantly. In the variable conditions, they switched back and forth between their optics and the naked eye.

The distant drone of the LC-130's engines faded, leaving only the pulsing keen of the wind sweeping over the frozen sea. It was as quiet as this place could be.

Kasey scanned for threats as well, yet she couldn't stop snatching glances at the sky. She willed the Hercules to appear soon. To come out of the gloom with lights blazing and set down to a landing. Because if that didn't happen immediately, the shooting would begin.

CHAPTER 74

Driscoll was in a pitched battle with the controls. He had slowed the aircraft to configure for landing, deploying the skis and lowering the flaps, and at the lower speed the aircraft reacted more sluggishly to his inputs.

They were two miles from touchdown, 800 feet above the ice and descending.

After performing the landing checklist, Driscoll said, "Give me the lights at three hundred feet."

"That's pretty low, boss."

"It's one of the few things we can do to keep people from shooting at us."

He was glad they'd at least been told that an enemy force was in the area. It negated any thought of another low pass to inspect the surface and left them with a simple go/no-go decision. And here they were. The quicker they landed, the quicker they could leave.

Driscoll had ordered every navigation and strobe light be turned off, "going black" for their final approach. He could barely make out the surface below in the ambient light, and his primary focus was on his instruments—Harrison had programmed both lateral and vertical paths from the threshold, and as long as Driscoll stayed on them, they would be in the ballpark. They would turn on the landing lights one minute from touchdown, and from there Driscoll would transition to outside references.

The plan had sounded solid when he and Harrison briefed it minutes earlier. Now, poised above the Arctic icecap in a sixty-ton behemoth, battling a sporadic blizzard, it felt suicidal.

"Five hundred feet," Harrison called out.

Both pilots kept glancing out the side windows, their senses on high alert.

At 300 feet, Harrison flicked on the landing lights. Again the LEDs shone with a solar intensity. The sudden illumination had a startle effect, the ice seeming to rush at them. Driscoll held steady.

Harrison suddenly saw flickers of light in the distance on the right. "We're taking fire!" he said.

Driscoll didn't respond. Either he'd been expecting it, or he was so engrossed in fighting the flight controls he couldn't process the news. A sound like a hammer hitting a block of wood rang out. Harrison looked over his shoulder and saw a shattered side window. He didn't even mention it to his aircraft commander, who had his hands full.

The Hercules skimmed in over the red threshold lights and touched down firmly—this was intentional to give the skis solid footing, as well as to dissipate energy. The aircraft began to slow, passing through 100 knots.

At that point they were along for the ride. Harrison watched in horror out the spiderwebbed side window as the small-arms fire became a nearly continuous flicker. Driscoll could change nothing in the situation as he tried to wrestle the skidding giant to a stop.

Neither man had ever felt so helpless. Finally, the Hercules came to a halt.

"Parking brake is set," Driscoll called immediately over the intercom to Carruthers. "We're taking fire—open that door and get our exfils on board!"

The loadmaster rushed to the side entry door and flung it open. He looked out into the gloom, and the first thing he saw was a sea of distant muzzle flashes. Then a flashlight beam, much closer, caught his eye. He discerned a half dozen shapes moving closer. He hadn't been given any prearranged signal for the recognition of friendlies, but the fact that this group was the right size and not shooting at them filled all his squares.

He waved them closer, and was about to head down to the ice to act as escort when a bright flash in the distance cut through the mist. It was quickly followed by two more flashes. Carruthers realized instantly what it was.

He dove headlong back into the cargo bay.

CHAPTER 75

Kasey was elated when she saw the LC-130 touch down, its brilliant landing lights turning night into day. Her excitement swung to alarm when the crackle of small-arms fire registered above the sound of the Herc's engines.

She looked over her shoulder and saw the source. Halfway back to the weather station, she spotted what looked like a kicked anthill—dark shapes swarming, gunfire blinking in the darkness. With the aircraft being the obvious target, bullets were flying over their heads. *But not for long*, she thought.

Before the Hercules had even slid to a stop, Drake was shouting for everyone to move. Kasey didn't have to be told twice. She and Sharpe leapt to their feet, and set out as fast as they could, keeping their heads down. She saw a crewman, probably the loadmaster, standing at the aircraft's open side door.

They'd barely gotten up to speed when Kasey sensed a brilliant flash from behind. As she turned to look, she heard a *swoosh* overhead as something flew past. Then two more flashes appeared in the vicinity of the weather station.

Kasey's alarm went to dread.

She looked back ahead and saw a projectile, most likely a rocket-propelled grenade, barely miss the LC-130's nose and denotate in a pile of snow. A second struck short of the aircraft, exploding on the barren ice. The third RPG, however, proved devastating. It struck the LC-130 in the right wing between the two engines. It penetrated the wing, which had to be filled with thousands of gallons of jet fuel, before the warhead exploded.

From a hundred yards away, the shock wave of the explosion slammed in, a body blow that rocked Kasey from head to toe. Moments later, an intense wave of heat washed over her face. A roiling pillar of flames leapt into the sky as fragments of white-hot metal flew outward and went spinning across the ice. The fuselage collapsed and both wings separated. A secondary explosion then sent the flaming cockpit hurtling away in pieces. The pilots never had a chance.

The sight left Kasey frozen. Her body seemed to hover for a moment, as if the ice had fallen away beneath her. It took every ounce of willpower to pry her eyes away from the horrific scene. There was nothing she could do for the crew. Their ride home was in ruins. It was a terrible and sudden twist of fortune. The only thing that mattered now was staying alive. She, Chen, and the rest of the team were in for the fight of their lives.

Ice chips began erupting more closely. At first the incoming fire had been directed at the landing airplane. Now, as the SEALs began to return fire, more came their way.

Everyone, including Sharpe, was flat on the ice to compensate for the lack of cover. The only salvation was that their enemy faced the same lack of protection. Kasey saw small groups of men darting in the distance. They looked professional, staying low, and using fire and maneuver tactics in an attempt to outflank them on the right. She saw one of them fall, but his brethren simply ran past him and kept moving. The SEALs engaged ferociously, their fire tight and disciplined. Kasey kept her SIG at the ready, but it wasn't an effective weapon against moving targets at a hundred yards.

She heard a cry from her right and saw Sharpe writhing on the ice. She fast-crawled toward him, and moments later a hail of bullets ripped into the spot where she'd just been. Splinters of ice sprayed in every direction, peppering her outer layers.

"Are you hit?" she asked, pulling up on his right side.

"Yeah, in the leg," he said through gritted teeth. Kasey checked for a wound. She couldn't see it directly, but there was a ragged tear in his pants and a dark spot that had to be blood.

She resisted an urge to give aid, knowing that dealing with the threats took priority. The Hercules was burning brilliantly, and somewhere in the back of her mind Kasey recognized this as a disadvantage—she and the others were backlit by the blaze, meaning the enemy would see them more easily.

"Here," he said, pushing the Winchester across the ice. "You'll probably do better with this."

She didn't argue. A grimacing Sharpe reached into his jacket pocket and handed over the box of cartridges. Kasey had been hauling Sky Fire, and she pushed it toward him. "Keep an eye on this."

"Roger that."

She settled into a shooting position and used the scope to search for targets. All of her senses were on overload. She heard the incoming fire zing overhead. Muzzle flashes flickered like a fireworks display. The fires behind her stained the air with a caustic odor.

She spotted a shadowed figure crouching in the distance, took careful aim, and fired. The gun bucked, and with her naked eye she saw the shape tumble back. The man started crawling to one side. Kasey lined up a follow-on shot, fired, and the figure went still. She was searching for the next target when she felt a sudden slap on her ankle.

She turned to see Drake crouching. "How's his wound?" the SEAL said, nodding toward Sharpe.

"I'll be fine," Sharpe replied.

"Okay, good. Think you can move?"

"Move where?"

"We're sitting ducks out here. We need to pull back toward the wreckage."

Kasey shot a glance at the flaming debris, and his logic became clear. The debris field was a hazard, with uncontrolled fires and minor secondary explosions. On top of that, if they tried to reach it, they would be highlighting themselves to an ever greater degree against the light of the flames. But the wreckage also had one huge advantage: It was the only solid cover within miles. If they could reach it and take up protected positions, it could shift the odds in their favor.

But first they would have to cross a hundred yards of open ground.

"Sounds good," she said. "I'll help Sharpe."

"Okay, you ready?"

Kasey took the rifle in one hand. Realizing Sharpe might not be able to carry Sky Fire, she grabbed the sling they'd attached and hauled it over her left shoulder. Then she helped him to his feet. "Are you sure you can do this?" she asked.

"I think so."

"Stay as low as you can." She then shouted over the din, "Ready!"

Drake rolled to a prone position and began firing fast-paced sighted rounds. "Go, go, go!"

They hobbled away as quickly as they could, Kasey supporting Sharpe on the side of his bad leg. Together they staggered like a pair of drunks in a three-legged race, but the erratic movement was actually a positive—it would make it difficult for anyone trying to sight on them. To her right she saw Williams and Raine running low with Chen on the stretcher. Drake and Juri picked up their rate of fire, doing their best to provide suppression. She saw Williams stagger and drop to the ground, the end of the stretcher he was carrying falling to the ice. But he popped right back up and began moving again. The SEALs were wearing body armor, and it had just proved to be a lifesaver.

As she closed in on the wreckage, the scene of devastation separated into individual plots of debris. Kasey discerned dozens of sections of various sizes and shapes, some of them burning intensely. She tried to pick out solid cover—ideally a spot on the perimeter to her left—that would provide a good firing position from which to repel the oncoming force. A large portion of a wing lay upside down, but it was burning with threatening intensity. A pair of wheels lay entangled with a bent ski assembly. Kasey saw Williams and Raine head for that with Chen. She kept looking. Dispersing for varied angles of fire would provide the best defense.

Then she spotted an ideal hide. One of the big turboprop engines lay on the ground, its propeller blades bent and mangled but still attached. The engine was smoldering but not on fire, and she reckoned there was no denser mass of metal to be had. It had also come to rest in a good position to cover their right flank.

The stench of burning jet fuel tore at her lungs. Smoke swept past in acrid waves. She steered Sharpe toward the engine as bullets pinged into the wreckage behind them. They literally fell behind the engine, Sharpe grunting as he hit the ice awkwardly on his injured leg. Kasey made sure he was in cover, then brought the Winchester up and immediately began searching for targets. She spotted two men approaching from the right. She settled her sight squarely on one of them and fired. He dropped like a felled tree and his partner dropped to his belly.

Kasey was increasingly comfortable with the rifle. Her motions became smoother, which made her faster as she searched, sighted, and fired. It was as if her brain had been rewired, the situation drawing out a tactical fluidity she never knew she possessed.

Drake and Juri were now beelining toward the wreckage, Williams and Raine laying down cover fire. Kasey, pausing to reload, did her best to add to their effort, but the Winchester's bolt action was a limitation. It struck her that the enemy force had looked bigger at first. They had to be whittling them down. Ever so slowly, the odds were turning in their favor.

Kasey had just managed two hits in three shots when an explosion rocked the darkness.

CHAPTER 76

Langley

Where's our close air support?" Flynn snapped at the videoconference screen at the front of the ops center.

It was a secure video link, and framed in the picture was the general running the show at JSOC. He said, "They've been flying at max speed, but they're still twenty minutes out."

The frustration in the man's voice was clear, and Flynn didn't have the heart to complain. The general was viewing the same satellite feed of the running gun battle. And he had combatants of his own on the ground. If there had been any way to get the F-35s on station faster, Flynn knew, the man would have moved heaven and earth to do it.

The satellite feed was vexingly spotty, the video repeatedly breaking up. Even so, the essential elements of the battle were clear. The LC-130 had crashed during landing after taking a hit from enemy fire, most likely an RPG. The aircraft was now in flaming ruins, and it didn't seem possible that the crew could have survived. The team on the ground were engaging a much larger force, yet they seemed to be holding their own. Unfortunately, even if they somehow repelled this assault, a far larger force was right behind it.

The grave silence that enveloped the room felt like defeat itself. Only now did Flynn realize how completely they had been relying on the LC-130 to rescue their people. With that option gone, the search for alternatives grew increasingly desperate.

"What about the F-35s?" the DDO asked. "Is there some way they could tip things in our favor?"

"Once they're on station, sure," the JSOC general replied. "We could use them to help repel the next attack, if that's what comes. But if our estimate about the size of the next wave of Chinese forces is right, I don't see these four jets being a difference-maker."

"What other assets are available out of Alaska?"

"There's a whole wing of F-35s, minus the four already en route. Also some F-22s down in Anchorage. But we're up against the same problem we've had all along. By the time they reach the target area, it'll be too late. These three Chinese transports are closing in fast."

Flynn had a terrible feeling he'd been outfoxed. Whoever was running the show on the Chinese side—he guessed it was the Seventh Bureau of the MSS, headed by Zhang Tao, which would have been responsible for keeping tabs on Chen—had committed a large military force. And they had traveled much farther than his own units to reach the Arctic. Indeed, the inbound Y-20 transports, according to their signals intelligence, had taken off eight hours ago to reach this remote ice floe.

How did Zhang see this coming? And why didn't I?

The live feed began streaming again after a temporary loss of signal. In the high-definition images, Flynn saw tiny shapes scurrying across the ice, the infrared flicker of muzzle flashes.

"What about the *Cheyenne*?" the general asked. Flynn had been coordinating the submarine's involvement through Pacific Fleet Headquarters.

"She's right where we left her, twenty-eight miles east. The ice is too thick for her to surface any closer, and there's no way our team can outrun the Chinese over such a long distance."

The general was silent for a moment. The he said speculatively, "There is one thing that might change the equation."

Flynn sensed the JSOC commander's tentativeness but invited him to continue.

"We could have our F-35s engage the Chinese transports. We

make radio contact on the guard emergency frequency and order them to turn around."

"And if they don't comply?"

"We shoot them down."

A long hush ensued as Flynn considered it. "Are they armed to do that?"

"They're each carrying two AIM-9X missiles, and of course they have their guns. But they'd have to get close to use either. We'd have to make this decision almost immediately to give them time to pull it off. If we wait even five minutes, I doubt they'd be able to track down the transports prior to the drop point. Our window for action is closing fast."

Flynn felt a massive weight, like the world was imploding. *Shoot down three Chinese transports full of troops?* That would be an act of war.

"We need to make a phone call," the general said, as if reading his mind.

"Agreed," Flynn replied quickly.

The president and his national security staff were in the White House Situation Room. They were following the mission remotely, but not linked in on the command line Flynn and the JSOC general were sharing. In essence, they were out of the decision loop. That was about to change; the extraction mission in the Arctic had gone critical.

It struck Flynn that ever since Chen and Sky Fire had left Hong Kong, the ante had been getting upped continuously. The downing of a civilian airliner, it turned out, had only been the beginning. The United States and China had both committed combat forces, and for reasons that were likely coincidental, the Russians had also become involved. Now all three nations had suffered casualties, and an intense firefight on the top of the world was playing out before his eyes.

The decisions were becoming so fraught with risk, they now exceeded his authority. The question of what escalations could be contemplated, and what gambles were acceptable, could only be answered at the highest levels in Washington, D.C. Not to mention Beijing and Moscow.

The call to the White House was initiated, but before Flynn had even reached for the handset, a brilliant flash of light filled one side of the main screen—the feed from the Arctic. It was central in the area where their team had taken cover.

"What was that?" the DDO asked.

The ISR analyst said, "I could be mistaken, sir . . . but I think it was a mortar."

CHAPTER 77

Arctic

Kasey was on her back looking up at the sky. She lay stunned and still, a ringing in her ears drowning out every other sound. She felt pinprick pains on one thigh and on her back. An acrid chemical odor assailed her nostrils.

She looked down and saw fiery embers of some kind melting through the fabric of her pants along her right hip and leg. She rolled in the snow, trying to douse whatever it was, then wiped away as much as she could with her gloved hand. The stinging abated, and she realized some kind of burning liquid had sprayed over her in the explosion.

The ice all around her was covered with sheets of twisted metal and chunks of ice. She figured the explosion had been instigated by either an RPG or a mortar, then accelerated by jet fuel. Since she hadn't seen any incoming round, she guessed the latter. It had struck fifty feet to her right, a direct hit on a burning section of wing. After a quick self-assessment, Kasey decided she'd suffered no serious injuries. She looked back at Sharpe. He was holding his hands to his ears, probably fighting the same cymbals she was. Otherwise, he appeared the same.

She tried to think things through.

If they were being targeted by a mortar team, her initial take was that it might change the game. But then she reconsidered. It could also signal desperation. If this attacking force was platoon-size, as they'd been told to expect, they could only be carrying a limited number of rounds. The fact that no more RPGs seemed to be coming their way implied the enemy had run out of them. The ringing began to lessen, and she admonished herself.

Now wasn't the time for analysis.

Kasey rolled onto her stomach and took hold of the Winchester again. As she put the stock to her shoulder, she noticed blood on her glove. Then a tingle of nerve pain in her left hand. It wasn't affecting her motion, so she ignored it and started seeking out targets.

She heard metered fire to her left and saw Juri concealed neatly behind a car-size fragment of jagged metal. The barrel of his weapon moved with liquid silkiness as he transitioned from one target to the next. She looked where he was aiming and saw a man running at full speed toward them, perhaps eighty yards away. Juri fired and the man went down clutching his throat.

Because a hit in the throat takes body armor out of the equation.

Kasey went back to searching, but targets were harder to find. She heard a distinct whistling sound and put her head down. Another mortar landed far behind them, a minor torrent of ice fragments being the only result. The blast did, however, rekindle the ringing in her ears. Kasey spotted a glint of movement well behind the other targets she'd seen. Using her scope, she identified two men working a mortar tube. She was lining up the crosshairs, trying to hold steady for a long-range shot, when one of them fell backward—also clutching his throat. Before he hit the ground, the second man fell. Both shots had come from Juri.

There was no longer any doubt in Kasey's mind. The Finn next to her was an incredible sniper, and he was decimating this Chinese force.

With each minute, the gunfire continued to ebb. Soon the inbound fire stopped completely, only an occasional outbound shot seeking a stray figure. Everyone kept watching, checking through scopes and scanning with sharp eyes. There was soon no movement at all in the distance.

Kasey turned her attention to Sharpe. She had no trouble finding his wound. A bullet appeared to have grazed his leg at a low angle and possibly damaged his knee. The good news was that the bleeding looked limited. Altogether, painful but probably not life-threatening.

"I don't see any pulsing," she said. "I think you're good."

After five minutes, Kasey saw the SEALs begin to emerge from their concealed positions. Raine was limping and held his weapon in an unnatural way. All of them remained alert, their eyes fixed on the distant ice field. They joined up behind a large section of charred fuselage, and Kasey saw Drake beckon her and Sharpe to join them.

She helped Sharpe stand, and together they hobbled to the meeting. All around them was a dystopian scene: mangled wreckage, plots of fire, churning columns of smoke. By the time they reached the others, Juri and Raine had taken up watch positions—they were standing on the perimeter, their gazes directed outward but still within earshot. Kasey saw that everyone had suffered some kind of damage—bloodstained uniforms, injured appendages, charred outerwear. Everyone, that is, except Juri, who had nothing more than a light dusting of snow on his shoulders.

Drake didn't rely on appearances. He asked who was injured, and the report was as positive as could be expected. There were a number of wounds, but no fatalities—a minor miracle given the intensity of the assault they'd just faced. He inspected Sharpe's leg and came to the same conclusion Kasey had—it was a serious hit, but not life-threatening.

Kasey looked over at Chen. His eyes were open but unfocused. He was barely hanging on. She took off her glove and saw a ragged gash on the back of her left hand. It had stopped bleeding, so she put the glove back on. It could be dealt with later.

Right after we get the hell out of here.

"All right," Drake said, "we did well. But we're still in the shit. We've lost our ride out, there's more enemy inbound, and the nearest friendly force is a submarine that's almost thirty miles away. I don't think we're up for that kind of hike right now, so I need to get with JSOC and come up with an alternate exfil plan."

Nothing Drake had just said was news to Kasey. Yet hearing it all at once, in such blunt terms, brought a massive wave of frustration. Or possibly anger. After so much sacrifice, so much pain and suffering, she couldn't fathom the idea that they could still lose Chen and Sky Fire. But that *was* the reality—they were running out of options.

The only person missing from the group, Williams, had been sent on an errand by Drake. He reappeared now with a somber look on his face. "None of the crew from the Herc made it," he announced. "I found all three bodies."

It wasn't a surprise, but it enraged Kasey that much more. The Air Force crew had attempted a landing in terrible conditions. They had put their lives on the line and almost pulled it off. Then their luck had simply run out.

Drake pulled out his satphone to initiate the call to headquarters.

He was working on getting a good signal when gunfire erupted in the distance. Everyone instinctively ducked lower. Juri shifted his aim with clockwork smoothness and said, "I've got him, Captain. Single target, moving away."

"Take him down!" Drake ordered as the sequence of roughly a dozen shots ended abruptly.

The Finn seemed to hesitate. "Actually . . . he's not an immediate threat."

"What? How can you know that?"

"Because he's using a handgun when he needs a rifle. And I'm one hundred percent sure he just ran out of ammunition."

Drake squinted into the distance. The others mirrored his move, concentrating on the area where Juri's barrel was directed.

Kasey saw one of the Chinese in the distance. He appeared to be sprinting toward the weather station shed. Then out of nowhere a massive form overtook him.

The huge polar bear lunged at the scrambling man and swatted him to the ground with its massive paws. Even from such a great distance, what had to be at least three hundred yards, the man's screams resounded across the ice.

CHAPTER 78

Beijing

The last injection was always the worst. When the needle sank into his cheek, destined for a raw nerve bundle, Zhang let out a long, low groan. Seconds later, although it seemed far longer, the procedure was complete. He had tried the botulinum toxin before to ease his suffering, and although it had never seemed particularly effective, he was desperate for any relief. The spikes of pain had become too intense, too distracting. He had to do something.

The doctor was a quack whose medical license had been rescinded. Zhang, of course, hadn't chosen the man for his medical expertise. He had made two things clear at the outset of their relationship. When Zhang wanted relief, he would pay cash and was not to be kept waiting. Even more important, his treatments could never be mentioned to anyone. To the best of his knowledge—which, as the head of the Seventh Bureau of the MSS, was unrivaled—the doctor had never deviated from their arrangement.

The man pushed his wire-framed glasses higher on his nose, packed up his kit, and, with nothing more than an obsequious bow, retreated into the hallway. Zhang heaved a sigh, hoping the injections would work better than last time. It irked him to put his ongoing Arctic disaster on hold, but he simply hadn't been able to think straight.

He had set up a private viewing area in a side room to follow the events in the Arctic. Wu and the operations center chief had joined him for a time, but he'd sent them to the hallway when the doctor arrived. He knew they were waiting outside, but he didn't summon them just yet. He needed a moment alone to ruminate about what had become of the Ice Wolves.

For as long as he could bear it, Zhang had followed the engagement in real time. There was no God's-eye view of the battle because they had no reliable imaging satellite coverage. Yet he *had* watched it unfold. The commander of the Ice Wolves had been wearing a body camera, and it clearly streamed the opening minutes of the fight. The system was something new—according to Wu, the video uplinked via a low-earth-orbit communications relay.

The scene had been brutal. Zhang had never been a soldier, and seeing the frenetic action from the captain's point of view made him glad he'd ducked that career. He had watched one man get shot straight through the throat, specks of blood splattering the camera lens. He'd heard the captain's desperate commands as he tried to rally his troops to victory. Then, a few minutes into the battle, the video had been rendered useless. He'd heard a loud clang and a grunt, and soon Zhang was left staring at an opaque blackness. If he wasn't mistaken, it was the dark sky above the Ice Wolves' commander.

The stillness of that scene, of the camera itself, told him all he needed to know. Yet the audio kept coming. Zhang heard the clatter of battle rifles firing, and the occasional distant explosion. Once or twice, he heard breathless words as men ran past. Eventually, the face of a man in full combat rig filled the screen as he knelt above his commander.

"*The captain is dead*," the man said, pulling his microphone closer to his mouth. "*I am now in command.*" And then he was gone.

And so it went. Ten minutes, fifteen, until the distant gunfire went sporadic.

At that point, the ops center chief had tried to raise the team on the tactical network. There was no reply, even though every man was tied to the comm link. The implication could not have been clearer.

Zhang sat dumbfounded. When it came to winter warfare, there was no better fighting unit in the People's Liberation Army than the Ice Wolves. Yet by all evidence, they had suffered a colossal defeat. He recalled one of the last overhead images they'd been able to capture—the four men standing next to the *Cheyenne*, rigged in skis and winter gear. Evidently they were not ordinary sailors after all.

He shut his eyes reflexively, and another electric bolt of pain zinged across his face. It was just as before: The Botox was useless for immediate relief. He waited and prayed for the agony to pass.

As it did, Zhang began to think more broadly.

Not all the news was bad. At the outset of the battle, the Ice Wolves had scored one significant victory. An American transport, some version of the C-130 that was actually configured to land on skis, had been destroyed. That, surely, would knock the Americans back. He recalled the track they had built using Sky Fire's position data. Chen, and probably his CIA minders, had trekked out into the icy wilderness from the crash site. It had to have been more than simply escaping the *Snow Dragon 2*. There had been a purpose to their movement, an objective. Now Zhang knew what it was—a rendezvous with an aircraft on skis. That was something he had never foreseen. Yet he *had* dealt with it. The CIA was unpredictable, but he sensed they were running out of options.

And he was not.

Zhang weighed what would come next. The *Snow Dragon 1* was battering toward the area, expected to arrive sometime the next day. More important, the three Y-20s carrying a formidable airborne force were nearing the drop point. The Americans had put up a good fight, but they would also have taken casualties and expended much of their ammunition. The next altercation could have only one outcome.

He called Wu and the ops center chief into the room.

Zhang asked for an update on the situation—the interlude with the doctor had only lasted ten minutes, but that could be an eternity in battle.

"There are no significant changes," the chief replied. "Our second wave of airborne troops will be overhead in twenty-nine minutes."

Zhang stifled a smile, not wanting to suffer the pain it would incur. "Excellent. Sky Fire will soon be back in our hands."

"Do you have anything you wish me to relay to the commander of the unit?"

Zhang thought about it, recalling the video footage of the first battle. "Yes. Tell them Sky Fire and Dr. Chen are to be found and repatriated. As for the Americans—no prisoners are to be taken."

CHAPTER 79

Arctic

Kasey and the others were silent after witnessing the distant mauling. She wondered if it was the same beast she and Sharpe had already encountered twice. The one she'd wounded in the shoulder. It didn't matter. Nature had taken its course and had done so with cold indifference.

When Drake finalized his connection to JSOC headquarters, he said, "I'm going to put this on speaker. I want everyone to have the big picture."

A general on the other end introduced himself and confirmed that the CIA's deputy director of operations was also on the call. He then got straight down to business.

"We're trying to come up with an alternate extraction plan, but there are serious constraints. The second wave of Chinese troops is inbound on three Y-20 transports. We believe they will airdrop elements of the 134th Airborne Brigade in roughly half an hour. This is a much larger force than what you just faced. They'll have more equipment and heavier weapons, and the sheer numbers alone will make repelling them by force almost impossible."

"Which leaves us where?" asked Drake.

"The only ideas we've come up with are extreme. As you know, a flight of four F-35s is approaching your area. The original intent was for them to provide close air support during your initial engagement, protecting a window in which you could evacuate on the Hercules. With that off the table, we're exploring other ways to utilize these fighters. In particular, we are weighing an air-to-air intervention."

"Air-to-air?" Drake repeated. "You're saying you want to shoot down three Chinese Air Force transports?"

"We have presented that option to the president. It would require his authority, and honestly, as I think you can understand, he didn't sound very receptive. He, the DNI, and other national security staff are debating the issue as we speak. The obvious concern is to avoid escalating this confrontation into a broader shooting war. We expect an answer within minutes, and if we get a thumbs-down, as I expect, we'll need to come up with other alternatives."

DDO Flynn broke in, "Kasey, are you there?"

"Yes, sir, I am."

"Good to hear. Fine work until now, and I don't want it to go to waste."

"Nor do I."

"General," Flynn continued, "is there any chance of beating back this incoming force after they get on the ground using close air support from the F-35s?"

Before the JSOC general could answer, Drake broke in. "If this airborne force is as large as you project, there's not a chance in hell of us coming out on top. Four F-35s would bring some pain on the enemy, but they wouldn't have enough ordnance to change the eventual outcome. On top of that, my guys are already beat up, and we've got injured civilians. What we could really use is some method of transport to reach the *Cheyenne*. If we had a half dozen snowmobiles, I could make it all work. But there's no way we can cover almost thirty miles on foot in our present condition."

A spirited debate ran, yet Kasey found herself tuning it out. Something had clicked in her head when Drake mentioned reaching the *Cheyenne*. The seed of an idea. She challenged the concept to the limits of her expertise and saw no reason why it wouldn't work. But there could be fatal flaws she hadn't thought of.

The JSOC commander was saying something about splitting the team when Kasey interrupted. "I think we can do it," she said excitedly.

The general paused at her interruption, and finally said, "Do what?"

"Use the F-35s."

Flynn interjected, "We just received word that the president doesn't want to shoot down any Chinese aircraft."

"No, we don't have to," Kasey insisted. "And no close air support either. We tell the *Cheyenne* to hightail over to our present position, then use the bombs from the F-35s to blow a hole in the ice big enough for her to surface."

A silence descended as everyone digested her idea.

The first to speak was Flynn. "Could that work?"

"Stand by," the general said. "I've got an Air Force pilot in the room who's a weapons expert."

In the subsequent pause, Kasey felt everyone's eyes on her. She chose to look at Sharpe. He said, "That's not an out-of-the-box idea, Kasey. That's an out-of-this-friggin'-universe idea. Having flown fighters and dropped a few bombs . . . I think it could actually work."

"It sacrifices our other options," she said. "But it also gives us a chance to get out of here without starting a war."

The general came back online. "Our resident expert says it might work, although nobody's ever tried something like that. I'm going to run it up the chain to the president. It would be an all-or-nothing option, but I suspect the possibility of getting out of Dodge with no more casualties on either side is going to win him over."

Flynn said, "The timing is going to be extremely close. We'd need to get the *Cheyenne* headed in your direction immediately to have any hope of pulling this off."

The general concurred. "I'm sending the order now. Regardless of whether this gets approved, she's not doing any good where she is."

The general elected to end the call, with an expected update in five minutes. Drake cut the connection.

Sharpe caught Kasey's eye. "Great idea. I'm sure they're going to run with it."

She nodded. "Most likely."

"Which means in half an hour we'll either be on our way home or waving a white flag."

Kasey grinned humorlessly. "Actually . . . I don't think I'm wearing anything white that would work."

"Yeah, come to think of it . . . me neither."

CHAPTER 80

28 NM Northeast of Weather Station

All that was necessary was to retract two masts. The *Cheyenne* was underway in less than a minute, her reactor ginning up for full speed. Her props shook from maximum revolutions, no attempt whatsoever was made to minimize her noise signature. They knew precisely where they were going, and that they had to get there fast. Only after the *Cheyenne* was speeding through black water was there time to critique the rushed plan.

"Blast a hole in the ice with thousand-pound bombs?" Bennett remarked.

He and Hansen had recused themselves to the wardroom once they were underway.

"I guess it might work."

"It reminds me of what that reporter asked you in San Diego last week. I thought it was a dumb question at the time."

Hansen remembered. It had been Fleet Week, and he'd been giving tours of the boat. A local reporter had posed a question about Arctic operations: Could the *Cheyenne*'s torpedoes be used to breach the pack ice?

Hansen's answer had been quick and definitive. Torpedoes were a horizontal weapon meant to hunt down ships, he'd said. The warheads fused on or near steel hulls, and gave straight-line penetration—

the destructive energy funneled in the wrong plane of motion. It might shake up the ice on the surface, but there was no way a torpedo could create a hole big enough for surfacing a submarine.

"Come to think of it, it might work with a Mark 48," Bennett said with a grin. He was referring to the Navy's torpedo type that was capped with a nuclear warhead.

Hansen didn't smile. "We're not carrying any of those . . . and anyway, I don't think that would set a very good precedent."

"Do you really think these fighters can blast open a breach that's big enough?"

"Three hundred and sixty feet long, thirty-two feet wide? It'll be a challenge. But they're carrying thousand-pounders, and those pack a punch. It also doesn't have to be a perfect fit."

"I'll bet we could get by with a lot less, especially on the beam. The ice on the sides will be weak—I figure it might fracture pretty easily if we come up fast."

"True," Hansen agreed. "And if we put a few scratches on the hull, I don't think anybody will raise a fuss. We just need to get high enough to open the deck hatch and take on seven people. Then we dive and go deep. After that, we're home free."

"How do you figure?" Bennett asked.

"According to headquarters, the *Laika* we saw earlier just stumbled into this whole mess. They said it was the only Russian boat in the area, and now it's on the bottom. We're up against the Chinese here, and while they're a definite threat to our people on the surface, they won't be once we're submerged."

"Their subs rarely come up this way."

"Exactly. Right now, they're focusing on the Pacific and Indian Oceans. In particular, the South China Sea. Once we go deep and quiet, nobody's going to find us."

The two officers went over logistics. The last thing they covered was the plan to address injuries, Bennett having been busy during that part of the headquarters briefing.

"How many wounded are we talking about?" he asked.

"There are seven individuals, and it sounds like most of them have some sort of injury."

This brought a weighted silence. The two SEALs and their Finnish counterparts had spent weeks on board *Cheyenne*. They'd mingled with the crew and shared meals. The four operators were universally liked and respected. The idea that they had been injured in the line of duty cast a pall over the proceedings.

Bennett's reaction, therefore, was perfectly natural. "We're going to get them out," he said. "Whatever it takes."

"My thoughts exactly," Hansen said. "*Whatever* it takes."

CHAPTER 81

It was the longest half hour of Kasey's life.

Drake had given her a combat first-aid kit, and she'd tended to the wounded. This mostly involved hemostatic agents and bandaging to stanch bleeding, including taking care of her own hand. In Raine's case, she had fashioned a sling to immobilize his left arm—he'd taken shrapnel near the elbow and didn't have full functionality. She had also done her best to keep Chen warm, rewrapping the mylar blankets and activating more chemical heat packs. He was marginally coherent but desperately needed a warmer environment. Kasey assured him they were nearly safe, hoping it was a promise she could keep.

She didn't mind that Drake had appointed her to be the medic—it was, she knew, the correct tactical call. She had come through the engagement in better shape than most, and she was trained in combat medicine. Williams and Juri, who were also relatively unscathed, were the natural choices to be assigned guard duty.

As she worked, Kasey tried to listen in as Drake coordinated their extraction via his comm network. He'd been working on it nonstop for ten minutes.

"Copy, fighters almost overhead," he said into his mic. "Standing by for handoff."

Sensing a pause in his workload, Kasey asked, "How's it coming?"

"As well as can be expected. The F-35s are in the area. I'm going to talk to them directly to coordinate the strike."

"A nine-line briefing?" she asked, referring to the standard briefing format for close air support.

"With some modifications. This comm unit will allow me to talk to the pilots directly. I can also uplink our precise position, which is important given the close quarters we're going to have on this strike."

"Any concerns?"

"I want us to reposition before the bombs start raining down. They'll be laying down thousand-pounders danger close, roughly four hundred meters away. I'm confident they'll hit the right coordinates, but we're keeping it intentionally tight—I want to be as close as possible to the *Cheyenne* when she surfaces. The thing is, I've never seen bombs hit pack ice before, so I have no idea what the blast effects will be. Seems like taking cover is a reasonable precaution."

"Okay. Where do you want to move?"

He looked out across the wreckage field and Kasey saw his eyes settle on the largest piece of debris. The LC-130's tail section had cracked off and come to rest mostly intact. It hadn't caught fire and was resting crookedly on the ice, an upside-down T peppered with random shrapnel holes.

"Tail section?" she asked.

"Yeah, let's do it."

If took five minutes to get everyone to the new staging area. They took up a position such that the tail would protect them from any blast fragments, but not so close that the structure would be a hazard if it shifted from the concussive effect of the bombs. As soon as they got into place, Drake made radio contact with the F-35 flight lead.

As he began his briefing, Kasey looked up at the sky.

It seemed to change continuously, and at the moment a murky gray void predominated. The question of what those clouds shrouded, however, hung heavy. Somewhere above, four sleek fighters were arming tons of smart bombs. Not far away, three Y-20 transports were preparing to unleash a very different load. She imagined a sky full of parachutes, hordes of paratroopers raining down on them. Both drops were going to happen, the only questions being who would be more precise and who would arrive first.

She glanced at the others and sensed everyone having parallel thoughts. Sharpe and Raine were scanning the dense overcast sky, and Drake also naturally looked skyward as he briefed the F-35s. There had been no trace of reengagement from the Ice Wolves, and Kasey was increasingly confident they were no longer a threat. Juri and Williams, apparently, were of the same mind. Even they, acting as sentries, were looking more upward than outward.

"Heads up," Drake announced. "I just spoke to the lead pilot. They've got radar contact on the inbound transports. Right now they're about eight minutes from a projected drop. Things are about to accelerate."

"What do you think the Chinese will use as a drop point?" Williams asked.

"Their current course will take them right over the weather station. That's roughly where the Ice Wolves landed. It's conceivable the Y-20 pilots could shift their drop point based on what happened half an hour ago—but that would require some initiative and decision-making in the field, which isn't a PLA strength. Fortunately, they can't see the ground, which means we don't have to worry about these fires giving away our position. That said, with the winds as strong as they are, this airborne force could come down right on top of us."

"Now there's a pleasant thought," Williams deadpanned.

"We need to focus on what we can control. The plan is for the lead F-35 to drop its stick first."

"Stick?" Raine queried.

"Sorry, Air Force slang. The bombs will be sequenced to drop in a straight line—not a cluster or multiple strikes on the same point."

Raine nodded. "There, after four weeks I've finally learned something from you."

Drake couldn't contain a grin. "The objective is to create a four-hundred-foot stretch of more-or-less open water. That's what I'm told the *Cheyenne* needs."

"How will we know whether we have that?" Kasey asked.

"The fighters can map the ice with their radar, but not with enough detail to give a definitive answer. JSOC has decided there's only one surefire way to know if the bombs are carving out a berth in the ice that's sufficient. After the first stick hits home, I'm going to haul ass over, take a good look, and pass on a report. If we need a bigger hole, I'll provide directions referenced to the original strike, and a second aircraft will drop. We'll have four iterations to work with."

"Won't all that take time?" Williams asked.

"Unfortunately, yes. We're hoping that one or two passes will do it."

"How will the *Cheyenne* know that it's safe to surface?" Juri asked.

"Excellent question. We don't know exactly where she is, and she doesn't have comm while she's submerged. But somebody at JSOC was thinking ahead. This whole shooting match is going to sound like a nuclear war on *Cheyenne*'s sonar. The last jet is keeping two bombs in reserve and will drop them five seconds apart. That's the signal to the *Cheyenne* that it's safe to surface. They shouldn't have any trouble finding the breach."

With the plan laid out in full, Kasey was of two opinions. On one hand she was impressed by its intricacy and innovation. On the other she was fearful of its intricacy and innovation. It was a military operation no one had ever imagined, let alone executed before. And if it didn't work, for any reason, they would be up against insurmountable odds.

Her musings were interrupted by a subtle change in the world around her. The source didn't register right away—Kasey only knew that something was different. Then it hit her. Prior to the arrival of the LC-130, and the subsequent firefight, the predominant sound for hours had been the howling Arctic wind. Yet now a different sound reached from the sky. It was faint at first, then grew more distinct. The sound of a jet engine. Possibly multiple jet engines.

In an instant, her mental circuitry switched from medic to warrior. Was she hearing four F-35 fighters coming to their rescue? Or three Y-20 transports disgorging paratroopers bent on their demise?

With that, the longest half hour of Kasey's life ended. The next one, she suspected, was going to move at the speed of light.

CHAPTER 82

One, three. Our bogeys are now twenty miles west. No transponders and they're down at five thousand feet."

"Looks like our Chinese friends are serious," the flight lead responded on their discreet frequency. "Go ahead, light 'em up."

Ever since receiving orders to blast a hole in the frozen Arctic Ocean, twenty minutes earlier, the F-35 pilots had been planning a strike like none they'd ever contemplated. And they were doing it, quite literally, on the fly. The manuals didn't cover it, and none of them had ever dropped a bomb on an ice field. Every aspect of this new tasking was pure improvisation.

But improvising was what fighter pilots did best.

To begin, on reaching the target area, they had split into two flights of two, intentionally dividing their focus. The second element, led by number three, was flying high and concentrating on the approaching Chinese transports. They had been tracking the Y-20s for over a hundred miles, but now, as they closed in on their drop zone, it was time to screw with their minds.

Both jets in the higher element locked up the inbound transports with their radar. Because the Y-20s were military aircraft, they would carry radar warning receivers. And with two AN/APG-81 radars suddenly targeting them out of the blue, warnings would be blaring in all three Chinese cockpits. The F-35 pilots didn't intend to launch any missiles—that option was expressly off the table, orders straight from the commander in chief.

But the Chinese pilots didn't know that.

The major leading the high two-ship grinned. He was a graduate of the Air Force's Fighter Weapons School—in essence, a fighter pilot's PhD program covering weapons employment and tactics—and he could only imagine the chaos their move must be causing on the three distant flight decks. On shock value alone, it would be a massive distraction. The Chinese wouldn't have been expecting enemy fighters in the area, let alone missile launch warnings.

The major watched his radar display closely. He anticipated one of two possible outcomes. If the transport pilots became sufficiently spooked by the radar warning, they would turn away. And that, at the very least, would delay the impending airdrop. If they kept coming, however, it would suggest they recognized the warning for the ruse that it was. *Or*, the major mused, *there's some kind of political officer on the flight deck with a gun pointed at the pilots' heads.*

A minute later, the answer was clear. Gun to their heads or not, the Chinese hadn't altered course.

"One, three," the major said. "I show no change in the course of our targets."

"One copies," the flight lead replied. "Hopefully it won't matter. One's rolling in hot."

The lead F-35 pilot rolled into a 20-degree dive and lined up the flight path vector with the programmed target symbol. His weapons were armed and his eyes glued to his heads-up display. Five seconds later he hit his "pickle" button and recovered from the dive.

Six GBU-32 JDAMs dropped in a precise sequence, separated by an interval measured in milliseconds. Each weighed half a ton, and their guidance packages steered them toward the triple-checked coordinates. They flew with the precision of military-grade GPS. The only hint that they were inbound was the engine noise of the receding F-35, and that soon abated.

As if mocking their potential destructive force, the bombs glided toward the polar ice cap in absolute silence.

CHAPTER 83

The explosions were literally earth-shattering—Kasey didn't as much hear the blasts as *feel* them. She instinctively recoiled as six bombs struck home in less than two seconds—a machine gun–worthy burst of devastation.

From behind the broken tail section, she couldn't see the detonations. But they seemed a lot closer than 400 meters. Seconds after the blast, she heard a rattling sound, and she realized that the area around them was being peppered by fragments of ice, a man-made hailstorm. As soon as it ended, Drake moved to get a look at the results. Kasey followed him to the edge of the fractured tail section, and together they strained to see through the smoke.

"I can't tell if it worked," she said.

"Yeah, that's how it usually works—we won't get a clear look for a few minutes." He made a radio call to the fighters, telling them that he was heading out for a damage assessment. They acknowledged that they would remain cold, not releasing again until he confirmed he was clear.

Drake set out on a dead run, sprinting toward what they hoped was an extended breach in the ice sheet. For Kasey it was an interminable wait.

"I've dropped a lot of bombs before, but I never realized how loud they are."

She turned and saw Sharpe behind her.

"I guess it's one of those things you don't want to experience firsthand."

Her eyes alternated between Drake and the sky. She watched him disappear into a curtain of smoke and mist near the target area. When he finally reemerged, he was again running flat out.

When the SEAL was halfway back, she saw him slow slightly—she could tell he was talking into his mic. By now everyone had joined to watch the show, except Chen, who remained immobile.

Drake skidded to a stop in front of them. "It's working!" he said breathlessly. "There were a lot of floating ice chunks, but we've got a solid channel of clear water. Right now the width is great, but it's not long enough. I called the fighters in for one more pass—they'll hit along the same line but offset fifty meters beyond the first reference point. Hopefully that'll do it. Everybody back in cover!"

They all complied quickly, and a minute later a second barrage of massive explosions rocked the air. Drake went through his drill a second time, ensuring the area was safe before sprinting out and returning.

"We're a go!" he shouted as soon as he was within earshot. "The channel is big enough and the fighters are clear. Let's move!"

Everyone had their assignment: Chen's stretcher, assisting the wounded, vital equipment. Kasey would aid Sharpe, and she'd insisted on carrying Sky Fire herself. There was no sign of the *Cheyenne* yet, but the breach was still partially obscured by smoke. They simply had to trust that she would appear.

Kasey had just started out, with Sky Fire strapped to her back and an arm around Sharpe, when a single explosion sounded. This one was more distant, and she saw the aftermath of the blast flaring two miles to the south. Five seconds later, a second bomb landed in the same place. This was the signal they'd been briefed to expect.

Then came a sound she hadn't anticipated.

Gunfire to her left.

Kasey's head whipped to the side, and she saw Williams in a crouch. He was firing into the distance, although at what she couldn't see. Then she looked up at the sky and saw a nightmare. Dozens of dark shapes floating down on parachutes.

Sharpe saw it as well, and their progress slowed.

"Keep moving!" Kasey shouted.

"I'm trying."

She saw Raine and Drake pause to engage, but everyone else kept moving. Shooting back at the oncoming Chinese wasn't a strategy to win—only a tactic to buy time. Kasey pulled Sharpe ahead with all her strength, but she knew that if she pushed too hard, he might stumble, putting them both on the ground.

Every time she looked up, there seemed to be more parachutes. Most of them were on their left. She hoped the next wave didn't come on the right, or worse yet, straight ahead. If they had to fight their way through to reach the *Cheyenne*, things would go to the next level. And she wasn't sure how many more levels existed before it was game over.

The smoke above the breach began to dissipate, and to her horror Kasey saw nothing but what looked like a ten-yard-wide lead. No submarine. The only option was to keep going, hope that salvation appeared in the time it took to cover the last hundred yards. She'd run that distance a thousand times in college. Never had it looked so far.

The staccato sound of the gunfire grew denser, more constant. The Chinese were on the ground, massing in numbers and organizing. Rounds chipped at the ice around them. She saw Drake go down ahead of her, but then realized he was only taking a low-profile position to provide cover fire. She felt Sharpe stumble and strained to keep him upright, hoping he hadn't taken a hit. She tried to look him over, but it was impossible as they ran.

"Are you okay?" she shouted over the din.

"I'm good," he responded. "Look!"

He pointed slightly to the left and Kasey saw it. Two massive masts rising out of the ice-clad sea. The sight impelled them forward, Sharpe nearly matching her for speed in spite of his injured leg.

Soon the *Cheyenne* was fully surfaced, her hull hard against the frozen edge of the breach. They weaved amid virtual boulders of ice that had been blown clear. Kasey saw a hatch fly open and four crewmen emerged. They were wearing body armor and carried weapons.

As she and Sharpe closed in on the breach, the ice turned into a hill of white rubble nesting to the hull. Splinters of white flew skyward as rounds struck left and right. Kasey felt a jolt in her back but didn't feel any pain. She kept going, pushing hard. With a glance back she saw the SEALs pulling in right behind them, alternating between running and shooting.

One of the crewmen on deck dropped a rope ladder—the deck would be a ten-foot climb up the boat's curved steel hull. She steered Sharpe toward it as an RPG flew overhead and detonated on the ice field beyond.

Juri and Williams were right behind her, hauling Chen's stretcher. The operators' forethought of having secured Chen to the stretcher paid dividends as crewmen hauled him up the angled side to deck level. Moments later, they were carrying Chen toward the hatch. Juri and Williams immediately turned and began returning fire, providing cover for Raine and Drake.

Kasey helped Sharpe up the ladder, then hauled herself up behind him. She heard the metallic clang of bullets ricochetting off the sub's pressure hull. Sharpe disappeared down the hatch, and the last two crewmen went with him. Kasey was next.

She took one last look back. The ice-scape was a raging battle, scores of dark shapes firing and moving. Another RPG hit short, blasting a curtain of ice into the air. The four SEALs clambered up the rope ladder. She saw Drake detach the rope net and let it fall to the ice.

Kasey descended down a steel ladder and found herself near the control room. Orders were being barked as the crew prepared to dive. A crewman ushered her to one side, and she saw the SEALs appear on the ladder. Drake was the last man down. Everyone was amped up and out of breath. Drake and Raine were bloody, and Williams was grimacing. Once again, Juri seemed inexplicably unscathed.

She heard the hatch clang shut and commands were given. She felt the boat vibrate, pumps moving water and ice crumbling outside. The faint pinging of inbound rounds striking the hull soon dissipated. Thirty seconds later, the utter chaos of the surface gave way to near silence. A few hushed commands, the whirring of valves, the snap of switches. Aside from the quiet, Kasey sensed that something else had vastly changed, yet it took a moment for her to realize what it was.

For the first time in days, she was warm. There was no ice, no wind, no cold. The relief was overwhelming.

She saw Chen being assisted down a passageway by two crewmen, no doubt to get medical attention. Sharpe was right behind them, and the four operators followed. Kasey simply stood still. She backed into a small recess and took a deep breath.

"You must be our VIP," said an engaging voice. She looked up and saw a Navy commander approaching.

"Right now, I'm feeling more like a very important target."

He offered up his hand. "Trent Hansen, commanding officer."

"Kasey Sheridan," she replied, shaking his hand.

The captain glanced up the passageway. "Looks like we have some injuries to deal with. You come through okay?"

"No serious issues. What about your crew?"

"All safe and accounted for."

"And *Cheyenne*? Seemed like she was taking some hits up there."

"I doubt there's any serious damage, but we'll keep an eye on things."

"So that's it? We're in the clear now?"

"Unless these Chinese paratroopers brought along some depth charges . . . I think we're good to go." His gaze went behind her. "So that's what this is all about?"

Kasey had almost forgotten that Sky Fire was still strapped to her back. "Yep, that's it."

He shook his head. "Doesn't look like much, but I'll assume it's important."

"Like they say, dynamite comes in small packages."

"Then maybe I should put it somewhere safe—I can lock it up in a secure room."

"That'd be great."

"Is there anything special I should know about it? It's not like radioactive or anything?"

"No, nothing like that."

Kasey shrugged the black case off her shoulder and handed it to the captain.

"Well, I'll be damned," he said. He turned Sky Fire around and showed her a jagged hole in its black case. A bullet hole. Kasey remembered the jolt in the back she'd felt as she and Sharpe had approached the boat.

"I hope it didn't do any serious damage," Hansen said.

Kasey shook her head. "I'm sure it's salvageable. And we also have the guy who built it on board."

He put a finger on the ragged hole. "Kinda fitting, if you think about it. You sacrificed a lot to get this thing home. Looks like in the end, it took a bullet for you."

Kasey couldn't contain a broad smile. "Yeah, I guess it did."

CHAPTER 84

Beijing

Unlike the Ice Wolves' captain, the commander of the 134th Airborne Brigade did not wear a body camera. This left Zhang with only one fragile link to what was happening in the Arctic. The force on the ground carried standard VHF radios, and these enabled contact with the Y-20 transports overhead. As long as the jets remained within line of sight, which wouldn't be long since they were departing, messages could be relayed to Beijing. It was a cumbersome means of communication, and only marginally secure.

But as it turned out, within minutes Zhang learned all he needed to know.

We lost them . . .

Those three simple words, relayed over thousands of miles, landed in the operations center with the weight of a judge pronouncing a death sentence.

More messages, describing what had happened, arrived in the following minutes. One mentioned bombs blowing a hole in the ice sheet. Another claimed that a submarine had appeared out of nowhere. Zhang registered none of it. Chen, Sky Fire, the group of Americans. All were now out of his grasp.

We lost them . . .

He stared at the big screen. Choppy video obtained earlier from the Ice Wolves' body cameras ran continuously: the wreckage of the American cargo aircraft burning pyre-like in the distance. The footage looped time and again, as if it represented some kind of runners-up medal.

In Zhang's cutthroat world, there was no such thing. His rivals, his underlings, his enemies—all of which were plentiful—would smell blood in the water. And they would be circling, just as he himself had done for so many years. Zhang's mission had been clear. Protect Sky Fire at all costs. Yet he had reached for more. He'd let Chen run after realizing he intended to defect, hoping to foil the CIA's plans and turn his victory into a career stepping stone. Had he succeeded, he would have been a favorite to head the entire ministry.

But now? Zhang had failed completely. Irrevocably. And for that, there could be only one consequence.

His facial muscles tightened, which produced more than the usual agony. The pain radiated throughout his body, and his hands and feet began trembling.

It occurred to him that the operations center had gone quiet around him. He stood slowly, both to minimize the pain and maintain his dignity. He walked toward the hall, not because he had anywhere to go, but because he couldn't fathom staying here. He was like an elite athlete leaving a field after a crushing defeat in his final game.

He entered the hallway and immediately encountered Wu. She looked older somehow, more mature. Or perhaps . . . concerned.

"It's over," he said.

"I know."

Her voice was reedy, brittle. Zhang realized she wasn't carrying her laptop, but he noticed a smartphone in her hand. It somehow minimized her presence. "You can go," he said. "I no longer need your services."

"I think you do."

He paused to look at her. Wu glanced up and down the hall, apparently checking to see if they were alone. They were.

She put a hand to his shoulder and pushed him—pushed *him*—into the wall. "I can get us out!" she whispered into his ear.

The combination of her touch, her words, rattled Zhang to the core. "What are you talking about?"

Another glance up the hall. "I am in this as deeply as you are, and I feared it might come to this. I have been in touch with the Americans."

"What? The . . . the CIA?"

"Is there anyone else in the world who would have a use for us now?"

Zhang opened his mouth, but no words came. His thoughts seemed to seize, either because of his meds or the impact of what Wu was suggesting. Probably both.

"If we go now, go *right* now," she implored in a hushed voice, "they can get us out."

"Out? You're saying I should follow Chen, defect to America?"

"I'm saying *we* should. But it can't wait another minute. If we stay here, you know what will become of us. There is a car waiting outside."

Zhang's thoughts lurched. His face was on fire. There was so much to think about, so many angles to measure. And no time to consider any of it.

"It's now or never," Wu said, starting to back away down the hall.

Zhang was overcome. "Yes, America. That is our only chance."

They hurried to the stairs and descended to the first floor, each step an odyssey of pain for Zhang. He expected Wu to lead him out the main entrance, but instead she turned toward the subterranean parking garage. They were nearly running by the time they reached the garage connector. Zhang gasped for air and his heart rate was spiking, not used to such exertion.

Wu burst through a set of fire doors into the cavernous garage, Zhang right on her heels. A large black sedan stood before them. The engine was running, but Zhang saw no one outside. The windows were tinted dark. He was craning his neck to see the license plates, searching for something to mark it as a diplomatic vehicle, when he realized that Wu had fallen behind. He looked back and saw her standing by the doors. The urgency that had enveloped her was completely gone.

Two doors on the sedan opened simultaneously. From the front came a large Chinese man he recognized immediately—the head of ministry security. His open jacket displayed a holstered weapon. From the back came another familiar face. The Minister of State Security himself. A second security man appeared from behind a pillar.

Zhang instantly deflated, the adrenaline of hope giving way to the bile of defeat. The pain in his face barely registered, as if the nerves had disconnected. He felt nothing at all, fate becoming an anesthetic.

Wu walked past him calmly, confidently, and handed the minister the phone she'd been holding.

The minister tapped the screen and a recording began to play—Zhang's conversation with Wu in the hall minutes earlier. The audio ran all the way to the noose at the end.

Yes, America. That is our only chance . . .

The director stopped the playback. He looked up at Zhang. "Not that we needed this, but it does make my job easier." He stepped closer, reached into Zhang's jacket pocket, and pulled out the bottle of pills. The minister shook his head scornfully. "You have lost a step, Tao. Actually, you've lost several. I should have recognized it sooner."

He pocketed the phone, tossed the pill bottle away, and gave a flicking hand gesture.

The two security men closed in on Zhang, took him by the shoulders, and shoved him into the back seat. As the minister and Wu watched, the black car shot toward the exit and out to the street, the squeals of its tires echoing like screams.

CHAPTER 85

Crystal City, Virginia
Two Weeks Later

Kasey picked up her pace, not wanting to fall behind. She watched her target cross Crystal Drive and turn right, weaving amid concrete planters. She followed him through the Water Park, its paths arcing around fountains in the high midday sun. The cherry blossoms were near peak and verdant spring foliage created canyons of green.

The sidewalks were busy on the warm spring day, people finding any excuse to get out of apartments and offices. Kasey noted more than the usual share of regulation haircuts in the neighborhood—just over a mile from the Pentagon, Crystal City was heavily populated by active-duty military personnel who, after putting their lives on the line overseas, had no wish to battle with Beltway traffic.

The man moved quickly, smoothly, through the crowds as he neared his destination. In the fifteen minutes Kasey had been trailing him, he'd taken no countermeasures to either detect or evade surveillance. That was a mistake on his part. And it would be in her report.

Two blocks later, he turned under a jade awning and disappeared into a brownstone building. Kasey wouldn't make the same mistakes her quarry had. She spent the next ten minutes moving and watching. As surveillance detection routes, or SDRs, went, it was a minimalist effort, but still the best she could allow given her time constraints. She next stopped in a small store she'd spotted and purchased a stuffed bear. She wedged it in her purse and headed back out to the sidewalk.

Ending where she started, she crossed to the jade awning and turned inside. Kasey had never been to this restaurant, but it was familiar all the same. Dark wood, weighty fixtures, a brass-and-mirror bar. The liquor was top shelf, and rows of wineglasses were sorted by size, shape, and thickness—tailored to bring out the best in different varietals. This was D.C. at its most elemental, a place where deals were done. Where congresspeople and justices held court, and where lobbyists and paramours were at their persuasive best.

The maître d' pointed her in the right direction, and turning the first corner, she saw Sharpe sitting at a corner table. Next to his table, an ornamental fireplace flickered a natural gas glow. No coincidence, she was sure. He did a double take when he saw her. If there was surprise, it was fleeting and quickly replaced by a knowing grin.

He stood to greet her, and they shared a warm hug.

"I take it there's no NTSB investigator coming to meet me?" he asked as they both sat down.

"Sorry, I had to be a little indirect."

He smiled again and shook his head, something between admiration and disbelief. Kasey couldn't help noticing that it was a nice smile. Rugged and handsome, and subtly different from the one she'd occasionally seen on the top of the world. He looked more relaxed now, less troubled by duty and conscience.

"Indirect?" he said. "Is that the agency term for having someone impersonate a government investigator and arrange a meeting under false pretenses?"

Kasey shrugged. Sharpe had received a call from a man, purporting to be an NTSB inspector, who wanted to schedule a series of interviews. The investigators hadn't yet talked to Sharpe about the downing of Hemisphere Flight 777. "The guy who called was a friend of mine from work, somebody who understands the need to bend the rules a little now and again. The agency wouldn't approve of my meeting with you—we're supposed to keep our distance from one another until things settle down."

"I was given the same briefing. Are they worried we're going to cook up alternate versions of what happened?"

"I don't think it's that as much as . . . well, we can talk about that later." She glanced down and asked, "How's your leg? I didn't see you limping."

He paused a beat. "You were following me?"

"Old habits."

"Guess I forgot who I'm dealing with."

A waitress appeared and took their drink order.

"I'll take a Stella," Sharpe said.

"Just tap water," Kasey replied. "Oh, and *absolutely* no ice."

Sharpe couldn't contain a laugh as the waitress departed.

"The leg is good. A partial tear to a ligament, but it should heal. I'm set to do a little PT. My feet were on the edge of frostbite, but no damage done."

"Good to hear."

"You?"

She saw him looking at her left hand, which was resting on the table. A small bandage ran down to the top of one finger.

"Nothing serious. But I guess it's kind of symbolic. Ring finger, left hand?"

"Better that than your trigger finger."

"True."

He glanced at the menu but ignored it. "It's good to see you, Kasey." His tone was heartfelt, real.

"You too."

"This is the first time they've let me out and about. But then, I'm guessing you know that."

"I know the agency put you up in a safe house out west in Fairfax County. Isolation debriefs aren't usually this long—they're playing this one particularly tight. It's my first time out as well. After I see you, I'm going to stop to see Walter's wife."

"I hope she's holding up okay."

"Me too. But I hope she doesn't press me too much about what happened. I don't think I could tell her anything but the truth. And the truth is pretty explosive."

"The stakes are high, I know. But I have to say, I've found the debriefing process frustrating. The flow of information has been a one-way street. All I know about the fallout from our Arctic adventure is what I've seen on the news."

"And what you've seen on the news is all fabricated."

"Pretty much. This whole thing has been whitewashed. At least, by everyone except the Russians. They're pissed that they lost a cutting-edge submarine, and behind closed doors they're holding the Chinese responsible."

"No surprises there. At least they were able to pick up everyone from the original crash site. Your passengers have all been treated for injuries and repatriated."

"What about the crew from *Snow Dragon 2*?"

"The Russians are still holding them—bargaining chips. But that'll all get sorted out. None of it affects us."

"Which implies you're going to tell me what *does* affect us."

She gave him an appraising look. She had been getting constant updates on the aftermath of the mission. As a civilian, however, Sharpe had been kept in the dark. The security clearance he'd held as an Air Force officer had expired, and anyway, he had no "need to know" what was going on behind the scenes. On the other hand, Kasey knew she wouldn't be here today if he hadn't voluntarily put his life on the line for his country, and for her. She felt like she owed him the truth.

"There was a very tense call between the presidents—ours and China's. They agreed to sweep as much of what happened as possible under the carpet. The Chinese are in an untenable position. To begin, they brought down a civilian airliner—and we hinted that we could prove it."

"Can we?" As the aircraft's copilot, he had a deeply vested interest in knowing the truth.

"Honestly, I don't know. With time, and with Chen's help, I'm sure we'll figure out how they made the engines fail."

"Speaking of Chen," Sharpe interjected. "How's he's doing?"

"Better. From what I hear, he's recuperating in a secure, undisclosed location. If I had to guess, I think DARPA has him."

"Makes sense. Hopefully, he'll help expose the truth. The world needs to know."

Kasey shook her head. "Look, I know it sucks. But sometimes bad things that happen in the dark have to be left in the dark."

"For what? The good of the nation?"

"In this case, yes. The NTSB is taking the lead on the crash. We've advised them of our suspicions about a malware affecting the engines, and also that national security interests demand that they can't go public with it. They're going to make sure the vulnerability is identified and fixed. I can also tell you that no blame will be assigned to you or the other pilots."

Kasey went silent as the waitress set down their drinks. Sharpe took a long pull on his beer, his smile gone.

"From China's point of view," Kasey continued, "this whole affair was a disaster. It makes the regime look incompetent. Sky Fire and its chief designer disappeared from right under their noses. The *Snow Dragon 2* ended up as a fiasco. Then one of their most elite spec ops units got obliterated in a gunfight. Saving face is critical in that part of the world, and this was a failure on every level."

"So what? We all just pretend none of it happened?"

"Publicly, yes. The Chinese have already announced that a platoon from the Ice Wolves was lost in a training accident. The passengers from the crash have all been interviewed. Some knew more about what really happened than others, but they've all signed nondisclosure agreements based on national security concerns. The only exception is the older Asian couple who were returned to Hong Kong. They're now in the hands of the Chinese authorities, and they'll be managed even more tightly."

"I saw a news article that claimed the *Snow Dragon 2* sank in a storm trying to reach the crash site."

"A big lie backed by small truths—welcome to the world of smoke and mirrors. By the way, she did eventually sink. Our analysts think she was salvageable, but the Russians most likely scuttled her after their own icebreaker arrived to recover everyone."

"Out of spite for what happened to the *Aurora*?"

"You and I met Captain Khurtin. He didn't strike me as the live-and-let-live type."

Sharpe spun his beer on the table and gazed at the fireplace. "What about our LC-130 crew? I read some bull about that being a training accident."

"Brett, I know—"

"Those families," he said, cutting her off in a low voice, "will never know how valiantly their husbands, sons, and fathers died."

"Actually, they will. There were three widows. The president himself is going to meet with each of them. Without giving details, he will explain that these men made the ultimate sacrifice on a mission that was vital to our national interests. He will say, correctly, that others are alive today because of their actions."

Sharpe looked at her searchingly. Kasey knew what he was thinking. *Nobody knows better than us how true that is.*

He let out an exasperated sigh. "What about the thing that started all this?"

"Sky Fire?"

Sharpe nodded.

"It's secure. Our people are going over it, and soon Chen will help them dig deeper. It shifts the playing field massively. We'll have a huge advantage for years to come on the tactical applications of AI."

She saw him wrestle with that. He was wondering if it could possibly be worth the loss of life. Worth nearing the brink of war. Kasey had endured the same doubts. But it was time to move on. Time to explain why she was here.

"Look, there's another reason I wanted to see you today . . . it's important." He looked up, and she could tell she had his full attention. "We need to think forward—you and I."

"If you're about to ask me out on a date, that was the worst opener I've even heard."

Kasey couldn't contain a slight smile. But when she spoke again, her tone was all business. "The Russians are going to move past all of this. They lost a valuable naval asset, but they also came out as heroes in the rescue operation."

"And the Chinese?"

"They're a very different story. They were beaten on every level, and they'll be mad as hell about losing Sky Fire. There's nothing they can do about that, but I've been told by a number of analysts, people who know the regime inside and out, that they will make a serious effort to discourage this kind of thing in the future." Kasey let that hang in the air for a moment.

"Discourage how?" he asked.

"Something that's been in the Russian playbook for a long time—retribution."

"Retribution?"

She nodded.

"You mean like . . . coming after us?"

"Dr. Chen would be the obvious target, and I would definitely be on their radar. Chen will get a new identity and have security for the rest of his life. As for me, I'm a moving target and I'm trained in countersurveillance—complications like this are part of my life."

He watched her intently, taking in every word. He finally knew where she was going. "But I'm different."

"The Chinese will have interviewed the older Chinese couple who returned to Hong Kong. They would not only know that you survived the crash, but also that you left the crash site shortly after Chen and I did."

"You think the Chinese take me for some kind of CIA asset?"

"I'm not sure how they might connect it all . . . but yes, the Chinese could come to that conclusion. You need to understand the potential risks."

"You're saying Chinese assassins might come gunning for me?"

"Crudely put . . . yes."

After a thoughtful moment, Sharpe said, "I guess I won't be bidding the Hong Kong route anytime soon." His attempt at a grin fell flat.

"I am dead serious about this."

"So what would you have me do? Quit my job? Find a new career?"

"Exactly."

He looked at her incredulously.

Then Kasey said, "And maybe the agency could help you with that . . ."

ACKNOWLEDGMENTS

Brad's Acknowledgments

I have wanted to write *Cold Zero* for years. The key to getting it absolutely perfect, however, had always been finding the right cowriter. When I started reading Ward Larsen's books, I knew I had discovered someone sensational. From start to finish, the creation of this book has been a fantastic experience, and I hope you have enjoyed reading it.

Right off the bat, I want to thank **Ward** for his talent, professionalism, and great sense of humor.

Without our wonderful **readers** and **booksellers**, none of this would be possible. Thank you for taking this ride with us.

I want to thank all of my amazing colleagues at Simon & Schuster—president and CEO **Jon Karp**; our editor and publisher, **Emily Bestler**; the entire **Emily Bestler Books team**, including **Lara Jones** and **Hydia Scott-Riley**; Atria Books publisher **Libby McGuire**; associate publisher **Dana Trocker**; publicity and marketing director **David Brown**; senior VP of sales **Kim Shannon**, as well as her entire **sales team**; **Jen Long** and her team at **Pocket Books**; and **Jason Chappell** and **Paige Lytle**, along with the entire **Atria/Emily Bestler Books production departments**. I also want to extend my heartfelt thanks to the superb **Suzanne Donahue**, **Karlyn Hixon**, the **Atria/Emily Bestler Books and Pocket Books sales teams**; the **Atria/Emily Bestler Books and Pocket Books art departments**, especially **Jimmy Iacobelli**; and the **Simon & Schuster audio team**, including **Chris Lynch**,

Tom Spain, **Sarah Lieberman**, **Desiree Vecchio**, and our narrator, **Armand Schultz**.

My agent and dear friend, **Heide Lange**, and the entire team at **Sanford J. Greenburger Associates**—including **Iwalani Kim**, **Madeline Wallace**, and **Charles Loffredo**—have once again been absolutely brilliant. Thank you all very much.

This book is dedicated to the incredible **Yvonne Ralsky**, who was a leading force in making it happen. Thank you, YBR, for your exceptional vision, wisdom, and support.

My outstanding attorney and longtime friend, **Scott Schwimer**, remains one of the key people I would never go into battle without. Thank you, Scottie.

Finally, I want to thank my beautiful **wife and family**. You are the engine that keeps everything running. I love you all beyond measure. Thank you for everything you do for me.

Ward's Acknowledgments

Brad and I have been writing thrillers for more than twenty years, although each in our respective universe. Neither of us has previously partnered with another writer, and when we dove into this collaboration, more than a year ago, I don't think either of us knew quite what to expect.

Looking back now, I'm glad we took the plunge. Having been immersed in a long-running series, I found that creating new characters and working from a clean slate was profoundly liberating. Brad and I pinged ideas off each other for countless hours, yet the positive mood never wavered. All in all, it turned out to be the most fun I've had creating a story. Thank you, Brad, for making it so easy. I trust that our readers will sense the energy and enthusiasm we felt as we wrote this book.

Cold Zero is a work of fiction, but it reflects the harsh dynamics of what is taking place at the top of our world. I hope this story raises awareness of the importance of the Arctic, a delicate strategic battleground that deserves our continued attention.

This story would never have come to pass without the support of others. Sadly, my expressions of gratitude begin on a somber note. My agent of some years, Scott Miller of Trident Media Group, passed away during the writing of this book. If I have any regret regarding the project, it is that Scott wasn't able to see the end result. *Cold Zero* is a direct product of his hard work and encouragement, and his easy smile will be sorely missed.

As ever, I am deeply indebted to the wonderful booksellers, reviewers, and fellow authors who help spread the word about my books. Though you are too numerous to be mentioned individually, your contributions are essential. Thank you, most sincerely, for all that you do.

On the matter of publicity, I must single out James Abt of BestThrillerBooks.com. I have been working with James for many years, and he is the best in the business.

Much appreciation to the team at Simon & Schuster for bringing this project to life, and also to Robert Davis at TOR/Forge for blasting the hole in my schedule that made it possible. You are professionals from top to bottom, and a pleasure to work with.

Finally, as ever, thanks to my family for their enduring support. You are my source material, my coaches, and my true north. Pizza is on me—again!